ABOUT THE AUTHOR

Ryan Jennings Peterson was born and raised in the south
suburbs of Chicago. His debut novel, *On the Ladder of
Humanity*, the first Jolene Hartley Novel and Book 1 of The
Humanities Saga, was completed in 2012, followed months
later by Book 2, *On the Edge of Greed*. The third in the series,
On the Road Through Chaos, was completed two years later.
Ryan currently resides in the suburbs of Chicago with his wife
and two daughters.

I0633917

BOOKS BY
RYAN JENNINGS PETERSON

The Humanities Saga

On the Ladder of Humanity
On the Edge of Greed
On the Road through Chaos

ON THE ROAD
THROUGH CHAOS

ON THE ROAD THROUGH CHAOS

THE HUMANITIES SAGA
BOOK THREE

A Jolene Hartley Novel

RYAN JENNINGS PETERSON

ASIN : B00LLJH7ZA
ISBN-10 : 0692242147
ISBN-13 : 978-0692242148

Cover design by: Ryan Jennings Peterson

Cover photography from Pexels.com used under Pexels License.
https://www.pexels.com/@karolina-grabowska
https://www.pexels.com/@benjaminjsuter
https://www.pexels.com/@agafonova-photo-3500249
https://www.pexels.com/@zachtheshooter
https://www.pexels.com/@ivaoo

FOR

Dad. The original RJP. My personal hero.

ON THE ROAD
THROUGH CHAOS

PROLOGUE

JANUARY ...

The air was humid, more so than earlier in the day thanks to the combination of a late-afternoon thunderstorm rolling slowly across the Caribbean and the above average temperature that had settled in over northern Jamaica and refused to budge. The weight of the atmosphere in Ocho Rios was palpable. It was as if one could reach out a hand and pull back with a fistful of sweaty heat, like a snowball made from tropical dew.

It was a change of pace that James Graiser welcomed. He had checked the weather patterns in the United States a time or two since being back in the Caribbean, noticing the mercury for the winter had remained far above average in Chicago than previous years. Yet other than a quick glance to stifle his meteorological inquiries, he forced his life in the States out of his mind. There were things there he did not want to remember. He had no intentions of heading back to his home base. He was even considering making Jamaica a permanent fixture in his life. Desmond Brown, his longtime friend, had even offered a room in his quaint, comfortable shack until James could find a pad of his own.

Like that was a problem for James. Graiser's financial limitations lacked one major thing: limitations. Finding a shack, tent, hut or beachside mansion was not something James needed to worry about. His bank account — or rather the funds in his hand-me-down account — was astronomical. Working at Desmond's small fruit plantation was by no means considered a job in James's mind. It was an activity to pass the time.

Graiser lifted a bottle of Red Stripe to his lips and continued down the beach, the darkening sky blending into the evening sea, millions of stars reflecting off the shifting surface of the ocean. The illusion of a never-ending sky before him made his already compromised equilibrium that much more unsteady. He turned his focus away from the sea and glanced over his shoulder at the raucous party underway a hundred yards back.

It was Desmond's friend's place, though for the life of him, James could not remember his name. Cortez? Curtis? Kirk? Either way, Desmond's pal was gracious with all he had. James was well beyond inebriated. He and Desmond had worked earlier in the day, walking through his fields and picking ripe fruit that they later sold at the market in town, a business that produced just enough to allow Desmond a spot in the tropics. They had retired in the late afternoon to Brown's abode to a meal of Ting soda and saltfish, followed immediately by several Red Stripes and an abundance of marijuana.

James had smoked pot before in his earlier days but had never found it to be his thing. His spirit was more aligned with that of a backpacking tree-hugger than a joint-rolling pot-smoker. Yet in recent months, he had fully embraced the drug, smoking with Desmond every chance he could. He got used to the feeling of paranoia until eventually he could comprehend what was happening around him, even shrugging off the inability to carry on a conversation in fear of saying something completely off the wall. He learned to function, if only to thank those passing him a smoking pipe or spliff. Within the six months he had been in Jamaica, James Graiser became a new man altogether.

James lifted the bottle of Red Stripe to his lips once more before tossing it among a grouping of palm trees. He stretched his arms high over his head and spun in a circle, feeling the much-needed breeze cross his sweaty face. His hair was longer than it had been while in the States, the wavy curls draping just below his eyes, a shag look he had not worn since his high school days. *Funny,* he thought. *That's the last time I smoked pot, too.*

His arms went wide and he continued in a slow spin, knowing full well that the motion would test his limits of balance as well as his gag reflex. He stopped after a moment and was surprised to see a vision before him, a hallucination obviously created by the past he wished to flee from. The brilliant white light silhouetting a woman's frame shined brightly against his face. He tried to focus his vision to her, tried to decipher who now stood before him. His eyes darted up her frame, sliding along the curve of her hips, meandering over the side of her breast and into the wind-blown, shoulder-length hair. James could judge against the backlight the jaw line, the high cheekbones underneath soul-penetrating eyes.

He fell to the sand, dropping ungracefully into the billions of grains below his feet and toppling to the side. He remained still, forehead resting on the coolness of the beach as he forced the vision from his sight. After several long moments he opened his eyes. All was dark, the light and silhouette once again replaced by the never-ending sky and the millions of stars reflecting off the sea.

* * * * *

James. Hey, it's me. Listen, we need to talk. Give me a call when you get back. I'll be around all night.

* * * * *

He sat there for a time, elbows resting on his knees as he cradled his head, uncontrollable thoughts swirling in the recesses of his mind like they always seemed to do while intoxicated. He glanced around, realizing his refreshment had run out. He really did not want to make the walk back to the party just yet. To his left, about a dozen yards away, sat an ATV packed with garbage cans and a red Igloo cooler, most likely leftovers from a reception or company outing that had long since called it a night.

James was not ready to follow suit. He stood, gathering himself for the short walk, steadying his legs and taking a deep breath before proceeding towards the vehicle. He smiled as he opened the cooler and eyed a dozen or so Real Rock Lagers. He grabbed one and popped the cap off, taking a long, slow sip from the bottle before turning and making his way towards his spot in the sand once again.

* * * * *

Hey, it's me again. I just wanted to make sure you're okay. I haven't heard from you yet and I need some rest. I'll have my phone by me all night, so please call when you get this. I'm not going in tomorrow. Or for a few days at least, so I'll be around if you want to talk. Okay. Bye.

* * * * *

James's mind began to race again, his thoughts flooding his vision, memories rushing to the surface with reckless abandon. His eyes glazed over as he stared to the sand, each of the grains before him spinning and morphing into a thought he tried to push away unsuccessfully.

He traveled back, swirling to a time just as chaotic and misplaced as the present. He looked out a window in an airplane somewhere over the Atlantic, the blackness interrupted by the intermittent red blinks from the light on the wing. He had been contacted the previous day via satellite phone by Daniel Vincent, a family friend, telling him he needed to end his excursion and fly back immediately. James had pushed the subject, knowing that Vincent calling meant only one thing: something had happened to his parents. He did not know if it was his mother or father. He played scenarios in his mind. House fire. Car crash. Heart attack. Nothing stuck, yet he knew without a doubt his return to Chicago was necessary. Backpacking would have to wait.

* * * * *

Where are you? It's been a week and I haven't heard from you. I'm thinking about having someone stop by your place. Guess that would be abusing my powers though, right? Can you please call me back? I'm going back to work tomorrow. I just … Please call. We need to talk.

* * * * *

He was vacant. Emptied completely. Sounds had crammed together to form what equated to an extremely slow motion record player, the polar opposite of the Chipmunks singing Christmas songs. Movements from those around him had trails, lagging entities trying to keep up with the present. He stared to the white carpet of Daniel Vincent's living room floor, not comprehending the words that had just passed from his parents' friend's mouth. "James, I'm sorry to tell you, but your parents are dead." *Your parents are dead.* James would have thought it cruel the way those words just fell from Vincent's tongue, yet the tears that dripped with them softened the blow. He appreciated Daniel. He appreciated the way Daniel spoke to him as if he were an equal. *Your parents are dead.* Just like that. No need to sugarcoat it.

* * * * *

Presently, James lifted the Real Rock to his lips again. A movement from his right caught his eye, pulling him momentarily from his reveries. He watched as Mattie moved towards him, unaware James was seated to her left fifty yards ahead. She was a pretty girl originally from Kingston, having moved to Ocho Rios to work at the tourist hotels in the area as a teenager. Her long dark legs reflected the moonlight and James watched her hips sway back and forth in a pair of khaki shorts. Mattie had a beautiful smile and blonde-tipped dreadlocks that fell just to her shoulders. He was unsure of her age but knew she could not be more than twenty-two or twenty-three.

* * * * *

James. It's me again. I'm not really sure if I did something to make you not take my calls, but we need to talk. Not about us, if that's what's worrying you. We need to talk about what I brought up the last time I saw you. It's important. Please call me back.

* * * * *

He was catapulted back to his parents' murders, the malleable sand beneath his feet transforming into a hard concrete floor. He sat in a morgue in Wisconsin next to Daniel Vincent and Ahmet Karaca, his father's business assistant. James did not bother to look to them, knowing each was thinking the exact same thing. They had repeated on numerous occasions on the flight into Rhinelander that he did not need to be here. They could identify the bodies. It was not something he needed to witness. James repeated himself each and every time. "I'll do it."

* * * * *

I stopped by your place a couple times over the last week or so. I'm assuming whatever's going on with you at the moment doesn't involve me personally. So until I hear back from you, I just want you to know that I'll be here for you. No matter what. I've got to go. Bye.

* * * * *

The bright lights over the silver tables reflected into his eyes as the Medical Examiner stood to his left, waiting for James's sign to pull back the white sheets. He breathed deeply, feeling as if he was caught between reality and a dream. No: a nightmare. The lab smelled of cleaning agents. The floors were spotless. Instruments lined perfectly organized tables. The eyes of the man to his left weighed heavily upon him, though, at a glance, held comfort. James gave the man a slight nod and waited as he pulled back the sheets.

* * * * *

"There you are," Mattie said, stepping towards him and stopping with a jutting hip, her sleek legs crossed. "You had me worried," she said with a smile and a cock of her head, the Caribbean accent heavy on her words. James forced a smile and sipped his beer, his eyes never leaving Mattie. "You all right?" she asked. He nodded and looked to the sea.

* * * * *

Are you all right? I don't know what to say anymore. Merry Christmas? Happy New Year, maybe? I don't know. I checked with the post office and they said you have them holding your mail. No forwarding address or anything. At least your disappearance seems to be on purpose. Gives me a little piece of mind, I guess. Happy New Year, James.

* * * * *

He remembered nodding to the medical examiner for each. They were definitely his parents, though his mother's face was badly bruised and swollen. The small, blue dove tattoo behind her right ear, however, was the calling card. He floated out of the room then, exiting the lab as the medical examiner spoke, the voice fading into the distance and two objects rising from chairs before him as he collapsed onto the linoleum floor and into darkness.

* * * * *

"I said where'd you get that?" Mattie asked again, nudging his knees as she knelt in front of him. James stared into her eyes before nodding his head in the direction of the ATV to his left. She chuckled. "Stealing beer from a wedding, huh? How about you give me a sip of yours?" She reached her hand out and grabbed onto the bottle, brushing her delicate fingers across his. She kept her eyes on him as she sipped the beverage, holding his inebriated, jumpy gaze as best she could.

Mattie leaned forward and put her lips to his, kissing him with a drunken lust as their tongues danced against one another. She pulled him up to her, wrapping her arms around his head and threading her hands through his wavy hair, her body pressed against his, their sweaty skin gliding together. She moved away and looked down to him, his lazy eyes opening and locking onto hers, her beautiful, sensual face and blonde-tipped dreads pulling him into the moment.

* * * * *

I won't call again, but I just wanted to let you know that you know where to find me. I hope you're all right. I'm sure you are. I miss ... I won't call again. Bye, James.

* * * * *

Mattie laid James down into the sand and unzipped his pants. She removed her khaki shorts and unbuttoned her thin, linen shirt, pulling James's hand up to cup her breast while she worked him into readiness. She leaned forward and kissed him again, this time James taking initiative to reach up and grab a fistful of Mattie's hair. He pulled her mouth into his, working frantically as this young beauty slid him into her and began to rock back and forth, the Caribbean night embracing them, the sea lapping onto the beach providing the soundtrack to their union.

ONE

LATE MARCH ...

The financial waters had swallowed Intervise Securities completely. Newspapers across the city — and even the nationwide journals — had descended upon the streets of Chicago in search of any juicy tidbit they could scrounge up regarding the company's unprecedented scandal. All the major media outlets were reporting the largest investment debacle in decades. And it was all thanks to a freelance investigative reporter by the name of Dane Hartley.

> *The rumor-mill has been buzzing since last September of an alleged embezzlement scheme gone seriously wrong. Now, as the year rolls along in what appears to be a citywide financial crisis, those indignities reported by Chicago's own Dane Hartley seem to have been confirmed by local authorities and money gurus alike.*

Intervise Securities, a once well-maintained and established financial entity in Chicago's fiscal realm, was rocked in the latter half of the year amidst a fraud scheme that reached out to encompass one of the cities most established magazines, State of Finance. *And in the wake of what allegedly spanned the better part of a decade, five people are now dead, and thousands more left to wonder if they were indeed victims of financial fraud.*

It was some of the best work Dane Hartley had ever done, though he treated it — and the media personnel now surrounding his everyday life — as nothing more than child's play. He had been thrust into the story through one of the murder victims, Bartholomew Reed, a man who worked for *State of Finance* at the time of his demise. Reed had been handed the evidence via a ghost, a source that hid in the shadows and lurked behind every corner, copying files and keeping a keen eye on the happenings between *State* and Intervise.

That ghost, it turned out, was a mole within the magazine, a woman by the name of Ann Carroll, who, over the years, kept the monetary ledgers in her sight and a Xerox machine at her fingertips. The jury — along with public opinion — was still out on Ann's role within the fraud, however, with the death count as it stood, an older woman blowing the proverbial whistle on the current scum of the financial world would hardly garner a mention in the bylines, much less a lengthy legal battle. Ann had been — and continued to be — a key part of the mounting story. Yet her cooperation and willingness to throw others under the bus had placed her in protective custody, at least until her day in the limelight.

Bart Reed, however, had not been so lucky. After learning of the connections to his bosses, *State of Finance* Editor-In-Chief, Seamus O'Dowd, and Assistant Editor, Kyle Walker, Reed hastily shoveled the mess to Dane. It had pulled Hartley into what would become, up to this point, the defining piece in an otherwise somewhat-successful career.

Dane had enjoyed writing the piece thoroughly.

> *Who knew that chaos and greed shared such a volatile edge? The line on which some individuals walk baffles me. As a journalist, I will be the first one to admit that corners need to be cut at certain times. Information needs to be disseminated on a timely basis to let the general public know the inner workings of the beast.*
>
> *Yet, the minds that conjured up this lust for money, this murderous rampage that would stop at nothing to fill already over-abundant bank accounts — these people are the epitome of trash. I know from first-hand experience. I was the intended victim of a motion-activated bomb that killed a dear friend. She was the*

*second person to be murdered in regards to this
influx of greed.*

Kelly Depler. The name resonated throughout his mind as he wrote the follow-up article to the Intervise-*State* scandal. She had been blown to bits in his apartment, a wrong-place-wrong-time individual wearing nothing but her skin. She had been Dane's neighbor, a lovely woman with a serious appetite for strings-free sex. Dane had been happy to oblige.

He had not attended her funeral, however, yet it was not something that pulled at his heartstrings too much. At the time of her burial, Dane had taken residence in a grimy motel room on the west side, lurching through file after file of the Reed documentation he had received from Ann Carroll. The documents had cast a shining light upon major players in the embezzlement scheme, yet there were definite holes. Seamus O'Dowd and Kyle Walker, however, had been slam-dunks.

*Upon receiving the documents from the late
Bart Reed, I weighed my options: take on the
work of a great journalist or let the story fade
into the abyss? In the end I chose to stand on
the shoulders of Reed, to continue his trek into
the dangerous underbelly of what would
become the financial crime of the decade. The
headquarters of* State of Finance *beckoned.
Little did I know I was walking blindly into the
line of fire, happening into a realm of greed and*

murder that encompassed not only O'Dowd and Walker, but also Mr. Damian Verland, former Vice President of the Chicago-based firm, Intervise Securities.

* * * * *

Damian Verland sat back on his leather couch and threw his feet onto the oversized ottoman before him, his eyes staring blankly to the muted television on the other side of the room. He was tired. His days had become monotonous, to say the least. There was not much to do when you were unemployed, on house arrest and readying a defense for what equated to the rest of your natural life.

He had been arrested on numerous charges: murder, conspiracy and fraud, to name a few. The list was long, and he knew his freedom was something that was dimming with each passing day. His bond had been set at a ridiculously high price, a death sentence for the average citizen. Yet Damian Verland was hardly that. The amount was pocket change for him, a slap on the wrist. He walked out that night, though not before that bitch detective recommended house arrest, a decision that was backed completely by the higher authorities.

Verland had already gone through his preliminary hearings, yet the trial was still not set in stone. He had faced the detectives in the courtroom and set a plea of not guilty to the judge. The battle for his freedom was on. His passport had been revoked and his name smeared across the tabloids as the next Bernie Madoff.

He sat up and leaned to his left, grabbing onto a crystal tumbler of scotch set near the base of the couch. He drank from the glass, savoring the taste as the liquor swished around his mouth. His eyes scanned the room. Stacks of papers loomed on every surface. Boxes upon boxes of financial documents cluttered the den, overflowing onto the dining room table.

Verland began to rise, yet retained his seat and turned the volume up as the news reporter began to interview Dane Hartley. The journalist was exiting a high-end restaurant, his aviator sunglasses out of place in the darkening night.

"Mr. Hartley, your publication has stirred up quite a controversy," the reporter said, her voice strong and flowing. "Is it true that Damian Verland was connected to Seamus O'Dowd and Kyle Walker of *State of Finance* magazine, and that they were siphoning money from Chicagoans for the past decade?"

"According to the documents from my source, absolutely," Dane said, removing his glasses and setting himself in the cameras light.

"Who is your source?"

Dane laughed. "Nice try."

"Is there any —"

"Look, look. You can read the piece. Everything is factual. The documents I have — the documents I gave the Chicago Police Department — prove it. I've fabricated nothing."

"Some people in the media world have looked down upon your report as being biased," the reporter pushed.

"Absolutely I'm biased," he replied, his brow furrowing slightly at the woman who shifted nervously. "Doesn't mean it isn't fact. This isn't like a normal investigation. This wasn't like me catching an interview from someone stepping out of a restaurant. I was targeted. I had my apartment bombed by a psychopath that left bodies throughout the city. How could I not be biased? I was targeted to be killed. Tell me how I'm supposed to look at that with an objective view."

"I read in your publication, as well as the reports last year, of the explosion at your apartment that killed Kelly Depler."

"That's right."

"Can you tell me what Ms. Depler was doing in your apartment?"

"Baking cookies," Dane answered quickly.

The reporter halted briefly, unsure how to follow up. "Cookies?" she questioned, stumbling.

"That's right. Cookies. What's it matter? Kelly Depler was a good woman. And she's dead now. She was an innocent bystander that was murdered due to the greed of a few people."

"Those people being Seamus O'Dowd, Kyle Walker and Damian Verland?"

"That's correct."

"Is it true —"

"Listen. The fraud that was perpetrated upon the clients of Intervise Securities is awful. Absolutely horrible. They deserve to have their day in court against Verland. But let's not forget the people that won't have their day in court. Let's not forget Bart Reed and his family. Let's not forget Kelly Depler. Those are the real victims, not some millionaire trust-funders that lost the keys to their second Lamborghini."

"Mr. Hartley, don't you —"

"Thank you, but that's it." Dane turned and walked away, waving to the camera one final time before lighting a cigarette and disappearing down the street.

Verland took another long drink from the tumbler, watching as the news program switched from the live feed back to the studio, the face of an attractive black woman filling the screen. "That was Monica Alvarez in Roscoe Village with investigative journalist Dane Hartley. Thank you, Monica." The anchorwoman turned to a new camera. "Hartley has experienced a sudden amount of fame over the last six months with his exclusive knowledge into the Intervise Securities scandal that shook the financial world here in Chicago. As he said just moments ago, the embezzlement scheme has taken center stage due in part to a string of killings that has followed it. Bartholomew Reed and Kelly Depler were two of the victims. Reed was allegedly murdered due to the documents he had in his possession, and Ms. Depler was mistakenly killed in an explosion at Mr. Hartley's apartment.

"Three other individuals were killed in connection with the Intervise scandal as well: Seamus O'Dowd, Editor-In-Chief of *State of Finance*, and his Assistant Editor, Kyle Walker, were both gunned down at the magazine's headquarters in a brutal slaying within O'Dowd's office. The gunman, Luke Moran, was later shot and killed in the magazine's printing warehouse by Chicago police. Moran had a record as a youth before joining the military and excelling as a soldier. He was killed while assaulting Detective Jolene Hartley, who, as we first reported, is the sister of Dane Hartley."

Again, to a new camera, a flashing smile welcoming the viewers to a new perspective. "Jolene Hartley, herself, has gained a decent amount of fame in Chicago since her inception into the police force. Detective Hartley's first case as a member of the homicide unit garnered national attention for the Chicago Police Department with the hunt and subsequent takedown of a well-known serial killer. Hartley's more recent escapades on Navy Pier at the end of last summer, and her latest attack in Lakeview, have garnered much attention in the media. Our investigative team learned of Hartley's involvement in the Korhan Karaca assault months ago, though no arrests have been made.

"Last year, Detective Hartley ended up shooting and killing Taylor Thames on Navy Pier, sparking an investigation into the murders of three Chicagoans, one of those being Alderman Daniel Vincent, who was found murdered in a parking garage five years ago. Taylor Thames, as you may have heard us report, has been linked with embattled Congressman Harold Johnston. Johnston is currently facing a number of legal issues, including being connected to the murder of Vincent. Authorities believe the Congressman to have ordered the hit that ended in Vincent's death."

Verland's eyes panned across the television while the anchorwoman spewed out her report, a collage of photographs displayed on the screen showing the bodies of Seamus O'Dowd and Kyle Walker as they were pulled from the *State of Finance* headquarters on gurneys, the black body bags shimmering in the Chicago sun. The images faded into the background as the mugshot of Luke Moran filled the area. Damian glared at the face, cursing under his breath at the man who led the detectives to his doorstep.

His blood began to boil as the collage slid stage left, immediately replaced by the still photograph of the lovely Detective Jolene Hartley. It was an image that had been taken before his time on her radar, though not by much. Detective Hartley was seen walking away from Navy Pier, her hand up in a defensive posture as the paparazzi flashed away at a maniacal speed. She was escorted by several medics and other officers, and followed by a man that looked as if he had been through a battle alongside the beautiful detective.

Damian lifted the tumbler to his lips and halted as he stared to the man, his eyes searching the face before returning to the female officer. He grumbled at the sight of her, downing the remaining scotch before turning the television off and tossing the remote on the ottoman before him. He sighed and glanced around, taking in the mountains of paperwork strewn through his once pristine home. His eyes traveled down the hallway and locked onto a wooden paneled wall and the notch just large enough for his pinky to slip into. He thought of rising and walking towards the section, a vision forming in his mind of him bending and pulling at the board until it popped off, revealing the mysterious contents within. He no longer had the strength, however. He was tired. Tired of the trial preparation. Tired of searching for the freedom he knew he would not find. The search was in vain, even with the information he still had up his sleeve.

* * * * *

The amber glass from the shattering beer bottle thundered throughout the garage, echoing in a singsong chime as the slivers rained down upon the concrete floor. He resumed his pacing, lifting the cigarette to his lips and taking a long, drawn-out drag before moving to the ancient refrigerator against the wall. He opened the door with a piercing squeak and retrieved another beer, popping the top and tossing it into a corner. His eyes fell to the television once more and he took a swig.

Things seemed surreal at the moment, like he had been transported into the past and was once again dealing with individuals he wanted nothing to do with. The image of the Graiser kid splashed across the TV was one thing. He had checked up on him from time to time, though not in the past several years. He hardly seemed to be any sort of threat. Yet the fact that he followed the young, pretty detective away from Navy Pier was something altogether different. It immediately raised a red flag. There were too many connections that led back to him.

The main one being Korhan Karaca.

Word on the street was Karaca — the fucking invalid junkie Turk — was wanted for attacking a police officer. There were things a criminal just did not do, he remembered thinking to himself. Messing with the cops did nothing but bring the heat on you. "Better to let the police do their thing and you get the fuck out of sight."

The quote was from his past as well, and, at this exact moment, his undeniable future. He took another drag from his cigarette before bending down to place the bottle of beer on the ground. He stood facing the television and pulled his cell phone from his pocket, eyeing the display and the numbers that stared back to him like a bad dream.

He did not have the number programmed into his phone, yet, for the years between the duo's last rendezvous, he had not forgotten the digits, or the hideous scar that graced his associate's left eyebrow, leaving a drooping lid over an evil orb. He punched them in and placed the phone to his ear, listening as the ringer chimed loudly, as if to remind him of what was about to happen. He was seconds away from connecting with the most dangerous man he had ever come across, a man that —

"What the fuck do you want?" a smooth, monotone voice answered from the other end of the line. The calmness sent a shiver down his spine. The last thing he had wanted in his life was to rekindle any form of relationship with this man. He was terrified of him. The things he could do, places he could reach. He was more than happy to rid himself of the dread that he had associated with in his youth.

That was not to say he was a saint these days. Far from it, in actuality. He ran with a crew that stayed in the shadows, lurking just beyond reach of the Chicago Police Department, ever present in the mind of a select few, yet wholly overlooked by the collective sum. On several occasions he had had to flee the city, taking shelter in the far south suburbs until the heat dissipated, relinquishing unto another guilty party that he, without hesitation, let take the fall. His name was out there, yet no more than any other common crook.

Yet these altogether new happenings had forced his hand. He had been required to make a move. The past decade had been beyond lucky. He knew that. Things had played out in their favor more than they could have ever hoped for. But their luck was running thin.

"You got your TV on?" he asked, his gruff voice trying unsuccessfully to hide the anxiety that spread throughout his body like wildfire.

"I'm watching it," came the response, followed by silence.

He waited briefly before continuing. "Well, did you see the picture?"

"There are a lot of fucking pictures." The humor in his tone was nothing but eerie.

"The one from Navy Pier."

"What about it?"

"Come on," he answered, pleading and bending for his bottle. "Tell me you don't recognize him."

"I'm not an idiot. But I am still wondering why the fuck you called me about it."

"Why I'm …?" He let the phrase hang in the uncomfortable air. "You know who the woman is?"

"Let me guess. Someone you're looking to hook up with. Tell me: you going to turn on your charm? Or use your fists?" The comment hit home hard. Apparently their time apart had done nothing to ease the tension that had built.

He chose to ignore the remark, changing the subject away from himself and back to the detective on TV. "Come on, man. It's the same cop. It's the one that they attacked."

"So?"

"So? *So* … She's the one that was there at the magazine." Another uncomfortable pause. "I'm hoping I don't have to explain it further."

"What do you want me to do about it?"

"I don't know. Maybe care a little fucking bit!" He tossed his cigarette to the floor and lit another. "Look," he began again, reigning in his irritation. "That fuck Karaca is unhinged. He attacked that cop and is running from every badge in the city. It's only a matter of time before he's caught and deals."

"If he's still in the city."

"My guess is he's still here. He's a fucking junkie. He's got to get his shit somewhere. Why start in a new place?" The question was rhetorical, yet the quiet that followed brought goosebumps. "What do you think we should do?"

"Look for the Turk," came the soothing voice. "If you find him, end him."

"What about the Graiser kid?"

"What about him?"

"Well, he's obviously talking to the cops."

"You don't know that. Don't go assuming anything until you know for sure. Killing Karaca is one thing. That fucker will do anything to get out of a lengthy jail sentence. You're right about him dealing."

"So we just leave the Graiser kid alone?"

"For the time being. Look, I'm out of town. I got shit to take care of and will be back in Chicago in about a week."

With that the phone went dead, leaving the man staring at the television screen as he lifted the beer to his lips once more. His hands were shaking.

TWO

"In related news," the anchorwoman continued, switching yet again to a new camera, "the mention of Congressman Harold Johnston comes on the cusp of his battle to clear his name from the murderous rampage caused by Taylor Thames. Thames is the son of Robert Thames, the one-time treasurer for Johnston who is currently serving the tail end of his stint in a federal penitentiary for corruption charges. According to Dane Hartley's report, Congressman Johnston, in the past, had money tied into Intervise Securities, though it is not known if he is a victim of fraud himself.

"Intervise Securities has since shut its doors following the termination and subsequent investigation into Damian Verland. Intervise's owner, Jacomo Rafaele Francesco, sold the company off after the scandal went public and Intervise has since been folded into numerous entities. Francesco, who hadn't given a public interview in over a decade, passed away shortly after the move in January in his homeland of Italy. Francesco was —"

Jolene Hartley switched the conference room television off and stood motionless, her hands locked and resting on the top of her head. She grinded her teeth, thinking back moments before to the image of her walking from Navy Pier, her hand up to deter the paparazzi, James Graiser close behind. She remembered it like it was yesterday. One does not easily forget killing another human being.

She took a step forward and laid the remote control on the gleaming conference room table, the noise as the plastic clicker made contact with the lacquered wooden surface extremely loud in the otherwise quiet precinct. Jolene ran her hands over her face, massaging her eyes before streaking her fingers through her long, dark locks. She clasped her hands behind her neck and lifted her face to the ceiling, exhaling slowly, her thin, supple neck reflecting the fluorescent lights over her desk outside the conference room.

The fracture of her left supraorbital ridge had healed perfectly and the small scar that still graced her eyebrow was disappearing ever so slowly over time. She was back to her old self after the encounter with Luke Moran in the *State of Finance* printing warehouse, a brutal meeting that almost left the detective with a shortened lifespan. If it were not for the tenacity of her partner, Jacoby Ratliff, Jolene's body would have been found battered and lifeless on the cold cement floor. It was not how the cards had been dealt, however. Ratliff, broken wrist and all, had torn through the warehouse wall and put a well-placed bullet through Moran's skull, saving Hartley from strangulation at the hands of the murderer.

Jolene still woke from time to time in a panicked sweat, her hands instinctively running across her neck where the white rope had been pressed into her skin. The burn mark left by the rough texture had long since disappeared from her throat, yet the emotional toll of once again being so close to death had settled in for the long haul. They were scars that came with the job, she told herself.

Jolene turned and exited the room, stopping to pull the door closed behind her. She halted as she caught her reflection in the glass to the left of the opening. For all the bumps and bruises and broken bones she had collected within the past year, Jolene Hartley had triumphed over them all, her durability surprising even herself at times. She was a young woman above average height, with a lean, toned body that most fashion models yearned for. Her flowing brunette hair sat atop a face that screamed beauty. Her eyes were piercing above high cheekbones; her full lips could crack a smile that brought the sun out, though her scowl could bring forth a tempest hardened sailors cowered from. She was the poster child of sheer elegance, yet cut with a hardness that rivaled even the toughest male officers.

She had spoken to her brother, Dane, only a few times since arresting Damian Verland at his pristine mansion months ago. The sequence of events had brought them together after years of silence, though each of them was still keen on keeping that distance. Dane was, as Jolene put it on numerous occasions, a pain in the ass. He was better on his own, and definitely something she did not want to deal with on a daily basis. She had kept up on his reports following the arrest, however, and could not help but chuckle as the story that played out on paper and in the studios painted Dane the immaculate hero.

He had been gracious enough to leave out the names of her and Ratliff — and James — yet the media, she knew, were anything but idle. They had scrounged around for the true story and eventually had come upon the fact that the very officer involved was none other than the hero's sister, a fantastic turn of events that brought a whole new twist to the scenario. As the news anchor had said: Jolene Hartley had made a name for herself throughout her career, yet it was not always something she was comfortable with. Being famous tended to put more bulls-eyes on your back.

Hartley stepped away from the conference room door and made her way to the desk she sometimes called home. She glanced to the wall clock as she took her seat, sighing noisily and shaking her head. It was 8:00 p.m. on a Friday evening, a scenario that had become all too familiar in the life of Detective Jolene Hartley. Her current case included a murdered grocery store clerk, a robbery gone badly that had led her and Ratliff on a wild goose chase throughout Chicago. They eventually made contact with a nineteen-year-old prostitute who had witnessed the get-away vehicle screeching away from the scene and took down the license plate number on the back of a bill she had just received for services rendered. Being in that particular line of work, "Chloe" knew having a security backup was something that could save her from a spell in the slammer. She had traded her first-hand knowledge of the murderous event for a clean slate after being picked up soliciting an undercover officer a day later.

After several interviews and stake-outs throughout the neighborhood, Hartley and Ratliff, along with a team of uniformed officers, had been graced with a name and picture, though their suspect, to this day, had eluded them, most likely shacking up with fellow hoodlums or perhaps escaping the city altogether.

Hartley looked down at the picture of Douglas Merlowe. They had no video of Douglas pulling the trigger, yet two of the four individuals tied to the crime had been nabbed — thanks in part to the license plate number from Chloe — and spilled the beans regarding their associate, saying the robbery was supposed to be just that: a robbery. They had had no intention of hurting anyone and had not even known Douglas had brought a loaded weapon with him. "The shooting happened after the employee ran his mouth. We were all heading to the door and we heard the shots. We turned around to see Doug standing about ten feet away. He shot him twice and we bolted. It was fucked up!"

Hartley tossed the picture on top of her desk and leaned back into her chair, eyes skyward. She thought for several moments before sitting up slightly and glancing around, checking the pit to see if anyone was making their way through at this late hour. When she determined the area was clear, she bent down and pulled a drawer open, retrieving several file folders and placing them before her. She breathed deeply, eyes scanning the worn surfaces of the folders. She ran her hand along the top file, her fingers brushing the label of the case she had taken from storage months ago:

GRAISER, MICHAEL A. & GRAISER, AMELIA H.

She had glanced through the paperwork numerous times, jotting down a note here or there, mentally collecting the evidence that had been passed along by a small Wisconsin police department to the Chicago PD some ten years ago. She had memorized the names of those involved: Keith Weitzel, caretaker of the property; Chris Pennington, a ten-year veteran and his rookie partner, Lindsey Pratt, first responders at the scene; Guy Finney, lead homicide detective; Emmet Eckland, medical examiner. The list went on, yet Hartley could determine the main players well enough.

The interior crime scene had been gruesome, to say the least. From the report Hartley had perused on multiple occasions, blood was smeared along walls, carpets, counters and even a splatter on the ceiling. Dishes were cracked and shattered. Silverware was found on the stone floor split in two. A rolling pin, possibly used by the victim in self-defense, had connected with the marble countertops and taken a chunk out of the wooden cylinder.

The coroner's report had Amelia H. Graiser's cause of death as extreme blood loss, coupled with intense internal bleeding from a vicious rape. She had contusions across her body. Several of her fingers had been broken. A tooth had been knocked clean out of her mouth and was found on the other side of the kitchen island. Amelia had been stabbed twice in the abdomen and left to die. Hartley's eyes had glazed over the first time she read through the report, and at this particular moment, she still fought the urge to weep. James's mother had held on for several hours before being found by the caretaker. Weitzel had called the authorities and they made it to the lakeside villa within the quarter hour, immediately hooking Amelia up to an IV and beginning the trek to the closest hospital. She died en route.

Michael Graiser was found minutes after the police arrived. The boathouse light was shining brightly and the officers made their way quickly down the path into the facility. Blood covered the wooden planks a dozen feet in front of them, an obvious sign of some horrible accident or, more likely than not, foul play. After searching the boathouse for several minutes, Michael's body was eventually found floating face down in the water next to the Lund fishing boat, stab wounds evident on his backside.

From behind her, Jolene heard the slam of a door, the noise bringing her to the present as she quickly shuffled the papers back into the file folder and placed the stack back in the drawer. "Jo, go home," came Captain Henry Nolan's voice. "It's Friday night. Girl like you should have something better to do than go through files."

"A girl like me, sir?" she questioned, glancing over her shoulder as he passed by.

He slowed as he turned to her, an expression of confusion and embarrassment spread across his face as he tried to right the ship. "Yeah. You know … Young and with a life. Someone that —"

"Just messing with you, sir," she replied with a chuckle.

"Well, I'm not. You've been here late every night for weeks. Go home. That's an order. I don't want to see you here for a couple days."

"Yes, sir," she answered, though remained in her seat.

Nolan also stayed put, eyeing his detective curiously. "How's that case coming along, by the way?"

"Which case is that?" Hartley asked cryptically.

"The only one you should be working on," he replied.

"It's coming along. Just waiting for some word on his whereabouts."

It was Nolan's turn to be cryptic. "And whose whereabouts are we looking into?"

Hartley understood the double meaning, knowing full well her superior was aware of her disconnect with James. "Douglas Merlowe."

"Good," he said and turned. "Hopefully he stays missing for at least the weekend. I really don't want to call you in on a Saturday night."

"No, sir," Hartley said. She watched the captain turn into his office without flipping on the light and retrieve his coat, spinning on a dime and closing the door behind him.

"Seriously, Hartley," he said as he passed by her once more. "Go home. Have a relaxing weekend."

"Yes, sir. Goodnight."

* * * * *

She moved from her desk and into the kitchen, opening the refrigerator and eyeing the can of soda on the upper shelf. It was not hers, however, at this moment Hartley did not care. *Finders, keepers*, she thought with a grin, popping the tab and bringing the can to her lips. She stood in the kitchen and gazed through the glass at the pit, her eyes falling on an empty desk from her past: Anthony Barailles.

Barailles had been her first partner as a rookie homicide detective. Her professional relationship with Anthony worked well, for a time. Each was a good cop, with Hartley becoming the main component of their duo early on. Barailles was accepting of his new confidante, even if that meant having to take a backseat to a female. Other members of the squad poked fun at him, yet Barailles knew without a doubt his partner was the best officer in the precinct.

It was when Jolene began a relationship with Ronny Debarsi that Barailles's true colors began to come through. The all-nighters in close proximity to one another; lunches and dinners — sometimes even breakfasts — kept Barailles at Hartley's side, and vice versa. Having another male enter into his territory was not something he looked favorably upon, even if he had a failing marriage and two children. Jolene picked up on the vibe sent out from her partner quickly, yet deflected it from herself, stating it was Barailles's problem alone. He was the one with the family. He was the one that needed to curb his feelings for her. They were partners on the job, not in life.

Yet four years later, fate stepped in. Through his outstanding work, Ronny Debarsi was given the opportunity to take a position as an agent of the FBI — in Philadelphia. He was to work on a task force chasing down some of the most notorious bank robbers in the country. The offer was too good to pass up. Hartley and Debarsi amicably said their goodbyes, each wanting nothing more than to remain together, yet knowing their lives in the service of others would pull them apart, leaving a happy, working relationship strained and bent.

Six months later disaster struck in the form of a retirement party. Hartley, in need of filling a void left by her ex, stepped into Barailles's apartment in an exchange that nearly led to them tangled in the heat of passion on his living room floor. At the cusp of utter sexual independence, Jolene made the decision to halt their lustful actions. Barailles, with the new bachelor pad and freedom to do as he pleased, was, nonetheless, still married. Anthony was smitten with Jolene; that much she was certain of. And there was an obvious connection felt from her as well. Yet, alcohol or not, she needed to curb her urges for someone with less to lose. She could not face the possibility of ruining a marriage completely.

Jolene walked back to her desk and sat. She bit her bottom lip, replaying the past year through her mind. She reached down once again and retrieved the Graiser files from the drawer, this time passing by the police reports. She was searching for a photo, an image she had come across when initially opening the folders, bypassing the crime scene pictures with little regard for the brutal display before her.

Hartley finally stopped on the one out of place picture in the whole set, placing it before her on the desk surface and pushing the files back into the drawer. The image was that of a young James Graiser, the only child of the murdered Michael and Amelia Graiser. He was no older than eighteen or nineteen, a cute, mop-haired young man that brought a fleeting smile to her face.

James had been thrust into her life the same day Anthony Barailles had been forced out. Their case into a murdered ex-gangbanger over the Dan Ryan led them to Graiser's apartment just at the right moment. Graiser had been stabbed by their suspect, Taylor Thames, yet had sidestepped the onslaught and retreated up the fire escape where he took refuge among the gigantic air conditioning units. Upon giving chase to Thames, Barailles was shot multiple times and rushed in for emergency surgery. Anthony remained in the hospital until his retirement from the force, leaving Hartley to fend for herself in regards to the case.

From the start James Graiser was someone special to Jolene. He had come into the station after fleeing the hospital and sought her out, helping her with the case amidst laughter and occasional flirtation. He brought smiles to her face and nervousness to her stomach, something she had not felt in quite some time. He was adorable in her eyes, an object that brought about a giddiness straight out of her high school days.

His carefree attitude was contagious and she welcomed it every chance she got.

Hartley sighed and placed the image back into the drawer. She thought for a moment and picked up her desk phone, dialing in a series of numbers and resting the receiver against her shoulder. A smile formed on her lips and she immediately forced it back from whence it came. The ringing continued in intermittent bursts, her anxiety growing between the intervals of noise. She brought her thumbnail between her teeth and bit down.

"Hey," came the reply from the other end of the line.

The smile forced its way back to the surface. "Hey, I'm at the station."

"Still? What are you doing? It's the weekend. Who knows when you'll have another one off?"

"Yeah. I know." She paused before continuing. "Listen, I doubt you're up for it, but I was thinking about grabbing some food. Would you want to —"

"Just tell me where," came the interjection.

Hartley laughed and her smile grew, the darkness of the precinct seemingly brightening as she made her plans for a late night dinner.

THREE

It was nearing 9:00 p.m. at the Caribbean Café in Ocho Rios, and a hazy dampness hung over the area like a blanket. James was accustomed to the sporadic downpours that frequented the island, carrying with them a humidity that clung to one's clothes and skin. He was entering into his seventh month in Jamaica, the longest he had stayed in a single spot in years, and he had lost himself here, sinking into a state of mind that lacked any semblance of the old James Graiser.

He had wanted to disappear altogether, blend into the world and never resurface again, yet word had snagged his attention of the happenings in Chicago. Desmond had made a point to watch the world news and caught the tail end of a segment on the Intervise Securities-*State of Finance* fiasco, a laugh escaping his gut as James sat next to him with his lips around an enormous joint. "Man, you're on the news!" he exclaimed, grabbing the remote and pumping up the volume as the image of Graiser being escorted from the Navy Pier shooting spread across the screen.

It had been the start of the itch that settled into James's system, a tickle that began to intensify as the weeks went on, culminating in a mental pros and cons list over whether or not to return to his home base and face the demons of his past. He was at a standstill, however, as each positive was made moot by an exact opposite. For example, returning home meant dealing with the possibility of opening his parents' case, an idea he absolutely did not wish to ponder. Yet on the same token, the possibility that the gun found at Hartley's apartment could shed light on the decade old horror that seized his life meant he could move on completely, and not in the haze of marijuana smoke. He could be free to know what had happened and who was accountable. He could have closure.

That is why he found himself once again stopping into the Caribbean Café, a coffee shop owned by an English gentleman by the name of Grant Wyatt, a thin, pale individual wanting nothing more than to spend the remainder of his life in the tropics. "Back again?" Grant said as James entered the store. He checked his watch. "Only about an hour till closing." James nodded. "Want your usual?"

"Please," James answered, stepping to the counter and pulling out a wad of sweaty American dollars.

"If you want to use the computers again, don't worry about the coffee. It's on the house. Just pay for the internet."

"Thanks, Grant. I won't be long."

"And hey. Maybe next time you're in the area, bring me some of that good green you and Desmond got your hands on." He smiled from ear to ear, patting his belly.

"We're in Jamaica, Grant. Everything is the good stuff."

He spent the first half hour running through his email account, mass deleting items in his swelling inbox that need not be opened. He had neglected his virtual mailbox since being in the Caribbean, needing a clean slate to fold himself into and start anew. However, after Desmond's rant regarding the picture of him following a beautiful police officer on Navy Pier, James's curiosities began to grow. He began surfing the web, touching base with articles posted on CNN and Yahoo!, filling the void of useless knowledge that he used to delve into.

The bell above the doorway chimed and pulled his eyes from the screen. Mattie stepped in, nodding her head to Grant as he waved back, checking the young vixen out quickly before returning to the dishes before him. "Hey, boy," she said, stepping next to James's station and leaning into the counter, her arms pressing her breasts together in an attempt at an early evening Caribbean seduction.

"Hey, Mattie," James answered, glancing from the computer screen to her and back. "What are you doing here?"

"You know, just looking for the guy that disappeared this morning. You see him?"

"Sorry."

"Why'd you leave so early?"

James scratched his head. "Just needed to get some things done. What are you doing out here?"

"Looking for you, of course. That and helping Desmond pick up some beer. You were supposed to help him out. You forget?"

"Shit, yeah. I was supposed to make it back over there. He's not too pissed, is he?"

"No, man. He's good. Said for me to kick you in the crotch, but I'd rather not mess with that area unless it's for other purposes." Mattie moved in close and wrapped her arms around James's shoulders, pulling him in for a lustful kiss, one he only half returned. It was not that he did not find Mattie enticing. He did. He liked her very much. Yet there was something still pulling him away. "Why don't you come back with me? We could lay in bed and skip the gathering."

"Sounds like a pretty good idea."

"It is, man. What do you say?"

James thought for a moment, his eyes glancing to the computer monitor and back to her. "I've got to look some things up right now. How about I meet you there in about an hour?"

"Ditching me for a computer?" Mattie laughed as she kissed him on the cheek. "That sounds fine. I'll stop in at Desmond's for a little bit. Meet me there." She turned her attention briefly to the computer display, her eyes scanning over the Google search box. "Who's Jolene Hartley?" she asked.

James bit down on his lip and looked to the floor. He had not heard her name spoken aloud — other than Desmond's incessant news programs — in half a year, and it sent shivers down his spine. "An old friend from back home. A cop in Chicago."

"A cop, huh? Well, you better not be bringing back any of Desmond's ganja to a cop. That wouldn't be a good idea."

"Yeah. Probably not," he agreed, forcing a smile to her.

"All right, man. I'll see you in a little while." She waved to him and stepped out into the street, disappearing from view around the corner.

James watched her leave before turning his attention back to the screen, his eyes hovering over the text of Jolene's printed name. He breathed deeply, surprised at how nervous he was to look up the detective, as if the information he read about her would immediately transport her back into his life.

He scanned the search results, flipping between pages before settling on an entry that rang a bell in his mind.

SHOOTOUT AT STATE OF FINANCE
SEVERAL DEAD, FEMALE COP INJURED

The story smashed into his body like a semi-truck. He remembered meeting with Jolene that day after the *State of Finance* shootout that left Luke Moran dead in the warehouse. Hartley had shared briefly with him the details of what had happened, yet left her injuries with the ambiguous, "I'll be fine." The article told a different story.

> *The details are unclear at this time, yet sources that witnessed the shooting say three people have been killed in the headquarters of Chicago-based financial magazine,* State of Finance. *Our source inside the building said the shooting started within the offices of Editor-*

In-Chief, Seamus O'Dowd, and escalated as the gunman made his way down the hall and into the printing warehouse on the ground floor. Apparently there are two bodies within O'Dowd's office, although we cannot verify at this time if the Editor-In-Chief is one of the deceased. The gunman was also killed by a Chicago police officer, though not after inflicting serious damage to another member of the force. A female officer, whose name has not been released, had been in the printing warehouse with the gunman and had apparently been in some sort of altercation with the perpetrator. We have confirmed with the local hospital that the female officer has sustained substantial injuries, though is in stable condition. Among those injuries are a fractured bone above her left eye, a concussion, multiple contusions from what doctors are calling a 'savage beating', and an injured leg, though we do not know at this time how severe that injury is.

James leaned back in his chair and ran his hand across his face, seemingly trying to brush the image from his memory. He could not, however. The wounds visible from that day were fresh in his mind. He could see the swollen, discolored left eye as Jolene approached. He watched as she limped up to him and sat at the outdoor patio seat. It was a day he would never forget.

It was the day Jolene Hartley asked him about his parents' murders.

She had told him new information had come to the surface, something about a gun found in her apartment after being mugged, a gun they traced to one Michael Graiser, his father. The gun, she had stated, had been purchased three days before the killings in their Wisconsin vacation home and taken after the gruesome deeds were committed, leaving James alone in the world at the age of twenty, a lost soul trying to right a ship that was quickly sinking.

James snapped out of his reverie and leaned forward, hands reaching out to the keys as he typed in a new query: *Korhan Karaca*. It was a name he had not heard since that day when he last saw Jolene. The gun found at the scene of her attack had been wielded by Luke Moran and tied to the murder of Bart Reed. Yet there had been two individuals who assaulted Hartley that evening, the other being identified through fingerprint analysis as one Korhan Karaca, the troubled son of Ahmet Karaca, Michael Graiser's personal assistant.

James scanned the page, clicking on the third item on the list and being immediately redirected to the Crime Section of the *Chicago Tribune*.

> *Fingerprint technicians have identified the*
> *suspect in the assault of a Chicago police officer*
> *in her home the other evening as thirty-eight*

year old Korhan Karaca. A warrant for Karaca's arrest has been issued. He is wanted for breaking and entering and battery to a Chicago police officer. Patrol units have been given Karaca's picture, as well as his known associates. Karaca has been in trouble with the law since his teenage years, in and out of county jails on charges from possession to assault and battery.

Ahmet Karaca, Korhan's father, was available for comment. When asked about his troubled past, Ahmet pleaded to his son. "I wish for Korhan to turn himself in. I love you and I do not want to see you hurt. Please, turn yourself in before it is too late."

Authorities believe Karaca to be armed and dangerous. If he should be seen by anyone, please call 9-1-1.

James stared at the screen for a moment longer before signing off and walking to the counter. Grant rose from his seat and looked to the clock. He turned with his mouth open, words stopping abruptly on the tip of his tongue as he watched James exiting onto the street. His eyes fell to the countertop and the crumbled fifty-dollar bill his patron had left.

FOUR

Jolene hung up the phone and grabbed her leather jacket from the wooden coat hanger just outside the conference room door. She began towards the steps but halted, instead veering between the unoccupied desks and to the restroom. Captain Nolan was right. She had been spending way too much time at the station. Researching cases and going through bundles of paperwork would only drive her mad if she continued at the frantic pace she was going. She needed to get away and not happen by for a quick glance at this file or a hasty chat with that suspect. Her weekend, although starting at nearly 9:00 p.m., was going to be just what she needed and Captain Nolan ordered: relaxing.

She gave herself an once-over in the large mirror, smoothing out her shirt and spinning to the left to take in the overall appearance. Jolene stopped and placed her hands on the countertop, laughing at the routine she stepped through just before a date, actions that seemed to be playing out at the moment. "Just go, dummy," she said aloud with a shake of her head and one last glance at her reflection.

* * * * *

He was waiting patiently outside Paradin's Restaurant, back resting against the brick and mortar exterior of the establishment. His right foot was crossed over his left, hands jammed into pockets in a pose that had been immortalized in every fashion magazine a hundred times over. Jolene stared at him as the cab pulled up to the corner, waiting for the light to turn green and the taxi in front to proceed through the busy Friday night intersection. He stared down to his feet and back up to the sidewalk as a group of young women passed by, each doing a double-take at the man standing guard. He did not give them a second look.

"This will be fine," Jolene said to the driver.

"You no want me drop you at corner?" he asked, his broken English causing her to pause before the words registered.

"No, thank you. This is good." She handed him the fare and tip and exited the vehicle behind a group of college kids already well into their evening, voices loud in the night air as they stumbled along the pavement.

"Good God!" one of them yelled as Jolene stepped out to the sidewalk.

"Dude, shut up!" another rebutted, glancing back and nearly walking into a signpost as he caught sight of her.

"What?" the first young male questioned. "She's fucking smoking hot!" He pushed his buddy and looked back to Hartley. "I'm sorry. I'm drunk. Is it wrong for me to tell you how good looking you are? I think it's a compliment, you know?"

"Matt, come on. Seriously. Leave her alone. Let's just get to the bar."

"Maybe I want to go with her," Matt replied in a slur. "How about that? Where are you going?"

Jolene could not help but grin as she pulled the bottom of her jacket to the side, pulling the lustful young man's eyes to her waist ... and to the police badge still dangling from her belt. "Oh, fuck! See, Matt! I told you. Leave her alone before she arrests you."

"Damn!" Matt said in a singsong tone, eyes slowly crawling up her torso. "Well, you're the hottest fucking cop I've ever seen."

"Have a good night, Matt," Jolene replied.

"You too, beautiful. Officer. Whatever." He turned and nearly collided with a parked car.

Jolene chuckled and ran her fingers through her hair as she took a step forward, smiling at the man standing post against the restaurant. He moved from his position near the wall, stopping several feet away and reaching his hand out in greeting. Jolene looked to it and smiled, extending her own for a shake, her vision sliding up his extremity, over his chest and neck, and falling upon the light green eyes of her partner.

"Having a little trouble with those guys?" Jacoby Ratliff asked.

"I had it under control," Jolene answered. They both laughed and moved to the restaurant entrance, Jacoby pulling the door open for her and an exiting couple. Before he could step through and join her, an elderly man with a cane approached, slowly edging his way closer to the door. Ratliff stepped back and remained stationary, holding his post as temporary bellboy. Hartley stood in the lobby and laughed, watching as her partner tried to maneuver his way through the threshold and to her side.

"May I take your bags?" he joked, his body inadvertently brushing hers.

"Always serving others," Jolene said, stepping to the hostess. "Two, please."

"Do you want a table or booth?" the teenage girl responded.

Jolene turned to Ratliff. "Table or booth? Or the circle top by the bar?"

"Yeah, let's do the circle top."

"Circle top?" the hostess repeated. "No problem. Follow me."

Hartley and Ratliff followed the girl through the restaurant and to their table. Paradin's was a nice establishment. It had opened several years ago to rave reviews, though, in Jolene's eyes, their crusted fish and steak were highlights of an otherwise mediocre menu. The ceilings were high and the lighting dim, candles on each table reflecting and dancing along the dark brown accented wood strategically placed along the walls and floor. An assortment of plants sectioned off the booths, the greenery shooting up from behind the red leather benches to grant each station a little privacy in an otherwise insanely busy atmosphere. The orange flickering flames of the kitchen could be seen rising high throughout the dining area as cooks and busboys ran hurriedly back and forth, dodging one another with a crate of dirty dishes and extremely sharp knives. A wine room to the left allowed the patrons of Paradin's firsthand access to bottles of merlot or Riesling or Shiraz, each with a taste test before purchase. Aromas of well-seasoned steaks and ocean fresh seafood hung in the fragrant air, carried throughout the establishment by an enormous fan that mixed the flavors together and gifted them to the throngs.

"You guys enjoy your meal! Your waiter will be with you shortly," the hostess said with a smile before bouncing back to her station.

"Bubbly," Jolene said, mocking the girl's smile with a tilt of her head.

"Like a high school version of you, I'm sure," Jacoby responded.

"Ha. Ha," she replied as Ratliff grabbed the wine menu and began perusing the selection. Jolene looked upon her preoccupied partner, watched his eyes scan across the pages, his face intense as if the decision were life and death. She had become accustomed to having Ratliff at her side. The murder of Bart Reed had brought him into her life just as she was getting used to being on her own. She did not shun the thought of a partner; Hartley actually liked the idea of a unit working in unison, watching one another's back while fighting the good fight. The thing she had dreaded was getting to know the inner workings of someone with that responsibility dropped into their laps, especially after her partnership with Barailles had turned sour. Jacoby had immediately fit right in. His demeanor, the way he moved about the case and sided with her regardless of the situation, were several of the reasons why she felt so comfortable with him.

And then there was, of course, his outward appearance, which definitely did not hurt matters. Jacoby was built like an Olympic gymnast: fine-tuned muscles stacked gracefully upon a frame that had been hardened by the military. He was the child of a white father and black mother, giving him the exotic appearance she had become smitten with on day one of their meeting. She had tried to resist his pull, yet there was a multitude of qualities he possessed that she yearned for in a man. It had sent Jolene into a tailspin that kept her in his orbit.

While his physical appeal screamed Abercrombie & Fitch, it was his moral character that set him apart from the rest of the attractive men Jolene Hartley had met in her time. He was kind and chivalrous, assets Jolene felt most individuals of the opposite sex in this day and age lacked. His attitude towards life in general was upbeat, though he was mature enough to know the world was anything but generous, making his own generosity that much more appealing. And he was *very* appealing to Jolene.

Their waiter approached with a smile and two menus, sliding them onto the table before setting a smaller, black specials book atop that. "Welcome to Paradin's. I'm Thomas. I'll be your waiter this evening. Can I get you some drinks to start off?"

"I'll take a glass of merlot," Jolene replied, feeling Ratliff's eyes on her.

"Absolutely," Thomas said. "And for you, sir?"

"The same, please," Jacoby answered.

"Great. Just to let you know, we have a couple specials not on the list here," he said, directing their attention to the black book. "The first is our chicken. It's a stuffed chicken breast in a chardonnay sauce served with lemon-pepper asparagus and wild rice. The other is our flank steak pinwheels, stuffed with spinach, feta cheese, and roasted red peppers over a bed of baby spinach leaves." He looked at the two momentarily before continuing. "I'll give you two a couple minutes. Be right back with your drinks."

"Thank you," Jolene said as Thomas turned and disappeared around a corner. She turned her attention back to Jacoby who sat still, hands folded before him. He cracked a smile at her as a busboy placed water in front of them.

Their partnership had been very successful since the beginning. There had been a plethora of cases assigned to the pair since the incident in the *State of Finance* warehouse, yet none measured up quite as well in Jolene's eyes. After all, he had saved her life. He had tenaciously bull-rushed the warehouse wall with a broken wrist until he successfully busted through and came to her rescue. Not many men would go to that extreme.

From her left, Thomas appeared yet again, his serving tray stacked tall with drinks. He placed the glasses of merlot in front of them and quickly excused himself, starting his trek through the section of tables he called home for the remainder of the evening. Jolene began to bring the glass to her lips, only to be caught off guard as Jacoby raised his in a toast. "To us," he said.

Jolene smirked at him, yet clinked her glass with his. "Us, huh?" she replied, feeling a little heat under her collar.

"Yep," he replied. "We make a good team. I've had a few not so great partnerships in the past, so it's nice to be able to come into work and not have to worry about stepping on your toes."

"Ah," she said with a nod. "Well, may want to keep an eye out for them anyway. Who knows when you'll screw up?"

They each took a long sip, their eyes never leaving the other's gaze. "Plus, let's face it: you *are* pretty damn easy on the eyes —"

"And there it is," Jolene said, shaking her head, though she could feel herself blush slightly as she smiled wide.

"— so that by far beats my old 250-pound partner from Narcotics," he added with a chuckle. "He had three missing teeth and a comb over that put Donald Trump to shame."

"Well, you're not too bad yourself."

"Not too bad? I clean up nicely and you know it."

Hartley squinted her eyes to him as if weighing her options. "Let's just eat," she said, picking up the menu before her and watching as his eyes hovered on her for a moment before turning down to his own.

She stared at him for a short time, her thoughts fading back into their relatively short existence and coming to rest on that day in the precinct sparring room where their lips first met. Jolene had thought about that moment almost every day, reliving the exact second when their tongues flicked and hands ran across each other's bodies. They had not had the chance, however, to test the boundaries of the physicality they found themselves delving into. A well-timed entrance by Kim Banneau halted all activity, pulling the new partners apart and into awkwardness. Banneau, at least, seemed amused, a smile spread across her face and witty comment waiting to erupt from her mouth. It had been an embarrassing episode for Jolene, mainly due to the fact that the previous evening had been spent rolling in a heated sexual exchange with James Graiser. She had been confused and vulnerable, and, at that exact moment, figured a romp in the sack, however forced it may be, would propel her and Graiser forward. It did not, unfortunately, instead leaving her in a state of limbo as to the control of her relationships.

"What are you thinking about?" Jacoby suddenly said, forcing her to regain the present at blinding speed.

"I'm sorry?" she replied, flustered for the moment as she shook her reveries from her brain.

"Food," he said. "What are you thinking about?"

"Oh," Jolene responded, dropping the menu onto the table. "I guess I'm going to go with the special. The stuffed chicken one. You?"

"I was thinking about that one too, but since you're going for it, I'll go with the flank steak. I'll just steal some of yours."

"You come near my plate and I may shoot you. I do still have my gun on me, so I'd think twice about reaching for a piece of asparagus."

"Well said," Jacoby smiled, turning as Thomas stepped to their station. They placed their orders and requested a refill on their wine, Ratliff suggesting Thomas bring the remainder of the bottle. "There's no chance in hell we're leaving here without finishing the wine." Jolene nodded her head, holding her glass up and downing the remainder of the liquid. Ratliff smiled and followed suit, his green eyes catching her gaze and holding onto it as the pair began their evening with one another.

* * * * *

"I'm pretty sure yours is better than mine," Jacoby said, wiping his mouth on the beige cotton napkin and swallowing the bite of chicken Jolene had offered him.

"Agreed," she said, lifting her glass of wine to her lips and glancing around the restaurant. The bottle they had just finished pouring was starting to go to her head, the slight relaxed feeling gracing her limbs. "That steak was a little too well done for me."

"Right? It was like you needed a chainsaw to cut through it."

"It had some good flavor though, regardless of the meat."

Jacoby laughed, receiving a wide-eyed *What did I say?* look from Hartley. "We sound like a bunch of food critics. Coming from a guy who eats McDonald's cheeseburgers by the dozen."

"Get out of here!" she responded. "With a body like that …" She trailed off, staring to the table as Jacoby smiled to her mischievously. "See, now that's the stuff that comes from my mouth when I've had too much wine."

"We should probably get you more then. I like hearing about myself from other people."

"What? Rather than it coming from your own humble lips to begin with?"

"Exactly."

Jolene could remember the time when her and Ratliff — accompanied by Kim Banneau, Virgil "Mac" McLourey and an assortment of other officers — began these excursions out for dinner and drinks. She had always done so with Banneau. Her raucous, shameless fellow detective could be crude and disgusting, and was known to share jokes that made the male officers near her cringe. She was more than Jolene's best friend. She was like a sister. Kim had been there for her through thick and thin. She had helped Hartley battle her way through the wounds received by both Taylor Thames and Luke Moran with a mixture of therapeutic conversation, laughter and alcohol. Banneau knew just how to make things better, and Hartley loved her for it.

Yet the comfort of evenings out with Ratliff alone had started just months ago with the decision to meet for drinks and laughs with the usual suspects at Freddy's Candy Shop, a bar frequented by the officers just down the street from Jolene's apartment. At the last moment, however, Jacoby had asked her to join him for dinner, an inquiry that had caused an involuntary reaction on Hartley's part: she had hung up the phone. Laughter had erupted from her being, though she could not quite put a finger on where it was coming from. She had been put on the spot with the question and, at that particular moment, a sudden dropped call seemed the best choice. She remembered weighing her options as the phone began to ring once more, answering the device with a decisive, "Sounds great." At the time she had been utterly flustered. Now, it only made her laugh. She was a Chicago police officer. The line of work required quick thinking. Too bad she could not do the same with her social life.

"So how come you were at the precinct so late?" Jacoby asked. "Anything new come up with Dougy Merlowe?"

Jolene shook her head. "No, nothing new. Just looking into a few things."

"Yeah? Like what? The Mystery Case?"

She smirked and furrowed her brow. "Mystery Case? What is this? *Scooby-doo*?"

"All right. Not ready to let me in on it? That's fine."

"There's not really anything to let you in on," Jolene said with a shrug.

He looked at her for a moment before conceding defeat. "Okay. Well, when there is, you just give me the word and I'll be there to help."

"Just like you're helping right now by letting my drink go empty?"

"Oh, well I didn't realize it was going to be that type of night," Jacoby answered, raising his hand to the closest waiter. "Can you bring us another bottle of this when you get a chance?"

"Absolutely, sir. Let me tell your waiter," the man responded.

"Oh, it's that type of weekend," Jolene said as the man retreated to the wine room. "I figure I'm in need of a nice relaxing — possibly drunk — weekend. Plus, Nolan kicked me out of the station and told me not to come back for a couple days."

"So you figured you'd listen for a change?"

"Hey, I listen to the Captain. I just don't listen to you."

"Well, I'm glad we got that straight," he said with the smile that melted her each and every time.

FIVE

EARLY APRIL ...

It was odd, him packing a bag. He had become so accustomed to packing bags throughout his years on the planet that it should not have felt foreign. Yet it did. Nearly eight months in the same location could do that to you. He had remained stationary the entire while, save for the weeklong trips to Kingston with Desmond and Mattie to visit her family on several occasions. He enjoyed it here. The weather, the people, all of it. James had not wanted to leave Jamaica. He felt like he had become one with the island, cherishing everything his life had become since he had made it his home.

Or had he? Smoking obscene amounts of ganja was hardly something he considered high on his life achievements list. He did not look down on his friends that were habitual potheads in the least. In fact, he considered them to be some of the most interesting people he had ever met, down-to-earth folk with peace and love on their minds. No, he enjoyed their company, and the island they called home. Yet there was an enormous pull from his past, a magnetism that beckoned him back with such force that he had found himself gathering the will to purchase his plane ticket into Chicago's O'Hare International Airport.

James suddenly jumped as he felt hands slide from his sides to his chest, wrapping around his torso in a gentle embrace that screamed of Mattie. He tilted his head back and leaned into her, her thick dreads acting as padding on his neck. "Hey boy," she said, her accent thick and soothing.

"Hey," he replied, turning his attention back to his belongings spread out before him.

"So you're really going, huh? Back to Chi-Town?"

"Yeah."

"You know you don't have to. You know you can stay here. Desmond doesn't care you're crashing with him."

"I know," he replied. "At least he doesn't tell me to my face."

"Seriously, James," she said, sliding underneath his arms and coming face to face with him. "Stay. Maybe you just need a change of scenery here. Maybe ... I don't know. Maybe you move out of Desmond's ... and me and you get a place." James forced a smile and looked to the floor. Mattie nodded her head sadly and took a step back. "Not enticing enough, huh?"

"No," he answered, bringing his eyes back to her. "No, it's not like that. There's just ... There's just a lot I need to deal with."

Mattie bit her lip, tears forming. "Is it that cop?"

"Yes," he answered, and then quickly added, "but not like that."

"Then like what?" He opened his mouth to speak, yet nothing came out. He sighed and glanced to the wall. "No one leaves for a girl if it's not like that."

"Mattie, listen," he said, pulling her close to him. "I promise you, I'll —"

"Hey, Jimmy," came a gruff voice from behind him." James turned to look upon his friend and roommate, Desmond Brown, his lengthy dreads pulled back and stuffed into a dilapidated tam. "Phone call, man." He handed James a cell phone.

"Yeah?" James answered, holding up a finger to Mattie.

The voice on the other end caused a smile to form. "You are a bloody tough man to get ahold of, you know that?"

"Sorry about that, Augie," James answered. "Been a bit busy these last couple weeks."

"Busy?" Augie replied with a chuckle. "What can you be busy doing in the tropics? Besides some busty broad." He had always had somewhat of an unfiltered personality. August Hughes was a friend from ages ago, a backpacking buddy from his time as a youth. Augie had been born and raised in London, and had worked throughout his teenage years to gain money for two things: European vacations and heroin. He had met James in the Alps on a skiing trip where he nearly died from an overdose in an expensive cabin filled with half empty beer bottles, smoldering cigarette butts and used syringes. James had been the only one to remain by his bedside at the hospital, Augie's other friends departing for the seedier areas and their next fix.

"Did you find him?" James asked, taking a seat on the bed and watching as Mattie turned to a pile of clean shirts. She began to fold them slowly, one at a time, the fabric sliding between her fingers as if it were the last time she would feel them. She placed each next to his bag, creating a stack of items ready for departure.

"I did," Augie answered, pulling James's attention away from Mattie. "And let me tell you: Korhan Karaca's a fucking surly dude!"

"Wait, wait. You've talked with him?"

"Yep."

"When did this happen?"

"Uh … I don't know. A couple weeks after checking out his parents' place."

"His parents' place? Why'd you go there?" James sounded almost upset.

"Have you ever tried to track down a junkie?" Augie questioned. "Because let me tell you, it's not an easy thing to do sometimes. I stopped over there to see if they could give me any information on where he was."

"Did they?"

Augie chuckled. "No. None. They saw right through my disguise. Apparently if you want to be a drug counselor, you shouldn't show up to places smelling like weed."

"What did they do?"

"Nothing. Well, the old man started yelling and told me to leave. So I did. Don't really want any trouble, you know?"

"Good."

"Yeah, well, I'm pretty sure he called the police. I made it to the bus stop just down the street and watched a squad car pull up. Guess I didn't make a good impression."

James thought for a moment before turning the conversation back to Korhan. "When you saw him, you didn't —"

"No, don't worry. I didn't mention you. Although I'm not really sure why you want me to keep you out of it. I thought his family and yours were pals."

"That was a while ago. I just figure with him on the news, and the pictures of me … It'll just sidestep some issues."

"Aye. I read you. Best to stay out of sight if you're a wanted fugitive, huh?"

James thought briefly of that long ago evening, of the destruction of Jolene's apartment and the subsequent sexual escapades that he found himself in. He shook the memory from his mind. "Yeah. It's just easier this way."

"Understood. Why didn't you tell me he was such a charming bloke, though?"

"I haven't really had any contact with him in a long time. I didn't know. Even back when … Even when my parents were around, he was having his own troubles."

"No worries, Jimmy. He's calm enough with some green in him."

"Augie, you think it's the best idea for you to be helping me out? You smoking with him and going into these neighborhoods —"

"Listen, you asked me to find him, and I did. I've just been gaining his trust."

"I know, Augie, but with your history and all —"

"Whoa, hold on. I'm not that person anymore, James."

"I know. Just be careful. I don't want you to put yourself in any bad situations, you know?"

"Trust me," Augie said. "I'm not touching any of the stuff he's been doing. Just smoking a little herb with the man afterward. That's it. I promise. What about you? When are you heading back to the States?"

James looked up to Mattie and locked eyes. "My flight's in a couple hours," he said reaching out to her and pulling her to him by her waist. She ran her fingers through his hair as he rested his forehead on her stomach. "I'll be back later tonight."

"Great. I should be connecting with Korhan later."

"Just keep me updated on where you are. I'll come and meet up with you two when I get back."

* * * * *

Hartley sauntered back to her desk and sat, waking her computer with a shake of the mouse. It was the first Friday in April and she had decided to take a half day, an idea that had popped into her mind the night before as she stared at her files while the clock slowly ticked closer to midnight. Nolan was all for the early release, excited himself at the night out he and his officers had planned. The majority of his team had the following day off, though those who were not lucky enough still had decided to make the venture out to Freddy's Candy Shop in hopes to enjoy the brief camaraderie before their Saturday shift began.

"Are you going to be joining us later?" Captain Nolan asked from the threshold of his office.

"Absolutely, sir," Hartley responded. "Just going to take it easy the rest of the day. What time's everyone thinking about getting to Freddy's?"

"I'd say about seven or seven-thirty. Does that sound about right?"

"Sounds perfect. I'll see you then." She reached up and flipped the monitor off, the screen buzzing as it faded into silence. Hartley enthusiastically popped up from her seat and retrieved her leather jacket from the back of the chair, turning to Ratliff as he picked up his ringing phone and put it to his ear.

"Ratliff," he said into the mouthpiece, his eyes meeting his partner's as she slid into the form-fitting coat.

"Are you going tonight?" she whispered to him, enunciating the words as they fell from her lips.

He nodded back to her as he continued to listen to the caller, covering the mouthpiece momentarily to respond. "Six-thirty? Want to maybe grab a bite?"

Hartley grinned and nodded. "See you there." She waved quickly to him as he began to speak into the phone, his eyes furrowing slightly at the caller on the line. Hartley moved towards the stairs, her body beginning to relax as the thought of a nap on her couch filled her mind. It was warm out today, the perfect scenario for a windows-opened snooze.

Just as she was about to disappear from view, Ratliff's voice echoed to her down the stairway. "Jo!" he yelled, coming from behind as she turned towards him. He stopped before descending the steps, looking down upon her. "We just got a tip on Merlowe. He's at Wentworth and 23rd, in Chinatown."

"Does patrol have him?" she asked, her relaxation beginning to stiffen as the blood began to pump, adrenaline starting to flow through her body.

Ratliff shook his head. "They're tailing him until we get there. Figured we've been searching for this guy for a while. Why not take him down, too? Unless you were really excited about sitting around and doing nothing the rest of the day? I can go handle this myself if you'd rather snuggle up on the couch with some popcorn and John Hughes movies."

"Not a chance in hell," she interrupted, moving back up the steps towards him. "Let's go get him. I wouldn't mind starting my weekend by bringing in a murderer."

* * * * *

They met the patrol units behind a Chinese restaurant on Wentworth Avenue near the corner of 23rd Street. Their fugitive and his cronies had been seen walking into an apartment complex overlooking the avenue. The tailing patrol unit could not be a hundred percent sure, but the officers thought that Doug Merlowe and his crew had entered into the second floor apartment and were now waiting to make their next move. "We watched them go in and about twenty seconds later, the lights in that unit came on. No one's gotten close enough to the window up there, so we can't be sure that's where they are. But patrol covering the back said no one's come out that way, so they're still in the building."

"How many?" Hartley asked.

"Three went up," the officer replied.

Ratliff thought for a moment before turning to his partner. "Maybe just go in quietly and take the apartment? Have some officers positioned strategically throughout the building in case they take off?"

Hartley looked around from behind the restaurant wall, taking in the surrounding area as she always did in cases like this. From where they now stood behind the restaurant, the immediate vicinity was wide open. The parking lot wrapped around the restaurant to their left and opened up to an intersecting alleyway just behind them. Next door to the right was an auto body shop that shared a chain link fence with the eatery, and to the left, a tall, red brick building with parking blocks lining the ground level, spots for either the residents of the apartments inside or that of the patrons of the restaurant they now hid behind.

From the corner of her eye she watched as a bent, elderly Chinese woman moved slowly through the restaurant parking lot, picking her way carefully between the stationary cars and towards the apartment complex. The large, brick structure faced Wentworth Avenue, however, the glass side door just off the sidewalk allowed residents to access the apartments above with relative ease and security from passersby.

"What do you think, Jo?" Ratliff asked, watching as his partner eyed the woman enter the complex next to them and begin the trek up the steps. "Jo?" he repeated after a moment's hesitation.

"Ratliff, I think the next time you call me Jo, I'm going to send you back to the car with a black eye." She said it without making eye contact, subsequently missing the chuckles and grins that formed on the uniformed officers' faces. Ratliff turned to the group and shrugged, conceding defeat in the particular war of wills. It took nearly a minute before a second floor light switched on in the building. From the pavement Hartley and Ratliff watched as the old woman made her way from her kitchen window to the adjoining room overlooking the avenue below.

Ratliff immediately understood. "You want me to go up or do you want to?"

Hartley turned and faced him. "You're with me." She glanced behind her partner and pointed to one of the uniformed officers that had been Merlowe's tail. "Officer Hill, go in through that side door right there and up to that woman's apartment. Should be the second floor, first apartment on your right. Take a look through her window and see where our guys are at in that building. I want a head count and their locations in the room. Ratliff, give him your number to call."

"Got it," Hill said, writing Ratliff's phone number on his hand before walking quickly towards the parked cars and the side glass door. Hartley remained immobile for another few seconds before moving back to the cruiser where she popped the trunk and retrieved her Kevlar vest. She did not want to go into the apartment across the street blind, nor did she want to place her life, and that of her partner's, on the hopes Doug Merlowe and his friends would lay down their arms and turn themselves in without a second thought. The idea was a nice one, but more times than not the suspect tied to a murder investigation seemed more inclined to flee, using any means necessary.

Ratliff's phone rang as he finished securing his bulletproof jacket to his frame. "Yeah," he answered. He listened for a moment before relaying the information to Hartley. "Our eye in the sky. He's got Merlowe in the apartment with three others. Merlowe's on the couch with another guy. Backs to the door. Two others are sitting at a table behind the couch, just left of the entrance."

Hartley nodded, pulling her firearm out and giving it a once over before placing it back in its holster. "Okay, tell him to come back down." Ratliff relayed the message and hung up, stuffing the phone deep into his pocket as Hartley looked back to the assembled team, a squad that included three other uniformed officers — four, counting Officer Hill — as well as a patrol unit on the next block over. "You all will come with us.

Vasser," she said, pointing out a rookie cop overly excited about the task at hand. "You'll remain on the ground floor once we get inside the building."

"Ma'am, I'd be better use with you apprehending —"

"This isn't a debate. And you call me ma'am again you'll be fetching coffee. Understand?" Vasser nodded. "Good. Ground floor. No one comes in, no one goes out. You three," she continued without missing a beat as Hill fell in line. "You'll be on our asses. We go in and get everyone on the ground. I don't want anyone getting jumpy in there, so we work quickly. Don't even give them time to think about arming themselves. Vasser, get on the horn to the patrol around the block. Tell them they need to secure the back of the building."

"Like they'll listen to me," he said with a laugh, deflating promptly as Hartley's gaze fell on him. "On it," he replied quickly, rushing to his squad car and connecting with their backup a block over. Hartley glanced over her shoulder one last time before sending her team into action. The uniformed officers quickly spread themselves out, fanning apart down the block to be less noticeable while making their way to their collective destination. Hartley and Ratliff threw jackets over their Kevlar and began to stroll down the sidewalk at a gingerly, yet focused pace, just two people out for a jaunt through the neighborhood on a warm, sunny afternoon.

As they converged on the building, Ratliff stepped to the glass door and opened it for the officers who hurriedly piled into the vestibule with anxious eyes and pounding chests.

Vasser reached up to his two-way and whispered into it. "Alpha Team in place, over."

A response came immediately. "Copy. Bravo in place, over."

The group halted all movement and looked to their leader who gave a quick grin through her nervousness and, with a subtle nod to Ratliff, brought her hand to her holster. "Let's go, people. Merlowe leaves this building walking and in handcuffs."

SIX

The plane ride was quiet, minus the occasional sob from the lone baby rows behind him, the young mother rocking ever so gently, back and forth, with a look of concern spread across her face, obviously worried about pestering other fliers. James had glanced her way on several occasions, giving her a relatively calming — yet forced — smile to ease her uncertainties.

The flight attendants came by intermittently, mostly leaving him to his own devices as he stared out the window, watching as the sky turned from a calming, light blue to an immense, deep blackness. James stared into the nothingness that became the evening, deep in thought of Mattie and Desmond, the embrace from each and the promise to return as soon as he took care of the business at hand. He had never spoken about his past with Mattie, though, through the constant barrage of United States television reports and internet stories that Desmond seemed enthralled with, James was sure she had pieced things together. There was enough out there to determine that the man she had begun to fall for had been through much in his youth.

Surprisingly, however, Mattie had never asked. He did not know if this was due to the fact that she did not wish to pry, or if she just did not care that much, though he found the latter difficult to swallow. Mattie was a compassionate, young woman. The way she acted towards him did not lead James to think she was in it for just the physical benefits. However, he completely understood the notion of wanting to keep what they had solely in the present, separated from the things she did not comprehend. If she had no control over it, was it really worth digging into? She had become enamored with James as he was now, not as he had been a year ago.

Yet James could not deny the fact that the man Mattie had come to share a bed with was, for all intents and purposes, something of a mystery even to himself. He had felt lost for a long while, drifting between the turbulence of his parents and the sandy beaches of Jamaica, a hazy, confused mindset encompassing him for the majority of the time. His last meeting with Jolene had shaken him to the core, changing the path of ignorance he had established himself on and turning him into a man running desperately away from any semblance of truth. Fight or flight. James had definitely taken off. And now was his chance to stand his ground, fight for the reality that he had denied himself for so long. It was time to fight for his parents.

He remembered walking away from Jolene, the anger and anxiety welling up inside him, her beautiful, battered existence fading into the distance as he continued down the pavement, eyes staring to the concrete yet focusing on the overwhelming whirl inside his brain. He could still hear her voice. "I'm not sure what any of this means ..." It was a phrase that he found comical at the moment. He had lived his life since that meeting by those words. James had not been sure what he was doing, where he was going or how he would be when he got there. It was a relaxing, carefree way to proceed through the world, and one he could envision himself returning to. His financial situation required no responsibility to a career, no qualms about picking up and moving on to better pastures. He was free to do as he wished, but only after he looked into the life he had left.

And that meant, at some point, crossing paths with Jolene, a thought he was both excited for and fearful of.

* * * * *

The shot glasses clinked above the heads of those surrounding the table nearest the front window of Freddy's Candy Shop. "To a job well done!" Captain Nolan shouted above the clamor floating on the bar's dense air.

"Well done!" came the response. There was a simultaneous tilt of heads as a dozen people downed their shots in unison. Jolene brought her hand to her mouth and swallowed the alcohol, not used to the strong flavor that Jameson brought. She was a tequila girl, and one that usually tried to tread lightly when dancing with other types of spirits, whiskey topping that list.

She felt a hand on her shoulder and turned to look upon her partner, Jacoby's smile gracing his face, his green eyes gazing down upon her. He had been conversing with several of the officers that had been with them earlier in the day, though his attention was now drawn to her. He smiled and nodded his personal approval of the work that had been done today in regards to Doug Merlowe. It *had* been a job well done, some of the best policing she had ever done while on the force, and all without her firearm. Doug Merlowe was in custody, pulled out of the apartment in the exact fashion she had planned on after her and her team had infiltrated the building: walking and in handcuffs.

The other members of Merlowe's group had been arrested as well, though some had since been released and were back to their lives. Merlowe, however, was going nowhere. The remainder of his future was tied up in the goings-on of prison, what with a murder conviction hanging over his head and all.

The typical night out with the officers had turned into somewhat of a celebratory party for Jolene and her team, a congratulations of sorts that spawned wholly from the fact that, while the apprehension of Doug Merlowe and his cronies did not go as smoothly as possible, Hartley had walked away from the skirmish within the Chinatown apartment with barely more than a scratch, something of a rarity within the past year.

Hartley had led her team quietly up the building steps, Ratliff and the three officers following close behind and leaving

Vasser in the small vestibule to cover their backs. They had weaved up the staircase with guns drawn, counting down the apartments until they came to the door closest to Wentworth Avenue. From the hall window, Hartley had seen the elderly Chinese woman's pad across the street. The woman had sat resting in a rocking chair as she stared out the window, oblivious to the action about to unfold.

Hartley readied the group, stepping back to allow one of the uniformed officers free reign at the white, wooden door. The entranceway exploded inward, bouncing off an interior wall that rose four feet and ended in a makeshift countertop stacked with ashtrays, car keys and random cell phones. Hartley entered first, gun raised and mouth shouting directives to the individuals inside, all of whom had either jumped to their feet in fright and now stood with hands high, or fell face first to the floor, obviously experienced in police interventions.

"Police! Get on the ground now! On the ground!" she screamed, moving into the space and to her left as her team filed in behind her, Ratliff tailing the group and stopping near the end of the half wall. The officers hurriedly moved around the couch and subdued an individual who had fallen to the floor out of sheer shock, pulling his arms back and handcuffing him with his face in the carpet. They next made their way to a Chinese man standing just to the left of the television, his eyes wide as he tried to register what was happening. He, too, was handcuffed and set down on his stomach.

From her left, Hartley watched as the two men seated at the dining table made a break for it, darting through the eat-in kitchen and towards the rooms down the hall. Hartley jumped into the path of one and threw a shoulder into him, tossing the scrawny individual into the kitchen counter with a crunch. He grunted before collapsing onto the linoleum floor, the air stripped from his lungs from the hockey check she inflicted.

The other man jumped the miniature wall in a quick bound and bounced off the hallway door, bolting into the corridor and towards the stairway. "Police! Don't move!" Ratliff yelled, raising his weapon at the fleeing man. "Hey!" The guy did not so much as glance the detective's way before darting towards the ground floor. Ratliff holstered his weapon and gave chase, skipping down the steps three at a time before sandwiching the escapee between the wall and his own body. Vasser stepped into the mix as well, placing a knee into the back of the fleeing man's neck as he fell to the floor, allowing Ratliff the chance to secure the handcuffs to his slim wrists.

Upstairs, Hartley moved cautiously down the hallway towards the rear corridor, gun extended before her as her eyes scanned the immediate area. Although Hartley and her crew had thus far successfully apprehended a handful of individuals with little to no resistance, there was one serious flaw that she had mentally taken note of: Douglas Merlowe was still unaccounted for. He had been in the apartment, that much was for sure. Officer Hill had identified their suspect. And their backup team, positioned at the rear of the building, had not reported anything unusual, including Merlowe walking out the doors. The building itself offered no easy access to adjoining structures, which meant one of two things: either Merlowe was hiding elsewhere in the building, biding his time to make an impromptu escape, or he was within one of the rooms before her.

Hartley moved into the hallway, checking and clearing a closet that housed the washer and dryer as well as a water heater. She continued forward, coming to the intersecting corridor and noticing a pair of closed doors to her right. She turned the opposite direction, deciding the opened entrances to her left posed more of a threat at the moment, figuring she could react to a doorknob being turned quicker than an ambush.

Hartley edged her way toward the first threshold, an opened entrance to her right that, although consumed in utter darkness, she could tell was the main bathroom of the large apartment. She slid her back against the opposite wall and pivoted towards it, taking a step forward just as a man entered the hall to her left. Hartley spun with her gun raised. "Stop!" she yelled, surprised to see his hands already in the air in surrender, his eyes wide in fright. "Where is Doug —" She did not get the remainder of the sentence out.

* * * * *

James stared up to the grungy, dented bronze plaque displaying the building's address and smirked. It was not an amused reaction. It had been performed more in line with sheer disbelief. He could not fathom that his first stop in the United States had been in a rundown, ramshackle neighborhood such as this. After over half a year abroad in a locale as sunshiny and tropical as Jamaica's northern coast, the cool, damp Chicago night was a surreal experience. The briny, humid air he had become accustomed to had now been replaced by a smoggy atmosphere laden with the overpowering odor of rotting garbage and urine.

James pulled out his cell phone and woke it with the press of a button. He navigated to his text messages and clicked on Augie's name, loading a thread of comments that had been sent on the cab ride from O'Hare. It was definitely the address, as much as he wished it were not. He hardly felt safe in this area. Even the cab driver had given him a double take after the destination was given. "You sure you got the right place?" the man had asked him. He had shaken his head and put the vehicle into drive, catapulting James rapidly into whatever lay ahead.

* * * * *

From the shadows of the bathroom, Douglas Merlowe shot out of the blackness like a cannon, ramming into Hartley as he reached for her extended firearm. The two careened off the corridor walls, the struggle for the gun brought with such intense desperation that it was violently wrenched from her grip, sailing through the air and bouncing to a halt at the frightened man's feet at the end of the hall.

Doug Merlowe was not a tall man, though he definitely had some weight behind him. As he watched the gun fly from the detective's hand, he did the one thing he thought would give him an advantage over the more petite woman: he tried to wrap her in a bear hug and toss her away from the firearm.

It was the worst move he could have possibly attempted.

Hartley reacted with lightning fast reflexes, using his grip around her body as leverage to push off the nearest wall with a power that sent Merlowe stumbling backward. His hold on her disappeared quickly as he crushed into the doorjamb of the bathroom he had just exited. Hartley dropped from his grasp and stumbled into his thick body, regaining her balance just as Merlowe reached out and locked onto her right shoulder. From the corner of her eye she watched as her suspect's gaze fell upon the gun. Allowing Doug to reach the weapon meant allowing her team the opportunity to take him out, ending her vision of the perfect arrest. Another dead body was not the way she had planned this outing.

As the sound of Officer Hill moving down the hallway resonated in her ears, Hartley hastily took matters into her own hands, spinning the left side of her body clockwise towards the fugitive and extending an elbow at his exposed nose. The strike connected, jerking Doug's head back viciously as he tried to claw at any part of the detective, his hand reaching out desperately to grasp onto her jacket as his eyes clouded with tears. Hartley deflected his attempt, grasping onto his thumb and pulling it back as she catapulted him forward and into the other side of the bathroom threshold. A groan escaped his mouth as he slammed into the corner and fell into the hallway, his face contorted in a bloody mask of pain as he gripped his broken thumb.

"Don't move!" Hill had yelled as he stepped into the corridor, gun aimed at Merlowe.

Hartley took a deep breath and turned, her eyes ablaze as she looked to the man still standing post at the end of the hall, her firearm resting a foot away from him. His gaze rose from the weapon and fell onto the woman before him, as well as the mess that was Doug Merlowe. He had glanced one last time at the firearm before making his move. With only a moment's hesitation, he had stepped back and put his hands in the air, his eyes falling one last time on the female detective. "Smart choice," Hartley had said, stepping forward and retrieving her service piece.

SEVEN

"Smart choice?" Kim Banneau laughed from across the table. "Please tell me you didn't say that?"

"She did," Officer Toby Hill said as he stepped up from his position next to Jacoby. "You should have seen the kid's face, too. I'm pretty sure if you would've handed him the cuffs, he'd have graciously put them on himself."

Jolene laughed. "It's true. Whatever thoughts that kid had going through his head about running quickly disappeared."

"Well, it was a successful takedown," Nolan added from his seat next to Mac, the Medical Examiner woozily swaying to the music pumping from the jukebox.

"Can I get anyone another round?" Jacoby said as he moved behind Jolene's left shoulder.

Kim raised her hand. "I'll take another. Jo, shot of tequila?"

Hartley shook her head. "Absolutely not. I think I've had enough shots."

"Okay, so that'll be another round of tequila, too, Jay," Kim continued. "Since I didn't hear any complaints."

"Kim!" Jolene exclaimed.

"Shut up," Banneau fired back. "We're all off tomorrow."

Hartley was about to respond when she felt a hand lightly touch her back. She peered over her shoulder at her partner. "One more and then I'm calling it quits with shots, too," he said to her quietly.

She eyed him with a humorous scowl. "Whatever, Ratliff," she finally said, leaning back ever so slightly into the palm of his hand. "Just trying to get me drunk. I understand how guys work."

"Absolutely," he replied. "How else am I going to take advantage of you?" He smiled wide and stepped back as she swung a light-hearted backhand at his chest.

"Just get the drinks, buddy," she answered, watching as he moved off to the bar.

Jolene returned to the table and skidded right into the waiting grin of Kim.

"You look like you're enjoying yourself," Banneau said, patting the seat next to her.

Hartley guzzled the remaining beer in her glass and slid over to her friend, leaning into Kim's awaiting arms. "I think I have the right to be," she said.

"Not saying you don't. Just thought I'd say it aloud to you. Maybe hearing it will bring it into the open a little more."

Jolene separated herself from her friend and leaned on an elbow. "What? Don't I appear happy?"

"You appear … drunk."

"Not what I —"

"I know. Yes, you look happy. Happier than I can remember you being in a long time. I'm just glad you're giving yourself a little break."

"What do you mean?"

"Come on. You've been pining over what you should and shouldn't do concerning that fine-ass partner of yours for the last six months. It's about time you let yourself just live a little. No more worrying about … you know."

* * * * *

The building reeked like nothing James had ever smelled before. He could faintly distinguish the aroma of marijuana smoke drifting through the corridors, yet it was quickly overrun by a pungent mildew odor mixed with the rancid, toxic stench of crack. A haziness draped heavily throughout the hallway, the fumes so thick that the white wallpaper had long ago turned a sickly yellow, drooping and dangling in a lethargic, inevitable tumble to the stained, dingy outdoor carpeting. Burn marks from extinguished cigarettes created a connect-the-dots effect across the surfaces of both floor and walls, some so deep and dark that it was only a matter of time before the cockroaches infesting the establishment had a new entry into the bowels of the building.

James turned the corner and entered the dilapidated stairwell, pushing the door open onto the boot of a young junkie. He looked down upon the woman, stopping briefly as she stared up to him with bloodshot eyes and a jagged, gaping maw. "Hey!" she forced out, her raspy voice like nails on a chalkboard.

"Sorry," James replied, inching his way around her.

"Watch where you're going next time. Goddamn it!" James edged his way up the stairs and nearly made it past her before he felt a hand grab his shin. "Hey, I'm sorry," the woman said apologetically. "Been a rough day. Look, I'm trying to get to my boyfriend's place. I got dropped off by a cab just around the block, but it's not right. It's the wrong neighborhood. You wouldn't have a couple bucks, would you? I just need to get out of here." James shook his head no. "Wait, wait," she said as he began up the stairs once more. She stood, revealing a body that at one time had been voluptuous and beautiful. "Listen, maybe we can work something out. Maybe I can earn the money."

"No —" James began.

"I'm not looking for a lot. Just enough, you know? How about you give me twenty bucks. I'll suck your dick for twenty."

"I'm not interested —"

"Fifteen," she interrupted, the volume of her voice increasing with her desperation. "Fifteen and I'll let you fuck me. Please!"

James turned and took a few steps down, stopping as the woman bit her lip and rested her dirty, brittle fingers on his belt buckle. James reached down and grabbed her wrists, pulling her frightened eyes to him. "I'm not interested," he said again. "I'll give you five dollars if you tell me where apartment

2C is." She stared to him, mulling over her options. "That's all I'm offering and wanting."

"Up these stairs and down the hall to the left," she answered, putting her hand out as James reached into his pocket.

"Thanks," he said quietly. He pulled out a five dollar bill and set it in her palm, looking into her eyes for a brief second before spinning on his heels and heading in the direction given.

James followed the hall to the left, reading the numbers that remained on each door until he reached apartment 2C. He stopped before it, staring at the rusted letters and numbers and paint-peeled entrance that separated him from the first stop into the truth of his tragic past.

* * * * *

Jolene's smile faded at the suggestion of James. "I've been looking into the murder of his parents," she said, the admission falling from her lips hastily, as if the words were themselves taboo.

"No shit," Kim answered plainly, taking a sip from her glass.

"Wait, you know?"

"Seriously? I'm pretty sure everyone knows."

Jolene cast a glance to her superior. "I figured Henry knew. Didn't know about the rest of the world though."

"Well, you didn't really hide the fact that you were snooping around that well. Shit! You had a box of files under your desk for two months!"

"What? That wasn't a good hiding place?" Jolene joked, forcing a smile as she turned her attention toward the bar and her partner now making his way back to the table, a serving tray stocked full of beer mugs and shot glasses precariously balanced overhead. He weaved through the patrons of Freddy's Candy Shop, seemingly dancing his way between the swaying crowds.

"You let him in on it yet?" Kim asked after a moment.

Jolene shrugged, her eyes remaining fixed on him. "He tried to bring it up. I just …"

"Thought not. Look, it was a trying time after James left. But that's the main point you have to take from it. *James* left. *He* was the one that made that decision. Gone. Vanished into thin air." She snapped her fingers, as if putting on a magic show. "As much as everyone liked him, you just don't do that to someone."

"In his defense, he had a lot going on," Jolene tried.

"Bullshit," Kim added quickly. "He had a lot going on ten years ago when his parents were killed. Island hopping in the Caribbean for the past decade is not considered *a lot going on*." Kim quieted as Jacoby approached the table and slid the serving tray onto the surface. Those nearest moved in, hands eagerly grasping for the closest beer or shot.

"Hold on, you vultures!" he said loudly, swatting those that had not succeeded in procuring a drink. Jacoby grabbed a beer and shot and placed them in front of his partner who looked up to him with kind eyes. "A toast!" he yelled, picking up his own glass and allowing those around him time to retrieve their own. "To Detective Jolene Hartley. The best police officer I know, the best partner anyone could have, and more than anything, one of the best people I have ever come across. I'm lucky to have you as my partner. Cheers!"

"Cheers!" the group yelled. Jacoby reached forward and held his drink aloft. Jolene remained still, staring intently to him with her own tequila sitting before her, the liquor swaying gently within its container. After several moments she reached down and raised it to his, the glasses chiming together as they downed the liquid in unison.

* * * * *

The door opened quickly and James looked upon a small blonde-headed man with severely crossed eyes and a twitch that began at the corner of his mouth and reverberated throughout his upper body. He stared at James for a split second before uttering his greetings. "What the fuck do you want? Are you the cops?"

"What? No. I'm looking for —"

"Paw-Paw," came the familiar British accent from around the corner, a comfortable tone in an otherwise strange atmosphere. Augie stepped into sight and placed a hand on Paw-Paw's shoulder. "He's with me."

"You didn't say your buddy was a fucking cop!" he said, a twitch shaking his frame.

"Wait. What?" Augie said, trying to hold back a smile. "No, Paw-Paw, he's not a bloody cop." He looked to James. "Did you say you were a cop?"

"I didn't say anything," James responded.

"See," Augie replied, smacking Paw-Paw on the back and turning him into the apartment. "He's not a cop. Just … Just go do your thing." They waited a moment before Augie turned to him and laughed. "That bloody guy is the most paranoid son of a bitch I've ever seen when he smokes." Augie's smile, even through the clouds of mind-altering drugs floating from the open apartment door, made James feel relatively at ease.

He had always been something of an older brother figure to Augie, even though James was two years his junior. The aspects that made up Graiser's life had, unfortunately, forced him to grow up at a quicker pace than his one-time addict friend from London, compelling him to face responsibilities that Augie shunned at every chance.

Augie was an odd looking man with a weaselly appearance that made him a memorable figure for all the wrong reasons. He was thin, with a long, pointed nose he had dubbed his own personal ski slope, a double-edged joke he had used from time to time to express his adoration of snow-topped mountains as well as cocaine-laden tabletops. His eyes were sunken into his head, two dark orbs staring at the world from beneath a mop of deep, reddish brown locks, a mane that had given him the nickname of "Red" in the drug circles he had routinely visited back in the days when he used.

"It's great to finally see you, mate!" Augie said, stepping into the hall and wrapping his arms around James. James hugged him back, yet the weight of the task at hand allowed no more than a brief sense of camaraderie. Augie pulled back and stared to his friend's emotionless countenance.

"Is he in there?" James said quietly.

Augie nodded slowly. "You want to do this?"

James sighed heavily before answering, "No. But I have to."

"Understood. Well, come on." Augie stepped aside to allow James entry. He closed the door and set the locks before leading James down a short hall and into an adjoining kitchen. From the room before them, James could hear Paw-Paw's hysterical laughter, his paranoia obviously evaporating into the smog that floated near the apartment's ceiling.

James stepped into the room and froze, his eyes falling upon Korhan Karaca, the child of his father's former personal assistant, a man he had not seen in what seemed like two lifetimes. Korhan chuckled with Paw-Paw as he lifted a bowl to his lips and fired up a lighter, pulling the flame into the nearly cached weed that began to glow a brilliant orange. The slow burn of the marijuana lit up Karaca's face like a campfire, allowing James to witness the pockmarks and scars that littered his skin, a gift given by Jolene on the night Korhan and Luke Moran had attacked her. He felt angry then, knowing full well this man was the reason for his exodus from his life in the

States, the indirect cause of his unbearable pain that forced him from Chicago, and from Jolene Hartley.

James wanted nothing more than to fly across the room and pummel Korhan, to rain fists and kicks down upon the man until he was nothing more than a bloody pulp seeping into the grungy couch cushions he now sat on. However, that was not his planned course of action. At least not yet, anyway. He needed answers. He needed someone to provide a clue, a fragment of a lead, as to *why* this deed had been done to his parents. He needed to figure out the reasons behind the attack that left him alone in the world.

And he needed to find out who was responsible.

James stood still at the end of the hallway, unable to will himself to take a step into the room. He stared at Korhan as Augie stepped around him and walked to the seated felon, grabbing the pipe from him and putting it to his own lips. Karaca leaned his head back and rubbed his eyes, the smile sliding from his face immediately as his eyes fell upon the familiar figure across the room. He recognized him, yet could not place him for several seconds. Finally, it hit him, and his eyes grew glassy and tears began to stream.

EIGHT

James bolted through the doorway and into the night, head up with eyes wide as he sucked in the crisp evening air. He felt out of breath, as if he had sprinted a half mile with no relent. His legs grew shaky and his hands began to tremble as he leaned into the building, bracing his body as stars formed in his eyes. He suddenly felt his stomach heave towards the heavens and a rush of vomit escaped his mouth and splashed onto the pavement below. He let loose again and reached out to grasp onto a metal handrail jutting from the brick wall, steadying himself for a brief moment before a succession of dry heaves doubled him over.

The door to the building opened once more and James sat up, wiping the tears from his cheeks and spitting away the residual vomit from his lips. "Hey," Augie said as he approached, placing a hand on James's back. "You okay, mate?" James nodded, the perspiration across his face and back cooling his body instantly. The stars that had formed in his vision faded, leaving him staring up at his friend. "You sure?" Augie asked.

James grabbed onto Augie's shoulder and pulled himself up. "I'm fine," he answered, running his fingers through his mop of hair.

Augie glanced around before speaking again. "I, uh … I didn't see that coming at all." James looked to him, his face expressionless. The exchange of dialogue within the rundown apartment building had shook James to the core. It had taken everything he had to not storm across the room and pummel Korhan into a bloody, lifeless mess. At one point, Augie had inched his way between the pair, feeling as if his longtime friend would become unhinged and do something he would no doubt regret. James's better judgment had prevailed, however, and he had come away with something far better than winning a physical battle with a hysterical junkie. He had come away with information and a name: Millers.

"I have to go," James said suddenly, pushing away from the building and past his friend.

"Where to?" Augie asked, arms wide.

"I have to go. I have to see someone," James replied, beginning to walk down the street towards a busier intersection and the possible taxis he could hail.

"James!" Augie yelled after him. "What do you want me to do?"

James halted and thought for a moment. He had not envisioned things going as they had. He had pictured things in his mind stalling and him catching the first flight back to

Jamaica. Yet fate had played a far different series of events. He walked back to Augie and pulled out a wad of cash, stuffing the bills into his hand. "What the fuck is this for?"

"Listen. Give it to him."

"What?"

"Just do it."

Augie's mouth dropped open and his eyes went wide. "You want me to give him —" He counted the bills in his hand. "— four hundred dollars? Are you serious? After what he —"

"Just do it, Augie!" James said with a growl. He closed his eyes and took a deep breath. "I'm sorry. Just give him the money. Tell him I need his help. I'll keep giving him whatever he needs, if he can help me find this Millers guy."

"Okay," Augie said, nodding in understanding. "But where are you going?"

James turned and began down the street once more. "I need to go see someone."

August Hughes watched as James departed, his friend's gait filled with determination as he disappeared down the sidewalk and into the night.

* * * * *

Jolene bit her lip and watched as Jacoby Ratliff made his way to the door of Freddy's Candy Shop, his frame swaying back and forth as he slipped between the patrons of the establishment. He had completed his goodbyes for the evening moments ago, making his last stop by her side. She had felt —

and welcomed — the hand he had placed gently upon the small of her back that pulled her attention from Kim. They had held each other's gaze momentarily before he smiled wide and extended his hand to her. She had eyed him up through a slightly drunken fog with a thumbnail between her teeth and Banneau chuckling from her side. "Good work today, detective," he had said as they shook.

"You too," she had replied.

"Have a good weekend. I'll see you on Monday."

"Yeah. See you Monday." They had held on to the handshake for a moment longer, their fingers gripping, eyes locked, words fighting to escape into the atmosphere and ride high on the alcoholic breeze created by the wooden ceiling fans.

"What are you doing?" Kim said suddenly, pulling Jolene's thoughts out of the recent past.

"What?"

"Why are you still sitting here?"

"What do you mean?" Hartley asked.

"I mean everyone's going to be out of here soon anyway. Go! Go get an escort home. Enough staring at his ass! Go bite it!"

"Kim!" Jolene laughed, turning her attention back to her partner as he stepped through the threshold and onto the pavement. Jolene spun around to Kim quickly and grinned nervously, springing into action and moving between the tables as she slid into her coat.

"Happy hunting!" Kim yelled after her.

Jolene weaved between the groups packing every inch of the bar, waving to this person with a smile or patting that person's shoulder as a sign of goodbye, as well as to part the way. She was surprised to only have a mild level of anxiety rising. Under normal circumstances, the butterflies in her stomach would have been working in overdrive, however, at this moment, it felt like a leisurely flutter. The alcohol surely did not hurt, though Jolene could not help but think the collected way in which her and her partner had been dealing with each other on and off the job also played a significant role. She was definitely comfortable around him. Her sense of self had become much more aware of the flirtatious side that had appeared with Jacoby Ratliff. *Jay.* That evolution had taken a while. She still needed a small amount of push to let his nickname fall from her lips, though each time it became easier and easier. He, on the other hand, had no problems with using her abbreviated, off-duty *Jo*, even while on the job, a notion that still riled her blood for good reason. Sometimes it felt the job would follow her home, cling to her skin and not let the cop side fall to the floor until a new day. Sometimes *Jo* was all that made her feel like a normal human being instead of a silver star.

She speedily made it to the doorway and pushed it open, the crisp, cool night blasting into the heated establishment for a couple seconds of refreshment before once again putting the lid on the boiling stockpot that was Freddy's Candy Shop. Jolene moved onto the sidewalk and glanced in both directions. She felt heated, as if missing Ratliff by milliseconds would force her into confronting the patrons of the bar once more, all eyes on her as she made the shameful, embarrassed entrance without the man she had just ran after.

Jolene sighed at her missed opportunity and turned back towards the doorway. As her finger fell on the cold, metal handle, a taxi slowed through the intersection and stopped just behind her. She let go of the knob and moved towards the street, watching as Ratliff stepped up to the rear passenger door and began to climb in.

"Jay!" she shouted, her heart thumping as he stood and looked around for the source. "Ratliff!"

"Hey," he replied, holding a finger up to the driver as Hartley made her way to him, hands in either jacket pocket, a grin spread across her face. "What's up? I thought you were staying a while longer?"

"Well," Jolene replied, glancing over her shoulder. "Kim's about to take off too, so I thought … I thought maybe you'd want to escort a lady home? Wouldn't want anything to happen to the best partner you've ever had." She said the last part in a mocking tone, pulling a chuckle from herself as well as her partner.

"No, I guess not," he agreed, turning to the cab driver. "Sorry, pal. I'm actually going to walk." He closed the door without waiting for a response. Ratliff approached his partner and stopped, glancing down at the glossy eyes and happy grin crossing her face. "Shall we?" he said, swinging his arm wide.

Hartley brought her shoulders up in a shrug and pivoted on her heels. They began in silence, their footfalls echoing on the gritty pavement, breath visible in the coolness of the night. Jolene had no plan formed in her mind, no pre-meditated arrangement that ended in her blurting out a rehearsed invitation. She was not worried about the walk home and what might come after. She was playing it by ear, flying by the seat of her pants into semi-unknown territory. Over the months of getting to know Jacoby through their professional partnership — as well as the blooming flirtation that had broken into the open — Hartley had become what she had been hoping for since the moment Ronny Debarsi left Chicago: independent. She liked Jacoby as a partner on the job, as well as a friend and possibly more. He was a kind individual with an edge that sparked her bad-boy interest. He was not afraid of her stubbornness or beauty, as many men in her past were. He was equally hardheaded and handsome, which set their collaboration on a level playing field. In her eyes, they complimented each other perfectly.

"So, you really beat some ass today," Jacoby said, breaking the silence. "Merlowe didn't stand a chance!"

"Yeah, well, after last year's trips to the hospital, I figured I was sick of getting pummeled. You didn't fair too badly either. I saw the hole in the drywall where that kid's head went through. Nice work."

Jacoby laughed. "Hill kept saying it looked like a cartoon when someone runs through a wall and just leaves an outline." Her childhood memories of *Tom and Jerry* and *Looney Tunes* raced to the surface.

"Well, apparently we do make a good team then," she said, glancing up to him with sparkling eyes.

"I wasn't lying," he said, looking to her. "It's a good situation when you get to work and learn about the job from someone just as passionate as you. It's not work to me."

"Me neither," she agreed, biting the bullet and reaching out to him, grabbing onto his right arm and holding tight. It was a move that caused the nervousness to rise. She was an independent woman, yet here she was, opening up, showing her vulnerability as a human being, something she did not like to do. She was tough. She was firm on the job and liked the respect she received through her hard work and level attitude. And she reveled in the looks of utter awe from people like Douglas Merlowe's associate in the hallway earlier in the day. She did not like to drop that edge. Yet she had just now with Jacoby, and it was something she could tell he appreciated as he glanced out of the corner of his eye to her.

"So, what else is new?" she asked with a sigh as they neared her apartment building entrance.

"What else is new, huh? That's what you're going with? Have we reached that point in our friendship where we have nothing to say to each other?"

"Shut up," she responded, letting go of his arm and stepping in front of him with an anxious sigh. "Just trying to make conversation."

"Just giving you a hard time." He looked to her building door and back as Jolene reached into her pocket and retrieved her keys.

"Well, I ..." She trailed off, looking up to him. "Thanks for walking me —" She stopped as Jacoby moved closer, placing his left hand gently on her neck, his thumb grazing her jaw line while his right slid across her back and pulled her to him. Their mouths met, lips pressing against one another in the cool night. The butterflies in Jolene's stomach vanished immediately, replaced by an excited heat from the exchange as their tongues danced together. Jolene reached up and wrapped her arm around his shoulders, her key-wielding hand running through his hair carefully and pulling his face to hers. It had been over half a year since their meeting in the sparring room and she would be lying if she said she had not been longing for this moment of unbridled passion since then.

The kiss slowed, lips closing yet still pressed to one another, grips loosening until they separated. Jolene opened her eyes and looked into his green orbs. She could not help but smile up at him as she took a step away, her hand running a course across his shoulder and coming to rest on his chest. "I know it's late, but ... Would you want to maybe ...?" Her words faded as she looked up to him, her eyes nervously catching his gaze before sliding to the right and falling upon a figure standing near the back of a stopped cab across the street.

Jacoby watched as she transformed from nervous delight to utter confusion. Her eyebrows furrowed. Her face contorted as the drunken glaze over her eyes gave way to a puzzling clarity. It was as if a ghost had appeared before her, sucking the attention away from their perfect exchange with absolutely no apologies.

It took Jacoby a moment before he realized something was wrong. He turned and followed her gaze, his heart sinking the moment his eyes fell on the mop-haired man standing at the back of the taxi. He was tan, much more so than when Ratliff had seen him last. His eyes seemed slightly sunken and the expression on his face was like that of someone who had been through recent hardships. The man's eyes looked to Jacoby briefly before retreating back to Hartley.

Ratliff turned back to Jolene and dropped his hand from her side as the name fell from her lips. "James?" she said quietly. She watched as Graiser's stance became rigid, his eyes reflecting the street lamps and displaying a hurt that went well below the surface. He set his jaw and entered the cab once more with a last glance to Jolene. The taxi raced off down the street, the detectives staring after it in the awkwardness that had settled in.

NINE

Shock, confusion and anger. An excess of mixed emotions had erupted within Jolene the moment she had seen him, yet those were the trio that had encompassed her mind, body and soul. James Graiser. *Her* James Graiser. Back in Chicago. But for how long? Had he been here the entire time? Had he been shacked up in some suburban bunker for the past half year just waiting for the opportunity to step into the light and shake her foundation?

No. She had determined his whereabouts for the last seven months — although unknown — were most definitely not in Chicago. The tanned complexion he sported screamed of the south and Jolene had a solid notion that the Caribbean had cradled him throughout the mild winter and physical or mental breakdown he evidently now wore.

It had been a shock to see him, no doubt about it. Jacoby, too, seemed a little thrown off by James's sudden appearance in the dark of night next to a stationary taxi. And his physical stature seemed ... off. His demeanor, based on the seconds they shared staring at one another from across the street, lacked an ingredient that made James … well, James. His eyes, usually innocent and bright, seemed to carry a hefty dimness that blocked out the world around him. His adorable smile that pulled outsiders in seemed to be lost, the carefree attitude pulled down and restricted.

Ratliff could tell his and Jolene's night of flirtation had met its end. He had stated he would love to come up, though circumstances as they were, he did not wish to cause more confusion to an already chaotic ending to an evening. He had kissed her on the cheek and said he would see her Monday.

Jolene made it up the stairs and to her apartment wearing the same expression she had when James took off down the street in the taxi. She was confused. Why now? Why show up after almost eight full months of complete and utter silence? Why come back into her life only to show face for a fleeting instant? What was the point? Had he come to the conclusion that things needed to be settled between them? Was he drunk to the point that he thought an impromptu appearance would lead to a conversation and forgiveness?

She had absolutely not forgotten about him over his absence. There had been a residual longing for him that had settled into her bones and brought his face swirling back to her consciousness every once in a while, like that of a high school sweetheart or one's first love.

However, she had moved on. Kim was absolutely, one hundred percent right: *James* had left. *He* was the one that had made the decision to end their budding relationship. Granted,

Jolene's mind had already begun the process of halting whatever was going on between them, yet that had not been set in stone. Their night of lustful passion in his apartment had been a mistake in her mind. And Jacoby's entrance into her life had definitely set in motion actions that led to James's exit. Yet, as she knew, anything could happen. Her job had taught her that much.

Jolene sat on her couch in the glow of the kitchen track lighting, sipping a tall glass of water and staring out the window into the extremely early morning darkness. Her eyes were tired. The inebriation of the evening had vaulted her into a whirlwind of lust with Jacoby and ended on the chaos that had become James Graiser. Yet behind the closing lids was a fire that had become ignited, driven by anger she could not hide even in the wee hours of the morning.

She was irritated with her one-time friend and fling. It had taken a lot of questioning and late night voicemails to realize James was choosing to no longer be part of her life. She had come to the eventual conclusion that she was okay with it. The human side of her being wanted an explanation, some sort of closure as to why he had chosen this path, even if she had, herself, decided that their time together needed to be put on indefinite hiatus. It was not so much that she cared as she just needed to know. However, the cop side wanted answers. Not to their relationship status, but to the decade-old cold investigation into his parents' murders. Why had he bolted after she confronted him that day? What was the cause behind his sudden, lengthy exodus?

Sure, at first her calls to his home phone and cell line were as a friend, albeit one that had been dropped without warning. Though as the months grew and the calls became less frequent, the cop in her had come through, wanting more of a connection to possibly push along the cold case. She wanted to know he was okay, but she was angry enough to leave it at that.

Over the last several months, however, her agitation had subsided, fading into her past along with James and leaving in its wake a budding personal and professional relationship that brought a smile to her face and excitement to her heart. Jacoby had given her the space she needed to deal with her emotions, as he had earlier in the evening. Yet, like he had said to her at one point in the past, he was confident enough to go after what he wanted, and he remained in the picture as her partner and a man that whole-heartedly cared for her well-being.

She shook her head and sighed, running her hand through her hair as she looked to her phone. She should have shrugged off the immediate shock of seeing James and reiterated the offer to Ratliff to join her for another drink. She wanted nothing more than to sit and talk with him, cut a rug on her living room floor and continue the party that had started at Freddy's Candy Shop and ended with their zealous kiss.

She settled onto the couch and pulled a blanket over her tired body, her thoughts racing from Jacoby's lips to the taxi and the ghost from her past. *James*, she thought to herself, eyelids drooping, the windows across the room blurring in her vision. *Why now, James?*

* * * * *

Jolene spent the rest of the weekend in a relaxed state, save for Saturday morning, which was split between the fluffy covers of her bed and the cool tiles of the bathroom floor. She remembered days like this in college, curled on the ground in the fetal position promising never to drink again if the cosmos would remove the deathly sick that consumed her body. She had learned since then that the best cure was aspirin, water and motion. *If you're going to be sick, you're going to be sick,* she thought to herself. Better to get it out than hope and pray for a miracle.

She was awakened Monday morning by the incessant ringing of her cell phone on the end table, the vibrating buzz pulling her from a deep sleep to stare at her clock that was twenty minutes from beeping. She reached out and stared to the screen. Jacoby.

"You better have a damn good reason for calling and waking me up before —"

"They found him," Ratliff interrupted quickly.

"Found who?" Jolene asked.

"Karaca." She sat up in her bed, the comforter falling to her waist as she stared at the armoire directly across from her. "Hello?"

"Yeah. No, I'm here. Just processing." She swung her legs from beneath the blankets and stood. "Where's he at? Who's tailing him?"

"On the west side. He was seen going into a crack house by Parsons about ten minutes ago."

"Who?"

"Andy Parsons. Old buddy from Narcotics. He knew about our interest in Korhan from the attack. Gave me a call to see if we wanted to be there when he was picked up. What do you say?"

Hartley cracked a smile. "Absolutely."

"That's what I told him. I'm on my way to get you. Can you be ready in fifteen?"

"See you then," she said, disconnecting from the call and making her way to the bathroom where she cranked on the water full blast, the superheated steam flowing from the shower as she pulled off her pajamas and stepped into the cauldron.

* * * * *

Hartley was waiting on the sidewalk fifteen minutes later with two to-go cups of coffee when Ratliff pulled up in his ancient Jeep Wrangler. He reached over and pulled the lever to open the door and Jolene stepped in, glancing around the cabin for a cup holder to place the drinks in. "Good luck," he said with a grin. The interior had been long ago stripped clean of any furnishings, the doors nothing more than a metal shield to ward off the ever-changing Chicago weather. Hartley imagined the vehicle to be one of two things: an oven roasting its riders in the summertime or an icebox during the winters, freezing the inhabitants into human icicles.

"Do the seatbelts work at least?" she retorted playfully.

"Mine does. Yours? Not so sure."

"Great." She handed him his coffee as he pulled away from the curb and headed into the early morning commute. "You hear anything more from your Narcotics buddy?"

"I texted him after I talked to you. He said Karaca hasn't left the building. But we need to get over there in a hurry. If he hits the street, they'll have to move on him."

"Swing by the precinct."

"What for?"

Jolene eyed him for a moment. "I'm not going in without a vest."

A smirk formed across his face. "I called Hill. He's on his way out there with them."

"Guess you've thought of everything then, huh?"

"Everything but what you're going to say to Karaca when he's arrested."

Jolene focused out the windshield before responding. "Maybe I'll start out by asking how his face is."

Ratliff chuckled, the image of Jolene smashing the Waterford crystal vase across Korhan's face bringing even more excitement to the morning. "I'd say that's a good start."

* * * * *

Ratliff pulled his Jeep into a small gravel lot surrounded on two sides by an overgrowth of trees and an abandoned, burned-out building to the north. Officer Hill, on loan to the Narcotics Division for the duration of the takedown of Korhan Karaca, walked over with another man in street clothes, the Kevlar vest wrapped tightly over his solid frame.

"Nice to see you," Hill said, handing the body armor to the detectives as they rounded the Jeep and halted near the rear bumper.

"Thanks," Ratliff replied.

"He still up there?" Hartley asked the other man, nodding her thanks to Hill and strapping the vest to her body.

"Yep," the man said. "Hasn't moved yet. We figure he's getting his fix and will be out soon. How's it going, Jay?" He stuck out his hand and shook Ratliff's firmly.

"Can't complain." He looked to his partner. "Hartley, this is Andy Parsons. AP, my partner, Jolene Hartley."

"Detective," Parsons replied, grasping onto her hand.

"Pleasure," Jolene said, pulling her firearm from her holster to check the magazine. "Thanks for letting us tag along."

"Absolutely. After what this shithead tried on you, I wouldn't have it any other way. Jay was pretty adamant about us holding still until you could get here."

"Well, I appreciate it."

"So what's the deal here?" Ratliff asked.

They began around the Jeep and backtracked in the direction of the exit, halting behind a tangle of vines that had overtaken the chain-link fence, providing the group of four a hidden vantage point of the building before them. The structure sat about forty yards away, directly in line with the street just outside of the gravel parking lot. The area was a ghost town, save for the sporadic vehicles traveling down the intersecting avenue at leisurely paces.

"Well, for personnel," Parsons said, "there's us and another team across the way in the laundromat waiting instructions from me. Strategically, we're going to wait for Karaca to show face and start down the sidewalk. We don't know who or what is in that building, so we figured that course of action the least hazardous."

"Do we know if he has associates with him?" Hartley asked.

"Not when he went in. But if he's with someone when he hits the pavement, we plan to get everyone on the ground."

"No plans to go into the building afterward?" Ratliff questioned.

Parsons shook his head. "Bigger fish to fry. We figure, if anything, the arrest will spook whoever's in there. We'll take our suspect back to the station and the other team will hang around and take inventory on whoever comes out of there. Maybe we'll get lucky and one of them will lead us to someone higher up the food chain."

"And you're sure you don't mind us taking part?" Hartley pushed.

Parsons smiled to her. "Like I said, with the shit he tried to pull, I'm happy with you making the arrest."

"Hey, hey," Ratliff said, peering towards the building. "Looks like the time may be now. That him?"

Hartley and Parsons moved closer to the fence and peered through the metal and vines. The door to the building swung open and Karaca stepped onto the pavement, phone in hand and cigarette to his lips. Hartley's blood boiled immediately, memories of the attack flooding her mind. She forced them to the backburner, needing her wits as a police officer to drive her rather than her pent-up emotions. "That's him," she said. "That's Karaca."

TEN

Be outside in a second.

Augie read the text and swore under his breath. His hope had been that Korhan was either too busy or too inebriated to join him, hopefully huddled in a closet someplace with a needle in his arm and foam dripping from the corners of his mouth. Augie had learned that the junkie was a despicable human being, and did not like him in the least. Since meeting Karaca, he had been forced to split his time between dim lit strip clubs packed with miscreants of all sorts, and shady crack houses filled with delinquents he knew all too well from his youth. Augie had cleaned his life up long ago, yet the fact that drugs of any kind were at his disposal had become a mental battle he found himself waging while in Karaca's presence. He found himself needing all the focus and determination he could summon to rid himself of the demon that reared its ugly, drug-craved head.

The bottom line, however, was James. He had asked this favor of him, and Augie felt obliged to fulfill it. *Keep an eye on him,* was the directive that had been dished out, and it was the least he could do.

As Augie approached the decrepit building to meet his least favorite person, he halted near a solid, concrete cylinder that once held an operational streetlight and took out his cellular. He punched in a series of digits and leaned back, letting the phone ring while he spent his remaining minute in peace. "Hey," he said into the mouthpiece as James answered. "I'm getting this asshole right now. When're you free?"

"I'm not sure," James replied, monotone. "I've got some running around to do this morning."

"Everything okay?" James remained silent, his breath the only sound crossing the airwaves. "Listen, mate. I know what he gave you was pretty heavy. I can't imagine —"

"Yeah," James interrupted. "I, uh … I have to go. Just … I'll call you later. Sorry, Augie."

"No. It's fine. I'll take him to breakfast. See if I can get anything from him, you know? You go do what you need to."

"Thanks, Augie."

"Yeah. No worries, mate." He disconnected. James was definitely hurting, that much he could tell. Yet there was absolutely nothing he could do about it. A shoulder to cry on just would not cut it, not after what Korhan had let loose the other night. The admission of truth that had fallen from the junkie's mouth had not only shocked both James and himself, but even Paw-Paw, who quickly gathered his things and left the premises. It was the reason, even if Augie had wanted to, that he could not abandon the plan James had concocted, even if that plan had not been fully shared as of yet.

Augie slid the device into his pocket and ran his hand across his face, yawning in the early morning light. He turned to his right at the metallic grind of a door opening and watched as Korhan exited the building with his eyes down to his own cell phone. Karaca stopped just outside of the building, swaying gently with the breeze, back and forth like a leaf on a tree, as he took a drag of his cigarette. Augie sighed and forced a smile to his face, compelling himself to appear much more excited than he actually was. He stalled for a moment and spread his arms wide, yelling down the pavement to his apparently newfound friend. "You in the mood for some eggs and bacon? My treat!"

* * * * *

"Jo," Ratliff said as they pulled their firearms and readied themselves. "Are you sure you want to do this?" He could see the fire ignite within her.

She turned sharply to him, glaring in his direction momentarily before focusing once again to their target. Parsons chuckled. "I think she's ready, Jay." Ratliff nodded his head in approval. Parsons grabbed his two-way. "All right, people. This is it. Alpha unit will move down the east sidewalk. I want Bravo down the alley behind the buildings. We converge on our guy as quickly as possible."

"Copy that," came the coarse response.

Parsons pulled his own weapon and looked to his team. "Okay. Let's get this motherfucker."

* * * * *

The sound of Augie's British accent should have been enough to garner some sort of immediate reaction from Korhan. The odds that he associated with another Londoner in this part of the city were extremely slim. Yet, Karaca lifted his lethargic eyes slowly, trying to determine — through whatever high he was currently wallowing in — who was beckoning him, and from what direction.

Augie could not help but laugh, waving a hand in the air to draw his attention. Korhan caught sight of the movement and bobbed his head in acknowledgment. "Absolutely ... my friend," he said at length, the drawn out words and deep tone reminding Augie somewhat of André the Giant. Karaca moved forward, slowly and methodically placing one heavy foot in front of the other as he sucked deeply on the cigarette dangling between his lips.

He stumbled on the uneven walk, the concrete slabs jutting up at random angles from the roots of long-gone trees that had once lined the avenue. Korhan slid down the sloped curb and into the street, catching himself on a nearby signpost, the illegible traffic directive faded from the intense sun and covered in bright gang tags. He looked up and smiled dumbly at Augie, mumbling something under his breath that, no doubt, was meant to be a conversation starter. Augie ignored it, not bothering to ask him to repeat.

And that was when it happened, the quizzical look spreading rapidly across Karaca's face mirrored by Augie's perplexed countenance. The latter felt in the universe that something was just not right. Things were out of place, not in line with the usual goings-on of the neighborhood. Korhan, on the other hand, looked as if he had seen a ghost.

Augie turned slightly as the growl of a vehicle approached from his left. He glanced towards it and watched as an old, blue conversion van slowly made its way down the street, the driver sporting a goatee, bug-eyed glasses and long, black hair. He stared for several moments before focusing once again down the sidewalk, noticing for the first time the pair of individuals moving towards him from behind Korhan.

Something was definitely not right.

* * * * *

"Whoa, whoa," Parsons said, halting the group as their collective gaze fell upon the two men making their way towards the building from behind their subject. He pressed the button on his two-way and connected with the other group of officers. "Bravo team, do you have a visual on two civilians on the sidewalk?"

The static-filled response came quickly. "Negative. We're coming up to the street now. Will have a visual in a second."

"Copy that," Parsons said.

"Should we hold our positions?" Parson thought for a moment, glancing from the suspect and back to the pair of men.

"They look familiar to you?" Ratliff asked.

Parsons shook his head. "No one that I've seen out here before. That's not to say they aren't heading to that same building our suspect just came out of." He stalled again, obviously weighing his options, a decision made that much more difficult as a blue van appeared from the right, revealing to the team another civilian, this one with his arms wide and apparently speaking with Karaca. "Fuck," Parsons whispered under his breath. He reached for the two-way and opened his mouth to speak, yet was interrupted by Hartley.

"Keep them moving," she said, her eyes down the street at the scene. Parsons turned back to her. She focused on him briefly before returning to the thoughts racing through her head. "Get your team to move into position and lock down Korhan's escape. They can clear the sidewalk when they get to it."

"You're putting a lot of faith in our suspect not being armed," Parsons stated.

"Our suspect can barely smoke a cigarette. I really doubt he's going to be able to pull a gun from underneath his shirt before we get to him. And I don't think the other people on the sidewalk are going to run towards Karaca."

"What about the red-headed guy?" Ratliff asked.

"We'll focus on him," Hartley added. "Let Andy and his team take down Karaca. We'll grab his associate." They eyed

Parsons and waited, the team lead debating internally on the best course of action.

He reached down and spoke into his two-way. "Bravo team, keep moving towards the target."

* * * * *

Things were definitely out of place in the early morning sun. The blue van that inched past Augie could have been searching for drugs. The long-haired driver seemed to fit the mold of other users Augie had associated with in his former life, and he knew all too well that it was never too early for a fix.

Yet the speed of the vehicle was not the reason for Augie's hesitation: it was the driver's focus. Someone moseying through the seedier city streets in desperate search of rocks or powder would have been doing just that: *searching*. Eyes would have been scanning the pavement. A head would have turned and acknowledged Augie, wondering if the slim, mop-haired red-head was the dealer they were eagerly hunting for. Instead, the driver remained still, face forward to the street before him, the direction of his focus giving the impression he was staring at Korhan or the individuals approaching him.

And the two men were hardly without question. They did not at all appear to be your typical junkies. *Augie*, out of anyone loitering on the sidewalk, would have been tagged as the druggie. Even Korhan, with years of abuse under his belt, was thick, carrying a weight that should have been eaten away by the constant needles and powders coursing through his veins. Augie's exterior, in his own mind, was the epitome of a man in the clutches of abuse. His skinny frame and rat-like appearance had always been mistaken for someone looking to score. These men, however, were filled out, bodies that were well-nourished, if not muscular.

From the corner of his eye, Augie caught movement, dragging his attention from the approaching men to the intersecting avenue. It was not the slow gate of a recently stoned individual stumbling down the city street that caught his vision and refused to let go. Nor was it the flutter of wind-blown refuse floating on the breeze that pulled his eyes from his unwanted associate. On the contrary, this was precise, well-practiced. These actions had been repeated over and over until nearly perfect. And when he lifted a hand to his brow to ward off the brilliant light of the sun, the weight of the situation hit him, though not fully at first. Twenty-five yards up the intersecting street, moving at a steady pace along the sidewalk, a group of officers approached, weapons drawn, eyes steady.

Augie came to the rapid conclusion that the female officer amongst the assemblage was Jolene Hartley. He had never met the detective before. However, through media outlets within the city, and James's own personal account from the Navy Pier episode, her beauty could not be mistaken. She moved gracefully, with a purpose that screamed professionalism. Her long, dark locks were pulled back. Her eyes were intense, moving from Korhan to himself in a matter of moments, sending a shiver of nervousness through his limbs as the action unfolded before him.

Augie caught his breath instantly as her fiery eyes locked onto him, the penetrating glare seemingly burning into his soul as the officers surrounding her lifted their guns slightly, faces expressing a concern that he could only assume meant Korhan was making a pathetically useless break for it.

He could not have been more wrong.

"Get down!" The words from the female officer's lips rang out just before the concussion of gunfire erupted, yanking his concentration back to Korhan at the exact moment blood and tissue exploded from Karaca's neck.

ELEVEN

"Down! Down!" Hartley yelled, moving hurriedly up the sidewalk with the rest of the team and halting near the entrance of an abandoned floral shop, the ancient window busted out long ago, revealing a dusty, dingy interior overtaken by intrusive vines and filthy rodents. Her words had come out in a rush, directed to the red-headed man standing directly in the line of fire, a confused expression smeared across his face as the two men approaching from behind Korhan pulled their weapons and fired.

"Shots fired! Repeat: shots fired!" Parsons yelled into his two-way, following up his narrative with their current location and the need for backup. The series of events up to this point had surprised not only the red-haired man, but Hartley as well. What should have been a relatively easy takedown of an intoxicated junkie, now seemed to be turning into a life or death situation for everyone involved. The group of officers had watched as the blue van inched slowly along the concrete, suddenly revving its engine before screeching to a stop a dozen yards beyond where Korhan had been standing.

"Police!" Parsons had yelled, spooking the two men as they each squeezed off a few rounds. They jumped at the sudden appearance of the officers, a surprised, wide-eyed stare etched onto each of their faces as they realized their plan to remove Karaca had somehow gone seriously awry. They were shocked, to say the least, that the police were present while their murderous task was being played out. Not only present, but armed and vested in what seemed to be a premeditated strategy aimed in their direction.

"Drop your weapons!" Parsons yelled once more, causing the shooters to glance questioningly at one another. The pause allowed the officers enough time to advance several more yards, placing themselves dangerously close to the gunmen as they neared the edge of the floral shop and the adjacent intersection. They were walking into no-man's land, an opened juncture of the city streets that offered no protection or cover from the armed men standing on the sidewalk before them. It was definitely a precarious situation, one that was trumped by the inaudible growl heard from within the blue van just prior to the barrel of an assault rifle suddenly jutting from the driver's side window.

The continuous release of ammunition that spewed forth was nothing Hartley had ever experienced before. She fell helplessly into the building next to her, arms up in a pathetic attempt to cover herself from the bits of brick and glass that showered down from above. She could hear the bullets impact the façade, felt the whiz of the projectiles fly past her at a furious pace. She could feel Ratliff beside her, his body pressed against hers, heels pushing into the uneven pavement as if his desperate shoves would propel them into the relative safety of the rats' nests and vines of the building's interior and away from the speeding bullets heading in their direction.

After what felt like minutes of constant assault and praying, the gunfire halted, allowing the officers time to gather themselves and open their eyes to a haze of brick and mortar that floated in the air. Hill regained his footing first, glancing quickly around the wall and moving nimbly to take position behind a large maple tree that had somehow survived in the shadows of its current location. "You guys okay?" Parsons said, reaching down to pull Hartley to her feet.

"I'm good," she answered, wiping her forehead with an arm and spitting whatever debris that had settled on her tongue. "Jay?"

Ratliff rose and moved into position behind his partner. "Fine. Where's —"

Shots rang out once again, the officers flinching instinctively at the loud popping before realizing the assault was directed elsewhere. Hartley peered around the wall, watching as a battle rose between the gunmen and what must have been Bravo Team. The driver of the vehicle held down the trigger without relent, the constant bombardment allowing not a single shot from the officers, who, no doubt, were pinned down in the alleyway, waiting, as she had been, for a break in the assault.

Hartley watched the shadows of the gunmen slide along the pavement, their bodies making brief appearances at the rear of the van before once more disappearing behind the vehicle. Loud pops could be heard, a sign that the men, too, had turned their attention away from the injured Karaca and were focused on halting the officers' progress, a necessity as they were vulnerable on the open sidewalk.

Hartley's eyes scanned the horizon, falling upon a figure writhing in pain in the street's gutter, a puddle of blood seeming to grow as the seconds ticked by. Korhan still lay where he had fallen. She had watched as the initial shots had connected with his thick body, sending the big man tumbling onto the pavement in sheer agony, the excruciating burn of the bullets within his skin sending him into uncontrollable fits. She moved her gaze to the right, half expecting the red-haired man to be stationed yet again on the sidewalk, a statue in a chaotic atmosphere of danger.

He was nowhere to be found.

* * * * *

He was gone. The initial gunfire. The screaming. "Get down! Get down!" Augie cursed himself for reacting so slowly. In his abusive days, he had always prided himself with the ability to react when things were out of sorts, to move on from a deal when the hair on the back of his neck stood up. Yet this time, he had stalled. He had waited, taking in everything that was happening before him until it was almost too late.

If it were not for the detective, who knows what would have become of him? The odds he would have been hit by the onslaught of bullets were high. Yet she had pulled him from the confusion that had clouded his mind, yanked him into the frightening present and the reality that his life was in actual jeopardy at that very instant.

So he ran. He turned and bolted down the sidewalk, crossing the street at a certain point and continuing down the opposite walkway. He did not quite know where he was going. Augie had taken a cab to the neighborhood, always exiting the vehicle a block or two down to gather piece of mind before meeting with the shithead he had been forced to associate with. The shithead that had just been shot multiple times in the chest and neck.

It was definitely not something Augie had ever been privy to before. He had seen overdoses occur, in addition to his own. He had even seen someone stabbed in the streets of Amsterdam on a wild trip that included skiing, hallucinogenic mushrooms and three hits of acid. Yet the suddenness of the gunfire and the instantaneous expulsion of fluid and tissue from a human body, he had never witnessed prior to the day's events.

And it was something he did not want to witness again, either. The events played in his head, like a broken phonograph repeating the same six seconds over and over.

Wide eyes. Jolene Hartley. Blood.

Wide eyes. Jolene Hartley. Blood.

So he ran.

* * * * *

The first shot from the officers was taken by Parsons, a decision that allowed relief to the men in Bravo Team, yet pissed off the driver of the blue van to no extent. Andy released a bullet that entered the driver's side window of the vehicle and struck the windshield, hitting neither weapon nor suspect, yet causing a break in the assault that held down the other half of the team.

Ratliff followed suit, aiming towards the side of the van and letting loose several shots that connected with the metal exterior. Hartley moved down the sidewalk with Officer Hill, guns at the ready for when the men on the sidewalk appeared. It did not take long. Screams were heard from behind the van, and with a furious assault, the men stepped into the open, firearms raised and blasting towards the officers.

Hartley dove to the side, rolling across her back and coming to a halt on her stomach, weapon raised to the individuals firing upon them. She pulled the trigger twice, both bullets sailing wide of the target as he ducked behind the vehicle. Hill dropped to one knee, aiming his service piece to the back of the van while his eyes focused on the front, waiting for the moment when the machine gun popped into view once more.

He saw movement, a black jacketed being jumping into view and raising his hands. Hill reacted on instinct, pulling the trigger and sending one of the men toppling over, the bullet embedding into the stomach in a heated intensity that pulled from his soul a scream that lingered in the air.

"Hill!" Parson yelled, pulling the officer's eyes to the left just as Andy collided with him and knocked him to the pavement, the pair tumbling out of the line of fire as the driver let loose another manic round. Ratliff took aim and pulled the trigger, the bullets once more entering the van's window and exiting the shattered windshield, forcing the driver to retreat for the moment.

Hartley watched as Parsons and Hill came to a grinding halt. She rose to her knees and began forward, stopping suddenly as the wounded man on the sidewalk reached out towards the back of the van. From the protection of the vehicle stepped the other shooter, hand extended towards his accomplice, an action of sympathy that did not fit whatsoever with their murderous endeavor. "Put the fucking gun down!" Hartley yelled, grabbing the man's attention as he dropped to one knee and turned, right arm extended towards her with gun in hand.

Hartley fired, sending the missile speeding through the air towards her assailant. The bullet connected, though only grazing the man's cheek and temple enough to spin him to the sidewalk, his gun dropping to the pavement as he reached to the fresh wound. He yelled in pain, yet continued moving, grasping onto his associate's jacket and pulling him towards the safety of the van.

Hartley began to rise, yet was jerked to the ground as Ratliff moved to her side, pulling her out of the way as the incessant barrage of gunfire erupted from the driver's side window once more. As they covered their heads, they heard the rev of an engine, the obvious sign of a vehicle beginning its retreat, the exodus that Hartley and her team dreaded and thanked all in one thought. The van sped away, firing into the alley where Bravo Team had held its ground. Tires squealed. Smoke rose into the morning air, slowly disappearing as the officers of the two squads rose from their positions and began to try to come to terms with what had just occurred.

Two things rose to the forefront of Hartley's mind as she stood in the middle of the street and holstered her weapon.

One: someone had wanted Korhan dead.

Two: they had succeeded.

TWELVE

James sat underneath an umbrella on the patio of a coffee shop and ran his finger along the flaky, metal grating of the tabletop surface, his eyes slightly swollen and red from the emotions that had been stripping him bare over the last several days. The early morning establishment was speckled with patrons, all downing their chai lattes or vanilla cappuccinos before the long day of work began anew. Newspaper corners flapped in the slight breeze, pages held down by the quick forearms of their respective readers. The traffic on the city streets moved at a snail's pace, inching along the pavement in front of James as he focused on issues not concerning the daily commute.

In his mind, he knew coming back to the States would require mental toughness. He realized the reality that came with digging up the truth to his parents' demise would most likely carry with it some form of renewed pain. This trip was not going to be a vacation. It was not a brief getaway from the life he currently led in the sun-soaked waters of the tropics. He knew what he was getting into, to a certain extent.

That first night back in Chicago, that unwanted evening with Korhan Karaca in the belly of a drug den, had almost pushed James past his physical and mental limitations. He had felt helpless, a man sizing up an opponent far superior than himself, knowing, without a doubt, that the possibility he was getting in over his head was something very real.

He could still envision the tears streaming down Korhan's face as his eyes locked with Graiser's and the recognition set in. "What the fuck is this?" Korhan had yelled at Augie, who easily pushed the inebriated man back to the filthy couch cushions with little effort as he tried to rise. "I know you! I know you!" James's extremities had shook as Karaca turned his deep, guttural growl to him, an overwhelming overflow of emotion pouring out from the junkie as the seconds ticked by, a thick, jittery finger waving in Graiser's direction all the while. "Why are you here? Why is he here?" The angered, desperate tone had been aimed at anyone who could answer.

"Mate," Augie answered calmly. "He just wants to talk."

"I don't want to fucking talk to him!" Korhan yelled, trying unsuccessfully to rise once again. "Let me the fuck —"

"Do you know who I am?" James asked, his tone a mixture of fright and forced confidence. Karaca lashed out at Augie, flipping the Londoner's hand from his shoulder and falling back into the cushions once more. "Korhan," James said loudly. "Do you know me?"

Paw-Paw stood silent in the corner, his nervous, over-stimulated eyes jumping from the members in the room. James watched as he slowly inched his way towards the hallway, badly wanting to be rid of the chaos that had risen within the last several minutes.

"I know you," Korhan finally replied. "You're the Graiser kid."

* * * * *

His phone, which he had successfully chosen to ignore since disconnecting with his British counterpart earlier, had begun to ring and vibrate against the metal table with a ferocity that garnered several discerning looks of disapproval within the last couple of minutes. James had looked down on each occasion and sighed, Augie's name and image spread across the display for the few seconds before Graiser pushed ignore.

Now, however, with the sixth call in just as many minutes, James felt forced to answer. What could compel his friend to try and connect with him this much was beyond him, though the nearby patrons of the coffee shop felt it best if he either accommodated the person on the other end, or excused himself from the premises. James chose to answer. "Augie, I told you I had some things —"

"They bloody shot him, Jimmy!" Augie said hurriedly into the mouthpiece. "I can't believe —"

"Whoa! Whoa, wait," James said, sitting up in his chair, the obvious severity of the situation pulling him from the slump he had found himself in since the meeting with Karaca. "What are you talking about?"

"They fucking shot him ... on the sidewalk. I was right there! I saw every —"

"Shot who? I don't understand —" The question pulled curious eyes and ears once more towards him.

"Korhan!"

"What? When?"

"Just now!"

"Wait, wait, wait." James ran a hand over his face, wiping his eyes. "Settle down and tell me —"

"Don't tell me to settle down, Jimmy!" Augie interrupted. "They just fucking shot Korhan ... and I saw it all. So don't tell me ... to settle down." His jagged speech and frantic breathing pattern led James to believe Augie was on the move at a furious pace, something that was, in itself, out of the ordinary with his friend's normal lackadaisical, by-the-seat-of-your-pants way of life.

"Jesus Christ!" James said, hands shaking as he looked around the patio to the other individuals. He stood quickly and gathered his things, moving away from the coffee shop and taking a spot next to a nearby alleyway. "Tell me what happened." he said, leaning into a nearby building.

"Oy!" Augie yelled. James could hear the squeak of a vehicle's breaks approach as Augie spit out a destination to the driver, followed instantly by the slam of a door. A crescendo of foreign music filled the background.

"Augie?" James said loudly into the phone.

He could barely make out Augie's voice over the racket of the cab. "I'm here," he said. "Fuck! What was that, James? Why … Why shoot him, man?"

"Augie, tell me what happened," James responded in a calm tone, though his nerves were as on edge as Augie's. "Just tell me what happened to Korhan."

* * * * *

The blue van slid to a grinding halt in the shadows of a ramshackle industrial warehouse overlooking the North Branch of the Chicago River. Smoke poured from the hood and flooded the cabin, choking the three men who had successfully outrun the throngs of officers that, no doubt, were spreading throughout the city on the lookout for them. The front right tire had been shot out and was now nothing more than a frayed mess of smoldering rubber. Bullet holes lined the cabin walls. Glass sparkled on the dashboard.

The driver's side door flung wide with a jarring crunch, squeaking noisily as the long-haired man hopped out onto the concrete. He removed his sunglasses to reveal a long, hideous scar cutting through his left eyebrow, and ran a hand over his face, wiping away the residual engine smoke and glass fragments and auto fluids that had collected on his skin. He summoned a large wad of spit and sent it shooting into the distance with a disgusting splat, glancing around hurriedly to determine whether anyone was in the near vicinity to witness the eyesore that was the getaway vehicle to the murder of Korhan Karaca. They were alone.

He rounded the front of the automobile and reached into the shattered passenger window, retrieving the assault rifle from the seat, the lengthy barrel of the weapon rising vertically from the floor. The cabin door suddenly burst open and his bloodied companion fell onto the pavement with a grunt, a filthy towel held firmly against the graze wound.

The driver loathed this man. He hated everything about him: the smirk he seemingly wore at all times; his close-cropped hair that resembled the strict military background of his own father; the smugness that enveloped every action he had conducted since their reunion. He shook his head, wishing the bullet had been more than just a graze, more than just a mere flesh wound that allowed him the chance to groan and grunt incessantly. For a moment he stood there, staring as his accomplice rose to his feet, his pained expression falling to the rear of the cabin and the injured third individual writhing in agony. He envisioned himself lifting the gun once more and pulling the trigger, embedding bullet after bullet in the space between his associate's ears. Yet he did not. He could not, at least not yet. Things had gone seriously awry today, and the fact of the matter was he might still need his services in the near future.

A gurgling, blood-laden cough pulled his attention to the rear of the vehicle. The driver moved away from the front window and stationed himself over the shoulder of his accomplice, both individuals staring to the crimson pool forming underneath their wounded third party.

"Guys … I need … a … hospital." His breathing was rapid, eyes jumping anxiously from the men before him to the dark life pouring from his midsection. "P … Please. I swear … I swear … I won't say anything. I don't … I don't know anything."

"What do we do?" the short-haired, bullet-grazed man asked, turning his gaze towards the driver. He pulled the towel from his wound and winced in pain, shouting an expletive into the Chicago breeze as he looked to the blood-soaked rag.

"We get rid of the fucking evidence," the driver said calmly.

"What about him?"

The driver remained silent for a moment, weighing the options before him. He stepped forward and shouldered his accomplice out of the way, reaching to the doorway and pulling the handle to open to left side of the entry. The injured man in the interior let loose a series of fitful coughs, blood exploding from his mouth and running down chin. "Just … drop me … Just drop me … at the hospital. I won't say … I won't say … anything. I … promise."

"Maybe we should take him," the injured man behind him said.

The driver turned and glared at him, his eyes piercing. He glanced back to the wounded man in the van and smiled. "And you don't think he'll say anything, huh?"

"I won't," the man said from the cabin. "I won't. I promise. Just ... drop me at —"

"We were just in a shootout with the cops!" the driver yelled. "Do you not remember getting grazed by a fucking bullet?"

"Of course, but —"

"We just whacked someone, with the cops there! Why were the cops there?" He stepped forward, causing the short-haired man to shy away. "This has been royally fucked beyond belief!"

"What do you want me to say?"

"I want some fucking answers! You and that fuck were supposed to find Karaca, not bring the cops with you."

"We weren't followed! I swear!"

"Then what was that? Why are we exchanging fire with the Chicago Police Department? Tell me that."

"Guys," came the plea from the van's cabin. "Guys ... I really ... I need a —"

They were the last words that ever fell from his mouth. The concussion of a half dozen gunshots from the driver's weapon echoed throughout the area, bouncing from the sides of the abandoned warehouses and dissipating into the Chicago River. The bullets pierced internal organs and arteries, killing the man instantly. "What the fuck?" yelled the short-haired man.

The driver turned quickly and aimed the barrel of the weapon at him, his stone-cold gaze silencing the friction of the moment. "What? What the fuck do you have to say?" The lapping of the water and horns from the city beyond filled the air. "That's right. Keep your fucking mouth shut! You see your friend there? That piece of shit was shot by the cops at the scene of a murder. Karaca's dead. That's the only good thing that came out of today so far. We've got fucking heat up our ass right now that's going to make it difficult to move around and conduct business as usual. So no, I don't think it's the best idea to drop your pal at the hospital. Use your fucking head! The cops are going to be looking at all hospitals and clinics. They'll be waiting for someone to come in with a gunshot wound to the stomach. And once they find him, I'm pretty sure a reduced sentence would look like free pussy to a guy like that. Don't forget the reason we're even associating with one another again. It's not because of your charming fucking personality. It's because Karaca's situation forced our hand before he got nabbed and dealt with the cops." He paused and lowered the weapon to his side. "Looks like we made it in the nick of time too, wouldn't you say?"

He stepped away from the van, positioning himself next to the bullet-grazed man, sighing. "Who was the red-head on the sidewalk?"

"I don't know," was the defeated response. "Another junkie?"

The driver chuckled. "Doubt that," he said. The other individual gave him a brief questioning look. "If he was a junkie, he'd have been in the building with our man."

They stood there for several moments, each reliving the past hour in their own way, the scenes of the shooting shuffling through their minds, as well as the events leading up to their recently deceased associate. "What now?" the injured man asked.

"We need to find Graiser," was the matter-of-fact answer.

"Why?"

The driver turned and stared at his accomplice. "Because the woman cop that almost shot you in the face was the same one pictured on the news with him. That's one hell of a fucking coincidence that she shows up today."

"So what do we do when we find him?"

"Figure out if he's talking to the cops or not."

"Why not just take him out?"

"Because killing Karaca is no big deal. No one's going to miss that shithead. Taking out James — if this is all connected — makes it seem like there's something bigger going on. Personally, I don't want that heat at my front door. Do you?"

"No."

"Good. Now, give me your gun." He reached his hand out.

"What for?"

The driver's eyes grew cold. "Because I don't want it being traced back to you. If that happens, you may be on the other end of my next shot. Now give me your gun."

The injured man raised the towel to his face once more, this time in an effort to buy him a little more time rather than stem the flow of blood from his face. The fact of the matter was he did not have his gun. It had been dislodged from his grasp when the bullet sliced through his flesh, and now, most likely, was within an evidence bag on its way to the forensic laboratory.

"Give it to me," the driver said once more, this time with an insistence that called for action.

The man patted his waist, feigning a search for the weapon that bought him a few more seconds and a possible way out of the current situation. "It, uh … It must have fallen out in the van."

The driver smiled and extended his arm towards the vehicle. "Well, by all means. Go and fetch it." He sidestepped as the short-haired individual moved into the cabin, searching around the area for his deceased companion's piece, which he found lodged between the floor and a bloodied boot. He retrieved it and turned, nearly running into the driver as he snatched up the gun with a curious look. He stared to his accomplice, seemingly trying to piece something together. The injured man felt the hair stand up on his neck, felt the perspiration moisten his brow.

The driver stepped forward, sliding the firearm into his belt. "Now, let's get rid of the fucking evidence."

THIRTEEN

The scene was like something out of a warzone. Glass from the abandoned floral shop up the road littered the sidewalk. Chunks of red brick from the building walls were scattered in every direction and dust from the mortar hovered in the air. Branches from a nearby tree were strewn about the walkway and leaned precariously on an ancient mailbox. Craters covered the street where the driver of the van had peppered the area around the fleeing officers. And Korhan Karaca, the man Hartley had so wanted to face down in the interrogation room, laid motionless, lifeless, in the gutter of the warm Chicago afternoon.

Hartley was confused as to what had occurred here today, as was the entire team. No one — besides their suspect and the two gunmen — had been seriously injured in the assault, which was a win in itself. Two of the officers pinned down in the alleyway had taken direct hits to the chest, though the Kevlar vests had softened the blows as much as possible, offering the men some serious bruising and soreness rather than shortened lives.

Hartley sat on the hood of a nearby cruiser, elbows resting on knees with folded hands as she bounced her feet up and down on the vehicle's fender. She watched as Ratliff exchanged dialogue with Parsons and a grouping of officers, no doubt answering questions as to the screw-up that had occurred within the past hours. News vans had shown up within the first half hour after the incident, and each had tried to procure — unsuccessfully — an interview with Chicago's most notorious female cop. Parsons, immediately noticing the burden that was placed upon Hartley's shoulders just from her association with the takedown of Karaca, had set up a two block perimeter, fanning out the team that had just recently taken fire into the surrounding vicinity to halt any media that felt ballsy enough to advance.

Mac had shown up just after the news vans and reporters set up their stations, weaving the forensic vehicle through the throngs of cameras and microphones and short-skirted field reporters looking for any juicy tidbit to boost their fame within the city. He had parked the truck in the middle of the street and exited onto the pavement with searching eyes, his gaze finally resting on Jolene with a relieved smile.

"You okay?" he asked as he approached, resting his hands on her arms as an uncle to his favorite niece. "You're not hurt, are you?"

"No," Hartley answered. "I'm good."

"Good." He stepped back and glanced over his shoulder towards the body lying near an ancient signpost. "I know you'd rather have him alive, but with what he and Moran did to you last year, I'd be lying if I said part of me wasn't relieved." Hartley forced a smile and nodded her head, a thank you of sorts to a man only looking out for her best interest. She, however, had not wanted Korhan Karaca dead. He deserved to spend a good deal of time in jail, locked behind bars with no access to the things that drove him to attack police officers in their own homes. Wishing death upon someone was just not part of her. Justice was.

After a few minutes, Ratliff walked over and handed Jolene a cup of coffee. "Here you go."

"Where'd you get this from?" Hartley asked, sliding down from the cruiser's hood to stand before him.

"One of Parsons's guys. He had him pick it up on the way. Thought you could use one." He took a long sip from his drink and turned as Mac approached from the left. "I know I can."

"Thanks," Hartley said. "Find anything useful?" she asked the ME.

Mac shrugged. "Depends on what you mean by *useful*. Found a couple used syringes and a half-full twenty bag of coke near the building entrance. I'm sure that's *useful* around here. Other than that, Julian's sweeping the area and taking inventory." He sighed and glanced around. "So what happened here?" Hartley looked to him and shrugged. "I mean, what do you guys think? Was this a drug-related hit? Mr. Karaca piss off the wrong junkie?"

Ratliff shook his head. "Those guys were definitely not junkies. This looked too planned out to be one druggie against another."

"Agreed," Hartley said. "With that van pulling up and everything, it just seemed like too planned out a hit."

"Some sort of retaliation, maybe? Didn't this guy run in some pretty shady circles?"

"Yeah," Hartley added. "That's a definite possibility. Guy in Karaca's position surely made some enemies along the way. We'll have to look around and see who those people are. Until then, we're hoping maybe you can shine some light on the situation?"

"What would you do without me, Detective Hartley?" Mac smiled.

"Live an unfulfilled life," Hartley replied with a tilt of her head.

"Very sweet," Ratliff added.

"And full of shit." The response jerked the detectives' heads around, each pair of eyes settling on Captain Nolan as he stopped in front of the group with hands on hips. His face displayed a combination of anger and relief. He lifted a hand to his face and rubbed his chin, his focus jumping between the duo and the Medical Examiner. "You find anything useful?" he finally asked.

"Seems like the question of the day," Mac replied. "How about you go first, Henry. I can wait. Plus, I need to check and see that Julian isn't messing up my scene."

Nolan's head began to nod slowly at first, as if he was weighing the order of how the next segment of this conversation should go and realizing his longtime friend was correct. He turned to Hartley with fiery eyes as Mac moved away from the group and towards the body of Karaca. "What are you two doing here?"

"Sir?" she replied, the question more in response to his aggressive tone than the actual inquiry.

"There are other, more important, things you two should be doing. Why are two of my homicide detectives busy with a routine arrest?"

"With all due respect, sir," Hartley said, the drive within her matching her superior's. "This was hardly a routine arrest. I —"

"Which makes it all the more reason why you shouldn't have been involved, Detective Hartley. Is the current spotlight shining down upon you not enough at the moment?"

"That's not fair, Cap," Ratliff stated, coming to his partner's defense.

"And isn't that your Jeep I saw in the parking lot over there?" Nolan ignored his comment, turning his cold eyes to his detective. "I was at the station early this morning. I didn't see either of you two picking up your armor."

"I asked Hill to bring it over," Ratliff said. "He was on loan to Parsons's team today, so —"

"*He* was on loan. *He* was. Not you two."

Hartley calmly stepped forward, her slow movement pulling everyone's eyes to her. She stopped directly in front of her superior and looked up to him with a soft, focused gaze. "If we had brought him in without incident, would this still be an issue, Henry?"

Nolan closed his mouth and thought for a moment. "The *issue*, Jo, is that there's a lot of focus on you and Jay at the moment. The *issue* is you're a homicide detective under my supervision, not part of this task force taking down a random drug addict and criminal."

Hartley blinked slowly and took a deep breath, her composed demeanor soaking up whatever hostility had been building. When she finally spoke, it was with a soothing, yet succinct tone. "He's not a random drug addict and criminal, Henry. He's the man that attacked me in my own apartment. In my home, sir. He and Luke Moran would have killed me."

"Which makes you too close to this assignment," Nolan tried.

Hartley nodded her head in agreement. "Probably. But either way, it was an arrest that the task force was going to make. We were just backing them up."

"Jo, what happened here this morning —"

"Was a complete surprise and beyond our control. From our perspective, we had a suspect wanted in connection with attacking a police officer in our sights. The fact that he was shot and killed was beyond our scope. Now, I'm sorry that we didn't fill you in, sir. But, Henry, I needed to see him brought in. I needed to be here for this."

Nolan locked his eyes on her, his intense glare and steadfastness faltering as the seconds ticked by. He was indeed disappointed, though the foundation of the feeling came from the fact that she had once again been targeted in the media's spotlight. Nolan understood her resolve, her absolute, unwavering need to be present at the apprehension of Karaca. He was, after all, the last standing individual who had forced his brutality upon her, though, in the grand scheme of things, it was she who had gotten the upper hand.

Nolan began to open his mouth but halted as Mac approached yet again, this time followed by Julian, his lead technician and the butt of the majority of his jokes. "So, who wants to know if we found anything useful?" he said with a wink and a smile. The group remained silent. "Okay. Lively bunch here. Anyway, we've actually got a couple good pieces here. Follow me." He turned on his heels, not waiting for anyone as he proceeded back towards the body.

Hartley and Ratliff fell in line as Nolan backed away. "I need to get back to the precinct," he said. "Keep me posted." Hartley nodded her understanding and forced a smile. "Jo," Henry said, pulling her attention to him once more. "You guys are on this one." The phrase seemed forced, as if other words had edged their way back into his thoughts and were replaced by these.

Hartley looked to him momentarily before responding. "Yes, sir."

Mac, Julian and Ratliff waited patiently for Jolene to join them, positioning themselves amidst a splattering of blood, bullet casings and tire marks, as well as Karaca's bloodied body just to their right. "Ready?" Mac asked.

"Let's go."

"Okay. We have a couple things that I'm sure will have you jumping for joy. First: blood." He pointed to the sidewalk. "Not only do we have a pool from our victim, we have random splatters in multiple locations from what I'm assuming is our suspect."

"Two of the guys were hit," Ratliff chimed in. "You think it's from both of them?"

Mac shrugged. "Possible. We'll have to get some samples and test them out to be certain. But the blood over here is definitely not from Mr. Karaca." He paused and lifted his hand in the air, a plastic evidence bag containing a firearm being set on his fingertips by Julian.

"Ah! That's helpful," Ratliff said with a grin.

"It's just what I do," Mac replied, matter-of-factly. "Second. We have a firearm. Nice piece, too. SIG Mosquito, with .22 cartridges. Was it the murder weapon? We'll see. Again, we'll have to get some ballistics done and get the bullets from our vic. But the surprise," he added, turning the bag around to display a thin layer of powder, "is a nice fingerprint. We can run this through the system to see if anyone pops up."

"Seems like a great start," Hartley said. "Think we can push these through quickly?"

Mac nodded. "For you, I'm sure we can figure something out. There is one more thing, though I'm not sure what, if anything, we'll be able to get off of it." Mac pointed to Julian, who raised yet another plastic evidence bag up. Inside, covered in a layer of dried blood, was Karaca's cell phone, the screen and casing cracked and chipped, a bullet hole apparent on the edge of the device. "It's in pretty bad shape, but there's always a chance."

"He was on that when he came out of the building. Let's see if we can't pull anything from it. Maybe it'll tell us what Karaca's been up to."

"Will do, Detective Hartley," Julian answered.

"Ratliff," she said, turning to her partner. "We should probably try and get in touch with his next of kin. Korhan didn't have any siblings, and from what I've researched, he wasn't married or anything. Let's try and connect with his parents. See if they can shine any light on what this was all about."

"I'll get a patrol unit to head over there right now," he said, stepping away and pulling out his phone.

Hartley turned her attention to Mac, who smirked and nodded his head. "I'll put a rush on everything and get back to you. Give me an hour or so and Mr. Karaca will be in the lab."

"Thanks, Mac," Hartley answered, spinning on her heels and walking slowly towards her partner and the bare-bones Jeep Wrangler in the hidden parking lot.

FOURTEEN

James blew into the small drinking hole of his coffee lid, the steam escaping quickly into the breeze and becoming lost in the tumultuous Chicago he had descended upon. He took a long sip, the hot liquid swishing around his mouth and awakening his taste buds. He set the cup on the bench next to him and rubbed his eyes, running his fingers through his greasy, dirty hair as he sighed. Korhan Karaca was dead.

James was tired. No, tired was not a strong enough word for it. He was exasperated, burnt out, longing for a new existence that did not have him wrapped up in the deeds he currently found himself. He yearned for happier times, a period when he and his parents sat looking out upon a Wisconsin lake and the millions of ripples that slowly made their way towards shore. Or the skiing trips to the Alps that ended in the trio watching the sky darken beyond the roaring flames of a peaceful bonfire. He wanted things to go back to normal, although he was not sure what exactly that was anymore. It was definitely not the life he was leading currently.

James shifted his weight and looked around, eyeing the address he had written down after much research. The cab he had taken had dropped him at the corner of East Cedar Street and North Lake Shore Drive, the heart of the Gold Coast, a neighborhood James had not frequented all that often. He knew his way around Chicago, yet with the impromptu vacations that lasted months on end, his adventurous nature allowed his hometown curiosity little room to roam. He had exited the vehicle and found the building just north of the intersection at Lake Shore and East Division, a large, white structure with long balconies overlooking the renowned street and shoreline. His eyes had scanned the exterior, taking in the trees and flowering shrubs that were obviously tended to by professionals. A large, two-lane drive entered and exited the property from Lake Shore, cutting and curving through the pristine landscape and under the welcoming overhang to a valet podium stocked full of workers.

James had slowly walked the sidewalk, glancing as guests moved towards the building entrance and were greeted immediately by a well-dressed concierge. "Good afternoon," the man said to the people. "Can I help you?" At the distance James stood, the response was inaudible, lost in the Chicago breeze. The attendant nodded his head and opened a case near the entryway, retrieving a black phone and waiting for the connection. "Mr. Glover," he said in a chipper voice. "I have a Mr. and Mrs. Shane at the entrance … Yes. Great, sir." He returned the receiver to its base and smiled wide to the couple as he opened the door into what appeared to be a beautifully designed, well-lit lobby. "Do you know where you're going?" The couple nodded their heads in unison as they passed into the spacious interior. "Great. Have a good one," he said as they moved out of earshot. The attendant turned again and greeted another couple as they exited a red Lexus, the valet workers immediately jumping into action to bring the luxury sedan to a more secure location. "Good afternoon," the attendant began again.

James had glanced around quickly, leaving the exchange behind him and turning back to cross Division once more. He had stopped at the corner and taken a seat on a nearby bench, his eyes watching the building in wait for the man he had come to see, an individual with the ability to find things out much better than he could himself.

* * * * *

There had not been much to go on, that was for certain. James had never wandered into the realm of his parents' murders for an extended period of time. Most occurrences were conjured subconsciously, rising to the surface suddenly to swirl the senses briefly before being pushed deep into the recesses of his mind.

Yet things had changed for him that fateful day when Jolene Hartley had called to meet him for lunch, showing up looking as if she were on the losing end of a championship bout. James had resigned himself to life without family. He had had faith in the Minocqua Police Department to do what could be done to shed light upon the situation. And when the leads dried up and the case was shrugged to the side, he did not hold a grudge. He had accepted the route the investigation had gone and the subsequent dead-end that stopped it. Sometimes things were just not meant to be.

Throughout the initial phases of the case — and against the better judgment of both Daniel Vincent and Ahmet Karaca — James had dealt personally with Guy Finney, lead homicide detective, and Emmitt Eckland, Medical Examiner of Oneida County, Wisconsin. The pair of seasoned veterans had filled him in on anything prudent to the investigation, including the details into how each of his parents was killed. Daniel had erupted in outrage that night in the Minocqua precinct, unable to hold back his feelings that James, although twenty at the time, was too young to hear such things. The young man had calmed his older confidant with a soft glance and asked the detective to continue.

After that, things had quieted. James no longer heard anything from Eckland and Finney's calls became few and far between. Graiser moved into an apartment Daniel Vincent had offered him and began his new life alone. He was the inheritor of extreme wealth, all of which he would have given up for his parents' return. It was not to be, however. They were gone, taken from him entirely too early, leaving him with an emptiness he filled by hopping throughout the country and the rest of the world, a lonely man filling a void with whatever he could find.

He had not moved in nearly forty-five minutes, enough time to allow an attractive jogger and her svelte greyhound to pass by a half dozen times on their route through the neighborhood. He glanced the runner's way with each lap, but never so much as returned the smile the cougar sent his way. He was not interested in her spandex-covered ass or the cleavage that grew at each passing from underneath the half-zipped shirt. James was there for one reason only.

As he waited, he ran through the series of events that had led him to the Gold Coast, to this spot overlooking LSD and the expansive Lake Michigan beyond. His research at the Caribbean Café in Ocho Rios long ago had come up empty, revealing nothing more than an internal war being waged within himself. He had eventually given in, coming to the conclusion that Chicago and his past would not disappear from his sight unless he had closure from what had happened so long ago.

And it had all been churned up by Jolene Hartley.

He had been angered at her that day, the sudden irritation rising above the longing he normally felt for her. To him, the words falling from her mouth had dripped poison. They had echoed in his ears like a howling wind threatening to blow him over, toppling him to the earth and the past he had nearly escaped from. *What do you remember of your parents' murders?* Everything. Nothing. What did it matter? They were dead, and neither Jolene Hartley nor Jacoby Ratliff could bring them back. Both the Minocqua and Chicago police departments had previously done their jobs. There was no reason to begin poking at an investigation that had long ago dried up.

"Are you looking for something?" a raspy, feminine voice said from behind him. James turned and once more laid eyes upon the jogger and her dog. She was an attractive woman with blonde highlights over dyed brown hair. The gray roots just peeking out, as well as the crow's feet at the corners of her eyes, let James know she was most likely pushing fifty, if not just over. "Or someone?" she said as she patted her greyhound's head, bending over slightly to reveal the canyon of cleavage once more.

James smiled and shook his head. "I'm okay. Thank you," he replied as he focused once more across the intersection.

"You've been standing here for a while. Didn't know if I could help with something."

"I appreciate it, but, really, I'm all right. Just waiting for someone."

"Friend? Girlfriend?" James turned and eyed the woman again. She smiled and ran her hand across her sweat-covered brow. James took note of the enormous diamond on her ring finger. "You stand here long enough, cops might pick you up for loitering."

James forced a smirk and shook his head. "I think I'll take my chances, thanks."

The woman shrugged and walked towards him. As she passed him by, she spun to face him, her thin, toned legs walking backwards, hips swaying seductively as the greyhound followed reluctantly. "Good luck. Maybe I'll come check on you in a little bit." She smiled and waved before beginning down the sidewalk. James glanced her way one last time before turning his attention solely on the building opposite him.

* * * * *

The man James had been waiting for finally exited a cab with his cell phone to his ear, turning nonchalantly to throw the fare and tip through the opened passenger window. He looked exactly the same: sport coat clinging to a muscular frame; dark brown locks, slightly longer than when James had seen him last; and the ever-present cigarette between lips that had no filter when spewing forth chosen words to those that crossed his path. James knew why he had come searching for this man, yet the butterflies in his stomach let him know it was possibly a huge mistake. The individual paced back and forth slowly, gesticulating as he spoke loudly into the mouthpiece of his cell phone, unaware — or uncaring — that Graiser was approaching.

The look in Dane Hartley's eyes as he hung up the phone and turned to watch James step forward led Graiser to believe that he, indeed, had not seen him coming up the sidewalk. The reaction, however, said otherwise. Dane looked at James with searching eyes as he sucked on the cigarette between his lips. He exhaled the smoke and said, "You look like shit."

James could not help but smirk at the comment. He did not know Dane well, just the brief couple times they had met during his fleeting relationship with the reporter's sister. Yet he knew Dane to be temperamental and unfriendly, a man that Jolene had had no problems detaching herself from with little to no thought. "What the fuck do you want?" Hartley asked, flicking the cigarette to James's shoes, a shower of ash and ember cascading around him.

James stepped out with his right toe and smashed the butt into the pavement, the willowy wisps of smoke dancing into the air before disappearing in the breeze. He looked up to Dane momentarily before reaching into his coat with his right hand and retrieving a large envelope. James shifted the contents in the container before tossing it to the reporter, who caught it with a steady hand and quizzical expression. Dane smirked and opened the envelope, the smile sliding from his face slightly as he looked upon a stack of crisp one hundred dollar bills. He glanced up quickly, his eyes still searching Graiser's for a sign as to what exactly was going on. "What is —"

"Ten thousand dollars," James interrupted. "That's what it is."

"For what?"

"Help."

FIFTEEN

The view was phenomenal. Crisp blue waters and whitecaps swayed and danced for as far as the eye could see, blending into the sky seamlessly as if on an artist's canvas. The sunlight shining down upon Lake Shore Drive sparkled off the windshields and roofs of speeding vehicles, bringing him back to the days when his parents would take him up and down Michigan Avenue during the Christmas holiday, his young eyes mesmerized by the twinkling display dangling from the trees. It was refreshing, and a sight that caught James off-guard and had him reconsidering his permanent departure from Chicago. If only things had been different, he could see himself living in a condo such as this one day. Not that he was unable to afford it now. He could purchase the entire top floor of the building with plenty of wiggle room to spare. Yet with the direction his life was heading, he was unsure where he would end up.

"Got to say," came the voice from behind him, rousing James from his reveries. "I wrote you up to be a rich dickhead."

James turned to stare at Dane as he exited the massive kitchen and made his way towards him. "Probably still are," Hartley continued, stopping near an end table to retrieve the envelope James had tossed his way earlier. "But you definitely know how to get my attention." He laughed as he glanced to the stack of bills momentarily before tossing the money nonchalantly back to the table's surface. "So what do you want? Got to be something that your little toy doesn't want to be a part of. Huh? Otherwise, why come to me?" He stared at James with a smirk. "How is my little sister doing anyway?"

James gritted his teeth and forced the conversation elsewhere. "I didn't come to talk about Jo," he said coldly.

"Yeah? Then why the fuck did you? I've been kind of busy lately, if you haven't heard."

"I haven't," James responded quickly. "I try not to follow reality star train wrecks."

Dane nodded his head approvingly and raised the glass of scotch to his lips, his eyes never leaving the disheveled man before him. "Speaking of train wrecks, what the fuck happened to you? Are you following every other spoiled, rich kid down the wrong path?" Dane laughed. "I mean, believe me. I've run across plenty of junkie assholes in my line of work. If you're looking for a new supply line, just say the word. I'll drop you wherever you want. As long as you curl up in whatever gutter you find and leave me the fuck alone."

"I'm not looking for drugs, Dane," James said with a hiss.

"Then what? You show up with a fucking sack full of ten thousand dollars, asking for help? Figure you'd just get help from Jo and —" He stopped speaking as a crooked, evil grin formed on his face. Dane lifted the glass of scotch to his lips once more and took a large gulp. "Unless that's what you need help with? Is it?"

James looked at him quizzically. "I'm not really sure what you —"

"It's my sister, huh? That's what you need help with?" He laughed as he made his way into the kitchen and the bottle of scotch on the marble countertop. "What happened, Jimmy? You and her not on the same page anymore? Things go south for you?"

"This has nothing to do with —"

"Yeah," Dane cut in. "I bet it doesn't. Just like I bet it has nothing to do with that asshole partner of hers either." The mention of Ratliff caused James's blood pressure to rise, his thoughts racing back to the moment when his eyes fell upon Jacoby and Jolene locked in a kiss. He had not known they were an item. How could he? His abrupt disappearance had cut ties to many things that had been happening in his life. Mainly Jolene.

The display of affection between the pair had seemed like an awful dream. He knew from the increasingly bitter messages Jolene had left that she had moved on from him. It was something he had brought upon himself, and he was now destined to deal with. Yet he was not ready for the scene he had witnessed, another man's lips pressed to hers, arms interlocked, lust and want apparent on both individuals.

"Figured as much," Dane said, pulling James's eyes from the floor to the kitchen once more. "Got to hand it to her. I didn't think she had it in her to be fucking both of you at the same time. Apparently she's growing up."

"Fuck you," James heard himself say, the words dripping venom.

Dane shrugged the expletive to the hardwood floor beneath him. "So what do you want to know about her?" He smiled as he made his way to a stool and took a seat, one leg extended to the ground, elbow resting on the marble island as his hand gently swirled the liquor. "Where her favorite restaurant is? Coffee shop? I'm sure you know where she lives. So does her detective friend. If you're looking for how often they're together or the best spot to see them in action, I can't help you there. I got pull, but not that much. You'll have to find some other way to act out your peeping-tom fantasy. I'm sure you'll find it fulfilling. With the way those two were trying not to tear each other's clothes —"

"I'm not here for Jolene, although I can see why she thinks you're a dick."

Dane shrugged once more as he sipped his drink. "Well, the feeling's mutual, I can tell you that much."

"I came here for help."

"Yeah? And you think you came to the right guy?"

"For the ten thousand I just gave you, yeah. And if it's worth my while, I'll hand you another ten grand."

Dane stared at him with a confused look. "What do you think I have that's worth twenty thousand dollars? Man, I don't know what happened to you, but you are a fucking nut these days!"

"It's money in your pocket. Or nothing."

"I'm not really hurting for cash right now, if you can tell," Dane said, lifting his arm wide as if to display his new abode and the furnishings within.

"Couldn't hurt though, could it? Take it or leave it, Dane."

Dane stared at the man before him, this fragment of an individual from days past. He took another drink and stood from the stool, turning over the situation in his mind. Finally he smiled and pointed to James, saying, "You want a drink?"

"I want to get past this macho crap and talk."

"Then talk. Give me something that makes me inviting you up here worth my fucking while. Stop beating around the bush and give me something." James thought for a moment, dredging up the last several months in his mind as coherent thoughts, collecting the fragments of conversation from his meeting with Korhan. "Come on!" Dane said loudly, his face a display of frustration and annoyance.

"All right!" James said, moving towards the couch. He stopped before he got to the sofa and turned. "I'll take a drink," he said, receiving a slight nod as Dane emptied some scotch into a crystal tumbler. He walked the cup to his unwanted guest and handed it to him. The liquor burned as it coursed down James's throat, the heat of the alcohol pulling Graiser, for a brief moment, back to his drunken nights in the Caribbean. "I don't know really where to start."

"How about by not saying that?" Dane replied, walking to the nearest wall and leaning into it, his legs crossing along with his arms as he stared down to James. "Bottom line: what's this about?"

"My family."

"Your family." It was more of a statement to begin the process of weighing the story before him, something Dane did unknowingly at the beginning of every possible assignment.

"My parents, actually."

"What about them?"

James took a calculated sip before responding. "They were killed. Ten years ago."

"So what?"

The comment struck a nerve, yet James took a deep breath. "*So*, I'm looking for who did it."

"Then why come here? Go to the fucking cops."

"I tried … I can't."

"Stop mumbling. Why not?"

"The case was closed years ago. They haven't opened it back up. What's to say they would now?"

"Evidence," Dane replied, the sarcastic tone making James want to hurl the heavy tumbler at his face. "Let's go about this another way. You're coming to me — wasting my time — asking what would make the cops open up a cold case for your dead parents that you're looking into. Right?" He did not wait for an answer. "What do *you* have that might make them think about it?"

James thought. "I have a name. Millers."

Dane's brow furrowed. "*Millers*? That's it?" He laughed. "You want the Chicago fucking Police Department to open up a case based on you having part of a name? Is that what you're telling me?" It took him a moment to compose himself. "And where'd you get the name Millers from?"

"Korhan Karaca."

"Oh my fucking God!" he yelled into the room's atmosphere, the volume of his voice causing James to jump. "Are you kidding me? The same Korhan Karaca that attacked Jo? Man! No wonder you two are on the outs."

"Screw you," James said emphatically.

"Listen, listen, listen." He moved away from the wall and grabbed the drink from James's hands. "Let's face the obvious facts here. I don't give a shit about any of this. This Intervise-*State* scandal — this financial crisis with an epicenter that, in some ways, points to me — that's what I care about. So excuse me if I don't fucking jump at the chance to help you out. My advice: go back to your junkie, cokehead buddy and get his help."

"I can't," James said, his anger rising. "He was killed a couple hours ago."

Dane turned and stared to him. "Then you're really up the creek, aren't you?"

"Look," James replied, standing. "I know this isn't your thing, but I'm desperate right now."

"Then give me something useful or fucking leave!"

James stammered, trying to come up with his train of thought as of late. "It was the gun. When Jo was attacked, they left a gun."

"What about it?"

"Apparently it belonged to my father and was taken the night of the murders."

"By who?"

"I don't know."

"So that's a dead end. Next."

"I don't ..." Dane raised his arm towards the door. "Wait. I did some digging into the people involved in the investigation in Wisconsin. You know, I thought I could maybe contact them again. See if anything has come up on their end. They're gone."

"What do you mean by *gone*?"

"Chris Pennington — one of two first responders — was shot and killed just three months after my parents. Lindsey Pratt, his partner, quit the force two years later and re-enlisted in the army where she was killed by a roadside bomb in Pakistan. Then there was Emmett Eckland. He was the medical examiner. He was found five years later floating in a johnboat on a lake."

"What happened to him?"

"From what I found, he apparently had a heart attack. And then Guy Finney, the lead detective, was charged with an assortment of crimes and is now in some penitentiary in northern Wisconsin."

"So pretty much what you're telling me is you have a whole list of assholes that dealt with your parents' case that are all either dead or rotting in some jail. Is that right?" James nodded his head. Dane smirked and stepped aside, revealing the doorway that would lead Graiser out of the building, and hopefully out of his life forever. James remained where he was, a look of resolution and turmoil spread across his face. Dane placed his hands on his hips and stared at his unwanted guest. "What else do you have, James?" he said, his tone pressing, yet encouraging, as if he knew there was something brewing just beneath the surface.

James's eyes became glassy and he set his jaw. He looked away from Dane and to the large windows overlooking the lakefront. When he turned his gaze back to the reporter, a quiet anger rose to the surface along with the tears. "Korhan Karaca and Luke Moran were there the night my parents were murdered."

SIXTEEN

Dane peered through his gleaming, oversized windows overlooking Lake Michigan to his surprise guest leaning against the wrought iron balcony railing, his shaggy hair swinging in the breeze of the fading Chicago afternoon. He had always prided himself on being a man with his eye on the prize. Little affected him. Only a handful of times in his life had he been caught in an emotional battle being waged within his soul. Life, in general, seemed easiest when it was confronted with the "Fuck off world, here I come" mantra he so typically used.

Yet here he was, standing in his den, scotch in hand, eyes to James Graiser, in a wrestling match with an emotional uproar that had clouded his mind for the last fifteen minutes or so. The tears had streamed down James's face after the admission that his now recently-deceased, druggie contact had been present at the killing of his family members. Dane could not quite put his finger on it, but there had been something violently intense in Graiser's countenance, a look that had crossed the boundary of sanity and gave Hartley pause for a brief moment. He had remained stationary in the room, looking upon the mess that was his sister's ex-fling, and come to the conclusion that, regardless of his personal feelings towards the "rich prick," he deserved to be heard.

At least the story did. Dane was no fool. Although, in truth, he did not really care for the plights of this wrecked human being, he did find the demise of one of Chicago's uber-wealthy intriguing. The Intervise-*State of Finance* debacle was his prize pig, yet every reporter needed that follow-up piece. His narration of the financial world of Chicago would only go on for so long. The public would grow tired of the schemes and frauds and political implications that went along with it. Yet, the murders of the Windy City's rich? A slaying of a pair of Second City sweethearts? And to add to the sum of it all, the antagonist of his story, the monster in his dreams, Luke Moran, intertwined the narratives beautifully. Who would have thought the ex-Marine's tale would continue, albeit in a retrograde fashion? He could almost taste the Pulitzer.

Part of Dane felt some sort of newfound respect towards James. It was not because Graiser had earned it through his pleas of assistance to the journalist, and it definitely fell short of pulling at his heartstrings. It was wholly based on the fact that James Graiser, island-hopping, never-had-a-real-job-wealthy-prick of a Chicagoan, had used the exact same means he himself would have. He found someone with more connections and surmised to use that individual to the fullest extent.

Dane filled up the tumbler on the counter and walked it onto the balcony. He handed it to James without a word, eyes staring intently as if trying to deduce Graiser's next step. They stood silent, the wind lifting off of the waters before them and cooling the intensity that had been carried into the apartment earlier in the day with James's entrance. Dane placed his own crystal tumbler on a small metal and glass table and pulled a pack of Marlboro's from his pocket, offering one up to James. To his surprise, his guest accepted, fumbling through the nearly full pack with jittery fingers before successfully procuring a cigarette. "Thanks," he said, taking the lighter from his host.

"Don't mention it," Dane replied, retrieving one of his own. He watched as James lit the end, sucking in cautiously, as if the act were new to him. He did not choke or begin a coughing fit, but Dane could tell the smoke streaming into his lungs caused a slight uneasy feeling within James. Hartley smirked and shook his head, lighting his and pulling a long, relieving drag into his system. "You know," he began, breaking the silence, "that bit of information could have possibly set your parents' case in motion again. You know that, right?"

James looked up to him with tired eyes. "How so?"

"Well, to begin with, you have — had, I guess I should say — two individuals with firsthand knowledge into the murders. That usually tends to garner some sort of reaction."

"It wouldn't have helped," James answered, a defeated tone settling in.

"Why the hell not?"

"Because Korhan wasn't in the house." Dane lifted an eyebrow, a subtle, yet confused sign for James to continue. Graiser turned and brought the cigarette to his lips once more, exhaling a swirling cloud of smoke into the air. "When I met with him, he said he wasn't actually in the house when it happened."

"Where was he then?"

"In the car. Keeping lookout."

"And Moran?" James shrugged. "Well, if he wasn't in the car with your friend, then I'd guess he was in the house."

"I don't know. I'd assume so, but —"

"Why was your buddy left in the car?"

"Stop calling him that," James warned.

"Relax. So Karaca was left in the car." It was more of a statement than anything else. "Why?"

"He told me that he was told to stay put and keep an eye out on the driveway."

"By who? Moran?"

"He didn't say. Korhan seemed to have trouble remembering things. It *was* a while ago."

"Bullshit," Dane stated bluntly. "It was all the fucking dope he did. Tends to affect the memory a little bit. So, based on him not knowing who gave him the babysitting job, I'd assume there was more than just him and Moran there, right?"

James nodded. "Said he clearly remembered two other guys, besides Moran."

"One of them being this Millers character?"

"Yep."

"And the other guy?"

"Couldn't remember his name."

"What'd he look like? White? Black? Tattoos?"

James shook his head. "It was a pretty intense meeting. He kept saying he didn't even know where he was at or whose house they were robbing. Other than that, I didn't get him talking that in-depth."

Dane sighed, taking a sip from his drink before saying, "Guess we can't ask him again, huh?" James remained silent, turning his attention back to the lake and the stream of cars outlining its curves. "How'd you know he was killed?" Dane asked suddenly.

James looked his way. "What?"

"Karaca. How'd you know he'd been killed?"

"An old friend. August Hughes. When I was in Jamaica, I found out he was moving to the city, so I asked him for a favor."

"To kill Korhan? Seems counterproductive." Dane smirked. James did not.

"Augie's a recovering addict. He kind of knows the ins-and-outs of the seedier sides of places. He was able to track him down and start gaining his trust."

"And I'm assuming this …"

"Augie."

"Right. I'm assuming Augie was meeting with him at the time he was killed then?"

"Yeah."

"What was the purpose of getting in touch with him? Korhan, I mean? What did you hope to gain?"

James looked out to the water before responding. "I don't know."

Dane stared at him for a minute before continuing. "What's the purpose of coming to me? Besides whatever sources I have? You have enough information to go to the cops with. With Moran in the news since last year, any police officer would be willing to at least take a look into the validity of what you claim. Coming to me might get you to another step, but what then? Where does James Graiser go from there? Because what I know is this: you're a rich kid. You've had no responsibility your whole life. You get in trouble, mommy and daddy send out the fucking cavalry." James turned to him, anger in his eyes. "What you're dealing with are people who actually give a shit. They gave enough of a shit about something ten years ago to kill for it. Now, we all know that I don't much get along with Jo, but, man, you think long and hard about what your intentions are here. This may be something you need to talk with her about." He waited a moment and locked eyes with Graiser. "Or her fuck buddy partner." He smiled, unable to halt the jab at James's already bruised ego.

James took a drink from the tumbler with eyes still locked on Dane. "You're a prick, you know that?"

Dane shrugged. "Yeah, but I haven't kicked you out yet, so you can take that as something." He threw his smoldering cigarette on the balcony floor and squashed out the embers with the toe of his shoe before returning his stare to James.

James swallowed hard and continued. "I came here to see what I can find out through you. I went to see Jolene but … It just didn't work. Figured I'd take my chances here. See if you can help me scrounge up any more information on this Millers guy. I'd have a better shot of getting the police involved if I had more than just a first name."

Dane toyed with the idea, pulling James along on a ride that he already knew he would take. "Listen, man. I can help, but it's going to be a little while."

"I don't have a little while," James pressed.

"You think I'm going to just drop everything because you show up with a story ten years old and a dead link in Luke Moran? I've got a lot of other shit going on right now, kid. If you haven't been reading the papers — which is likely since you've been hiding in the fucking Caribbean — you'll see that Damian Verland and his shithead lawyer, Greg Faulk, are working night and day to try and clear his name. This may get interesting for me, so excuse me if I can't jump at your beck and call. I really —" Dane stopped his tirade as James's face grew taut, his eyes becoming hazy as he seemingly lost himself in a series of thoughts. "What?"

"Faulk? Gregory Faulk?" James asked.

Dane paused before nodding. "Yeah. He's the head of Verland's legal team."

"He was also on my father's legal squad ten years ago."

It was Dane's turn to look confused. "Come again?"

173

"Gregory Faulk was a research assistant for my father before the murders. He was hired on by Ahmet Karaca to help oversee the legal workings of *Streets of Unity*."

"What's *Streets of Unity*?"

"It was a subsidiary that dealt with impoverished communities. It was created to help neighborhoods get back a sense of self and hope."

"I don't speak hippie," Dane replied.

It was James's turn to smirk. "How about this? *Streets of Unity* had a plan in front of the city council that was about to be approved."

"What was the plan?"

"To build a community center that would allow thousands to benefit from for little-to-no cost."

"So what?"

"So, the community center was set to break ground the following fall. In the exact spot the Silver Ray Casino now stands."

SEVENTEEN

Jolene awoke the next morning and made it to the precinct in a zombie-like state. She had not slept well, fitful dreams of whizzing bullets and blue vans around every corner clouded her frenzied thoughts. She had awoken in numerous cold sweats, jolting her body upright from her mountainous comforter in a gasp. Her eyes had searched the room instinctively, focusing on the shadows that morphed into masked men looking for false documentation. Luke Moran and Korhan Karaca. The nightmares still hovered just below the surface.

Luckily, the barista at her local coffee joint — an early-twentysomething sporting a curly afro and designer frames, with a youthful lust for the detective that started in his groin — had her drink ready and waiting. He took her money at the counter and handed her back the change, his number written on the receipt, as usual, and the flirtatious smile spread across his face. "Still a little too young for me, Sammy," Jolene had said as she waved her thanks and turned for the exit.

"Still worth a shot," Sammy had responded. "See you tomorrow."

As Hartley walked the pit in the direction of her partner, she yawned and rubbed the residual sleep from her eyes. Ratliff sat at his desk, the clean-shaven, alertness letting her know that he had not had the same night she had been privy to. "Ready to go?" he asked as he stood.

"Give me a minute to check messages," she replied, taking a seat and waking her computer with a shake of the mouse. She dialed into her voicemail and listened with slumped shoulders as Mac relayed nothing new as of the previous evening. Korhan Karaca had died as a result of the gunshot wound to the throat, with severe blood loss. Samples of blood from other locations not pooled under Karaca's body had been sent for testing, and the print taken from the gun left at the scene was next in line for analysis. The tire marks from the vehicle, unfortunately, were a dead-end. They were available at hundreds of auto stores throughout the Chicagoland area, and were best sellers, which meant untraceable. Last, but not least, Korhan's phone had been handed over to the tech team to see what, if anything, could be salvaged.

Hartley hung up the phone and signed into her email account, running her eyes over the items in her inbox before reaching up and switching off the monitor. She turned to her partner who was ready and waiting. "Let's go."

* * * * *

Ahmet and Esra Karaca lived in a quaint bungalow in Norwood Park, miles down the Kennedy Expressway, northwest of the city. The neighborhood, with its dense population of Chicago's firefighters and police officers, was a particularly lovely area, known for the abundance of vegetation in an otherwise overrun concrete jungle. Hartley had always found the area to be a pleasant getaway from the grittiness of the city interior, a place she had frequented from time to time just to gain a sense of peace in her chaotic life.

The expressway, as usual, was slow going, allowing the partners time to relive the bedlam from the previous day. The patrol unit Ratliff had dispatched to the Karaca's home had learned from the couple's neighbors that Korhan's parents were out of town on vacation, and should be returning the following morning. There had been no talk amongst the uniformed officers and the neighbors regarding the reason for the visit, though there was definite concern spread across their faces.

Ratliff steered the cruiser up the ramp leading to Harlem Avenue and merged onto West Bryn Mawr. They weaved through the neighborhoods, watching as children played in small yards with friends, tossing baseballs between mitts or twirling hula-hoops around waists and arms. Hartley smiled, remembering long gone times when the world seemed much smaller and safer, when the anarchy of others had not yet treaded into her personal space with a ferocity that, sometimes, left her breathless.

"That's it," Hartley said, pointing out her window at the home.

Ratliff pulled the vehicle to the curb and killed the engine. He glanced through her window at the house with a furrowed brow. "Doesn't look like they're home yet, does it?"

"Won't know until we knock." They exited the car and made their way up the steps and to the front door. Hartley rang the doorbell, the chime echoing throughout the interior. Ratliff placed his hand on the storm door to ward off the reflection of the sun and peered in through the small glass lookout. The room was dark and still.

"Still haven't gotten back." The detectives turned in the direction of the voice, their eyes falling on a squat, elderly woman standing on her porch to their left. "They were supposed to be back sometime earlier, but obviously they must be running a little behind schedule."

"Have you spoken to them?" Hartley asked, moving away from the Karaca's door and towards the woman.

"Are you the police?" the lady asked, ignoring Hartley's question.

"Yes, ma'am," Ratliff answered, showing her his badge.

"I have not, no," she finally stated, looking back to the female detective as she made her way down the Karaca's steps and crossed the lawn. "They just asked me to take in their mail while they were away."

"Any idea where they went to?"

"Lake Lawn Resort." Hartley glanced to her partner, who shrugged his shoulders. The neighbor smiled. "It's in Delevan,

Wisconsin. Nice place. Paul and I have been there a couple times ourselves."

"And Paul is your …?"

"My husband. He's not here right now, or I'd have him come out."

"What's your name again?" Ratliff asked, stopping next to Hartley in the lawn.

"I'm Gertie. Gertrude, actually. Gertie just seems to have a bit more pep to it though." She smiled wide.

"I'm Detective Ratliff. This is my partner, Detective Hartley."

"Hello."

"Are you the neighbor who talked to the police yesterday?" Hartley asked.

"Yes. Paul and I did. We saw the young officer walking between the houses and looking into the Esra's windows. Thought something was strange about that, so we met him out on the lawn here. He didn't really let us in on what was going on. But I'd assume something happened. Get some patrol officers yesterday followed by detectives today. Is everything all right?"

Hartley looked to Ratliff quickly before engaging Gertie again. "We're not really at liberty to say at this moment. We're involved in an investigation and it wouldn't be right to divulge any information without speaking with the Karacas first. I'm sure —"

"Is it Korhan?" Hartley quieted, glancing to Ratliff before connecting with Gertie once more. "Is it their son?" Silence.

Gertie continued. "Paul and I were talking yesterday after the officer left. Figured it has to be Korhan. The Karacas are on vacation. If something happened to them, doubt the officer would be snooping around like that."

"I'm sure the Karacas are fine," Hartley quickly added.

"So it is Korhan, then." There was no inflection in her voice. "I figured something would happen to that boy. So sad. Is he … dead?"

"Miss —"

"Gertie," she quickly corrected.

"Gertie," Hartley said. "I can't share anything at the moment. Once we speak with the Karacas, then you can feel free to ask them. But until then, I'm sorry."

Gertie nodded her head in understanding. She turned her focus to the right and watched as an ancient, flawless Buick pulled up to the curb, its gleaming white exterior glimmering in the sun. Hartley and Ratliff followed her stare and watched as an elderly couple emerged, their eyes to the detectives in wonder. "Well," Gertie said, "here's your chance."

* * * * *

James walked the edge of Belmont Harbor, hands in pockets as he scanned the area. Ahead and to the right, dogs yelped and pawed at one another on a designated beach. Bicyclists and joggers passed him by hurriedly, the determination of a morning workout plastered on their faces. To the left, cars lazily made their way on Lake Shore Drive.

It was in the serenity of the ever-moving city that James inched along, his eyes coming to rest on Augie nearly thirty yards away, a wisp of curly smoke rising above his head into the atmosphere. His friend, like himself, did not smoke cigarettes. Weed was the drug of choice for Augie. He had given up tobacco years ago in the midst of a stint in rehab, determining swapping one crutch for another was not the way he wanted to go about his newfound sobriety. However, circumstances as they were, James was hardly the individual to broach the subject.

Augie glanced his way and acknowledged his presence, yet returned his gaze to the water before him, the shifting surface acting as some form of relief for the Londoner. He lifted the cigarette to his lips with nervous hands, drawing in a long pull that he released in a slow, extended cloud. "So what now?" he asked as James crouched next to him, hands folded before him for balance.

James did not avert his eyes from the ground. "Not sure," he answered. "What about you?"

"Fuck, mate," Augie responded, shaking his head. "I don't know. All I know is I have one more night in the motel, then I need to figure something out."

"Just extend your stay."

"Easy for you to say, Moneybags." For the first time in nearly twenty-four hours, Augie let a chuckle slip from his being. James glanced up and smirked. He stood and reached out for the cigarette in Augie's hand, taking a drag from the stick and handing it back. "I can't afford another night in the place. And, to be honest, it's kind of a shithole. I'll find something else."

"I'll pay for it —"

"No," Augie said quickly. "I'm not going to become your charity case. I can find something."

James thought for a moment. "Go to my apartment."

"You mean the apartment that you haven't been to in a year?"

James thought back to his Chicago base: the small apartment where he avoided certain death from Taylor Thames; the place where he first laid eyes on Jolene Hartley; the couch and bed where they had writhed in ecstasy and sweat. "It hasn't been a year," was all he said.

"Whatever. Are you not heading back there? You don't mind?"

"I'm getting sick of the daily massages and indoor swimming pool at the hotel I'm at. Might as well return to reality, right?"

"You're a bloody dickhead, you know that?" Augie said with a grin.

James forced a smile. "Go. Crash at my place. I'll be there in the next couple of days. I've got to take care of some things first." He reached into his pocket and pulled out a tangle of keys. He unhooked one and handed it to his friend. "You remember how to get there?"

"I just survived not getting my bloody head shot off. I think I can handle finding your place. Cheers."

EIGHTEEN

He pulled the car to a stop just around the corner from the address he had been given and threw it in park, surveying the area and noting the minimal pedestrian activity on the street in front of the apartment building he had been told to stake out. It was definitely not the place he wanted to be, especially with a graze wound to the face that crossed over his temple in a grotesque mash of coagulated blood and hair.

However, there was not much he could do at the moment. His associate had told him to make an appearance at Graiser's home and see what he could find out, and declining such a request could end in him being removed completely from the current situation. He knew beyond a shadow of a doubt that, given the chance — or reason — his counterpart would not hesitate to put a bullet between his eyes. It was the way he was. The way he had always been. There was no way around it. He needed to tread lightly, and bide his time.

* * * * *

Esra Karaca set a silver tray of ceramic mugs in front of the assembled group and waddled back into the kitchen for the carafe of steaming coffee. Esra and Ahmet were an elderly couple, yet the love apparent between the two was still palpable and playful. They matched one another equally in looks — both frumpy characters with a rotund quality about their physical appearances — and mannerisms, balancing each other in a way that spoke of an eternal connection that had lasted decades.

Esra returned with the carafe and set it down on the dining room table before taking her seat next to her husband. Ahmet's face mirrored his wife's. Their countenances verged on the edge of worry, yet their eyes gave way to an understanding that something serious had indeed happened. Like their neighbors, the Karacas led with the first thing that came to mind. "It's Korhan, isn't it?" Ahmet asked. His gaze focused on Hartley from beneath bushy, salt-and-pepper eyebrows and a shiny bald head. He fidgeted with the well-trimmed beard he kept, pulling the fine hairs of his moustache into his mouth with cracked lips. Esra reached over and grasped tightly onto his hand.

Hartley swallowed hard and steadied her gaze, wanting to appear confident as she relayed the news of their son. "Yes, sir," she began. "I'm sorry to tell you this, Mr. and Mrs. Karaca, but your son was killed yesterday morning."

Tears formed in the couples' eyes, hands brought to mouths to stifle any crude noises that usually escaped in times such as this. Yet, to the detectives' surprise, Esra rose and reached for the carafe, clearing her throat loudly before asking, "Would you like some coffee, dear?"

"Oh," Hartley said. "Uh … yes, please."

The elderly woman poured and asked Ratliff the same. He accepted, dropping a cube of sugar into the vessel as Esra tilted the decanter once more. "How did this happen?" Ahmet asked, forcing a smile of thanks to his wife as she returned to her seat and filled his mug, adding the sweetener and cream like she had for the last fifty years.

"There was a shootout, sir, and —"

"Between whom? The police and my son?"

Hartley shook her head. "No, sir," she answered. "As you know, sir, Korhan was wanted for attacking an officer last year. We had been looking for him for a while and had a tip where he was."

"So, why not arrest him?"

"That's what we were there for," Ratliff chimed in.

"So, what happened?"

"There were some unforeseeable obstacles that arose," Hartley said, trying to take the reins of the conversation back. "Korhan was shot and killed by several men while we were advancing on him. A shootout ensued between the police and the perpetrators, but we were unable to take anyone into custody."

"They're still on the run? Do you know where?"

"We don't sir, no. There are plenty of officers patrolling the area looking for the getaway vehicle at this moment."

"What type of vehicle?"

"It was a blue conversion van," Ratliff answered. "There was extensive damage to it, so it's only a matter of time before it's found."

There was a brief pause as the elderly couple looked to one another, a subtle exchange of comfort amid the awful circumstances. "And you're sure it was my son?" Hartley nodded. "How can you be so sure?"

Hartley folded her hands on the table and looked to her partner before responding. "I know who your son is, Mr. Karaca. I'm the officer he attacked."

* * * * *

He pulled the baseball cap down on his forehead, wincing from the sting as the elastic strap scraped painfully across the graze wound. He walked the sidewalk opposite the apartment building, glancing from the entrance to the street, taking in the movement from cars and pedestrians. An ambush from the police was not expected, yet the odds of the events that transpired the other day were minimal as well. Something had gone wrong, and until they figured out what, he had to stay on top of his game, working the scenery and situation as best he could.

He moved down the street and stopped across from the building where James Graiser was said to live. He pulled a cigarette from the wrinkled soft pack in his jacket pocket and lit it, sidestepping a woman as she barreled forward, waving a hand in the air to ward off the smoke. He apologized for the inconvenience as he turned, not wanting the woman to catch a glimpse of his face and thus tie him to the area.

He had nervously watched the news the previous evening and, besides mention of the shootout that left one man dead, descriptions of him and his associates had yet to be distributed to the public. Yet he still needed to show precaution. The fact of the matter was there had, indeed, been two murders yesterday morning, one already in the lab and another shoved deep within a dumpster behind an obscure warehouse. The van had been wiped clean as best they could, and doused with bleach his associate had found within the warehouse's locked cargo bay. DNA matches were highly unlikely at this point, a calming thought for the man since his was, no doubt, spread throughout the cabin. The vehicle itself had been moved into an alleyway a block from where they had dumped the body, a locale that offered it a brief hiding spot for the time being. It would be found, eventually, and easily tied to the shootout that left Korhan Karaca dead.

However, that was the least of his problems. Unbeknownst to his associate, the gun which he had yielded when embedding a bullet into Korhan's neck now rested in police possession, most likely being subjected to a bombardment of tests, one of which he realized could cause him possible dismay: fingerprint analysis.

* * * * *

The detectives excused themselves briefly from the dining room table and stepped outside, leaving the two elderly individuals to grieve as they needed for the moment. Esra was, by far, more emotional than her husband. Hartley glanced in through the front window at the pair and watched as Ahmet reached to his wife and held her in an embrace, her tears soaking into his shirt just above her wrinkled hand that clutched to him as if she would never let go. She seemed a sweet woman, the grandmotherly figure Hartley had known in her youth that knew her way around the kitchen and showered the kids with treats they hid from their parents. Yet the time and place Esra now found herself in brought an ache that was deafening. She could not breathe. Her inhales appeared sharp, her squat frame shaking and swaying as Ahmet wrapped his arms around her.

"Again, I'm sorry for your loss," Hartley said as they sat once more across from the couple. "It's a horrible thing to have to go through."

"It could be worse," Ahmet said, wiping his nose with a tissue.

Hartley threw a quick glance her partner's way before responding. "How's that?" she asked.

Ahmet looked up to her with bloodshot, yet serious, eyes. "He could have been a good son." The admission shocked the detectives, yet neither Ahmet nor Esra shirked at the comment. Ahmet forced a smile. "Do you have children? Either of you?" Both shook their heads. "Well, let me be the first to tell you: they are a gift from God. Thirty-nine years ago, the Almighty blessed my wife and me with a beautiful baby boy." He clasped hands with Esra.

"I had had trouble conceiving, you see," she stated. "We had tried for years and years. Nothing. No children. Three miscarriages."

"It's a hell of a thing to see your friends start families and raise their children. You're happy and angry at the same instant."

There was a brief pause before Esra looked into her husband's eyes. "We almost gave up." Hartley could not tell, but the exchange looked almost cathartic, like the very thought of quitting on procreation was something they had almost succeeded in doing.

"And then a miracle happened," Ahmet said, turning his attention back to the detectives. "Esra became pregnant."

"The Almighty answered my prayers," Esra said, though her words lacked the enthusiasm Hartley knew had been there long ago. "A baby boy. A child of our own to raise and teach."

"And then he became a nightmare," Ahmet said, his lower lip quivering with emotion contradicting the anger that welled in his eyes.

* * * * *

The lobby of the building was nothing more than a twelve-foot by eight-foot alcove with mailboxes lining one wall and an empty, dark office the other. A dim lit hallway led to a door with block white letters that read *Laundry Room*. Next to it, another entrance to the stairwell and the apartments above.

He glanced around quickly, keeping his hat low about his face. His eyes scanned the line where the ceiling met the walls, looking for a camera of any sort. Luckily for him, there were none. He spun on his heels and moved to the rows of locked mailboxes, his hands sliding across the shiny, brass surfaces and stopping as he reached the one he was searching for.

J Graiser.

He memorized the apartment number and turned into the hallway, stepping quietly down the corridor to the door leading to the stairwell. He reached his hand out grasped the knob, cursing as the locking mechanism held fast, disallowing him advancement.

He suddenly saw movement from the corner of his eye and watched an old man materialize behind the glass paned door leading into the laundry room. The old man's brow furrowed momentarily as he stared. He moved towards the intruder slowly, opening the laundry room entrance and speaking in a loud voice over the washing machines. "Can I help you?" he asked.

"No," was the response. "I'm fine."

The elderly man did not budge. "And I'm the Maintenance Supervisor. What can I do for you?" His tone was firm, yet friendly.

"I'm …" The man stalled, glancing back to the mailboxes before speaking. "I'm looking for Ricardo Perez. You know if he's home?"

The maintenance man shook his head slowly. "Sorry, son. No one named Perez lives here. What address are you —"

"That's okay," he interrupted. "Must be the wrong building. Thanks." He turned and hastily made an exit, glancing one last time into the building and the old man staring after him.

NINETEEN

Hartley and Ratliff made their way down the precinct steps and to the sidewalk below. They had just driven back from the Karacas home and brought the elderly couple in to identify the body of their son. The ride from the Norwood Park neighborhood back to the station had been a reserved, yet not too uncomfortable, trek. Ahmet and Esra had taken turns in telling stories regarding Korhan, everything from childhood spelling bees to adolescent mishaps, right into his early twenties and beyond when chaos ensued and drugs and criminal behavior reigned.

Ahmet had forced smiles from the back seat next to his wife, their wrinkled hands intertwined as he shared memories of the past. Yet his smile faded as he recalled the downward spiral. "My son," he had stated, "has had many problems. It's true. I'm sure the police in most counties surrounding Chicago could attest to that. I'm sure you, too, can attest to that, personally." Hartley nodded her head from behind the steering wheel, glancing back in the rearview mirror as he spoke. "I want you to know, detective, that I … we are truly sorry for the pain that Korhan caused you." She remained silent, the anger still within her being forced down by the grief these individuals now felt. Her personal feelings towards Korhan Karaca were just that: personal. And grudges had no business in her line of work.

"Korhan had a history," Esra said, miming her husband's sentiment. "He was a criminal and a drug addict. But he was still our son."

"And for that, we're sorry for your loss," Ratliff said solemnly, turning in his seat to look upon the couple with sympathetic eyes. He could see the emotion within the pair, yet knew the look of acceptance. He could tell they fully understood the extremes that Korhan had placed on himself for nearly half his life, the strained relationships of family and friends. Ratliff had been able to tell during the ride to the precinct that the Karacas were saddened, and rightfully so, yet they were not surprised by the outcome. If anything, there was a sense of relief. Relief that Korhan had made it this long on his downward spiral. Relief that the worry and fitful nights were all over, that the days of stomach wrenching unease at seeing an approaching police car were at an end.

They arrived at the precinct and escorted the couple to a waiting area, both detectives keeping a comforting distance until Mac appeared to lead the Karacas to their deceased son. Hartley leaned into the Medical Examiner. "Call me when they're through?" He nodded and disappeared down the hall.

"Where do you want to eat?" Hartley asked her partner as they glanced up and down the sidewalk just outside of the precinct.

Ratliff shrugged. "I don't care." He spun around and squinted to focus his vision down the street.

"Let's just go to the diner," Hartley said with an unsatisfactory sigh.

"Really?" he answered. "I was hoping for something a little more … edible."

Hartley laughed as they made their way towards the restaurant, an establishment frequented by what seemed like the entire police force at some point throughout the day. "It's just easier. Figured the Karacas will be up to talk with us some more soon. Rather be close by, you know?"

"Plus, Louie makes a damn good cup of coffee!"

It was Hartley's turn to furrow her brow. "Are you serious?"

"Hell no! It's worse than the break room. But it does wake you up."

* * * * *

"So, how do you think it's going in there?" Ratliff asked. Their waitress had just dropped off the food they had ordered nearly fifteen minutes prior and refilled their mugs, the bitter, burnt smell of coffee rising from the scalding hot ceramic vessels.

Hartley lifted hers to her lips and took a sip. She choked it down. "Probably about as well as any parent losing a child."

"They didn't seem that broken up about it." Hartley glanced up to him. "What I mean is I've seen worse. They seem like they knew it was going to happen."

"With the life Korhan led, they probably figured it would at some point. But just like Esra said: Korhan was still their son. There's an ache no matter what the current relationship status is."

Ratliff nodded and cut into his Salisbury steak, placing the morsel on his fork and dipping it into a mound of instant mashed potatoes. "We really could have found a better spot to eat," he replied as he shoveled the food into his mouth.

"I heard that!" shouted Louie, the establishment's owner and cook.

"I'm just messing with you," Ratliff said through a mouthful of food. He looked up to Hartley with wide eyes at having been busted bad-mouthing the diner.

Hartley laughed and dug into her own plate. "Let's talk about the case. What do we have to go on so far?" she asked after several bites.

Ratliff wiped his mouth and took a sip from the glass of water. "Well, I'd say there are a few main items. One: the Karacas. Maybe Esra and Ahmet can shed some light on what happened to their son. Maybe Korhan had some enemies that wanted payback."

"And you think the elderly parents might have something? They didn't seem too involved in his life."

"Look who's being pessimistic now." Hartley scrunched her nose at him. "I'm just saying, with Korhan's life the way it was, maybe he went to Ahmet early on for help. Who knows? But it's worth a look."

"Agreed. We also have the blood samples and the gun."

"Any word from Mac on those?"

Hartley shook her head. "Not yet. Left a message this morning saying he was on everyone's collective ass about it."

"What about Korhan's phone?"

"Same. His tech was trying to salvage anything he could. Still in limbo."

"Anything our victim can shed some light on?"

She shrugged. "We'll see. But we were both there. We saw what happened. I think whatever we get will come from Mac. Right now, I figure that's all we have to go on."

"There was that red-haired guy that took off," Ratliff added, remembering the man Korhan was seen speaking to moments before taking a bullet in the throat.

"Right. And him. But right now we don't have much to go on there, so we'll have to keep that one on the backburner. Hopefully we can get something off of Korhan's phone. Which reminds me: we need to put in a request to get his phone records."

"Way ahead of you," Ratliff said with a smirk. "Put the request in after you took off last night."

She smiled. "Do you really need me around, after all?" She brought the coffee mug to her lips once more, their eyes locking on one another for a brief moment.

Ratliff's phone suddenly chimed, vibrating across the table and startling both detectives. He broke focus with Hartley and looked to the screen. "It's Hill," he said. "Hey Toby," Ratliff answered. He leaned forward and held a hand in the air, summoning their waitress as he began to move. Instinctively, Hartley followed, knowing something was up. "Got it. Area's sectioned off? Great. Be there soon." He hung up the phone and stood, reaching into his pocket to throw a twenty dollar bill on the table. "They found the van," he said to his partner. "And a body."

* * * * *

Hartley phoned Mac on their way from the precinct to see what his plans were in regards to the new body found in the vicinity of their wanted blue van. "I'm already en route," the ME said. "Julian's back with the Karacas. I figure you two are on your way to the scene as well?"

"Yep," Hartley replied. With the route her investigation was taking at the moment, Ahmet and Esra would have to wait. Their testimony had the potential to be superbly important, however, the physical evidence within the van had become their new foundational block. "How were they?" she asked, referring to the elderly couple most likely staring down at their deceased son.

"Ah," he said, the shrug apparent on the other end of the line. "Obviously in pain, but not too surprised, I guess."

"Good. I'll see you at the scene." She hung up and placed the phone in her lap, her eyes staring into the Chicago sky.

* * * * *

The alleyway in which the blue van had been left abandoned had been sectioned off by the first responders at the scene. Mac had brought a sporadic collection of his evidence team with, dropping several of them at the van while he made his way to the body a block down. It was apparent that the van was indeed the vehicle from the firefight. Windows had been shot out. Bullet holes littered the exterior. A number of casings were strewn about the cabin.

But it was also evident that the likelihood of finding any solid evidence was slim. The vehicle reeked of bleach. The white plastic containers — at least a half dozen — were strewn within the interior of the van, and it appeared every handle, steering wheel and cup holder had been wiped down and doused with the cleaning agent. Hartley was stunned as she stared to the cabin and the pool of crimson tinged bleach settling in pools on the floor. She knew full well that two of the assailants had been shot, one in the gut, which tended to bleed profusely. She turned from the rear doors of the van and swore, kicking a chunk of asphalt farther into the alley to collide with a rotten wooden pallet. "Shit!" she said. "You guys finding anything?" she asked, glancing around the cabin towards a technician dusting the steering wheel for prints.

The tech shook her head. "Nothing yet," she said. "Seems whoever was in here did a bang-up job."

"No kidding," Hartley replied, though the comment was not directed to anyone in particular.

"I'll let you know if I find anything," the tech answered.

Hartley began down the alley, whistling to Ratliff and turning him away from whatever conversation he was immersed in with Officer Toby Hill.

Ratliff ran up beside her, his arm grazing hers as they made their way to Mac and the body. "Nothing, huh?"

"Nope. What did Hill have to say?"

"Not much," Ratliff replied. "Said they sectioned everything off when they found it. Ran into the body doing a canvass of the area. Looks to be one of the shooters. Guy Hill hit in the stomach."

"But it could have been the other dozen shots that were fatal," Mac said as they approached, his obvious keen sense of hearing bringing him right into their conversation.

"Whoa," Hartley replied. "How many times did Hill hit him?"

"Only the one time," Ratliff said.

"Well, looks to me that the threesome decided to cut their losses," Mac added. "The amount of blood this guy lost was irreversible. He would have perished anyway."

"No need to take him to the hospital," Hartley chimed in. "Just gives him a chance to spill the beans. Dealing with some pros here."

"Well, pros or not," Mac said, "they didn't do enough to leave us empty-handed."

"What do you mean?"

Mac smiled. "Well, they left a body, first off, which will allow us to do some DNA testing. Or fingerprint analysis. Whichever you'd like."

Hartley nodded with a smirk. "How about both?"

"Surely, my dear."

TWENTY

Hartley and Ratliff moved straight through the pit and into an interview room where Ahmet and Esra Karaca had been placed nearly forty-five minutes prior. Their eyes were bloodshot from the emotional toll that had taken place, yet their cheeks were dry. "I'm so sorry to keep you waiting, Mr. and Mrs. Karaca," she said as she took a seat across from the pair in one of the wooden chairs. Ratliff followed her in and pulled a seat from the corner of the room, taking position next to his partner.

"No," Ahmet said, waving his hand in the air. "Don't worry about it. We needed the time. It's the longest I've spent with my son in … must be fifteen years."

"I know it's been a very trying day for you both. I'd like to ask you a few questions, if that's okay with you." She pulled a pad of paper from her pocket and flipped it open to a clean page.

Before she could open her mouth, Ahmet spoke. "I always thought … well, hoped, I guess would be the correct word. I always hoped Korhan would get his act together. He was such a sweet boy." He looked up to the detectives. "Is it wrong for me to only want to remember him as that? Not as the monster he obviously became?"

Hartley displayed a sympathetic smile. "No. I think we remember those we lost as we need to."

"I guess so," Ahmet replied. "Have you ever lost anyone close to you?"

Hartley stalled, wishing the conversation would veer towards the less personal. "I'm around death every day, Mr. Karaca. I get to know those like your son well."

Ahmet smiled at her. "So I'll take that as a no. Let me tell you, it hurts. No matter the distance that's between you, or the friction or the discomfort. No matter what has happened between your good and bad times, it's a feeling that I wish upon no one. It takes your breath away."

"Again," Hartley said quietly, "I'm sorry for your loss."

"No you're not," he said. The comment caught everyone in the room by surprise, including his wife. He turned to look upon her and caught the shocked expression spread across her face. He glanced quickly back to the detectives. "Sorry," he said with flushed cheeks. "All I meant was that my son attacked you. He might have even tried to … tried to kill you. I would not be sorry for a man like that leaving this world."

"Mr. Karaca, regardless of my feelings towards your son for that event, I also don't wish the empty feeling of losing someone on anybody."

He looked into her eyes and studied them, nodding ever so slowly. "I believe you. And thank you." He smiled to his wife and then uttered a comment that nearly sent Hartley sprawling to the floor. "I understand why James would be working with you on his parents' case."

Ratliff stopped mid-yawn, his fist closing around his opened mouth, eyes darting from the elderly man to his motionless partner. Hartley's brow furrowed and her hands grasped onto her knees for stability.

The statement came from nowhere, in her mind, blurted into the room at random to throw her off balance and frazzle her senses. She took a moment to process, glancing sideways to her partner before connecting with the man before her. "I'm sorry. I … uh. I'm confused. Why do you …?" She paused again, gathering herself as an officer of the law and trying to regain her composure. She asked the first question that came to mind. "James who?"

"James," he said, as if she should know who he was talking about. "Graiser." Hartley remained fixed on him. "I recognized you. It took me a while, but I recognized you from the news programs." Ahmet nervously twisted to his wife, peeking to her quickly, a concerned look etched into his wrinkled face. "I'm sorry," he said, reaching a hand into midair to hover over the coffee table. "Maybe I said something I shouldn't?"

Ratliff leaned forward to pull Hartley's attention from whatever shock had befallen her. She blinked several times in succession and cleared her throat. "No, Mr. Karaca. No.

Everything's fine. I just ... I didn't expect you to mention him. James."

"Oh," he responded. "Well, I'm sorry if I threw you for a loop. Apologies."

"It's ... It's fine." She shifted in her spot, righting the ship and buckling down once more, though the line of questioning had been widened. "Mr. Karaca —"

"Ahmet."

"Ahmet," she obliged, "why would you think we're working on the Graiser case?"

"Well ... I don't know. I just assumed with you and him on the television together, I figured you were looking into it. You know, the pictures from the Navy Pier shooting? Are you not?"

Hartley shook her head. "Ahmet, I assure you that everything you've seen in the news is purely coincidental in regards to the Graiser case."

"Do you not know about his parents?"

"I know plenty. It's a cold case that hasn't seen any action for the past ten years. James and I ..." She halted, remembering how his sudden appearance ended the physicality between her and Ratliff in a heartbeat. "Mr. Graiser's involvement in our investigation last year had nothing to do with his parents."

Ahmet nodded his head slowly and slid back into the couch cushions. For the first time, Esra took the chance to speak up. "How is James?" she asked, a tiny light in her eye twinkling as she mentioned him. "Have you spoken to him recently?"

Ratliff eyed his partner with a quick glance. "His involvement in the investigation ended last year," Hartley said, not seeing the point in bringing up their brief fling to the elderly couple or her partner.

"He was always a good kid," Esra said, seemingly needing the moment of peace to balance the chaos that had been her recent life. Ahmet smirked as well, reaching out to grasp onto his wife's hand. "Bit of a drifter, I guess you could say. Seemed everyone gravitated towards him though, you know?" Hartley could not help but smile as her memories trailed to the not-so-distant past. While working the case that had brought them together, there had been a time where James stayed at the precinct, bunking up in this very chamber, seeking the safety of the police department's break room as the threat of Taylor Thames still loomed. At one point, Jolene had learned James had been allowed to roam the halls, making friends enough to be escorted down to the holding cells to play bridge with the officers ending their shifts. He definitely had had a way about him. "By the looks of it," Esra said, pulling Hartley from her reveries, "you do."

Jolene shifted in her chair, an uncomfortable heat rising from her collar. "He definitely had a likeable quality."

The couple agreed. "He had acquaintances all over the world. You know that James used to travel frequently, right?" Hartley nodded. "He used to backpack all over the place. If his parents were heading on vacation or a business meeting, he would almost always go with and disappear for days. Never missed the ride home though." She chuckled as her gaze fell to the table.

After a brief silence, Ratliff chimed in. "Mr. and Mrs. Karaca, if you don't mind, we'd like to ask you a few questions about your son."

"Absolutely."

"When was the last time you saw Korhan?"

Ahmet's face stiffened. "Years." He glanced to his wife. "Four? Five?"

"Five," she agreed. "It was right after Daniel's funeral."

"Daniel?" Hartley asked.

"Daniel Vincent. You remember the alderman, don't you?"

"I do. His case coincided with the investigation James helped us with."

"Do you remember the circumstances of that meeting with Korhan?" Ratliff questioned.

"I do," Ahmet said. "We had just gotten back from Daniel's funeral. I came in through the back door and noticed the window on our basement entry was broken. Came in to find him with a bag full of Esra's jewelry."

"What did you do?" Ratliff asked.

"Tried to talk to him, but it was useless. He was on drugs and not rational."

"Did you file a report?" Hartley inquired.

Ahmet shook his head. "He's my son. I exchanged the jewelry for a couple hundred dollars. Then he left. Just like that."

"No other meetings with him since then?"

"None."

"Anything else from your house missing since that time?" Ratliff asked.

"There've been things."

"What things?" Hartley pushed.

Ahmet shrugged. "Things. Jewelry. Some cash. Couple crystal vases from my wife's family. Just things he could sell for drug money."

"And you didn't report it?"

"No. I kept telling myself that this was it. This was the last time. He needed this vase or that watch for one last fix, then he'd clean himself up."

An emotional silence followed, broken up only by the inner workings of the officers in the pit. Hartley pressed on. "What about since then? Anything out of the ordinary regarding your son?"

"You mean besides him attacking a police officer?"

Hartley forced a quick smile. "Yes, besides that."

"There were a couple of visits to the house. People looking for him."

"Is that unusual?" Ratliff asked.

Ahmet nodded. "Sure. He hasn't lived there in over twenty years. I would assume his criminal friends know where to find him."

"Who was looking for him?"

"About a week ago, a police officer came by looking for Korhan. Seemed a little upset that I couldn't give him any information."

"What was the reason for the visit?"

"Didn't say. Just told me it was an important case and Korhan was an essential part of it."

"Did you catch his name?" Hartley asked.

Ahmet shook his head. "He said it in passing, but I can't recall. I do remember he was … an unconventional looking officer."

"How so?"

"Well, take him for example." Ahmet's eyes focused on Ratliff. "Clean-cut, handsome young man. Looks like a police officer. This guy was different. He didn't look like an officer."

"Uniform? Or plain clothes?"

"Plain. Kind of raggedy. And he wasn't driving one of the unmarked cruisers either. He took off in an older, rundown SUV."

"What did he look like?"

"Long, dark hair. It was pulled back in a ponytail. He had a thick goatee, as well. And a scar." He raised his hand and extended his index finger, dragging it straight through his left eyebrow. "Right through here. Must have had some sort of eye injury, because he kind of had a lazy eyelid."

Hartley looked to Ratliff, the long hair and goatee throwing a red flag. They remained quiet, yet both were thinking the same thing: the driver of the van. "Anything else you can think of?" Hartley asked.

Ahmet shook his head and then stopped abruptly, raising a finger in the air. "There was another guy who stopped by not too long ago. Kind of a weaselly character. He had reddish-brown hair. Deep set eyes. He was looking for Korhan as well, though I'm pretty sure he was one of Korhan's drug friends." Ahmet caught the second quick exchange between the detectives. "What? Do you know who these people are?"

Hartley took the lead. "We don't," she said. "But there were two individuals present at the time of your son's murder that match those descriptions. There was a red-haired man that appeared to be talking with Korhan."

"And the man with the scar?"

"We weren't able to see any scar, but the long, dark hair and goatee seem to be in line with the driver of the van." Ahmet looked to his wife and grasped her hand firmly, tears welling in their eyes as the thought of their son's possible murderer on their front porch filled their minds. "Mr. and Mrs. Karaca, we will do everything possible to find out who did this."

Just then the door to the break room burst open and Mac walked in, a manila folder in his hands. "Mr. and Mrs. Karaca," he said in greeting. He turned to Hartley and Ratliff. "Excuse me, but I think you need to see this."

The detectives excused themselves from the room and walked to her desk, stopping as Mac handed her the envelope. "We were able to access the call history of Korhan's phone."

"Even with all the damage?" Ratliff asked, an awestruck tone in his voice.

"What can I say? They are technological gurus." His smile faded. "Turn to the second page." Hartley followed his directive and scanned the sheet, her eyes finally falling on a number that was repeated several times. She stared up to Mac with intense eyes as Ratliff took the paper from her. "Figured you'd want to see that."

"What?" Ratliff said, running his finger down the surface. "Whose number is this?"

The number swirled ferociously in her mind. It drew the air sharply from the room, leaving in its wake a devastating quiet that left Hartley's head spinning. Jolene felt herself turn from her partner and the ME, even as Ratliff repeated her name over and over. She walked the length of the pit and began down the stairs, descending to the ground floor and out the precinct doors.

Ratliff turned to Mac and asked once more, "Whose number is this?"

The Medical Examiner took the folder from his hands and looked him in the eye. "It's James Graiser's."

TWENTY-ONE

Jolene had always prided herself on remaining professional, no matter what arose, yet she could do nothing about the surfacing of emotions at that particular moment. The fact that James had once again materialized was enough to cause her additional confusion and irritation. Yet it was the circumstances surrounding it that led her into complete, unadulterated rage. James Graiser — a man she had met during one of her most personally vicious and trying investigations, with whom she had developed feelings for and eventually slept with — had come back to Chicago without so much as a phone call, and now appeared to be in contact with the very same individual who had brutally attacked her in her own home.

And James knew it! On the day of the *State of Finance* shooting, when Jolene and Ratliff had shown up to meet with James, battered and bruised Hartley had told him the names of the men that had attacked her: Luke Moran and Korhan Karaca. And now, months later, after an exodus and what seemed like an eternal silence from James, he was spotted not only trudging around the city she served and protected, but fraternizing with her very own attacker. It had been enough to send her over the edge.

Her head was a twirling mess. The thought that her relationship with James had gone from person of interest in an investigation to possible special someone to consorting with a junkie criminal, simply blew her away. She felt sick to her stomach when she read the phone number on the pages Mac had shown her, and, as she exited the precinct and hit the sidewalk, she pulled her hair back from her face and ran them the length of her neck, grasping onto her shoulders as she tried to find some stability.

Her focus had retreated to that night in James's apartment, a magical, tragic evening in which she had pushed her failing relationship with Graiser into a heated, sexual exchange in an effort to connect with him in a way that would cast Jacoby Ratliff from her thoughts. She shook her head and cringed at the fact that she had allowed this man to run his fingers across her body, to play with her skin and lips and breasts. The union had been a charged display of passion, yet it now brought a tear to her eye that her one-time friend, an individual that had tasted the sweat on her skin and, for the majority of that night and early morning, had been inside her, had cast her away for a spot next to her past assailant.

Or so it would seem. Amidst her sudden and uncontrollable anger, the police officer in Jolene Hartley tried to break through to the surface. *You don't know the circumstances,* she thought to herself. *There could be a quality explanation for all of this.* She racked her brain to find one, yet the cop was pushed down, leaving only the irate, biased human being.

* * * * *

The brief hiatus to clarify the current situation with Mac had left Jacoby at a disadvantage as to where his partner had gone. He exited onto the large, concrete staircase leading to the street and paused, catching his breath from the speedy chase as he hit the sidewalk and glanced in either direction. He caught sight of Jolene just as she began to cross the intersection to his left. Ratliff began towards her, quickening his pace to a light jog as he maneuvered his way through the throngs of pedestrians and across the busy street. "Jo!" he shouted, his voice turning numerous heads as he cupped his palms around his mouth in a makeshift megaphone. "Jolene!"

She was still ahead of him, though Jacoby was sure she had heard him. The tears that had fallen from her fiery eyes had not been summoned by the fact that she was hurt. She was. She was sick to her stomach with the thought of James and Korhan chumming it up over beers at a local bar. She wanted nothing more than to walk in upon their friendly meeting and eye them both up with nothing more than an accusatory glance.

Yet there was nothing to accuse James of. He had not been there when Moran and Karaca had attacked her in her apartment. He had not known of Korhan's involvement in the grand scheme of things until the day she had confronted him about his father's gun. Hell, he had not even known about the gun! Yet there he was, his name mixed into the conversation right next to Korhan's, brought to the surface by the victim's very own phone records.

"Jo! Slow down!" came a yell from a few yards behind her. She slowed her pace as she turned, her hand rising to rub her forehead with eyes shut tight as if trying to corral the images and dialogue of the last year. "Jo," Ratliff said as he approached slightly out of breath. "Hold up a sec —"

"He was calling him," she interjected, talking aloud to no one in particular, not caring that she had just interrupted her partner.

"Jo, I know, but —"

"Korhan Karaca," she continued without hesitation. "James Graiser and Korhan Karaca." She opened her eyes and looked up to Jacoby, her beautiful, brown orbs reddened from the emotional overflow. Ratliff looked upon her and closed his mouth. "Jay, he doesn't contact me for over six months; no calls, no texts. No fucking postcards to say, 'Hey, I'm alive. Don't worry!' Nothing. But he keeps Korhan Karaca on speed dial." She paused and looked around.

"Look, Jo, I know your connection with James was —"

"No!" she responded immediately. "I don't give a shit about the connection I had with James! What I care about, Ratliff, is the fact that that piece of shit Karaca and Luke Moran almost killed me in my apartment. What I give a shit about is that James left town without a simple goodbye, only to show up randomly outside my apartment! And now I come to find out he's best buds with our vic!"

"I know!" Ratliff said loudly, stepping forward as he looked to his left and right at bystanders that had tuned into the conversation. He reached out his hand and placed it on Jolene's shoulder, pulling her slightly towards a storefront to his left. "Look, I know this is a shock. It's a shock to me, too. No one saw that coming."

"Jay," she said, arms wide in frustration. "It's in the phone records. His number is there! He knew Korhan was in my apartment. He knew!"

"I know. I know," he said. "Just take a deep breath and listen?" She looked to him with conceding — yet still angry — eyes. "Can you?"

"Yes," she replied forcefully.

"Okay. What we need to do is just focus on our case. Right now, *that* James we knew is in the past. *This* James — the James that's in Korhan's call history — is someone altogether different. Maybe someone we need to find to shed light on what happened to Karaca. Who knows? But we need to focus on the case. That's the bottom line."

Hartley shook her head rapidly and brought her hands to her face again, this time rubbing her temples as she listened to the words coming from her partner's mouth. "And you don't think James has anything to do with this?"

"Do you?"

"I don't know. This is way too much coincidence to —"

"I realize that," he responded calmly. "But it happens. Coincidences sometimes lead to the next step. So, that's what we need to focus on: what the next step is."

The silence that enveloped them was uncomfortable, to say the least. Jolene understood fully she needed to rein in her emotions and focus on the case at hand. She owed it to Ahmet and Esra to find out who killed their son and why, regardless of her personal feelings. Yet she was torn. The way things had been left between her and James — personally and regarding the murder of his parents — had set a fire in her early on. She had immersed herself in work, and, in the slow periods between cases, the files containing everything about Michael and Amelia Graiser. It was something she knew she needed to shake. However, with his appearance the other night in the vulnerable state she was in with Ratliff, and now the fact he was apparently connecting with Korhan, her mind was unwilling to let it go.

"Look," she said, glancing around before locking eyes with her partner. "I just need a little time to process this all. I'm sorry." She shook her head once more and stepped away.

"Where are you heading to?" Ratliff asked with a furrowed brow.

"I ... I don't know. Just give me a little time, Jay." He nodded his head as she turned and began down the sidewalk, disappearing into the crowds as they started their migrations from work to home, a mass of people oblivious to the war waging within Jolene's mind.

* * * * *

Ratliff made his way back into the precinct and to his desk. Mac approached, having taken it upon himself to reconnect with the Karacas and set them up with a ride to their home in Norwood Park. "Where is she?" he asked, his eyes moving to Captain Nolan as he exited his desk and moved towards them.

"She left," he said, watching his superior approach as well. "Needed some time to process."

"Jay," Nolan said, stopping in front of the pair. "Where'd Jo run to?"

"She wasn't feeling the best. Took off." Ratliff leaned forward and shuffled through a pile of printouts. He lifted them into the air and began to stack them neatly, his mind floating to what Mac had given them regarding the phone. It had been a shock to see James the night when he and Jolene had shared their second kiss. It was something that Jacoby completely wished had gone a different direction. Yet the thought of Graiser's mistimed interruption morphing into a product of their investigation was something altogether different. It put him on their collective radar, but not as a jilted ex-fling or hopeful friend. This set him up with a connection to Korhan Karaca, a connection that happened well after he knew what had transpired between the deceased druggie and Jolene. This set him up as a person of interest.

TWENTY-TWO

She sat poised in front of an oversized window in her quaint dining area, resting with her knees drawn tightly into her chest on the sill that easily fit her entire body. A crystal wine glass balanced in one hand and her steady eyes focused to the city before her, staring at nothing, yet catching every movement. Lackadaisical pedestrians sauntered sluggishly across eerily quiet intersections. Cars slowed at stop signs briefly before gunning down the pavement. Lights twinkled. Trees bent in the breeze.

And Jolene sat still, blinking occasionally as her much needed tipsiness settled into her body. She had done something that had never even crossed her mind since her days began on the force. Her normal evenings — when not parked before the white board full of clues and suspects — was to make it home and watch television with a glass of wine or, on occasion, a beer. Possibly an evening out with Kim would be in the cards. Yet tonight, after her impromptu, uncontrollable exit from the precinct, Jolene had found herself in a neighborhood bar, pushed up to the counter as the bartender fed her shots of tequila. The drinks had been on the house, as the youth tending the alcohol obviously had eyes for her. The fact that she still wore her badge must have encouraged the young man. Helping out an officer of the law would no doubt come full-circle for him, at some point. He only hoped, with the tequila being dealt out at such a rapid pace to this beauty before him, karma would catch up with him tonight.

Jolene gathered that the young man was all for liquoring her up. He flashed a smile and made comments regarding her appearance with a certain wit and charm, pouring a fresh shot for them both and toasting to their new found friendship. Hartley forced a smile and tapped glasses with him before throwing the drink down. "I'll be back in a minute for you, sweetie," he said as he moved to the end of the bar to serve the few patrons in the establishment, glancing over his shoulder at her from time to time.

The moment she realized she needed to leave was when he had asked for her number, inquiring as to her plans for the evening. "I live above the bar, so I'm here all the time." He looked around, a humorous action when thinking of the next question that fell from his lips and the fact that Jolene's silver star shined brightly in the overhead lights. "You want to come up and smoke a bowl?" Jolene squinted at him, unsure if the bartender did not realize she was a cop or just did not care.

"How much for a bottle of wine?" she asked instead.

"Depends. What do I get out of it?" he responded playfully.

Hartley remained stoic. "Money. That's usually how it goes."

The man smiled back, leaning into the bar directly in front of him, his grizzled, yet pleasant looking face, inches from hers. "How about you come upstairs and we can have all the wine we want."

"How about you just sell me a bottle of wine and I'll forget you asked an officer of the law to go smoke a bowl. Deal?"

It *had* been a deal. The bartender had smiled and, after a last-ditch effort, forked over two bottles for the price of one. Sure, it was the cheap house stuff, but Jolene was not searching for anything to tickle her palette, to make her taste buds stand at attention. She was looking for one thing at that moment: to get drunk.

She swallowed the last remaining alcohol in her glass and moved from her current spot on her windowsill towards the counter, trading the crystal vessel for the entire bottle. She lifted it to her lips and took a long drink before turning to face the far wall. Her focus settled on the distant corner of the room, the darkest portion of the apartment that seemingly sucked the light from the rest of the interior like a black hole.

Hold her still.

The words formed in her head and echoed throughout her thoughts, gaining strength enough to project into the space around her. She could visualize the black mask, his gruff-toned voice and the large, broad shoulders as he walked towards her. She felt the arms wrap around her from behind and lift her high into the air, her feet swaying beneath her hovering body.

Jolene lifted the bottle again and turned her head to the right to glance into the small foyer, her eyes searching the walls hugging the area. The hanging shelf that once housed a Waterford crystal vase was still present, although a vanilla scented candle now stood in its place. The bloodied wall left by Korhan Karaca's unsteady hand had taken a good scrubbing to get clean, and even then the colors looked like a bad tie-dye. Jolene had had to repaint the area, along with clean the floor due to the injuries she had dealt upon Karaca.

Don't fucking do anything! Stop moving!

She slowly made her way around the couch to stand in the empty spot where her coffee table once rested. The thought of Luke Moran's voice caused her to shudder. It had been the second time in a year that a gun had been pressed to her skin, a feeling she never wanted to flirt with again. The first had been with Taylor Thames, right before he pistol-whipped her into unconsciousness. Her meeting with Moran, however, had ended differently. She had told herself the situation with Thames was a one-time thing. To have your life in the hands of another was not something she was comfortable with outside of her partner on the force. And the fact that Moran and Karaca were indeed looking for something specific to her case against Seamus O'Dowd and Kyle Walker meant they were certainly not going to let her live.

But she had. She had survived the brawl in her apartment. She had made it through the battle within the *State of Finance* printing press warehouse. Jolene Hartley was not easily beaten. Yet, as she stood in her living room with her back to the television, eyes scanning the apartment before her as she lifted the bottle of wine to her lips, Jolene allowed tears to stream down her cheeks.

She remembered sitting there as the officer she knew only as Train led his team about the place, clearing rooms and containing the scene for when the forensics unit and paramedics arrived. She could recall the look on James's face as he came in through the opened doorway, the utter shock and disbelief that replaced the usual jovial countenance.

Who would have thought months later she would be lumping him into the same category with the same man who had attacked her? The notion was absurd, yet here she stood, figuratively and literally, in the place where it had all began. Korhan Karaca. James Graiser. Jolene Hartley.

She leaned forward and placed the bottle of wine on her couch before lifting her hands to her reddened eyes. Jolene wiped away the tears and took a deep breath while she lifted her face to the ceiling and ran her hands through her dark locks and down her neck, grasping onto her shoulders and tilting her head to the left and right.

The connection between James and Korhan was not such a stretch. In fact, it was an almost certainty. She had looked through the Graiser files many times, researched, little by little, the aspects surrounding their murders. The name Ahmet Karaca had been brought forth on numerous occasions by a plethora of different outlets, whether it be a police report or news article. The elder Karaca, after all, *had* been Michael Graiser's right-hand man, his helper and assistant who, as

James had put it, Michael had trusted with his life. To be that close and not know certain family members was almost unfathomable.

However, Jolene could not discount the fact that Korhan Karaca, a habitual drug user and lifelong criminal, was older than James. Through her talk with the Karacas, Hartley had learned that Korhan was thirty-nine, making him nine years older than Michael and Amelia's son, allowing enough time to let connections fade into oblivion.

Or eight. It could now be eight years older. She dropped her hands to her hips and shook her head. That was how it had progressed for her and James, from a person of interest to material witness to lover. And now? Just a one-time acquaintance who she could not pinpoint an exact age for.

Jolene moved to the couch and grabbed the bottle of wine, hoisting it in the air and taking another long sip. She shuddered as the alcohol burned her throat. Or was it because of the thoughts being violently wrenched from their place of rest in her mind? Either way, it was an uncomfortable feeling, one that led her to abandon the bottle on the countertop.

She sauntered into the kitchen, her feet sliding on the floor as she moved towards the refrigerator. The shelves were empty as she opened the doors, save for a bottle of tequila and some condiments. "Probably should go shopping at some point," she heard herself say aloud. She threw her head back and laughed, wondering if she was indeed losing her mind. She reached onto the top shelf and handled the bottle of Patrón, lifting the squat glass container in her hand for a brief moment before setting it down and closing the door.

Jolene lowered her head and stared to the kitchen floor, her hands still held firmly onto the refrigerator handles. She remembered completely the evening when her and James first locked lips, the alcohol that coursed through their bodies rooting them on as they threw back shots of tequila in a frenzy. The sexual tension in the room had been enough to suffocate them both, urging them into something that she would, later on, find out she was not ready for, yet at the time whole-heartedly willing to accept. It was one of the last times she felt somewhat in control of her social life.

But was that completely true? She lifted her head to the gleaming, white surface of the refrigerator and stared at her blurred outline, thoughts racing through her slightly inebriated mind. What about Jacoby? Had she not shown some form of restraint with her partner outside of work? Sure, things had gone haywire on that fateful day when they passionately kissed on the sparring pads. Yet had she not, since James's exodus, dealt with her surroundings with a good deal of dignity and grace?

Jolene laughed as she turned away from the refrigerator and moved back to the counter, picking up the bottle once more and this time pouring herself a glass. She brought the container to her lips and halted, unable to drink as a smile passed across her face.

She was happy with her life. Work — besides the current situation with James Graiser — was exactly what she needed.

Although homicides were not something she wanted the Chicago society to deal with, they were, no doubt, inevitable. Violence was never going to be stopped. She knew that. It was her only hope that she could deter it from arising at least for a given afternoon, enough for a kid to make it to his or her middle school, or a wife to curb the physical abuse from an alcoholic husband for at least one more day.

But her happiness — or content, if that was the correct word — came from more than just her career. In actuality, it had nothing to do with her job. Jolene Hartley, homicide detective for the Chicago Police Department, officer for a city that had given her so much and she swore to serve and protect, was, after nearly two years, enjoying something that overshadowed the badge, paling in comparison to an entity that excited and challenged her in the same breath.

That entity was Jacoby Ratliff, the same individual that had forced her thoughts away from her budding relationship with James Graiser. She remembered Jacoby's reaction as he stepped into her apartment after the attack. He displayed a sense of horrific awe, a catastrophic reverence that went beyond words and into an unspoken connection the settled between them and caused the most damage of all.

Or the most clarity.

To Jolene, it was a double-edged sword. At that particular time in life, her feelings were a jumbled mess. James Graiser or Jacoby Ratliff? Ratliff or Graiser? Heads or tails? Tails, in the end, seemed to be the most appealing. Jacoby, with the absolute flaw of being her partner on the job, turned out to be the savior she was searching for, that individual that restored her faith in the work she did and the connections she made there. He had reminded her of Ronny Debarsi, yet there was something that intrigued her and drew her in beyond her ex-boyfriend currently hunkered down in the Philadelphia FBI offices. Whether it was the soothing, light green eyes or the melting smile, she was not sure. Either way, her current partner was something that calmed her mind and comforted her ever-present edginess on the job.

Off the job, Jacoby Ratliff was an object of lust. He sat on the edge of star football quarterback and choir leader, yet he had an edge that caused Jolene to take notice. And that edge had been compromised the night of the attack in her apartment. As much as she remembered James walking into the room and gasping at the scene before him, her focus had been drawn completely to her new partner. Jacoby had been taken aback. He had entered her living space and nearly collapsed, his eyes scanning the blood-stained floor and walls, the out-of-line couch, demolished coffee table. He had been floored. Jolene had remembered connecting with him on numerous occasions that evening. In all, his passion seemed to be nearly taking over, strangling his detective senses and letting the emotions and feelings override whatever duties he felt he needed to display.

Yet there had been no homicide. Jolene, though rather beaten and bruised, was, without a doubt, still alive. And in his eyes, as she looked into hindsight, there an uncompromised glimmer of gratitude. She felt herself smile wide as she placed the glass of wine onto the counter, a happy medium that outweighed, for a time, the absolute confusion she had been feeling as of late.

A knock at her door roused her from the current, pleasant reverie, causing the detective in her to push past the romantic memory to face reality. Her apartment building — other than her nearest neighbors and the inhabitants below — was a closed community. A gate outside the building kept those from meandering into the establishment. That gate, however, was no more than a minimal obstruction. Anyone seeking access to the complex only needed to hop the five-foot fence and ring a variety of call buttons.

Jolene walked to her stairs and removed her firearm from the holster that sat on the third step. She had not quite made her complete entrance into her apartment to lock the gun in its box. However, at this moment, with the random knock at her front door and the thoughts in her head regarding Karaca and Moran, she was content with the fact that her firearm was within reach.

She moved hurriedly into the darkened foyer and took a deep breath, settling herself as much as she could before turning towards the door and quickly peering through the peephole. She stepped back with a smile and lowered her weapon, unable to stifle anything but a slight chuckle as she reached to the door and unlocked the mechanism.

TWENTY-THREE

James barely made it into the Starbucks before closing time. The barista in charge looked none too pleased, casting a glare in Graiser's direction before rolling her eyes and moving behind the bar. In his former life, James would have apologized and tucked-tail before moving back onto the sidewalk with a wave of his hand and a joyful smile. Yet those days were gone, and James was focused. He did not so much as think of the extra time the employees at the coffee shop would need to stay, mopping the floors, wiping down counters and tabletops, and, now, re-cleaning the machines. All he wanted was the vanilla latte he so needed at the moment.

He stepped to the curb as a yellow cab stopped to let him in, situating himself in the back seat and spitting out the address.

The cab driver nodded. "You have some wealthy friends there, huh?" he asked rhetorically as he pulled the vehicle from the curb.

James turned his focus out the window. "We'll see," he said quietly, taking a long sip of his latte, watching as the world sped by.

* * * * *

Monotony. The various dictionary definitions and thesaurus synonyms ran through his head as he brought the expensive crystal tumbler of scotch to his lips and took a long, calculated sip. Tediousness. Flatness. Lackluster. Uniformity. The words swirled to the forefront in a never-ending whirlpool of annoyance, blending with his seemingly constant alcoholic buzz.

Life had taken a turn. His bank accounts had been seized and subsequently frozen as the cases against him mounted. All assets hovered in a limbo just out of reach, taunting him as to the regal life he had once known, yet now crumbled around him.

The movement from his team of lawyers in the living room was barely recognized. He had grown so accustomed to the in-and-out of the legal team that he hardly paid them any mind, unless, of course, they needed his assistance, to which he would half-heartedly point them in the general vicinity. They became nothing more than obstacles he had to maneuver around whilst moving about his luxurious home.

And even that had grown into something he now loathed. His den, with its plush couches and expensive leather recliners sitting atop luxurious beige carpet, had been shifted and displaced to make room for a large card table and metal folding chairs. The oversized flat screen television mounted to the wall above the fireplace was now almost fully hidden behind an enormous whiteboard littered with important financial records worth noting. His dining area was non-existent underneath a mountain of brown boxes containing every last morsel of his personal and professional being.

And then there was the kitchen. He sighed and looked around, eyes falling on the currently darkened interior. It had always been his favorite room in the house. With the little time he spent outside of the office or congregating with clients at top restaurants throughout the city and beyond, one of his loves had always been to throw on an apron and create a wonderfully delectable, awe-inspiring meal. He could envision himself in times past, floating across the tiled floor to stir his homemade pasta sauce, or sauntering to the chopping block to slice the peppers and onions.

Now, the area before him was nothing more than a sanctuary, a less-than-tasteful escape from the uninteresting life he now found himself subjected to. Yet the room contained no files, no boxes of fiscal documents and, best of all, no lawyers or financial miscreants. They had been left to fend for themselves in the den, leaving Damian Verland to the peace and quiet that had infested his life and allowed no leeway whatsoever.

* * * * *

She looked beautiful as the door opened, her strong, slim frame resting against the entryway, eyes vulnerable and lazy, yet encompassing a steadiness that he had grown accustomed to. The short-sleeved, baby blue top she had changed into earlier in the day hung loosely about her shoulders, an extra button having been unlatched at some point since the time she had left the precinct.

Jolene smiled at Ratliff and stepped away from the door. His eyes immediately fell to the firearm at her side. "Are you expecting some trouble?"

"Never know," she responded. "When someone shows up to my door without me buzzing them in, it can be a little alarming. How'd you get into the building?"

"Apparently the sweet, old lady downstairs remembers us kissing. She said, and I quote, 'Any boyfriend of the detective must be trustworthy.'" He smiled at her. "Nice lady."

"Yeah. Apparently, Mrs. Gerard isn't the best judge of character in her old age."

"Well, she did conduct a thorough strip-search on me."

"She does that from time to time."

"It was definitely strange."

"I'll bet."

"Surprisingly gentle hands, though."

"Okay."

"I'm not sure the latex gloves were needed."

"Gross."

"Especially weird since she made me put them on and —"

"Stop it," Jo said with a shake of her head. Ratliff laughed with her. "What do you have there?" she asked, nodding in the direction of the large, brown paper bag he held at his side.

Jacoby lifted it to shoulder height and turned it towards her, revealing the imprinted Chinese crest on the stapled receipt. "Thought maybe you'd be hungry."

Jolene looked up from the container and into his green eyes. "You don't quite understand the concept of *needing a little time*, do you?"

"Of course I do," he replied. "But needing time still requires food. And last I checked we're not on the clock. It's just two people enjoying some good food and good company."

She smiled wide and stepped back into the foyer, extending her arm to let him pass. "And decent wine," she added.

"Great," he said with a grin, bending to extend his free hand toward the hallway floor and the bottle of merlot that sat near his feet. "Because this shit is awful!"

* * * * *

Damian Verland moved slowly around the butcher's block to the half-empty bottle of scotch on the countertop. The strong liquid swirling in the container had not been drained to its current state this evening alone, though he was definitely making a dent in it. Damian was just not that type of drinker. He enjoyed the flavor of liquor — mainly extremely expensive scotch or bourbon — as it churned over his taste buds. He reveled in the pleasure of the alcohol as it drained down his throat and warmed his insides. He did not, however, find the dizzying state of inebriation tied to overconsumption to be something of personal satisfaction. He felt out of control when anything surpassing mild tipsiness set in. His thoughts were incoherent to a point that made him paranoid, a feeling that the one-time Vice President of Intervise Securities was just not willing to let himself settle into on a frequent basis.

Yet, this evening was different. He had decided at some point within the lengthy meeting with his legal team and their financial advisors that he just did not care. His attitude had fallen into the gutter of life and there was little that could pull him out of it. He had lived in his house for an absurd amount of time and depression had long ago taken over his mind, turning him into a zombie-like creature that could be seen roaming the interior of the home. Verland soon learned to close his drapes, blocking out prying eyes of photographers, as well as any natural light that might have otherwise refreshed his senses. He was a recluse, though not by choice, and his wits and mental toughness were breaking under the scrutiny that had plagued him for months.

A muffled noise to his right caused him to look away from the kitchen window to a thin, salt-and-pepper-haired man with large glasses entering the darkened room. "Damian," the man said. "Did you hear me?" Verland stared to him without responding momentarily before turning his focus back to the exterior of the house, his eyes falling on the row of evergreens twenty yards away.

The kitchen light flipped on violently, the reflection off the window before him causing his eyes to shut tightly. "I need you to help out here," the man said, taking a step toward Damian.

"Greg," Verland replied, raising his fingers to his eyelids to rub the pain that his lead defense attorney had caused. "Could you please dim that a little?"

"No," Gregory Faulk replied. "I need you to help me. We've been pouring through the portion of files that we planned on tonight, but without your input, it's pointless! Now, could you please —"

"Yes, yes," Damian interrupted with a wave of his hand. "Just give me a minute longer."

"Damian, I'm serious. We need —"

Gregory Faulk quieted quickly as Verland glared to him, the look of absolute power within the ex-VP's eyes weighing on the attorney's shoulders. "I said give me a minute." Faulk nodded his head and turned on his heels, flipping off the overhead lights and leaving Damian Verland to his thoughts once more.

The last thing he wanted to do was dive headfirst into the legal issues he now faced. His team of lawyers working on freeing him from the bonds of the financial landslide pouring around him would do no good. The fact of the matter was he was guilty. There was no way the forensics teams of the state and federal governments were going to overlook the money he had siphoned from Intervise Securities clients for the past decade. Sure, he was a monetary mastermind and could hide the movement of some of his funds, yet the authorities looking into the files would no doubt find items that were well out of place, items he would have no excuse for. Regardless of whatever legal action taken against him in the future for his involvement in the murders of Seamus O'Dowd and Kyle Walker, his life as he knew it had ended. There was just too much stacked against him from the embezzlement scheme.

* * * * *

"This is it," the cab driver said as he drove slowly along the dim-lit road, his eyes peering out the windshield at the beautiful, immense houses lining the boulevard. James leaned forward and eyed the property numbers. It was definitely it, though, by the number of cars lining the driveway, the thought of ditching his current plan was on the forefront of his mind. He did not exactly *have* a plan. However, a mob of individuals was definitely out of the picture. He glanced around through the side windows of the cab until his eyes fell upon a white van kitty-corner to the house, a large man sleeping behind a dashboard littered with fast food wrappers and a variety of cameras.

"Keep going," James said to the driver, eager to get away from the photographer.

"You don't want to stop?" the man asked quizzically.

"Let's go to the next block. I'll get out there."

"Whatever you say," he answered, turning the wheel and continuing down the pavement. The driver took a right at the next intersection, following the road as it continued to weave through the neighborhood, the tree-lined streets quiet at the late hour save for the slight breeze that blew through the area from time to time. He began to slow as he reached another bend, this one jogging to the left away from the address his customer had given him.

"This is good," James said, leaning forward and handing the man a hundred dollar bill. "Hang out here and wait for me."

The man handled the money with wide eyes and a grin. "Listen, man. I'm pretty busy tonight. Maybe you could —"

"There's another hundred in it if you stay put," James interrupted quickly, receiving an approving shrug from the driver as Graiser opened the door and exited into the silent night. He shut the door as quietly as possible and began to walk the sidewalk, his eyes focused between the homes as he searched for his destination. He stopped after several dozen yards and gazed through a break in the lawns upon the evergreens he had seen from the front of the home, the huge trees rising up from the dirt to tickle the night sky.

James moved from the sidewalk into the yard before him and edged his way carefully across the pristine lawn, making sure to stay away from the motion-detecting security lights no doubt installed near the front door and garage of every home in the neighborhood. He did not know what he was going to find here. He was not even sure this would garner him any new information whatsoever. Yet, it was the only lead he had for himself, and he was set on seeing it through.

He approached the evergreen trees and stepped into them, the huge branches enveloping his frame, sending his thoughts into the past and the camping vacations his father and mother used to take him on. But they were no longer with him. His treks into the wilderness for the last decade had been by himself. No parents. No loved ones to sit by his side and stare into a gleaming fire. He was alone.

He was pulled from his reveries as a movement caught his eye from the darkened room twenty yards away. James could make out the silhouette of a man, the glass in his hand sparkling from the light over his right shoulder. He looked frail, as if time had caught up with him and now weighed heavily upon his frame. James had never met the man, so he did not have grounds for comparison, save for the pictures and video from the local news stations.

Graiser stepped forward from the evergreen trees and stood still, watching as another individual appeared in the room, an agitated look spread over his face. The man with the glass lifted it to his lips and mouthed words before turning his attention back towards the window and the world outside.

* * * * *

Damian Verland did not know what to think as his eyes turned to his backyard once more and fell on the vision amongst the evergreen trees. He could decipher the steady form from the swaying branches, the darker, blacker body from the green pine needles. It took him only seconds to recognize the figure as James Graiser, an individual he had never met, yet knew plenty about. The name resonated through his mind as their eyes met, dancing across his thoughts through the twisting, zigzagging mess that connected himself to Jolene Hartley and this man standing in his backyard.

The path was convoluted, to say the least, yet there was a definite, though indirect, link between the duo. The articles by Dane Hartley that had so ruined his reputation and prowess among the elite had also put the spotlight on the reporter's own sister, the same woman who had him arrested long ago for, among other things, the murders of the heads of *State of Finance.*

"Damian, I'm serious," Gregory Faulk said from over his shoulder, the tone mixed with annoyance and caution. "We need you. There are files we don't have."

"And?" Damian asked.

Faulk stared at him with utter contempt. "*And,*" he replied, "there's a possibility they could assist us. Doesn't that matter to you?"

Damian was surprised when a smirk crossed his face. "Will these missing files get me off? Will I be a free man with all of my riches at my disposal?"

Faulk removed his glasses and stared to his employer. "I think we're beyond that, don't you?" Damian remained silent, his eyes connecting with James outside as he brought the tumbler to his lips once more. "Look, if we can find the files, maybe we can get some sort of a deal going. I'm not sure exactly what the prosecution will accept, but —"

"I think that's it for tonight, Greg," Damian stated, bringing the attorney to a halt. "I'd like for you and the team to leave."

"Damian, I'm not sure —"

"I said get out," Verland repeated, this time with more force. "I need a night to myself. We'll pick this back up tomorrow."

Gregory Faulk glared at the ex-VP of Intervise Securities for several moments before moving back into the living room to corral the team. They gathered their belongings and made it to the door, each filing out hastily, wondering what the rush was, yet reveling in the fact that the evening had ended early. The weeks had blended together for them all. Family ties had been strained with the once-in-a-lifetime court case. Extra-curricular activities between team members had reached sexual heights as their lives revolved around the Verland estate and the nearest hotel. An early evening — albeit close to ten o'clock — was exactly what everyone needed, knowing the break would refresh all their senses before they started anew the next day.

TWENTY-FOUR

"Okay," Ratliff said as he moved from discarding the empty Chinese food cartons into the trash receptacle back towards the kitchen table. "Are you sure you want to play?"

"Absolutely," Jolene answered from her chair, a glass of wine to her lips.

"I've never played with wine before. It may be a little too —"

"Too what?" she asked with a sly smirk on her face. "Too much for you to handle? Maybe you should change out of your skirt and into some big boy pants." She laughed. "Now stop whining and tell me the rules."

"You said you played this before," he answered, both arms extended with index fingers pointing towards the drawers.

"Second on your right," Jolene said. "And I've played High-Low before. It's just everyone seems to have different rules. I'd like to hear yours so I can hold you to them."

Jacoby laughed heartily as he opened the designated drawer and shifted the random pens and pads of paper until he found the deck of cards he was searching for, the large Chicago

Blackhawks Indian head emblazoned on the back. "Is that so? Okay." He moved out of the kitchen in the direction of the table, pulling out the seat directly across from his partner as she cleared the paper plates and napkins left over from their meal. "Typical High-Low rules. I throw a card and you guess if the next one is higher or lower."

"No shit?" Jolene said sarcastically. "I don't think I'll remember that."

Ratliff shook his head. "Always the smartass. So, higher or lower. You can choose red or black, too. And if you really get a big head — which I'm sure will happen sooner than later with you — you can guess the color and, or, suit."

"In which case you drink if I get it right?"

"In which case I take a shot if you're right."

"Oh! You really found the big boy pants, huh?"

"That's right. Speaking of which, you have anything —"

"Tequila," Jo interrupted. "Back of the fridge." Ratliff hopped up and grabbed the bottle of Patrón before turning to watch his partner slide across the floor and retrieve two shot glasses from the cabinet next to the sink. "Okay, so how many in a row do I need to get right to change hands?"

Jacoby paused as his partner sauntered in front of him, each making their way back to their respective positions. "Three in a row to pass. Aces are a freebie."

"What about taking drinks?" Ratliff looked at her and smirked. "What?"

"How do you want to play it?"

241

"Whoa," she replied. "We're playing by your rules. I've already agreed to that. And don't go easy on me because of today."

"No, no," he answered. "That's not it. Just want to make sure you know what you're getting into here."

She squinted at him. "I understand the juvenile atmosphere I'm submersing myself in right now."

"Good enough for me. Okay, since we're dealing with wine and not beer, we'll take a drink after getting two wrong in a row. My buddies and I used to do every wrong guess, but I think that's kind of pushing it."

"Sounds good."

"We also used to do a shot guessing five straight wrong, but —"

"But what? Afraid you're going to wake up with a hangover tomorrow?"

"Well, I'm pretty certain that'll happen. I'm more worried about having to hold your hair back while you let loose."

"Bring it on!" Jolene pushed.

"Fine," he said, throwing his hands back in surrender. "Five straight guesses wrong and …" He picked up the bottle of Patrón and waved it in the air, the liquid swishing back and forth inside the glass container.

Jolene smiled wide and leaned forward, raising her wine glass towards him. Ratliff followed suit, touching crystal with her. "May the best cop win," she said, putting the glass to her lips and taking a long sip, her eyes locked on his.

* * * * *

Their meeting had not lasted long, and doubt, confusion and reasoning had been the prime leaders of the evening. Neither one really knew why they were standing at opposite ends of his kitchen, holding wine glasses and staring at one another. Their rendezvous at such a late hour was surprising, mainly because James Graiser and Damian Verland had never met. Each one knew factoids about the other, random bits of information gathered from news articles or *Dateline* episodes. James stared upon the face of Verland and noticed a past resoluteness outlined in now tired, surrendering eyes. He was older than he appeared on the television, the stress of becoming public enemy number one of the financial world sitting heavily on his shoulders.

Damian, on the other hand, eyed his guest with a heavy heart, one that he found, in a way, relieving, a sign that he still felt, still sensed the world about him more than the tingle of an alcoholic buzz. In his own eyes, James Graiser still held a youthfulness about him that had been portrayed in the Navy Pier photograph from the previous year. Yet there was something about the young man that displayed a grief that went beyond Verland's own, that sunk into the very soul of the individual before him and clung to every last aspect of his being. He, too, looked tired, yet it was an exhaustion that covered a longer timespan than the near year he had been forced into.

Damian Verland looked upon James Graiser and felt pity for him.

* * * * *

"I hate to say it," Jacoby said, swallowing the last bit of his wine. "But that's five wrong. Again." Jolene shook her head and reached out for the shot of tequila lying in wait near the center of the table. She was definitely feeling the tingling effects of the consumed alcohol, though she figured she was faring well at their seemingly never-ending game of High-Low, as Jacoby, himself, seemed to be catching up with her inebriated state of mind.

She fingered the full shot before her, eyes passing from her partner and back as she tried to force herself into action. The frequency of the last three drinks had come in such rapid succession that she had had no time to gather herself and now was facing the fact that one more could possibly send her over the edge. "Okay," she said after a moment. "I hate to admit it, but the shots are going to get to me here soon."

"Oh!" he said enthusiastically. "Ms. Tequila, with her taunting and trash talk, is starting to complain?"

"Oh, give me a break!"

"Correct me if I'm wrong, but I'm pretty sure you told me not to earlier."

She stared at him with thin eyes and a grin she could not suppress. "You're a shit, you know that?"

"Fine," he said, ignoring the accusatory comment. "The shots are slowing you down?"

"Yes," she answered, confidence and reality outshining her need to appear stoic.

"Well, I propose another way of paying the price, if you still want to play, that is."

"I'm not letting you win," she replied matter-of-factly.

"You do understand there's really no end to this, right?"

"Did I stutter?" Jolene smiled wide, her beauty shining as she pulled her hair up into a ponytail.

Ratliff looked her over. Her slim, supple neck, exquisite jawline, her penetrating, melting eyes, all of which made the pit of his stomach ache. "Okay," he finally said. "I haven't played this version of the game since visiting friends in college, but you've left me no choice." Jolene crossed her arms on the table and locked her focus onto him, as if challenging her partner. "Are you ready for it?"

"I'm listening, aren't I?"

"Well, since shots are obviously taking you out, the only other option is clothing?"

"Excuse me?" she said.

"That's right," he answered, throwing his arms wide. "You get five wrong in a row, you lose an article of clothing."

"Is that how you got all the girls in your college days?" Jolene asked with a humorous tone.

"I was in the military, but yes," he answered. "When I was on leave, I pulled plenty of tail using this method." They both laughed. "Unless you're too uncomfortable to continue, in which case I win."

Jolene stared to him, weighing her options as her eyes traveled his chiseled frame, her thoughts running furiously through her mind as the heat under her collar rose. She pulled the shot of tequila closer and toyed with the thick glass, the liquid swirling in anticipation. Jacoby chuckled to himself. "What?" she asked.

"Who's wearing the skirt now?" he replied mischievously.

Hartley set her jaw and glared at Jacoby through hazy eyes. His confidence and strong demeanor were irritatingly gripping. She wanted him to shut his mouth and cease any sort of noise, yet his voice and self-assured comments set her afire. With her focus locked on his, Jolene edged her chair back from the table and brought her hands to her waist and the small buttons holding her shirt together. As the last fasten was dislodged, she pulled the shirt back, the cotton sliding the length of her toned arms and dropping to the floor. Ratliff unapologetically scanned her body, his eyes falling like a waterfall off her lips, sliding across the tanned skin of her neck and down to her strong, toned shoulders. He hesitated as he made contact with her breasts, the Under Armour sports bra creating an exaggerated show of cleavage, one that he and Jolene were willing to accept at that particular moment.

The fact that she had chosen to remove her top had thrown Jacoby only slightly. What really got him, however, was what she did next. Jolene, vulnerable in nothing more that her jeans and a sports bra, cleavage in full view underneath a flawless façade, scooted her chair forward and reached out, pulling the tequila towards her and lifting it in the air. She smiled and tilted her head back as she took the shot down, her ponytail hanging between her shoulder blades. Hartley turned the glass upside down and slammed it on the table triumphantly, bringing a chuckle from Ratliff as he clapped his hands approvingly. "Let's just see who can keep their skirt on longest, okay?"

* * * * *

James rode back to his hotel room in silence, the thoughts of his meeting with Damian Verland clouding his thoughts. He had made it back through the yards to the waiting taxi, throwing the driver an extra two hundred dollars to return him to his hotel without any noise from the radio or pointless conversation. He had rolled down his window completely, tossing back his head and letting the cool Chicago night air work its magic.

He entered his plush hotel room and turned on the bathroom light, keeping the rest of the area shrouded in darkness while he walked over to the bar and grabbed a small bottle of scotch. James reached into a drawer and withdrew a pack of Parliaments, pulling a cigarette out and lighting it before retreating to the couch.

The cushions of the sofa cradled him as he sat, holding his frame erect enough so he could look at the coffee table before him. He brought the cigarette to his lips and took a long drag, blowing the blue-gray smoke into the room to be lost in the darkness. He sipped his scotch again and sat up, his eyes focusing on the brown file box Damian Verland had given him that sat beckoning from the armchair just to his left. He could see the sparkle of light on the top of the box, reflecting off of the dust that had accumulated over the years. "My time is done," Verland had said to him as he had bent over and removed the hidden panel from his wall, reaching in and pulling the box into the hallway. "Use this however you want. Just know it wasn't meant to happen this way." James lifted the cigarette to his lips once more, watching the orange glow of the embers spark to life.

TWENTY-FIVE

Things had grown to about even twenty minutes later. Each of the players had had a run at stringing together a lengthy number of correct guesses, both extending play at the risk of losing yet another article of clothing. Jacoby sat in nothing more than his boxer-briefs, waiting for Hartley to draw yet another card. Jolene, however, sat with eyes on her partner, waiting for him to guess on the mystery that she held in her hand. Her eyes and stature gave nothing away. Ratliff could not determine whether to go high or low on the eight of hearts that egged him on from the tabletop. He was a competitor, so losing the apparently never-ending battle that was High-Low was really not an option. Jacoby was in it for the victory, as much as seeing Jolene naked.

And he was close. Hartley sat back in her chair, eyes locked onto his, waiting for the next-to-last guess that would remove the Joe Boxers. He smiled at her playfully, his vision sliding down her neck and across her shoulders, hesitating slightly at her breasts before falling to her stomach. He shifted positions, leaning to his left to take in the sight that was Jolene Hartley, quickly glancing across her bare legs as she sat in anticipation in nothing more than her sports bra and panties. "Hey!" she said suddenly, pulling his attention back to her face. "Eyes up here, buddy! Let's keep this going."

"What?" he asked incredulously. "You expect me to focus on cards when you're sitting there like that?"

"You see me having a difficult time?"

"Fine." He leaned forward. "Black," he added quickly, though the confidence faded halfway through the word. The card fell to the table. Jack of hearts. "Fuck!" Jacoby yelled.

"Oh! One more and bye-bye boxers!" Jolene laughed, lifting her nearly empty wine glass to her lips.

"Not going to happen!" he replied, shifting in his spot and cocking his head to the left and right as if readying himself for strenuous activity. "I've never been naked first. I'm that good!" He laughed.

"We'll see. Red to you." Jacoby shook his hands and stared to the card, practically summoning courage from the image splashed across the surface. "Come on, Ratliff! Stop stalling."

He glanced to her and smiled, a display of confidence that brought her back to Debarsi. "Black," he said. "No! Wait a second." He paused, thoughts obviously flying through his mind. "Nine."

Jolene glanced to the card in hand for a second before shifting her focus to Ratliff. "You sure about that? This is it. No more clothes if you get this wrong."

"I'm sure," he said.

"If this isn't a nine, you lose and —"

"Flip the card!" he yelled, watching as his counterpart's face scrunched up and she threw the placard down furiously.

"How the fuck …?" she stated, letting the comment hang in the air as a nine of spades fell to the tabletop.

"Because I'm that good!" he answered back.

The next several turns went in rapid succession, each of the participants garnering one, maybe two, guesses wrong before predicting three in a row and passing hands.

"This is it," he said after nearly ten minutes of guessing. "Better make it a good one."

"Shut up," Jolene responded, staring nervously at the six of diamonds before her. Her body tingled with the buzz she had accomplished throughout the evening, yet there was still an anxiousness that caused the butterflies in her stomach to flutter. "Red," she stated confidently.

She watched as Ratliff smiled and slowly threw down the seven of spades. "So close," he said, setting the deck down before him and folding his hands, a smile crossing his face in anticipation of what he had looked forward to seeing.

Jolene rose several inches and quickly fell back to her seat, bending at the waist and finally pulling her underwear above the tabletop before throwing them to the side. "Wuss," Jacoby said as he retrieved the deck from the table, slightly perturbed at his misfortune and lack of view. "Seven of spades to you," he added quickly.

"High," she said. The six of hearts fell. "You've got to kidding me," she stated, foregoing the rules and lifting the wine glass to her lips. "Low."

Ten of diamonds.

"One more and it's lights out," he said.

"'Lights out'? Really?" She shook her head and turned her attention back to the table. "Okay. Red ten. Red ten," she repeated several times. After several moments she glanced up, locking eyes with her partner as she opened her mouth. "Low."

Jacoby glanced down and closed his eyes tightly, tilting his head slightly as a smile formed on his face. A rush of warmth filled Jolene's cheeks as she knew, without a doubt, she had lost the game. Ratliff set down the deck and tossed the card in question onto the surface.

Queen of clubs.

Hartley leaned into the table and placed her face in her palms, groaning as she realized her alcoholic bliss had finally led into a realm of no going back. Maybe it had been the wine. Or the day's events. Who knew? Yet in that moment, tequila shots and glasses of wine imbibed, she was suddenly uneasy. The fact that she was getting fully naked in front of Jacoby was not the issue. The problem was his patient, calm demeanor as he sat in his boxer-briefs just feet away with hands folded. She lifted her face just as he began to speak. "Have you ever played Horse?" he asked out of the blue.

"What?" she replied.

"Horse? With a basketball?"

"Sure," Jolene answered. "Why?"

"Well, when my brother and I play, we always gave an extra shot to the one about to lose."

"I don't need an —"

"It's not a matter of needing it or not," he interjected. "You said you're playing by my rules? This is part of the rules." He waited for a response. Jolene looked to him for several moments before nodding. "Okay," he continued. "You have to get the next three in a row. If so, the game continues. If not … Well, I can't help you then."

Hartley forced a smile. "What's it to me then?"

"Black queen," Jacoby answered.

She thought about it for a second before answering. "Low."

Ratliff paused before grabbing the first card off the top and tossing it to the surface, watching as his partner's eye's grew wide and she threw her head back, the muscles in her long neck bulging. "You've got to be kidding me!" she said quietly.

Jacoby looked down to the queen of diamonds and laughed, drawing her focus back to him. "I win," he said with a large grin.

"I guess you do," she answered with a hint of annoyance. Jolene stared to her partner for a moment before reaching to the bottle of Patrón and lifting it to her lips, the liquor pouring down her throat in a heated rush. She placed the container back to the table just as Jacoby reached out for it, gently lifting it to take a shot of his own.

The meeting of their eyes sent her into motion, an action even she was slightly surprised by. With nothing but her sports bra clothing her angelic form, Jolene Hartley pushed her seat back and stood, allowing her body to be in full view. She watched his eyes fall to her toned legs, traveling up her long limbs to her naked hips, sliding across her stomach and connecting once again with her gaze. Although she had been the one on display, Jolene felt empowered by her actions, putting herself on a pedestal rather than hiding in the shadows. She felt in control even as she lifted her arms and grasped onto the bottom of the Under Armour sports bra. "Wait," Jacoby said suddenly. "Wait."

Jolene halted as he rose. He moved to her slowly, the strength in his shoulders and arms apparent as he passed by her side and took up position directly behind her. She could feel his breath on her neck, sense his presence just inches from her own skin. She tilted her head forward as his hands slid up her back, his fingers gently gliding and tickling her skin as they maneuvered underneath the stretchy sports bra. With a quick tug, the material slide up her arms and off her body, leaving Jolene standing naked in her kitchen, the lone hair tie the only foreign article on her body. She slowly dropped her arms to her sides as her breathing became heavy. Jacoby's hands yielded a tender masculinity as they moved across her skin, caressing her shoulders, working their way over the indentations between her ribs and finally onto her breasts.

Jolene titled her head and his lips met her neck, drawing forth a moan from her as his hand inched down her side, flirting with her abs before turning to her hip and streaming down her thigh. Jolene pulled his left hand across her stomach, arching her head towards the ceiling. She reached back to tug on his boxer-briefs as his hand came up her inner thigh, massaging her body like she had wanted for some time. Hartley reached over and grasped the back of Jacoby's head, turning her own and pressing her mouth into his as his fingers played below, rubbing and manipulating her into a frenzied state that neither one could control.

* * * * *

He set the glass of wine on the edge of the Jacuzzi tub and disrobed, standing, drunkenly, in the bathroom of his home in nothing more than his skin. The heat of the water sent a mist into the air that clung to the hairs on his body, tickling his chest and legs. He breathed in deep, letting the warm vapors sooth his body, renew his monotonous existence.

Damian Verland grasped the wine glass and tilted it back, consuming the remainder of the liquid and reaching for the bottle on the counter for more. He filled the vessel nearly to the top and stepped back, looking at his increasingly foggy outline in the mirror. He was a sad looking man, lately, yet in this moment, Damian felt uplifted. He did not know what the future held for James Graiser or the box of files he had so willingly given him. All he knew was a portion of his past was gone, sent into the world that he had succeeded in for so long. He knew not where they would end up, nor did he care.

Damian sighed and stepped into the tub, the water sending goosebumps up his legs in spite of the extreme heat. For the first time in months, he felt himself smile. Sure, the possibility of the action could have begun with the inebriation he was wallowing in, yet Verland believed it had been conjured from someplace more meaningful, an abyss that held whatever comfort and solace and happiness that tried, unsuccessfully, to will itself to the surface. He felt it, now, definitely, even as the future loomed down upon him.

As he sat back into the water and situated himself in a relaxed position, his smile brought forth tears. And with the saltiness of his emotions soaking into his lips, Damian Verland lifted the straight razor to his wrist and gently pushed, slicing through skin easily, the pain of the wound drowned out by the alcohol embracing his weary frame. He switched hands and made the same incision on the other wrist, sighing and dipping the razor into the water to cleanse it of his blood. He sat back and smiled, envisioning himself in better times and places, free from the chaos and cruelty he had played a role in for way too long.

TWENTY-SIX

The sensual flick of a tongue on her stomach. Her abdominal muscles tightening involuntarily at the soft touch. An inexplicable need to stifle a sexually charged chuckle by biting her lip. Her nails scratching the hills and valleys of his broad, muscled shoulders. Her head thrown back in ecstasy as his fingers ran from her lips, down her neck and to her chest. Moans following giggles. Eyes meeting as they rocked back and forth, up and down, creating a heat with their sweaty bodies and dancing until they could move no more.

At least that is how the night's events replayed for the hundredth time in Jolene's mind. She was not far off. What had started as alcohol-fueled groping and toying in the kitchen, had quickly escalated into an overflow of sexual tension between her and Jacoby, their lust pouring onto the stairs as they tried to make it to the bedroom.

Jolene woke early, her eyes adjusting to the dim-lit room as the Chicago sun began to work its way into the city streets, warming the pavement and waking the masses in anticipation of the coming day. She rubbed her eyes and ran fingers through her hair, the wine-and-tequila headache present, yet not as intense as she would have thought. She bit down on her fingernail, realizing the savior from an absurd hangover was no doubt thanks to the workout she had had just hours before.

She turned to look upon Jacoby. His eyes remained closed in slumber, an arm thrown underneath his head in a makeshift cushion. She laughed as the memory of the brief pause they had taken during one of their intimate sessions entered her mind. She remembered kneeling near where her head now lay, her skin glistening with perspiration, body exposed to the room and Ratliff as he began to shift positions closer to the foot of the bed. He had lost his balance, quickly reaching out to grab hold of the comforter and save himself before falling head over heels to the floor. Jolene had hastily grasped a pillow and chucked it in his direction, hoping beyond hope that the object would connect with his torso with enough force to cause him to continue the inevitable, embarrassing tumble.

It did not, however, though the turn of events had proven even more pleasurable than she could have guessed. Jacoby had blocked the assault and lunged towards her, catching hold of her outstretched foot in his grasp and yanking her to him, his strength sliding her body underneath his as he pinned her wrists above her head, denying her any leeway to struggle. Not that she was trying. A playful wiggle here and there was enough to satisfy her attempt at freedom.

The clarity of that exact moment Jolene would never forget. The primal desires that had tried to overtake her body would stay with her forever. With her hands held fast above her head and her legs pinned between his, she was at his mercy. Not that she minded. Her playful grin had dropped away instantly, replaced by pure, unadulterated lust. Jacoby's eyes had locked onto hers for a moment before falling to trace the contours of her body along with his fingertips. It had been enough to drive her mad, which, in the end, was probably the exact thing he had wanted.

Ratliff suddenly shifted his head and yawned, pulling Jolene from her pleasant reveries into the present. She smiled and bit her bottom lip as she lifted the sheets and comforter to gain a glimpse at her partner's naked body. "Are you trying to figure out what happened last night? I really hope you just want another peek," he said with a laugh. "I'd hate to think you're trying to piece things together."

"It was a total drunken haze," she replied drolly. "How'd you get in here again?"

"Very funny," he replied, opening his eyes finally and turning. They stared at one another for several moments, Jolene gently grazing his shoulder with her fingers, her head propped in her palm. She finally let out a laugh. "What?" he asked.

"Nothing," she answered, covering her mouth with her palm.

"Seriously? Are we in high school now?"

Jolene shook her head. "I've ... We ... What we did has just been on my mind. For a while. Quite a while."

Jacoby smirked. "And?"

"It wasn't a mistake," she replied.

"That sounded like you were trying to convince someone."

"No," she replied quickly with a shake of her head. "I didn't mean it like that."

"I know."

"And I do remember everything. Well, almost everything."

"Yeah? What'd you forget?"

She smiled to him and leaned forward, placing her lips on his, shifting underneath the blankets until she was situated on top of him, their bodies once again morphing into a heated exchange, his free hand running up her thigh to rest upon her hip. "This," she answered.

* * * * *

The heated streams of water plummeting from the showerhead felt utterly fantastic. The steam that rose into the air was refreshing, mixing with the crisp draft coming from the slightly opened bathroom door. She lifted her face skyward and let the liquid soak into her hair, the locks falling about her shoulders in the cascading waterfalls that soothed her aching muscles.

She could not help but smile. Her night with Jacoby Ratliff had been perfect. It had not been just an intensely pleasurable sex romp between two individuals lusting for one another physically, writhing in a knot of glistening skin, lustful groans and intense stares. It had also become an emotional connection, a genuine link between the pair that had started with the turbulence that was James Graiser. As she stood in the shower, the thought of James made her itch. There was definitely still something there, however, she could not seem to put her finger on it. She remained hurt and confused as to his unexpected visibility in recent days, yet these hazy feelings had been nearly completely overshadowed by the display put forth by Ratliff.

In her time of need, he had shown up. Jacoby had been there for her, regardless of the direct request she had placed before him of needing some time and space to expel the demons battling within her. And not only had he come to her aid, he had done so bearing gifts of Chinese food and wine. He had not given the waters time to settle, instead braving the rapids and diving headfirst into a situation that could have been devastatingly awkward. Yet that was Jacoby Ratliff, at least as she had come to know him. He was unafraid to stick his nose into her business, to share his opinion on any number of matters that seemed to have nothing whatsoever to do with him. He had never flinched when standing toe-to-toe with her before. Why would he start now?

The fact of the matter was that, in her private life, she was enamored with him. She had been able to put the attraction on the backburner while on the job, however, as she realized, the past had not included an all-night sexual escapade. Would she be able to curb her fascination with him while at the precinct? Would her feelings for Jacoby be contained on the hunt for murderers? Or would this, like her past discretions, turn to bite her in the ass?

She smiled wide as she shrugged. At this moment, she did not care. She would deal with the repercussions of her actions as they came. Right now, the only thought that mattered was the intensity of their previous evening and the possibility of things to come.

Jolene blushed as a giggle escaped her, the vision of Ratliff nearly tumbling off the end of the bed once more at the forefront of her mind. An unexpected knock at the bathroom door brought her hands to her mouth. "Yeah?" she said anxiously, hoping her teenage behavior had gone unnoticed.

"Coffee filters?" Ratliff asked.

"Um … Try the cabinet to the left of the sink."

"Great," he answered. "You want some coffee, right?"

"Sure. Or we can get something on the way. Your choice. Whatever's easier."

He laughed. "If it was my choice, I wouldn't be getting ready for work. I'd be in that shower with you." Hartley smiled ear to ear.

* * * * *

The aromas traveling from the coffee pot to Jacoby's nose were exactly what he needed to start the morning off right. The flavors carried through the air tempted him to forego the final stages of the brewing process and swap the carafe with a dirtied wine glass. In the end, however, his willpower won out, replacing the urge for immediate caffeine gratification with the want to share the remainder of the morning with Jolene, which included a relaxing cup of coffee amidst the bent playing cards, puddles of tequila and merlot-encrusted wine glasses littering the near vicinity.

He slid his pants on as he rounded the table, collecting various aspects of his attire that had been hurriedly strewn about the apartment as a result of their frenzied High-Low game. He made his way to the kitchen table and bent over his evening's assigned seat, grasping onto his shirt that hung from the back of the neighboring chair. He pulled it over his head and reached into his pockets, searching for his cell phone that had been out of mind since he stepped through Jolene's door. On the countertop, he could see his partner's device blinking a bright green with waiting notifications, though his was nowhere to be found.

Jacoby spun in a circle, eyes scanning the ground until they fell on the phone hidden behind a table leg, a constant orange light shining dimly from the top of the device, letting him know the battery was about spent. He retrieved it and took a seat in the chair, waking the screen with the press of a button. The display lit up, the giant, red battery splashed across the glass. "I know," he said to himself, drawing his finger up in an effort to show the home screen.

The life of the phone lasted only a split second, although it proved to be just enough time for him to witness the number of voicemails lying in wait. He had friends in the city that would randomly call and leave a message in the early morning on their way to work or from a random bar at the wee hours of the morning. Yet having seven new messages was something different for Jacoby. He immediately thought the worst. A sick relative. An emergency at his apartment. Whatever it was, however, would have to wait. He did not want to jump to conclusions without checking into the voicemails first. And that would have to wait until the precinct, where he kept his spare charger.

From the hall above, Jolene appeared, smiling down at him in nothing but a bath towel, the fabric skimming her upper thighs, hair still damp and shoulders glistening from the water that was still present. "I'll be down in a second. Just let me get my things."

"Yeah," he replied, staring up to her. He rose and slid the phone into his pocket. "Coffee just got done brewing. Perfect timing."

"All right," she answered, disappearing into the bedroom as Jacoby made his way to the kitchen in search of coffee mugs. "Cabinet next to the fridge," Jolene yelled from upstairs.

"Thanks," Jacoby responded with a grin.

"There are a couple of to-go mugs in there. Why don't you grab those?"

"Yeah? Don't want to relax for a little longer?"

Jolene laughed loudly. "I don't really think I've relaxed in a couple days. If I start now, I'll be useless in this investigation."

"Refreshed and renewed, huh?"

Hartley appeared in the hallway and made her way to the steps. "Let's just say I have a new sense of purpose."

"Impressive. Last night you're swimming in Patrón, and now you're ready to take on a murder investigation? Very impressive."

"You can learn a lot from me, Ratliff," she chided, descending the last couple stairs and turning into the kitchen, her holstered firearm jutting from her hip, the silver star reflecting the overhead lights. She came up beside Jacoby and opened the refrigerator door, grabbing a bottle of water and unscrewing the top to take a long sip before placing it back on the shelf.

Ratliff handed her the to-go coffee mug as she spun on her heels and retrieved her cell phone. "Thanks," she said, waking the device and glancing down. "Whoa."

"What?" he asked.

"I've got a bunch of messages."

"I did too," he replied, coming up beside her and slipping his hand around her waist. He turned her towards him as she lifted the phone to her ear, half paying attention to it as he kissed her passionately. "What're they about?" he asked as their lips parted.

"What were yours about?" Jolene asked, tilting her head back as he placed his lips on her neck, peppering her skin with kisses, forcing her eyes to close as she pulled him in closer.

"My phone died," he answered.

"Shut up!" she replied, pushing his head back into her neck and pulling a chuckle from him. "No talking. More —" Her eyes shot open and she quickly dropped her head in consternation, shifting away from the affectionate display Jacoby was gracing her with.

"You tell me to shut up and keep —" He stopped as he gazed upon her stricken face, brow scrunched with eyes to the kitchen floor. "What's wrong?" he asked.

She held the phone to her ear for several moments longer, scooting away from him and towards the counter. She took a seat at one of the stools and pressed end on the connection, dropping the phone to the surface with a thud as she ran her fingers through her hair.

"Jo?" he repeated, stepping forward and pulling her attention from the countertop. "What's the matter?"

"That was Henry," she answered, staring intently at him, her eyes a mixture of annoyance and anger. "Damian Verland is dead."

TWENTY-SEVEN

Hartley sat still in the passenger seat of Ratliff's Jeep, eyes lost in the constant movement of pedestrians and street signs and buildings as they traversed through the city towards Damian Verland's home. Mac had left a message that he was on his way to the scene as well, and that initial reports were that Verland had slipped into a heated tub and cut his wrists with a straight razor.

"I can't believe Verland is dead," Ratliff said.

She lifted the to-go mug to her lips and took a long sip, her focus shifting to the inside of the vehicle and her partner. He had changed out of yesterday's shirt into a top that had been lying neatly in the backseat. Hartley had laughed at his misfortune of having to make a partial walk of shame, yet Ratliff immediately stated it was definitely the complete opposite of disgrace.

"Yeah, but is it really that shocking?" Hartley answered, pulling a quizzical look from her partner. "Look, he was a filthy rich businessman in the financial arena with skeletons that link him to the murders of Seamus O'Dowd and Kyle Walker. Not to mention the amount of money he siphoned from Intervise clients."

"Right, but he hasn't been found guilty of any of that yet," Ratliff responded. "Why take your life?"

"Because he *was* going to be found guilty. His assets had already been frozen."

"You don't know if he would've been found guilty." It was Hartley's turn to shoot a look at her partner. "Hey, stranger things have happened. Who knows what loophole he could have found?"

Hartley shrugged. "Possible, but doubtful. I'm just pissed he took the easy way out. The amount of damage he caused should've been paid back with his ass in a federal penitentiary. Broke and miserable. Slitting your wrists in a cozy bathtub with a glass of wine hardly seems fitting."

"With a glass of wine?" Ratliff asked with a grin.

Hartley nodded and took a sip of coffee. "That's what Mac said."

"Wow. He really knew how to make an exit, huh?"

* * * * *

Streets of Unity had been the initial idea of Amelia Graiser, a proposed plan to her husband to fund a project that dealt with the poor in Chicago and its surrounding suburbs. Amelia had always been a kind, giving soul, a saint in the otherwise greedy world of large business. She had brought the plan to her husband, not so much for approval, but for a unified blessing to venture forth into a project that, in no other terms, would make them wealthy in spirit only.

Streets of Unity would, of course, bring in money, however, the goal would be to put the majority of revenue back into the business, bolstering the employees with adequate pay and benefits before sending the rest back into the community in the form of free food, shelter and activities.

The Graiser Empire fell headfirst into the plan. Michael invested a great deal of his personal savings into *Streets of Unity* and, in turn, his wife, letting her run with ideas and schemes that would better the communities around Chicago. Alderman Daniel Vincent came to his friends with a possible location for their next endeavor, knowing full well that the proposition for the Silver Ray Casino within the city limits was upon the proverbial table.

Amelia and Michael, along with Alderman Vincent, felt their plans for the community center would reinforce the city's view of the impoverished neighborhoods, strengthening the mayor's approval rating and possible subsequent re-election. The Graisers were indeed giving individuals, however, knowing how to play the game was an absolute must in the business world.

Dane pulled a drag from his cigarette and exhaled into the stale condo air. His eyes burned from lack of sleep and tobacco smoke that swirled above his head. The stubble normally apparent on his chiseled jawline now appeared more as a purposeful beard that extended down his neck.

He had found himself thinking over his talk with James Graiser, wanting nothing more than to end his relationship with the story feeling only a miniscule amount of sorrow for James. Yet the notion that Gregory Faulk had ties to the Graiser Empire was something that he could not shake, no matter how hard he tried. The night James left his apartment, Dane had abandoned his plans for an evening on the town, instead, holing up with his bottle of scotch and getting obliterated in front of a marathon of *The Godfather*.

He awoke the following afternoon with a pounding headache, an empty bottle of liquor and a nagging clarity that he needed to — even wanted to — look into *Streets of Unity* and Gregory Faulk.

What he found was a possible trail into the past of Damian Verland, James Graiser and his parents, and a player that was all too familiar in the Chicago political scene.

* * * * *

The living room looked like a warehouse of an office supply chain. Brown cardboard boxes stacked four high, balancing uncertainly on small, rectangular card tables strewn about the room. Staplers, rubber bands and paperclip holders were everywhere, no doubt, at one point, strategically located throughout the den within arm's reach of the nearest researcher.

Hartley found the interior of Verland's home to be a contradiction in itself. The financial records that had been brought in to be scrutinized over and over lacked any sort of organization in her eyes, yet everything was compartmentalized in such a way that suggested a nightly cleaning from someone with a compulsion towards the systematic. Papers had been neatly stacked three inches from the corners of every table. Pens had caps replaced and set into specific slots within a metal-framed container. Even the paperclips had been lined up in a way that would have only been caught by the inspecting eye of a police officer.

Ratliff nudged her elbow and thumbed in the direction of an adjoining dining room where Verland's legal team was congregated, tears falling down cheeks, shocked looks of amazement spread across all those present.

"Morning," Mac said from down the hallway at the base of a long, spiraling wooden staircase. "How's everyone this morning?"

Hartley and Ratliff approached. "What's the story?" she said.

Mac feigned surprise. "Right to business? Okay! Follow me, if you will." He ascended the steps, carefully weaving between a pair of uniformed officers positioned halfway up the staircase. "Excuse me, gentlemen," he said as he passed. Hartley and Ratliff said their hellos to the men and continued to the second floor, following Mac along the lengthy plush carpeting and to the entrance of the enormous bathroom, where, situated in the center of the vicinity, sat the deceased Damian Verland, his head tilted sideways against the backrest, seemingly floating above the red-tinged waters that hid the rest of his body.

Hartley's eyes fell immediately to her surroundings, taking in what she could. Everything within the room seemed as it should, minus the straight razor set on the edge of the whirlpool tub, its blade clean and free of blood, even though it appeared to be the cause of Verland's demise. She eyed a three-quarters empty bottle of wine on the counter, its contents still apparent in the glass that sat at arm's length from the dead man in the water.

"So, it looks like your standard suicide," Mac said, matter-of-factly. "No signs of forced entry. No struggle. Nothing out of sorts, from my end."

"Who found him?" Hartley asked as she walked to the end of the bathtub and squatted. She stared ahead into the face of Damian Verland, death etched into his wrinkles, yet a calmness embedded into his skin. He seemed at peace, which churned up another round of anger in her body.

"Gregory Faulk," Mac replied. "That's what the responding officers told me, anyway."

"And who's that?" Ratliff asked.

"His lawyer. Well, one of his lawyers. Don't you follow current affairs?" Ratliff shrugged. "You'd think you'd have some interest in the case," Mac added with a smile.

"Would you mind pointing Mr. Faulk out to me?" Hartley asked, standing and moving away from the body. "I wouldn't mind asking him a few questions."

* * * * *

"What do you know about him?" Dane spoke into the phone at a frantic pace. His research had definitely turned up some interesting bits of information, all public knowledge, if said public was willing to do a little digging. Dane had called a few sources, making some deals that would get him deeper into what intrigued him about the subject. "Gregory Faulk. What do you know about him?" Dane repeated.

James rubbed the sleep from his eyes in his penthouse hotel room and lifted his head from the couch. He moved his cell phone from his head to stare at the time and yawn. "What I told you before. Faulk was on my father's legal team. He was a researcher at the time."

"What do you mean by *researcher*?"

"I don't know. I'm not a lawyer," James quickly rebutted. "I just know he was there. Behind the scenes. He wasn't someone who went to court and stood in front of a judge."

Dane sighed and brought a cigarette to his lips. He breathed in deeply, letting the silence on the phone reverberate in James's ear. "Look," Hartley finally said, a serious tone in his voice. "Whatever the fuck is going on here, you're going to need more help than just me."

"What's going on here?" James tried.

Dane ignored him. "You're going to need the police, man."

"What's going on? What did you find?"

Again, he danced around the question. "I don't know what all of this means in the grand scheme of things, but let's just say I think you may have yourself in some deep shit."

TWENTY-EIGHT

Gregory Faulk was a toothpick of a man. His salt-and-pepper hair sat atop a frame that lacked any sort of muscular composition. His shirt and tie clung about him in an emaciated display, causing Hartley to wonder if there was a medical condition that Mr. Faulk suffered from. As her and Ratliff approached, he glanced up from underneath oversized glasses and ran his skeletal hand through his hair.

"Mr. Faulk?" Hartley asked.

"Yes. That's me," he replied.

"Mr. Faulk, I'm Detective Hartley and this is Detective Ratliff."

"Ah! This gets even better!" he exclaimed, forcing a laugh and turning to his legal team just to his left.

"I'm sorry?" Hartley questioned, her brow furrowing.

"No, apologies, miss," he replied, wiping the smile from his face and placing a hand over his birdcage of a chest. "This has been a hell of a morning!"

"I'm sure," was all Hartley could reply.

"First my client decides to go out like Frank Pentangeli, and now his devil in the human form shows up to witness it all."

"Mr. Faulk," Hartley said, setting herself in front of the man and pulling his eyes to her. "I'm sorry for the troubling day you're having, but I'd advise you to watch what you say. Do we understand each other?"

Faulk glanced down to the floor quickly, catching the collective eye of his legal team. "I understand. I'm sorry, detective. Like I said, it's been a hell of a morning."

"I'd like to ask you a few questions, if you aren't too broken up at the moment," Hartley said, not waiting for a response and turning down the hall towards the kitchen. Ratliff waited with the attorney, swinging his arm in the direction of his partner as Faulk slowly fell in line.

* * * * *

From the confines of a research cubicle in the Harold Washington Library, James leaned back in his chair and rubbed his eyes, yawning. He stared ahead of him at the dividing wall lost in twirling thoughts he could not pin down. Each vision conjured danced in his mind for a miniscule amount of time before fading from whence they came. His parents. Daniel Vincent. Jolene. He reigned in enough attention to briefly halt upon the detective, the memory of her supple lips, curling into a smile before he kissed her passionately, pulling her into his embrace, hands running up her back and into the shoulder length dreads. Mattie. He felt himself crack a small smile, wondering how he always seemed to ruin special things in his life.

From behind him, James heard a rush of movement. He turned just in time to see Dane walk by, the journalist tapping him on the shoulder with a hurried, "This way." James glanced around quickly and pushed his chair out, hustling after, turning a corner and entering a room as Dane shut the door and flipped on the overhead fluorescents.

* * * * *

"Mr. Faulk," Hartley said, stopping in the kitchen, the only room that appeared somewhat organized and free of lawyers or police officers, save for themselves. "How about we start over?"

"Yes, please," he agreed, wiping his brow with a crisp handkerchief.

"Where were you last night?" she asked.

"Am I being investigated?" he replied.

"Did you do anything wrong that I should know about?"

"No, detective," he answered.

"Then, no. These questions are just from … a personal place."

Gregory Faulk laughed. "I bet," he answered. He shook his head and smiled. "Well, off the record, you'll be happy to know that Damian didn't stand much of a chance."

"With what? The murder charges or the fraud?"

"The fraud. You know as well as I do that the murder charges were flimsy at best."

"He had motive."

"Lots of people had motive. Those two guys at *State of Finance* weren't exactly heading up the list of Chicago's most ethical bachelors."

"Meaning?"

"Meaning they pissed countless people off. Any one of the corporations they helped crumble had motive. Presidents, vice presidents ... Shit. Even janitors were put out after those two got their hands on them."

"So," Hartley repeated, "where were you last night?"

"Here. We're always here. This place's turned into our second, hellish home."

"All of you were here?" Ratliff asked, pointing down the hall in the direction of the legal team. "How many nights a week?"

Hartley listened in as her eyes scanned the area, running along the smooth, pristine countertops. Her vision focused on the cabinets, the sparkling glass doors with lights that projected down onto the perfectly placed china. "Every night," she heard Faulk respond. "We've been here since you and your partner arrested him."

"Part of the job," Ratliff said. "Catching the bad guys." She looked across the island to where Verland had hung his aprons, various colors and material, all priced in the hundreds of dollars. "Do you know why Mr. Verland would kill himself?"

The appliances were spotless, stainless steel beasts with tinted black glass free of fingerprints.

"If we're being honest," Faulk replied, "then I'd say it had something to do with the impending move to a prison cell. That tends to put a damper on one's extravagant lifestyle."

Hartley held back a grin as she took the conversation and surroundings in. Just as she was about to turn back into the exchange, her eye caught something out of place, an object that stood out to her as would a red flag: a dirtied wine glass sitting upon the counter near the sink. She looked at the men before her with a quizzical expression. "Do you drink on the job, Mr. Faulk?"

* * * * *

"Sit down," Dane directed, sliding into the chair directly across from James and opening his leather shoulder bag. He removed a stack of papers and waited for James to take the chair. Graiser slowly sat, folding his hands and staring to the reporter. Dane held his gaze, trying to figure out the correct words to start the conversation. Instead, he looked upon his sister's ex fling and rested his chin in his hand.

"What?" James asked, confused.

Dane focused on him a moment longer before answering. "Tell me again what you know about Gregory Faulk."

James leaned forward and thought. "Just what I told you before."

"Then fucking tell me again," Dane pushed.

James nodded. "Okay. Well, Faulk was a researcher for my father's legal team."

"When?"

"Before the murders."

"What was he involved with?"

"What do you mean?"

"Was he involved with lawsuits? Or property? What?"

"I'm not sure," James said.

"Okay," Dane replied, taking a moment to think. "What else?"

James shrugged. "From my understanding, he was brought on by the legal team and worked as a researcher until the murders. From there, I have no idea what happened. Well, up until now, I guess."

"Right. And now he's Verland's lead counsel." Dane flipped a couple pages face down onto the table's surface and continued. "I found some interesting things about Gregory Faulk," he said. "You want to hear?"

* * * * *

Faulk shook his head vigorously, his graying mane swinging back and forth. "Absolutely not," he said adamantly. "We have a strict no drinking policy in the firm. Only time it's acceptable is after a win. I even ask my employees to refrain from drinking at all while on a case."

"That's a little extreme, don't you think?" Ratliff asked.

"In the line of work I'm in, one relaxing drink to take the edge off can turn into many in a hurry." He paused before pointing a finger in the detective's direction. "I'm sure you can attest to that as well."

"What about Damian?" Hartley asked, turning from the pair and eyeing the dirtied glass near the sink.

Faulk let out a loud guffaw. "Never seen that man drunk in my life until this whole thing started. He's like a fish nowadays!"

"Was he drunk all the time?"

"Well, maybe not drunk. But definitely ... in a daze. Either scotch or wine."

"And you say neither you nor your team drinks while you're here, is that correct?"

Faulk eyed her cautiously. "No, detective. We do not drink on the job."

Ratliff glanced his partner's way with curious eyes. "Did Damian have any guests over last night? Maybe after you all left?"

"Not while we were here, no. I couldn't tell you about after we left. It was odd that he kicked everyone out though."

"What time was this at?"

Faulk shrugged. "Late. Sorry, detective. The hours seem to blend together."

"What was odd about him kicking you out?" Ratliff asked.

"That he did it. Damian would just normally disappear. I'd find him sitting in the kitchen. Or upstairs walking the hall.

Couple times he just went to bed without telling anyone. But he never told us to get out before."

"Did Mr. Verland have a security system installed?" Hartley asked.

"Absolutely. Why?" She pointed to the wine glass, dragging Gregory Faulk's eyes towards it.

* * * * *

"Faulk left your father's legal team just before the murders," Dane said to James, both of the men sitting up straight in their chairs facing one another. "He ended up working for a firm called Haughlin & Conly, where he stayed on until three years ago before leaving to create his own firm with some others. Tanner, Lebowisz & Faulk." He paused to let the information sink in.

James nodded. "So what does that mean?"

"Nothing yet. But I tracked down some sources that were able to help me make this all a little more interesting. Seems that Haughlin & Conly was the firm that worked on the case against Robert Thames. Guess who took on the role of lead researcher?"

"Faulk."

Dane nodded. "It gets better. Haughlin & Conly was hired by none other than Congressman Harold Johnston during the investigation. They worked with outside financial consultants to skim through the mess and come to the conclusion that Thames was guilty."

"So, in essence, they wrote the script for Robert Thames." It was a statement.

Dane smiled. "With a little help from you and your squad on Daniel Vincent's side. The really intriguing piece of this to me is that Haughlin & Conly was looked into very briefly due to their connections with Johnston. Seems nothing stood out as strange to anyone, so there was really no coverage on it all." Dane paused, scratching his grizzled chin and leaning back with a sigh.

James looked to him, waiting for more with his hands clasped tight together. "Sorry, I'm following you, but I'm not sure what you're getting at."

"I'm just finding it hard to separate the fact that Faulk is connected to your parents. He's also connected to Harold Johnston, and now to Damian Verland as well." A series of chirps sounded from Dane's pocket, notifications of incoming messages. He tossed the remaining papers in his hand to the tabletop and retrieved the device. He stopped all movement suddenly and tilted forward.

James watched with worry as his counterpart's eyes scrunched up. "What?" he asked.

Dane shook his head and laughed, tossing the phone to the surface of the research table. "Verland fucking killed himself!"

"What?" James exclaimed, grabbing the phone and reading the text himself. "When?"

Dane shrugged. "Don't know," he said. "But with all this new shit, it would have been a great interview." James looked up in disgust. "Look, whatever's going on here could be connected to my Intervise-*State* story. Damian Verland was a slimy fuck. Who knows what skeletons he had in his closets? He could have possibly been able to help with whatever's going on now."

James thought for a moment before remembering the brown file box. He stared to Dane and smirked. "I might have something that could help out."

TWENTY-NINE

The security system was tied into a state-of-the-art computer in the upstairs closet, in the rear corner past Verland's row of thousand dollar apiece Armani suits and shelves of Movado and Rolex watches. With Faulk's permission, as he stood behind the detectives, Ratliff clicked away, locating the system's recording of the previous evening's events, in rewind. Faulk crossed his arms and leaned against the doorframe, toying with the bridge of his nose and making his large-framed glasses dance joyfully on his face. "What's the objective here again?" he finally asked.

"To see who was here last night," Hartley answered.

"How do you know someone was here?"

"Because it's my job to pay attention to details, Mr. Faulk," she replied, pulling a grin from Ratliff. "Keep backing it up, but make sure we can see everything," she said to her partner.

"And what details would those be?" Faulk answered, the tone of his voice verging on the edge of contempt.

Hartley turned to look at him. "Neither you or your team said you had anything to drink. Either someone in your group is lying to you, or there was someone here last night. I don't expect you to have noticed, Mr. Faulk, but that glass downstairs was sitting on the counter next to the sink with dried wine at the bottom."

"So what?" he asked.

"So, Mr. Faulk," she continued, "your employer was a meticulously clean man. Everything about him shies away from the fact that he would leave a dirty dish on the counter. Have you ever seen dishes stacked on the counter?" Faulk stalled, trying, unsuccessfully, to conjure up a memory of an abundance of food-encrusted silverware and china. He could not. "Right," Hartley said. "Even his tumbler — I'm assuming he used a crystal tumbler for his scotch?"

"Always."

"Even that tumbler had been washed and dried." She looked at the attorney before adding, "There's no way Damian Verland, a man who bordered on the obsessive, would have left a dirtied wine glass just to grab another for his trip to the bath. Even the straight razor he used to slit his wrists had been wiped clean."

* * * * *

James unlocked his penthouse and walked inside, holding the door open for Dane. Hartley's eyes traveled across the expanse that was the room and whistled. "Holy shit, man!" he exclaimed. "Instead of paying me another ten grand, why not just let me stay here? It'd be like a fucking vacation from my pad."

James looked to him. "Want to?"

Dane smirked and shook his head. "Don't take this the wrong way — or do — but I don't want to move into your life."

"Right now, I don't either," James said, throwing his keys to the counter and entering the kitchen. "You want something to drink?"

"You got some Jameson?" Dane asked.

"No, I don't," James answered. "Something else?"

"Why don't you call down for a bottle?"

James watched as Dane made his way through the living area, his eyes cursing the disrespect that seemed to cling to the journalist. Regardless of the recent connections he had seemed to make with Dane, James was still none too pleased to be standing in the same room as the man. He still found him to be a foul individual, a man of less than reputable standards. Yet he was a man that had opened a new lane for him in his parents' case, and that was worth the disgustingly charmless banter that he found himself charging through.

"This it?" Dane asked, his focus on the brown file box sitting in the corner of the room on a chair.

"Yep," James said, coming to a stop by his side and extending a beer to him. Dane grabbed the bottle and smiled, bringing it to his lips and taking a long swig.

* * * * *

The detectives sat for nearly an hour before coming upon anything out of the ordinary on the video monitor. Yet even that was relative. "See," Faulk said, pointing to the screen. "That's us leaving. That's when he kicked us out."

Hartley took note of the time and continued to survey the footage, watching the instances as a group of lawyers and researchers exited onto the front drive to light up cigarettes or stretch their limbs. She shook her head in frustration. "This isn't doing it. Is there another feed we can look at?"

Ratliff paused the video and clicked around. "Looks like there's a couple on either side of the house. And one over the back door."

"Try that one. Try the back door."

Ratliff switched the feed to the rear entrance and hit rewind. The darkness caught movements of opossums and raccoons traveling at quick, reversed paces, humorously moonwalking across the screen and into the shadows. Tree limbs twitched chaotically in the minimal, yet evident, breeze that blew. Yet nothing more came into view. Hartley reached over Ratliff's shoulder and grabbed the mouse, moving the cursor across the screen and clicking on the reverse button to speed it up.

The brief thought had arisen in her that it was a possibility Damian Verland *had* been drunk enough that he had left the dirtied wine glass on the counter, forgetting it in the fleeting seconds as he used the restroom or cleaned his scotch tumbler or —

"There!" Hartley said. Ratliff slowed the playback as his partner pointed to a figure stepping backwards from the evergreen trees and into the yard. A mumbled, yet unclear, curse fell from Gregory Faulk's lips as he stepped forward. The individual in the video had no descriptive characteristics about them at the moment, mainly due to the fact that they were facing away from the camera. Hartley did notice, however, the box within the figure's arms.

* * * * *

"I'll tell you what," Dane said after an hour at the dining room table, "I'm thinking about adding you as a fucking source from now on!" Papers from the file box were spread across the surface as both men rifled through the contents, wondering what their eyes were falling upon and what it all meant. Damian had given the box to James as a sort of parting gift, one that left the ex-VP of Intervise Securities dead and Graiser the inheritor of a mass of financial records that had filled their minds with figures and transactions that needed to be scrutinized with an expert's eye. One thing was for certain though: the contents of this box were meant to raise the cloud from over James's past, to shine light upon a period in his life that had been shoved into the recesses of his mind.

"What did he tell you when he gave you this?" Dane asked.

James placed the stack of papers he was searching through in front of him and rubbed his eyes. "He said there was a trail that led from his past that mixed with mine."

"Do you know what it is?"

James shrugged. "I can only guess that it has something to do with my parents, but who knows. Could be something with Daniel Vincent, too. I'm not sure."

"And he knows you had a connection with Vincent?"

"Yeah. It's not like it's something that was hidden from the public. Daniel was in the news all the time. My parents got their fair share of publicity, too."

"Okay," Dane said after a moment of silence, the words seemingly being thrown into the atmosphere to no one in particular. "Let's back up and consider what we have. There's the name Millers."

"Right."

"You get that from your junkie buddy who's gunned down in front of your ex-junkie buddy, who is … Where, exactly?"

"Augie. His name is Augie. And he's most likely checking out of his place and heading to my old apartment."

"You still have an apartment?" Dane looked around. "I'd sell that piece of shit and just stay here." He looked at James and his emotionless expression and waived a hand in the air. "Okay. So there's Millers. There's Augie. There's also this shithead, Gregory Faulk, who has a connection to your parents, Harold Johnston and Damian Verland. Johnston, as the world knows, also has a connection with Daniel Vincent, since you brought him up. Then, Verland has a link to Luke Moran and Korhan Karaca, them being the driving force of this whole bloodshed. Let's say, for argument's sake, that

Verland, through Moran and Karaca, now has an association with your parents."

"We don't know that for sure," James added quickly.

"We don't know anything for sure," Dane answered. "Everything here is just speculation. But, hell … It's better than what you had before. Am I right?" James did not respond. "So, if everyone is fucking everyone else in this whole spider web, then where's the common thread that ties it together?" Dane thought for a moment before looking up to James with a shit-eating grin. "There is one aspect to all of this that might be able to help." James caught on immediately, his hands beginning to sweat and a lump forming in his throat. "Might be time to check in with your ex." Dane could not stifle his amusement.

* * * * *

Ratliff, at Hartley's request, shifted the video feed to the interior of the home, reversing the stream ten-fold for any movement that would show their mystery guest's face. They found nothing of importance. Other than shifts in lighting, or shadows dancing along walls, the interior of the home, from the time their person of interest appeared in the backyard to the point where the legal team made their hasty retreat, showed nothing.

Hartley swore and forced Ratliff to go back to the backyard feed, watching again as the man slid into the screen and walked backwards towards the house. She could feel Faulk over her shoulder, his breath minty as he chewed on a fingernail and focused on the screen. Twice she stood up and looked at him, her penetrating eyes telling him, in no uncertain terms, to back off. He waived to her his apology and resumed his glare to the video monitor.

Just as she was about to swear at the amount of time the process was taking, Ratliff spoke up. "Here," he said, pointing to the lower part of the screen to the shoulders of their individual slowly backing out of the rear entry. The man stopped for a moment, obviously conversing with Verland in the kitchen. He stepped back, hand extended to the handle on the sliding door. The limb retracted, the file box non-existent.

Hartley turned to Faulk. "He got the box from here," she said matter-of-factly. "What was in that box?" Faulk looked stunned, his eyes not moving from the slow playback. "Mr. Faulk," Hartley said again, pulling him rapidly from the screen. "What was in that box?"

Faulk shrugged. "I would assume financial records of some sort."

"I need your team to go through what's downstairs and figure out what was taken. I'm sure you have an inventory of some —"

"Jo," Ratliff interrupted suddenly, the tone in his voice one of shock.

Hartley turned and glanced at him, her partner's eyes upon her, his hand holding the mouse, cursor hovering over the now paused video feed. She stepped closer and looked to the screen, her breath stripped the moment she recognized the face of

James Graiser walking into the kitchen of the now deceased Damian Verland.

THIRTY

The tires hummed along the pavement as they made their way back to the precinct, the constant buzz the only sound in the otherwise silent cruiser. Ratliff, at times, glanced to his partner in the passenger seat, waiting for a moment to bring up the conversation he knew was on the verge of spilling over, yet had somehow been kept at bay.

Hartley and he had left the Verland home shortly after watching James move into view. They had, with Gregory Faulk's permission, procured a digital copy of the security feeds, which Mac would be bringing back with him to the precinct once he had bagged the deceased ex-VP. Ratliff had asked Faulk some follow-up questions regarding the box that Graiser had exited with the previous evening, catching the attorney's evident dismay at the sight. It was something that had bothered Jacoby, a flinch or a tell that should have caused Hartley's senses to tingle as well, had it not been for, once again, James's sudden appearance.

The pair made it into the station and moved to the pit, each falling into the routine of checking voice messages and email inboxes. They spent several minutes unwinding, stopping into restrooms or kitchens, brewing a fresh pot of coffee or seizing a pastry leftover from the early morning shifts. As they made their way back to their respective desks, Captain Nolan peeked his head from his office door and summoned them. "Jo. Ratliff. Come on in here."

They stood as if they knew the meeting was coming, like it had been a scheduled assembly they had waited for all morning. They strolled into his office, Hartley setting herself next to one of the chairs facing his massive, cluttered desk. "Have a seat," their superior said as he sat back in his own. He folded his hands across his chest and reclined, waiting for his detectives to fall in line. "Let's get down to business," he said. "I want to know where we are with everything. What do we have to go on thus far in regards to the Karaca case?"

Hartley cleared her throat. "Well, besides having vague descriptions on our shooters, Mac was running a couple things."

"Like what?" Nolan asked quickly.

Hartley glanced to her partner before responding, wondering why her superior needed the information he already knew said aloud. She shrugged it off and obliged. "Blood from the scene. Mac said there were multiple locations where blood was found, and not all of it was Karaca's. Korhan was hit and dropped where he stood. The majority of blood loss was concentrated in a puddle underneath his body, of course, with blood splatter from the shots to the neck."

"What about the other locations?"

"Two of the shooters were struck. One in the face, which appeared to only graze the suspect. The other suffered a gunshot wound to the abdomen. He was the one they found in the dumpster."

"We're waiting on DNA analysis and fingerprints from him," Ratliff added. "And whatever they could pull from the van."

"Which didn't sound like a lot," Hartley said. "We also had fingerprints from the gun that was dropped at the scene. Not sure what they were able to pull from there."

The conversation halted for a moment while Nolan sat up and pulled a manila folder from a pile on the corner of his desk. "Well, you'll be happy to know that I'm the bearer of good news," he stated, turning the packet around and throwing it before them. Hartley sat up and pulled the papers to her. "Looks like Mac got this shit pushed through pretty quick for you. DNA analysis from the Karaca crime scene. Morgan Keller. He's our guy from the dumpster. Small time crook. Had a few priors in his twenties for drugs. One breaking and entering."

"Any family we could question? Girlfriends?"

"Nothing that we've found. Father died when he was three in a car accident. Mother passed away a couple years back from breast cancer. As for girlfriends or anything, I'll leave that up to you two."

"Thank you, sir," Hartley said. "It gives us a start at least."

"You're welcome," he said with a smile, reaching for yet another folder and tossing it in her direction. "But I've got something better."

"Sir?" she said as Ratliff reached over and pulled the documents out.

Captain Nolan pointed to the sheets of paper. "Again, thank Mac for getting these pushed through for you. The gun itself is registered to some trust fund baby in New York. Was stolen in a break in years ago. Doesn't lead anywhere. But there was a partial print that got a hit in the system."

"Who is it?" Hartley asked, leaning towards her partner and eyeing the paper.

"Guy by the name of Millers Renholm."

* * * * *

He reached up and ran his finger across the wound, grimacing as a fingernail caught on a section of coagulated blood and pulled at the scab. Millers Renholm swore aloud in his vehicle and rose in the driver's seat. He slammed his palm into the steering wheel ferociously. This whole series of events had made him sick to his stomach, an unnecessary stress that had not been needed in his life at this exact moment. There were countless other episodes that were playing out that needed his attention, deals and paybacks being dealt that he would have loved to accompany. He considered himself a major player in those circumstances.

And yet here he was, surveying an apartment building for the twentieth time, putting his face — and noticeable head wound — into the public eye for scrutiny. And for what? To see if the scrawny Graiser kid showed face? To see if he was indeed working with the cops? What then? What if he *was* working with Chicago's finest? Better yet, what if he was not? Millers could come to only one conclusion in regards to this whole affair. If James was searching for the truth with the help of the CPD, he needed to be dealt with. If not, he still, in Millers's mind, needed to be dealt with. There was no way around it. Either way, it seemed utterly pointless to him.

Millers wanted to just get back to his life. Yet, he knew that that was possibly something totally out of reach from here on out. He understood, to a certain extent, the mind in which he was dealing with. His long-haired partner was not someone who left gaping holes in an otherwise air-tight scene. Millers had, at times within the past, read of bodies found floating leisurely in the Kankakee River by fishermen wading through the waters, or of farmers nearly running over decapitated victims in their cornfields. The victims' names, once released, were members of the criminal society within Chicago that Millers recognized, and could easily place within the rolodex of his now unwanted partner.

Millers Renholm felt it was only a matter of time before it was his turn. And he did not intend to go swimming in the Kankakee. He intended to remain alive and well, which meant, for the unforeseeable future, he needed to remain open to the wishes of the man.

* * * * *

"What else?" Captain Nolan asked, folding his hands across his lap and staring to his detectives.

Ratliff glanced sideways to his partner and noticed her eyes turn to the floor. He did not want to out Hartley's one-time friend, especially since his role — although seemingly larger than either of them had expected — was, as of yet, undetermined. There were definitely signs that needed to be looked into, however, things as they were currently, Jacoby kept his mouth shut and relinquished the lead to Hartley.

Jolene, on the other hand, quickly battled with her personal and professional personalities, wanting more than anything to spill the beans on James's apparent involvement. Korhan's phone records and Verland's security videos proved that, coincidentally or not, James Graiser was indeed someone that needed to be questioned.

"Well?" Nolan repeated.

"Nothing else, sir," Hartley answered, her eyes connecting with her superior's.

They remained locked for several moments before Nolan unclasped his hands and said, "Okay. Keep me updated on everything."

The detectives rose and left the office, moving to their respective desks. Ratliff wheeled his chair over to Hartley and stopped, his elbow resting on the surface. Jolene could feel his eyes on her. She sighed and turned to him. "Look, I just need to check on it first," she stated. "By myself."

Ratliff nodded. "Understood," was all he said, yet remained in position.

She stared to him a moment longer before rising and pushing in her chair. "With everything that's going on, I need a personal answer from him. Not as a cop, you know?"

Ratliff wheeled his chair back to his desk and grabbed the cup of coffee that had reached room temperature. He took a step forward and stood before her. "I'll be here when you need me. Do what you need to." He smiled and squeezed her hand before turning towards the kitchen. Hartley stared after him for a moment before exiting the pit, her stomach churning as she descended the stairs in the direction of her recent past.

* * * * *

"Fuck this," he said, slipping from the stale air of the vehicle and onto the sidewalk to tread the thirty yards to the nearest Dunkin Donuts. He pulled his hat down low as he exited the establishment with a chocolate Long John and a large coffee, sipping the liquid and biting into the pastry with a hunger that matched his irritation.

Every day had been spent between a randomly stolen car in his partner's fleet, and the streets outside of James Graiser's apartment. Coffee. Donut. Coffee. Donut. Occasionally, walking the sidewalk, Millers would be graced with a beautiful college-aged woman in a short skirt and tight shirt, a girl that would pause every so often to stop into the coffee shop across from where he parked, or halt near his car for a cigarette before entering an alcove that led to the apartments above the restaurants and convenience stores that lined the avenue.

At the moment he stepped onto the sidewalk, Millers was confronted by just such woman. She did not notice him in the least, standing yards from the door and pressing a cigarette to her voluptuous lips and sucking in deeply. Renholm sidestepped an incoming patron and fixed his eyes on the beauty. She placed the cigarette in her mouth and reached up to move her long, bleach blonde hair from her face, the jet black eyebrows and liner framing intense blue orbs and high cheekbones. Her voice was raspy, though Millers could not focus on the words. His eyes slid down her frame, rolling across her blouse and skirt, to the slate gray tights that hugged her legs, her toned thighs and calves accentuated by the black heels.

Millers Renholm's eyes ran up her frame for several moments, his mind envisioning scenarios that would never be, his fingers and tongue running along smooth, soft skin that only belonged to his imagination. As he walked past her, he maneuvered between the girl and an approaching male, turning sideways and squeezing past, his one hand reaching up to pull the hat lower, the other going lower to slide across her ass as he produced an apology. His body shivered with excitement as the woman accepted the incident as nothing more than an accidental collision.

THIRTY-ONE

"Is there anything we can do to make your future stays more enjoyable?" the concierge asked as August Hughes exited his hotel.

He shook his head. "Been bloody peachy," he stated with a forced smile, the subdued lie almost breaking through and morphing into the verbal assault Augie had so wanted to spew forth. Instead, he successfully wrestled the urge down.

"Wonderful! I hope you enjoyed your stay. Please remember us on your next visit to Chicago!" It was a well-rehearsed speech for a less-than-knowledgeable tourist. Augie was anything but that.

"Cheers," was all he said as he grabbed his bag and slung it over his shoulder. He veered onto the sidewalk and moved twenty yards down, setting his luggage on the pavement and lighting a Marlboro.

He felt relieved. The hotel he had just exited, although comfortable in relativity to the others in the area, was, nonetheless, a shithole. His comforter consistently smelled of smoke — an offensive aroma he himself was responsible for — and twice he had had to dry off by employing the spare set of sheets thrown aimlessly on the closet floor by hotel maids that could not care less. Yet, when a turndown service and daily room pickup was on the brochure, one had the option to expect an up-to-par hygienic experience. The stained pair of silk boxers from a previous patron had sent that idea out the window within his first twenty seconds.

His thoughts, as he moseyed down the sidewalk in search of a cab, were on the dusty, long-since abandoned apartment of his close American friend. He had been to James's place a time or two before, though for not much longer than a day before moving along to the next phase of his vacation abroad. Augie had not been confident that his friend had still kept the abode, yet the mention of it during their last meeting made him a little happier since seeing a man's life drain into a gutter.

* * * * *

"I'm trying to get some information on a man you arrested a while back," Ratliff spoke into the phone.

The officer on the other end of the line responded in a rasp. "What's a *while back*?"

"About seven years."

"Whoa!" he said with a laugh. "I'll do my best. A lot's gone on since then. Who's the man?"

"Morgan Keller. You remember him?"

The officer thought for a moment. "A little bit. Typical troubled individual. Had some run-ins for drugs and petty theft. You guys have him for something now?"

"Actually, he was murdered."

"Really? You got anyone in custody?"

"Not yet," Ratliff replied. "His killing is part of a larger investigation we're dealing with. Just happened to be collateral damage that couldn't be left around, it would seem."

"You boys say it like it is downtown, huh?" the officer asked, somewhat rhetorically.

"He's part of the reason for the larger investigation," Ratliff responded.

"So, Keller graduated to bigger and better things, huh? Guess I never saw that coming?"

"No? Possible you remember him more than just a little, then?"

"Detective, I'm sure you know as well as I do that we see the same type of criminal day in and day out. I don't remember Keller more than I said. Those types of kids don't usually become your cold-blooded killers. At least not in this town."

"Yeah, well, anything goes here," Ratliff stated, holding his ground. "I appreciate the time though. Thanks."

"Yeah. Hey, listen," the officer said quickly before Ratliff could get off the line. "The arrest that we made a while back, we let go a girlfriend of his. Sarah Elizabeth Bernice. Pretty little thing. Nothing was ever tied to her. Don't even think we have a record on her."

"Do you know if they're still an item?" Ratliff asked.

"I don't think so. She moved to the city a year or two after Morgan's arrest."

"How do you know that?"

The officer chuckled. "The blessing of living in a small town," the officer said. "Everyone knows everyone else's business."

* * * * *

Jolene parked the vehicle on the opposite side of the street, an action she had done on purpose to walk the path that had led him into her life to begin with. She stepped onto the sidewalk and slowly made her way in the direction of James's apartment building, her heart fluttering slightly as she closed in on the alleyway where Barailles had been nearly killed. She glanced down the dingy, dumpster-lined lane, the flashbacks replaying in her mind as she stared to her bloody partner before spinning on her heels to chase her suspect into the warehouse door to the right.

Things had changed that day, some good, some bad, but all adding to the shift in her life, as if that fateful trip to connect with James Graiser had set off an earthquake that fixed around her being. She had become the proverbial epicenter that sent shockwaves throughout her personal and professional life.

Jolene turned from the alleyway and focused on the buildings before her. She scanned the top of the establishment adjacent to James's apartment complex, running her vision from the hotel windows she had chased Taylor Thames through, rewinding across the expansive terrain and to the fire escape of Graiser's pad. Flashes of James gripping his bloodied side as he maneuvered up the rusting metal path and to the roof crowded her vision briefly before she shook her head and stepped into the crosswalk.

* * * * *

The office building was on the sixtieth floor of the Willis Tower. Ratliff exited the elevator and walked into a lobby gleaming with flawlessly smooth granite countertops. The receptionist behind the massive desk turned her attention to the detective quickly with a confident — although overly intense — smile. "You must be Detective Ratliff," she stated as Jacoby approached.

"I am," he replied, eyes quickly taking in his surroundings.

"What can I do for you?"

"I'm here to see Sarah Bernice. Is she in?"

"Can I ask what it's about?"

"No." Ratliff surprised himself with the quick, to-the-point response.

The receptionist raised her hands in submission. "Say no more, officer. I'll see if she's available."

"Thank you," he answered. "And it's *detective*."

She forced a playful smirk and picked up the phone. After typing in a group of digits, she spoke quietly into the mouthpiece. Ratliff slowly made his round of the lobby, eyeing the Renaissance reprints on the wall, including a number of tapestries purchased by a senior partner who, no doubt, had an affinity to the Middle Ages. "Detective," the receptionist said, pulling his attention back to the desk. Ratliff turned and took a step forward. "Sarah will be with you in a moment."

* * * * *

He groaned loudly as the stream of urine splashed grotesquely on the pavement behind an overflowing garbage dumpster. Millers cocked his head back and held a cigarette between his lips, the smoke trails wafting into the rotten air, edging closer to the contours of his face until his eyes stung. He swore to himself and turned his head to the left, trying to ward off the burning tentacles from his Parliament.

He finished and zipped up, wiping the errant piss that dripped from his finger onto the side of his pants and walking slowly back to the sidewalk and the car parked just down the road from the Graiser apartment. He leaned against the vehicle door and turned away from the street as a police car drove by, the officer inside busy with the computer mounted to the center console.

Millers's eyes were drawn to a pair of young women making their way past him, their focus on the newly purchased handbag and pair of skinny jeans and not on the creepy, grizzled man with the head wound to their left. He watched them closely, his gaze sliding along the toned, tanned arms of the college-aged ladies that spent just enough time in the gym to maintain their beach-going bodies. He smiled at their perky breasts, the girl on the right showing just enough cleavage to let his imagination run wild. He felt himself become erect as they passed by completely, his gaze falling on the sway of their hips, the flick of their asses and, finally, the flex and release of their thigh muscles.

Millers glanced around quickly before tossing the cigarette butt to the sidewalk and moving back into the alleyway, stationing himself behind the dumpster in which he had just came, this time his thoughts on the college-aged girls, and, with the current situation he found himself in, someone from his past, someone whom he had dominated in a way in which brought out the pure evil that encompassed his soul.

His thoughts turned to Amelia Graiser.

* * * * *

"Oh my God!" Sarah Bernice exclaimed quietly, looking to the conference room table she and Ratliff sat at. "I can't believe he's dead."

"I'm sorry, Ms. Bernice," he said, giving her a moment to take it in.

"How? How'd it happen?"

"We're looking into everything right now." Ratliff stared to the woman for several seconds. She was a decent looking woman in her late-twenties, with a close-cropped pixie hairstyle the color of dark chocolate. Jacoby could see the gray coming through, and quietly put money on it that Sarah Bernice's style allowed her naturalness to shine. "Ms. Bernice, is it safe to say that you and Mr. Keller hadn't remained in touch since your break-up?"

Sarah nodded. "Yeah. Well, I had seen him a handful of times after that, but not for a while."

"What was the timeframe of those encounters?"

"A year or so after our split. Not since then though."

"And what were the reasons behind those meetings?"

Sarah flushed red and glanced to the detective. "Mainly we'd just meet to …"

Ratliff forced a smile and raised his hand. "Been there," he said. He changed the line of questioning. "In the incident report of Mr. Keller's last arrest, you were listed." Sarah's shoulders deflated slightly. "Ms. Bernice, just to clarify, this is not about you. I've read the report. I know you had nothing to do with his criminal activity. I'm just trying to get any information from you that I can about your ex."

"But I don't have any!" she said. "I haven't seen him in years. And the last time was a random night that I just happened to run into him. I swear! I want to help, detective, but I'm not sure I have anything."

"Anything can help," Ratliff assured her. "Anything from his past, which included you." He shifted in his seat. "Do you remember anyone that hung around when you were with him? Anyone that stood out?"

Sarah thought, the gears in her mind turning rapidly, her eyes wide as her head shook back and forth. "I'm sorry," she said, glancing to the conference room door. She sat forward and quieted. "Listen, I'm not proud of that time in my life.

Morgan was someone I had met in a period of my life when I was unemployed and going to school. He was a … well, a bad boy. He was someone who I would never deal with in my life now. He …" She stopped and looked to the conference room door again. "We did things … drugs and all that. I never disclosed that to my employer. Please, I —"

"Ms. Bernice, you have nothing to worry about. Like I said, this is not about you. Do you remember anyone ever meeting with him?"

She shook her head. "I'm sorry," she stated, tears forming in her eyes.

THIRTY-TWO

Nothing helpful.

They were the only words within the text message from Ratliff. Hartley figured as much. When couples broke up, it was usually for a reason, and in most cases, that reason was to get the other person out of one's life for good. She and Ratliff would just have to follow an alternate route.

Jolene stepped onto the far sidewalk and moved in the direction of James's building. She reached the entrance and tried the handle. The door was locked. Hartley stepped forward and put her hand to the glass in order to block out the sun. The interior room was vacant, just particles drifting in the shafts of light caused by her silhouette. Hartley tried the door once more before turning her attention to the callbox and the buttons lining it. She ran her fingers down the names, pausing at Graiser's momentarily before passing it by to stop over the last entry. *Maintenance.*

* * * * *

Millers relived the deed done to Amelia Graiser just over a decade ago. This time, however, there was no unwilling second party, no bloodied tears falling down swollen cheeks. This instance there was just Millers Renholm, his thoughts, and a putrid smelly dumpster stocked full of rotting garbage.

It was the self-inflicted, sexual adventure within the alleyway, brought on by college girls and former victims, which led Millers to the sidewalk just moments after Hartley entered the building where James Graiser lived. He had not seen her try the handle, nor had he witnessed her exchange with the maintenance man from his last visit. For all he knew, things on the Graiser Front were as they had been for the last several hours. He was bored, and figured a quick cigarette before taking the seat behind the wheel yet again was absolutely called for.

* * * * *

Jolene followed the maintenance man to the stairwell and smiled as he held the door for her. "You know where you're headed to, detective?"

"I do," Hartley responded. "Again, thank you. I know this is out of the ordinary, but —"

"Say no more, dear," he quickly answered. "If you need anything else, just knock on the maintenance door right there. Loudly. I'll be in there somewhere."

"Thank you." Hartley began up the steps, wondering what she would say to James. The thought had stalled briefly on the forefront of her mind to actually press Graiser's call button directly. However, with things as they were, she turned to the officer in her, the suggestion of surprising her one-time friend in order to put him on the spot seeming to be the better option. It was odd how he had been, at one point, a trusted associate of hers, now only a person of extreme interest in an on-going case that made little sense whatsoever.

Hartley finally reached his floor and turned down the corridor, stopping at his door and standing motionless. Inside, she did not know what she would find. Would James be there at all? What about the box of files that had apparently been taken from the Verland home? Or was everything up to this point an enormous misunderstanding, a weird series of coincidences put together to form a confusion unlike she had ever seen? She did not have the slightest clue, but knew, without a doubt, there was only one way to find out: knock.

* * * * *

Augie exited the cab in need of a coffee and cigarettes. He bought a pack of Marlboros from the convenience store on the corner and then crossed the street to Starbucks to get himself an egg and sausage sandwich and large, skinny mocha with an extra shot of espresso. He halted outside the coffee shop and lit his smoke, his thoughts rapidly drifting down the Chicago sidewalks, floating in the breeze that had become a conflicted mess surrounding him. His Windy City experience, thus far, had definitely not been what he had envisioned when he packed his bag in London. Drugs and blood and bodies had not really been mentioned within the itinerary set up by James.

* * * * *

"He's not there," a voice said from her left. Hartley looked upon an elderly man with disheveled hair, a grizzled chin and sporting a stained white tank top. He scratched his protruding stomach and leaned into his doorjamb. "Hasn't been around for a while."

"Do you know where he is?" Hartley asked.

He shook his head. "Just know it's been a while since I saw him. Too bad, too. He's a nice boy." The man tickled his chin before pointing to her. "Pardon the question, but how'd you get up here?"

Hartley forced a smile and turned. "I didn't break in or anything," she said, showing her badge.

"Oh," he said, straightening up. "Is he in trouble or something?"

"No, no," Hartley answered quickly. "James is … He's actually a friend of mine."

"Uh-huh," he replied, not convinced. "And by *friend*, you mean he's working with you, right? On a case?" Jolene said nothing. "I've been around a long time, officer. I get your drift."

Jolene allowed the misdirection. "Something like that." She paused and pressed her fingers to his doorway. "Well, I guess it was worth a shot." She stepped away and started towards the stairwell. "Thank you, sir."

"Uh-huh," he said. He reached out and touched Hartley's arm, stopping her for a moment. "Listen," he stated. "Like I said, Jimmy's a good kid, but I'm not one for hindering the processes of the law. I have a spare key he gave me a while back for emergencies. Does this constitute an emergency?"

Hartley nearly declined, yet thought better of it. James *was*, in fact, a person of interest in everything that was going on, from his apparent involvement with Korhan, to the inexplicable appearance at Damian Verland's property late at night. It was only right, in her position of authority, to investigate to the fullest, regardless if her cases were becoming muddled. The lack of a warrant would be something she would deal with if it arose, yet, she felt it would not come to that. "If it's not too much of a burden," she said.

The neighbor smiled and nodded. "Not at all. Just let me fetch my robe and the key."

* * * * *

There was a flood of euphoria as Jolene closed the door behind her, shutting the elderly man in the hallway. "I'll just be a few minutes," she had said. "I'll drop the key off when I leave."

"Take your time," he had responded. "I'm just starting *The Bourne Supremacy*. That Matt Damon sure is a tough S.O.B., huh?"

Now, as she turned into the darkened apartment, the memories rushed back, churning with the stale, undisturbed air of the interior. In the dimness, she felt as if she was somehow transported to the past. She could almost see her and James writhing on the couch, her naked body shifting above him, his hands running across her glistening, sweaty skin, breasts reflecting the ambient light streaming through the blinds. Jolene could feel his fingertips on her hips, running up her stomach and across the ridges of her ribcage. His lips pressing between her breasts, on her neck, her head thrown back in ecstasy.

She glanced around the room, her reveries dispersing into the air with the flick of a light switch. The apartment looked exactly as it had that night, although with a layer of dust that gave everything a fuzzy, gray appearance. She deduced no one had been here in a while. A quick glance into the refrigerator showed nothing but condiments, cans of soda and a jar of dill pickles that must have expired months prior. Jolene closed the door to a puff of dust, her fingers creating streaks on the handle.

She made her way down the hall and past the large bathtub extremely out of place in the otherwise mediocre pad. Hartley turned into the bedroom, her and James's third stop on their night of passion, the second being a heated exchange on the hallway floor. She began to reach for the light switch yet halted, her eye catching a piece of paper on the dresser. Next to the loose change and just to the right of an orange colored candle, she stared to her phone number, written in her handwriting from a time long past.

It was an odd sensation to be walking the apartment yet again, this time almost as a ghost that would disappear shortly into the Chicago streets once more. At one point she had been a factor in James's life, a sheet of paper with a number on his dresser top, ready at a moment's notice, if need be. Now, however, she could not fathom that existence. She was beyond that point. She was nothing more than a police officer checking on a person of interest, or, if the visit was mentioned without a warrant, someone trying to connect with an old friend. It was not beyond reason. James showing up outside her home gave her motive to come calling.

She averted her eyes from the piece of paper to a small stack of photos wedged between two books. She pulled the pictures free and began flipping through, smiling at some of the images as they displayed a younger James Graiser from random points in his past. Some showed him in forests, decked out in rain gear in the middle of massive pines, water droplets streaking across the frame and pooling around his feet. Another had the young man on a mountain, his face nearly hidden beneath an enormous, hooded parka and snow goggles.

Yet it was another photo that caught her eye, one that caused her to toss the building stack of pictures back to the surface of the dresser. She stared at the scene: James Graiser, backpacking in what she could only assume to be the European countryside, mountains looming high behind him. It was not her old friend that had pulled her in, however. Instead, it was who was in the picture with him, who James wrapped an arm around and smiled wide with.

Jolene reached out to the dresser top and tilted her head high, taking in a long breath as her anger and confusion once more nearly boiled over. She held fast to the picture, digging her fingers into the paper as if the pressure would disintegrate the image as well as the emotions rising to the surface. She glanced to it once more and pulled out her cell phone, waking it with the press of a button and scrolling through her call history until she found her partner. Hartley was just about to push the button to call Ratliff when the jingle of keys halted her, pulling her from James's bedroom for a moment and to the hallway. Her eyes scanned the doorway, coming to rest on the beam of light between it and the floor. Her breath caught as a shadow halted before the apartment entry, the quick clank of a key being inserted into the lock pushing the detective back into the room. Her mind was on overdrive, scenarios flying through her thoughts as she tried to determine her next move.

THIRTY-THREE

In this line of work, Ratliff knew not every connection to victims or suspects was bound to carry with it a plethora of new or useful information. It was just the way the world of law enforcement worked. He had wanted something better to go on than an ex-girlfriend from long ago, a woman who had, no doubt, just wanted to move on with her life. And Jacoby knew that an interrupted day at work did not sit well with many employers. Yet the move had been necessary. All paths needed to be checked. This one just happened to be a dead-end.

Before he had left to meet with Sarah Bernice, Ratliff had put out an APB on their known suspect, Millers Renholm. However, at this point, nothing new had come in. He and Hartley were at a standstill, which meant, whether they liked it or not, James Graiser was their biggest lead.

Ratliff stepped into the pit and waved hello to Officer Hill. "How's it going, buddy?" Hill said.

Ratliff shrugged. "Can't complain. You?"

"About the same," he responded, advancing down the steps. "You know where Hartley's at?"

Ratliff shrugged. "Had something to check up on. Should be back soon. Why? What's up?"

"Don't know. The captain just told me if I saw either of you, to let you know he's looking for you two."

"Yeah? What about?"

Officer Hill opened his mouth to respond, but said nothing, extending his finger towards their boss as he exited his office.

Ratliff turned. "Hey, Cap," he said. "You needed to see —" The words stuck in his throat as Dane Hartley followed his superior from the room, stopping in the pit just outside the doorway. He met the journalist's gaze momentarily before shifting to Nolan, whose own countenance was set in stone. "What's going on, Henry?"

* * * * *

August Hughes stepped into the dusty apartment and sneezed. He scanned the area, wiping his spilled coffee on his jeans before reaching into his pocket and procuring a cigarette. He stalled for a moment before shrugging off the guilt of lighting up in someone else's home without permission. The idea of smoke filling the room allowed Augie to get past the stale air. Besides, he really doubted James would mind.

A buzz in his pocket drew his attention from the interior of the room. He set his coffee cup on the nearby table and pulled out the device, inhaling a lengthy drag of the cigarette as he read the message. He chuckled and then coughed, smoke catching in his esophagus and being released into the dim apartment, floating into the space right in front of him and stinging his eyes. He rubbed his lids and started towards the window, pulling back the shade and squinting as the sunlight streamed in. Augie slid the bottom half up and felt the rush of air enter around him, a welcoming feeling in the dense atmosphere.

It was at that moment Augie realized something was off, something within the apartment was not as it should be. He had not thought about it upon entry, having been distracted by coffee and the urge for a cigarette, yet now, as he stood near the window and looked back into the space, his eyes fell to the kitchen and the shining overhead light. For a moment he thought, wondering if, indeed, he had switched it on as he stepped into the apartment. He quickly came to the conclusion he had not, as, from the hallway to his right, Detective Jolene Hartley of the Chicago Police Department entered the room, hand on her holstered firearm, eyes on the startled Londoner.

* * * * *

"Come on, buddy. Don't hold back your excitement." Dane smiled wide after the words slithered from his mouth. His unannounced, possibly unwelcome, showing at the precinct was something that had thrown off even Captain Nolan, and Dane was amused by all of it. The boss, at least, had shown a bit of couth, however, and allowed the sibling of his best asset to bring forth whatever had been on his mind, even if, after only ten seconds, he seemed on the verge of kicking the reporter out.

"Not the word I'd use for it," Ratliff replied, entering his superior's office as Nolan shut the door behind them. Dane sauntered to a chair he had obviously been seated in prior to Jacoby's arrival, and slid back into place. "Sir?" Ratliff said, remaining still and watching as Nolan walked around his large desk.

"Take a seat, Jay," the captain said, the tone in his voice laced with annoyance. Ratliff did as directed, hating the smirk that crossed Dane's face next to him.

"Yeah, make yourself comfortable," Dane replied. Ratliff cast him a sideways glance.

The room remained silent for a moment, the stall broken only by Nolan sucking in a gulp of air as he sat back in his chair. "Where's Jo?" was all he asked.

Ratliff shrugged, raising a hand slightly in a not-so-subtle attempt at uncertainty. "She said she was going to look into a couple things."

"Like what?" came the quick response.

"I don't know, cap. What's this —"

"Answer the question, Ratliff," Nolan interrupted.

Jacoby stalled, trying to think of something not so far from the truth as to not get his partner in trouble. "Come on, Jay," Dane said casually, mocking the captain as the reporter stared to the detective. "Where's my dear sister?"

"What do you care?" Ratliff said, eyes bouncing from his boss to Dane.

"She's my sister," he answered with hands raised, as if his unconditional love for Jolene had been violated.

"Yeah, I know how you treat your sister."

Dane smiled, shaking his head. "You know, Captain Nolan, some of these officers you have seem a little quick to judgment, don't you think?"

"Give it a rest, Mr. Hartley," Nolan said, rubbing his eyes and sitting forward. "Let's try this another way. Why are *you* here?"

Dane remained fixed on Ratliff momentarily before turning. "Because I've got something you may be interested in."

"Doubtful," Jacoby responded.

"Jay …" Nolan said with a quieting hand. He turned back to the journalist. "You've already said that. And let's be clear: that's the *only* reason why you're still in my precinct. We've got plenty to do around here, if you haven't noticed. Now, if you wouldn't mind getting on with it."

"Actually, Henry, I do mind. I'd love to wait for Jo to show face as well."

"Detective Hartley's busy," the captain replied, his voice stern enough to pull a little of the joy from Dane. "Get on with it, or leave. Your choice."

* * * * *

"Put the cigarette out, August," Hartley said, moving into the room with the Londoner and taking position between him and the doorway.

"How do you know my name?" he asked, voice shaky.

She held up the picture of James and him, arms thrown over each other's shoulders with the backdrop of a looming mountain range. "*James and August*," she read from the back of the photo. "*Massif des Cerces.*" Augie noticed her eyes quickly jump back to his. Her hand never left her hip. "Put out the cigarette, August," she repeated with force.

Augie nodded, reaching up to wipe the perspiration from his brow before extinguishing the cigarette in a small potted plant that had long since met its end, the leaves and stem shriveled and brown, dust clinging to the wrinkled surface. "Look," he began, shifting towards the detective. "I —"

"Don't move!" she stated, grasping her firearm in the chance the man before her made an attempt to flee. "Put your hands on your head!"

"Wait!" Augie replied, his voice cracking. "Wait! Jimmy said I can stay here. I swear to bloody Christ!"

"Put ... your hands ... on your head!" Hartley dropped the picture to the floor and stepped back, setting herself far enough away from the auburn-haired man to give herself some space.

"Okay, okay!" he answered, placing his hands on the top of his head.

"Get on your knees and lay down. Keep your hands on your head." Augie followed the directions given, dropping to the floor in a grunt. "Do not move!" Hartley said once more.

She moved closer, grasping one of his hands and pulling it to his lower back where she handcuffed it. Once secure, Hartley patted him down, running her hands across his body. "Do you have any weapons?"

"No," he replied. She reached into his pocket and pulled a pack of cigarettes out, opening the box to reveal a nearly full pack of smokes and a small bag of marijuana stuffed into the cellophane sleeve. "I can explain," Augie tried.

"Shut up." She brought her hands to his ankles, flipped off his shoes. When she was satisfied he was unarmed, Hartley grasped the handcuffs and brought the Londoner to his feet. She sat him in the middle of the couch, the edges of the cushions sinking in from his weight, making it harder for him to try anything, though, by the looks of it, she was sure he would not.

Hartley stared at him for a moment before stepping to the middle of the room and once more picking up the picture. She glanced down to it, her vision skimming past Augie and landing on James, a large, full of life smile spread across his face. It was a youthful aura she had once been used to.

Hartley turned the image to the man on the couch and held it aloft. "August, you've got one chance at this. Don't dick me around." His worried eyes met hers. "What is going on?"

THIRTY-FOUR

James stole a glance to the box next to him, the contents within the container weighing heavy on his mind. There were things in there that he did not understand. He was, by no means, a financial guru, and realized Dane, though more knowledgeable on the subject, was not one either. As much as he wanted to figure this whole mess on his own, he definitely needed help.

His phone vibrated in his pocket. James slipped the device out and read the message, a laugh escaping him as he typed in his response. *On my way.* He placed the phone back into his pocket and looked up just as an empty cab pulled to the corner. He raised his hand and the driver acknowledged him. James grabbed the brown file box and pulled the taxi door open, closing it with a jarring slam and giving the man behind the steering wheel his destination. The vehicle began down the road as James pulled out his phone once more and loaded his text messages.

* * * * *

The phone buzzed from the dusty tabletop in James Graiser's apartment, the intermittent drone breaking the silence in the room as Jolene's gaze bounced from the handcuffed August to the vibrating device. "Let me tell you what I see," Hartley began, pulling her subdued friend's eyes to her again. "I see a man who is part of an ongoing murder investigation, showing up at his associate's residence. His associate, although a one-time help for the Chicago Police Department, has recently been linked to the death of my victim. This doesn't look good for you."

"Please," Augie began. "Please, I can —"

"But," Hartley continued as if he had not spoken, "as coincidental as that seems, here's the catch: I have *you*, August, at the scene of Korhan Karaca's murder, which leaves you as a person of interest. What that interest is, we'll find out. But you were obviously in contact with my victim, and now, obviously, you're in contact with James Graiser."

"James has nothing to do with —"

"I beg to differ. See, August, the forensics team for the city of Chicago can do some magical work. Did you know that? They can, let me tell you." She paused, setting herself directly in front of Augie. "Now why don't you just save the bullshit for someone else, and tell me what's going on."

* * * * *

Dane shifted in his seat and looked squarely at Captain Nolan. "What I have for you might just help out on an old case."

"Which old case?" Nolan asked.

"One near and dear to all of us in this room. And Jo." He paused before adding, "Especially me." Nolan glanced to Ratliff who shrugged his shoulders. Dane caught the exchange and smiled. "So, what's your take on Damian Verland?"

"Dane," Nolan replied, rubbing his eyes. "What exactly —"

"I mean, it's kind of interesting that, on the night he decides to take the pussy way out, James Graiser shows up on his doorstep." The blunt phrase created a rise in the captain, and Ratliff could feel a heat rise from his body. Dane watched as Nolan's eyes snapped from him to his detective. "Oh, you didn't know that?" He turned to Ratliff, who remained stationary. "What about you?"

"Jay?" Nolan said, leaning forward.

* * * * *

"Okay, okay," Augie said, shaking his head. "I'll tell you what I know, but you have to believe me. Neither one of us had anything to do Korhan's murder."

"I'll be the judge of that," Hartley replied.

Augie drew in a breath and exhaled. "James and I are friends. We've been so since our backpacking days. James was the only bloke to stick by me when I was using."

"So you're an addict." It was a statement.

Augie shook his head. "*Ex*-addict," he corrected. Hartley looked to the bag of weed. "Come on. You can't really count that, can you?" The detective did not seem intrigued at having the legalization of pot conversation. "Years ago, he stayed by my side after I overdosed. He —"

"August," Hartley interjected, crossing her arms. "I'm not interested in your past. I don't care how you two met. I want to know why you two are showing up in my investigation."

"*I'm* showing up in your investigation," Augie tried. "Not James. I promise."

"August! You both are! Just because James was not at the scene doesn't mean I don't have him connected through different avenues. Now, tell me what I need to know!"

"Like what?"

"Like, when's the last time you spoke with him?"

"Just today."

"When?"

"Right before I got here."

"What did you talk about?"

"Him letting me stay here. He said I could stay as long as I want, rent-free."

"Where's he staying?"

Augie shrugged. "I don't know."

"Where's he right now?"

"I don't know."

Hartley bit her lip. "When is he getting here?" Augie looked nervous as he shook his head.

Hartley threw up her hands in disappointment, yet the Londoner hurriedly answered. "I swear. I don't know. If I knew, I'd tell you. That's the truth. He said he had to get something done, and then would be by."

"What was he going to do?" Hartley asked. His face told her before he opened his mouth. "What *has* he told you? Doesn't look like much."

"It hasn't been! He asked a favor."

"And you just accepted, without anything to go on?"

He stiffened up slightly. "I went on the fact that he's a friend. That's enough for me. He asked me to help him figure things out, and I said yes."

"What were you helping him out with?"

"Finding out who killed his parents."

* * * * *

"Jay, answer me," Nolan said.

"Yeah, Jay. Answer your boss." Dane could not help himself.

Ratliff set his jaw and stared to his superior. "I'd like to wait until Jo gets —"

"Jo's busy, right, detective?" Nolan said. "Isn't that what you said?"

"She is, sir, but she'll —"

"Then you better start explaining."

Ratliff blinked several times in succession, trying to erase the fact that his partner's ass of a brother was smiling wide. "Sir, I think maybe we should speak in private."

"I think you should tell me what the fuck is going on. Is there any truth to this?" Ratliff remained silent until the thundering fists of Captain Henry Nolan came crashing down upon his desk surface, shaking papers and pens alike, pulling from those sitting around the table an instinctive jerk.

Jacoby lowered his head and succumbed to the request of information. "Through the cell phone records of Korhan Karaca, we were able to determine that our vic and James Graiser had been in contact as of late. After hearing about Damian Verland, Jo and I went over there. The video surveillance showed James entering Verland's home through the rear door, empty-handed, and then leaving later on with a file box."

"What was in the box?" Nolan questioned.

"According to Verland's attorney, Gregory Faulk, probably some sort of financial records that they had been searching for. Everything else was accounted for."

Nolan thought for a moment. "So what does this have to do with your current case?"

"As far as we can tell at this moment, nothing."

"What about James? Where does he intersect with this?"

"Besides the phone records, we're not sure. It's something we're going to pursue, though. We know his family and Korhan's were close before the Graisers were killed. Maybe they keep in touch." He shrugged.

"James and a druggie criminal that attacks cops?" Dane asked.

"Stranger things have happened," Ratliff replied.

"Okay," Nolan said. "Where is Jo?"

"Sir, Detective Hartley wanted to confront James regarding his appearances in our cases before officially interviewing him."

"Our cases? And which cases are you talking about?"

"Karaca's and Verland's. I know, I know," he said, halting the interruption that was about to spew forth. "Verland was out of our hands. But it was a large case we were assigned to, and you know how Jolene works. She thought it better to speak to James face to face before pulling the cop routine." That seemed enough of a reason for Nolan, who rolled his eyes and nodded his head.

"Let's not forget their history, too," Dane said with a chuckle. "I mean, I would assume it would be hard to arrest someone you've fucked before, right?"

"Dane," Nolan said. "Shut up. I don't need your lip in here right now. What I want to know is how you knew James was at Verland's."

Dane continued to smile. "Because he came to see me, too."

"About what?" Ratliff asked.

"Well, about helping him, of course."

"And what are you helping him with?" Nolan questioned.

Dane glanced between the duo, a smirk slithering its way onto his face in a sickening manner. Ratliff immediately fought the urge to reach out and punch him once more.

THIRTY-FIVE

"Wait, wait, wait," Hartley said, the bridge of her nose wedged between a thumb and index finger. "What do you mean he's trying to figure out who killed his parents?"

"What's there to understand?" Augie boldly questioned. The look the detective sent his way curbed his confidence. "Look, he calls me one day and figures that, since I'm coming into town, he could depend on me to look for this guy."

"You mean Korhan," Hartley responded.

Augie nodded. "He said he needed me to find him to start connecting the dots back to his parents."

"Why now?"

Augie shrugged, a nervousness building under his collar due to the detective's obvious dislike of his ignorance. "All I can tell you is that when I found him, I immediately disliked him. Have you met that fuck?"

Hartley remained silent, remembering her confrontation with him in her apartment. Finally, she spoke. "Why were you meeting Karaca that day?"

"To take him to breakfast," Augie answered quickly.

"To take him to breakfast? August, you just told me you disliked him!"

He held up a finger. "First, it's Augie. Only my parents call me August. And second, it's what James asked me to do."

"Why?"

"He wanted him close. He was giving Korhan money to try and keep him around. He thought maybe the drug haze would go away long enough for him to remember something worthwhile."

"And what if he didn't?"

"I guess James was willing to part with his funds, if only for that chance."

"What was the money being used for?"

"What was Korhan using it for? I imagine it was for drugs."

"Did James know that?"

"I'm not sure what James thought. He's not stupid though. I would assume he knew what it was going towards."

"I'm sure he did," Jolene stated bluntly.

* * * * *

"I'm sorry, cap," Ratliff said, cutting off his superior. Nolan stalled and waved a hand in submission. Jacoby turned to Dane. "Why would James come to *you*? I have a hard time believing that you'd be his go-to guy."

"What, you expect him to come to you? You've been wanting to dip your pen in another man's ink since the day you got —"

"Fuck off, Dane! Just answer the question, will you?"

"Hey, from what I know, he did try to connect with you guys. He made an appearance at Jo's one night, but apparently things didn't go well for him." He looked at Ratliff, the detective raising his face toward the ceiling, a clarity rising to the surface.

"When was this?" Nolan asked, his weary eyes lowering to the desktop.

"The night we nabbed Doug Merlowe," Jacoby answered, rubbing his chin. The captain gave him a curious look. "After Freddy's," he continued. "Jolene asked me to walk her home and when we got there, James pulled up in a cab, saw both of us, and then took off."

"Why wasn't I told of it?"

"With all due respect, sir, there wasn't anything to report. He didn't say anything to either of us, and, at the time, he wasn't on our radar for anything. To be honest, Jolene and I were a little taken aback by it. We both figured he was there because …" He paused and made a quick sideways glance at the journalist, knowing full-well Dane was lying in wait for ammunition for his next verbal assault. "We figured he was there due to his past involvement with Jo, sir."

* * * * *

"So you were his contact when he was in the Caribbean," Jolene said aloud, though the comment was directed into the stale air of the apartment, a thought that was released into the universe as her mind tried to process what exactly was going on.

"How do you know he was in the Caribbean?"

Jolene turned to him and furrowed her brow. "Because I'm good at what I do, Augie," she replied. "He showed up one night at my place." Augie began to nod his head. "You already know that, don't you?"

"He came from a meeting with me and Korhan. It was his first night back in the States."

"What was the meeting about?" Hartley asked. Augie shook his head, though Jolene could tell it was not due to the fact he did not know. The look that spread across his face she had seen hundreds of times on others she had interviewed or interrogated over the span of her career. It was the look of complete understanding, a clearness that arose when one witnessed a horrendous crime, or knew too much that viciously ate away at them until one could bare it no more. "Augie," she said, pulling his eyes to her. She remained strong, yet allowed a subtle softness to sneak out and mask the detective in her. "What was said at your meeting?"

Augie tried to force a smirk, yet failed. Instead, he answered quickly. "Bloody crazy shit."

* * * * *

"You said you had something to help us out?" Nolan pushed. "Something about an old case?"

Dane nodded his head. "Absolutely. But before we get into it, let's clear up some things. Deal?" Nolan gave in, handing the floor, for the meantime, to the man before him. "Great. I'm a journalist, as you know. I've done some shitty things in my day to get information, but, I assure you, this is not one of those times. For once, you could say this evidence sort of fell into my lap. It's funny that —"

"Jesus, man!" Ratliff exclaimed.

"Ratliff," Nolan said, quieting his detective. He turned his attention back to Dane. "Get to the point."

"All I want is exclusives to interviews and an inside look at what goes on."

"Are you serious?" Ratliff asked incredulously.

"Hey, it fits in perfectly with what I do," the reporter answered, throwing his arms wide. "Trust me, you're going to want this shit!"

"Trust you? That's not going to happen anytime —"

"Calm down, both of you!" the captain yelled. The pair before him quieted and shifted in their respective seats. "Now, let's just deal with this in steps. You and I both know how this works. Obstruction of justice, freedom of the press ..." He waved his hand before him. "If it's worth our while, I'll allow a somewhat sidelined version of our leads. As long as you understand, Mr. Hartley, that, regardless of your family connections, if I see one iota of confidential information in print, I'll arrest your ass!"

Dane smiled. "I'm sure my family connection wouldn't think twice to give you her own handcuffs." He watched as Ratliff shook his head, obviously not in line with the current route of this conversation. Hartley had just the thing to reel him back in. "Anyone been looking into the Graiser case lately?"

* * * * *

Jolene sat at the kitchen table with her elbows on her knees and her hands folded before her, the words spoken by August Hughes racing through her mind at a whirlwind of a pace. She had never thought his world and hers would be so intertwined, so chaotically weaved together, professionally and personally. Yet here she was, months off from having spoken to the long-lost James, though feeling as if they were living the same effects of a past not so distant. The fact that James had come back to the city of Chicago to search out the events that led to his parents' murders was a heavy burden she, herself, knew too well. She had read the files, seen all the gruesome images within the folders.

Yet nothing could have led her to imagine the parallels between her own recent investigations and what James and Augie had heard directly from Korhan's mouth. Karaca, himself, had been there the night of Michael and Amelia Graiser's demise. Luke Moran had walked the halls of James's parents' vacation home that fateful evening, her very own recurring nightmare once more reaching out to her from the past.

Jolene lifted her head and stared through her handcuffed friend. Finally, she focused on him and said, "Augie, I need you to try and remember the other name." It had been a piece of information in which the Londoner could not bring to the surface, regardless of how hard he tried.

He shook his head. "I'm sorry, detective. I was pretty stoned. And it was a complete shock that Korhan was there himself. I just kind of zoned everything else out."

"Would James remember it?"

"Of course. I know he —" Just then Hartley turned her head to the right, her gaze falling to the floor and the space underneath the doorway that glowed with the hallway fluorescents. Augie leaned forward and followed her line of vision, noticing, as she had earlier, the light diminish as someone stepped in front of the entranceway.

"Looks like we can ask him now," Hartley said as she stood, nervousness at seeing her one-time lover creeping through her body, butterflies starting to swarm abruptly within her stomach. Augie stood as well, though the movements were labored with his hands secured behind his back. The moment Hartley turned to him to tell him to stay put, she could sense something was wrong. She gave him a questioning look just as the doorknob began to turn.

* * * * *

Before either of them could answer, a knock at the office door pulled Ratliff's and Nolan's attention away from Dane. The reporter glanced over his shoulder quickly before returning his gaze back to the officers. "See," he said, the smile spread across his face. "I told you I was his go-to guy."

James stepped into the room and placed a brown file box on the floor next to him. "More like my last ditch effort," he replied, throwing a condescending smirk Dane's way. He remained standing and looked among the group before turning and searching the pit. James turned back and met Ratliff's gaze. "Where's Jo?"

THIRTY-SIX

From Hartley's position, there had been just enough time and space to dart towards the door and flip the lock before the person on the other side made an appearance. She was unsure as to who was lurking just beyond the threshold, but Augie's look of downright confusion put her nerves on edge. Sure, the elderly next door neighbor could be making his rounds, checking on the detective as she sifted through the life of the long-gone James Graiser, seeing if she was nearing completion or needed assistance so he could return to his apartment with his spare key to enjoy a day jam-packed with movies and naps. Hartley hoped it was him. She wished the quick set of the bolt would only cause some mild irritation on the man's part, a hindrance in his otherwise leisurely day, a small setback that could be remedied with a clear of the throat and a request to unlock.

Yet, that was wishful thinking, and a pipedream Hartley did not receive. She noticed Augie moving cautiously toward the hall, stepping backward in a slow-motion moonwalk that leant, in itself, a certain eeriness to their current plight. She watched the handle jiggle ever so subtly, a few hasty twists in either direction that were thwarted by the bronze mechanism. Jolene glanced to Augie and motioned him to move into the bathroom as she reached to her hip and pulled her firearm. She quietly maneuvered into the space between the hallway wall and the table, setting herself just behind the hinges.

The detective glanced to the crack beneath the entrance once more, watching the darkened shadow shift lazily back and forth before giving way to yet another try at the handle. The knob turned slightly before halting, only to give way in the other direction with the same result. Hartley heard a grunt from the hallway, a possible curse or cough, a definite masculinity driving it. She began to reach out to the knob, yet halted as the shadow beneath the door began to lighten, giving way to the bright stream of sunshine and allowing Hartley and Augie a moment's relaxation as the thought of the curious individual walking back toward the stairwell or elevator filled their vision.

It was only a moment, however.

As Hartley glanced down the dim-lit hallway to where Augie waited, body half jutting out from the darkness that was James's bathroom, a loud concussion exploded to her right, the frame of the door cracking and shaking, the sound deafening as the man on the other side rammed into the entranceway. The first attack did not break through, though it did cause enough of an abrupt shock that Hartley instinctively folded herself into the wall, shoulders rising to protect her head as she leaned heavily against the drywall with her left leg flexed and nearly locked in place. Augie, startled, began to edge his way farther into the apartment, bouncing ungracefully off the walls as he tried move to James's bedroom while keeping an eye on the action just behind him.

The second attempt at the entrance did the trick, and it was employed with enough power to send the door slamming inward towards Hartley. She saw, just as the heavy, wooden panel collided with her elbow, the assailant burst forward, a gun in hand as he toppled into the apartment and landed near the end of the couch, eyes up and scanning the room until they found Augie near the back of the corridor. His momentum carried him to the floor, dislodging the firearm and sending it towards the edge of the room, just out of reach.

Hartley had tried to ward off the approaching gate, yet could not in the position she had taken during the initial bombardment. The knob came crashing in, striking her on the very top of the hip bone, a minor injury that caused an immediate and excruciating pain that burned into her thigh and pelvic area. The rest of the surface connected with her body and head, smashing her frame between it and the wall with enough force to push her right shoulder into the drywall. A muted screech escaped her body as the air in her lungs shot forward, bringing her to a knee as she tried to regain her breath and ward off the stars that began to swirl.

It took only a couple seconds for her to put the pain aside, lock it up in its rightful place, to be dealt with later. Now, as she pushed herself up, she watched as the intruder regained his feet, eyes still down the hall to Augie, who turned the corner and disappeared into the bedroom.

Hartley could not see the man's face as he made his first step towards the hall, yet, knew without a doubt, in his stumbling entrance, he also had not seen the detective. She raised up and lifted her gun. "Police! Don't move!"

The directive, spit into the suddenly active apartment, spun the man on his heels, nearly sending him off balance once again as he caught himself on the armrest of the sofa. His eyes locked with Hartley's, and at that exact moment, Jolene looked upon the scar zigzagging crudely across the man's temple, the wound she had inflicted the morning of Karaca's murder. His arms rose in the air in a submissive display.

"Millers Renholm, get on the —" The door came flying in her direction, caused by a quick grasp and throw by the intruder before her. Jolene squeezed the trigger just as the hinged wooden panel connected with her wrist. Hartley heard Millers growl, yet could not see the outcome of her shot as she staggered into the table next to her, almost losing her service piece while stumbling to a knee. Again and again, with rapid succession, the door was employed against her, kicked or thrown with a pitcher's velocity, connecting again and again with the detective's body as she tried to maneuver herself from her unwanted position between it and the kitchen table and chairs. The impacts were minimal, yet came with enough will that they kept Hartley off balance, one arm holding her body against a dining seat, the other raised in an attempt to soften the impression the door made.

Her situation was precarious, to say the least. She knew for a fact that Millers's gun lay just behind him, mere feet away, a close enough distance for him to attempt to dive for it. Yet, she also understood that he was not taking that chance. He realized, or so she thought, that the detective he now pummeled with an apartment door still had a grasp of her own weapon, and his odds of jumping into the center of the room, grabbing his gun from the floor and turning to use it, were some he did not wish to play. The only road for him, at the moment, was to keep her at bay, to try and dislodge her own service piece by whatever means necessary.

* * * * *

What the fuck? was all Millers could think as he repeatedly pushed the apartment door at her. *What the fuck is she doing here?* He grabbed the rebounding gate yet again, this time lining it up for a moment as he placed his foot on the surface and chucked it her way ferociously. He had wanted her to fall, to stumble, to lose balance and collide with the ground. Anything to give him a moment to do one of two things: turn to grab his weapon or bolt into the hallway and out of the apartment building.

She knew his name, which was not a total surprise in the grand scheme of things. There were multiple avenues that could have brought that realization to light. The one he chose to believe at the moment was that he had been too late in dealing with Karaca, that James and this fucking red-headed

346

nuisance had procured whatever information they had been searching for from the Turk and were in cahoots with the Chicago police.

Millers turned his attention back to the officer again, to her fleeting glances through dark locks at his scarred countenance, the grizzled face of what most likely appeared to be a madman, teeth displayed in a growl as he heaved the door again and again. His assault was working. The detective's hold on the table was faltering, and he could see the damage was being successfully inflicted.

He felt himself smile, the sweat running down his brow trickling to his lips, the saltiness tasted on his tongue. He felt a rush of adrenaline and euphoria take over his body. He felt invincible. And his eyes widened as he looked to the authoritative beauty before him, nearly crumbled to the ground in submission. His submission. He imagined one final thrust of the door, a weapon dislodged and sent skittering across the linoleum of the kitchen. He could see himself standing over the wounded officer, could feel the power in his hands as he bent her to his will, the desperate pleas falling from her lips like the tears from her eyes. He heard the raw slap against her skin, the successive blows he rained upon her as her clothes fell about her in torn ribbons. *The things I can do to you*, he thought. *The things I will do to you.*

His daydream ended abruptly, however, far short of the sick, disgusting hopes that clouded his vision, placing blinders on his focus and allowing the red-head down the hall a free run at him. The collision was jarring.

* * * * *

Hartley had finally gotten her left foot steadily underneath her. She was definitely in pain, though the majority of it reverberated from her hip. Her right elbow, the first point of contact for the barrage Millers sent her way, was split open, though she felt it was a wound that could be healed with a dap of antiseptic and a Band-Aid. Several of the connections had indeed been fiercer than the previous, a couple making contact with the crown of her head as she ducked it towards her shoulder for protection. However, due to the unusual stance she had found herself in, Hartley was able to set her right foot in a specific position, thus largely consuming some of the force that was meant to render her inactive.

She looked up to Millers between blows, glancing to his face, running her eyes across the snarl and to the scar slicing across the side of his head. His eyes were crazed, to say the least, and Hartley swore he was in another world, living a fantasy that existed somewhere in his thoughts.

Just as she was planning on throwing herself to the floor with her gun raised, she saw a flash of movement from the hallway. Augie, having stepped through his handcuffed wrists, sprinted from the corridor and rammed into Millers with a sickening crash, sending both men sprawling to the floor in opposite directions and affording Hartley the opportunity to take a breath. Augie slid to a stop near the weapon in the room, though, by his jerky movements and low-pitched whine, she could see he was in pain. Millers, being the thicker individual out of the two, bounced off the doorjamb and tumbled into the hallway, catching himself before he spilled onto the floor. It was at that moment, hand on the ground in a three-point stance to balance his weight, that Millers realized he had been shot, this time through the meaty section of his right shoulder. He winced in pain and pushed himself up, taking off down the hallway just as an elderly man stepped out to his right.

Hartley stepped towards the doorway and nearly collapsed, a searing burn shooting through her midsection as a result of her injured hip. She steadied herself on the closest chair and bit her lip. "Augie, are you okay?" The man rolled from his side and regained his knees, his head pressed to the floor as he waved her off.

Hartley gingerly took the few steps to the couch and raised her weapon, edging out into the hallway just as James's neighbor approached. He screamed and raised his arms in surrender as her gun turned in his direction. Hartley dropped it immediately and looked past him down the emptied corridor. "Where'd he go?" she asked the man. He pointed in the opposite direction, arms still held high. She breathed in deeply, exhaling the air slowly and placing her hands on her knees. "Shit!" she whispered, leaning carefully into the doorframe, eyes scanning her surroundings as thoughts swirled madly.

THIRTY-SEVEN

The papers James had brought in the brown box were still crisp, though slightly yellowed from time. There were smudges across many, and a stack of nearly two dozen had taken the brunt of a misplaced coffee mug. Yet everything was legible, at least from what Nolan and Ratliff could tell as they sifted through the contents with James and Dane hovering over their respective shoulders. Initials. Account numbers. Company names. Years. Dates. All were present, though, not being savvy in the finances other than balancing a checkbook, Nolan tossed his pile back to the surface. "What's all this mean?" Ratliff continued rifling through, shrugging the question to Dane, who was, as much as he hated to admit it, the obvious expert in the room. His answer shocked even Jacoby.

"I'm not sure exactly," the journalist responded, pulling Ratliff's eyes to him, as well as everyone else's in the room. "Listen," he replied quickly, "there's a lot going on in there, and over a long period of time. From what we can guess," he pointed at James, "whatever's in here will either lead us to whoever killed his family, or in the very least, give us some sort of clue."

"And you know that for sure?" Ratliff asked.

"Look, you fuck, I don't —"

"Easy," Ratliff stated, holding up the palm of his hand to Dane. "It's a serious question. This could give the case the kick in the ass it needs. For all I know, there could be a written, signed confession on one of these pages. But it could be a box of worthless files given to you by a desperate man."

"It's not worthless," James answered, defiantly.

"How do you know?" Nolan asked. James remained silent. "Listen, James, I hope you're right. I hope this leads us someplace. The gun from last year obviously didn't give us much to reopen the case. But maybe this will." He paused. "You have to understand though. Sometimes things just don't add up. Ratliff, myself — hell, even Jo! — we need to keep an open mind about everything. We need to figure out what exactly is going on. Why were you at Verland's? Why'd he give you a portion of files when, obviously, his legal situation requires him to pour through them? Are these files detrimental to the case? Is there damning evidence? This, if spun the correct way in court, will make you look like an accessory." He stopped the line of rhetorical questioning and let the words sink in. Dane remained still, an emotionless mask spread across his face.

Ratliff spoke finally. "James, there's things that have gone on, with your parents' case and our current investigation, that need answers. We're not trying to be pricks, regardless of what your new friend here says." Dane smirked and gave the detective the bird. "We're just doing our jobs."

James opened his mouth to speak yet turned his head towards the door and held his tongue. Ratliff and Nolan followed his gaze and watched as a uniformed officer entered with eyes wide and face stricken. "Jay. Sir," he said, looking at each in turn. "Just heard over the wire. Hartley's been in an altercation."

"What?" Ratliff said, standing quickly.

"Where is she?" the captain asked hastily, half rising himself. The uniform gave them the address that had come through. James froze as Ratliff glanced to him. Nolan and Dane remained puzzled. "Where's that? What's at that location?"

James finally answered. "That's my apartment building."

* * * * *

He made it to the bar he knew his associate owned, though the exterior and welcoming neon sign had changed since his last visit nearly a decade prior. Millers burst through the door in a sweat, blood coating his right shoulder and dripping from his hand. He groaned and he shifted his weight quickly, the movement sending a dull pain through his torso.

The establishment was relatively empty, minus a smattering of regulars and an elderly, though rough looking, woman tending the bar, her squat, rotund frame carrying a weight that matched the rest of the patrons. The interior was dark, only a half dozen lights above the tables working correctly. The others buzzed noisily or flickered in a sporadic display, a Morse code of lights grasping onto whatever life was left. The floor was wet, though Millers could not guess if it was from a recent mopping or the previous evening's overspill of beer. By the smell of things, he guessed the latter.

Ginger's Trap had never been in a prime location to become a hit in the city. It was barely a blip on the radar of most folks, the dingy, hole-in-the-wall institution on the other side of town that was unwelcoming of newcomers. Even the name of the place — Ginger's Trap — was wholly standoffish and carried with it a slew of different meanings. Ginger, a former hooker that used to walk the surrounding streets, had been his associate's lover for years. She had been caught transporting drugs into a nearby county and subsequently led police on a fifteen mile chase, in the end escaping her totaled vehicle and losing herself in a nearby city. She came to Millers's associate for assistance and was found two days later floating in the Fox River near St. Charles, two bullet holes evident in her head.

Millers walked to the bar and leaned over, grasping a bottle of vodka and a dirty towel as he sneered at the bartender. She closed her mouth and let his actions go, noticing his wounded arm and the sweat accumulating on his brow. It obviously was not the first time she had witnessed such a scene.

He hurried past two oversized bouncers and down a narrow hallway, coming to a shut wooden door with the word *Private* pasted on a smoky glass pane. Millers pushed through, coming to a halt in the middle of the room, his eyes falling upon his associate behind a rickety desk, a scantily clad, mascara-streaked girl of no more than twenty standing at attention before him. The long-haired man glared at Millers for several moments before reaching into his pocket and pulling out a wad of bills. He slid what appeared to be a couple hundred to her and patted her hand. "Go get yourself cleaned up. Get a good meal."

The girl nodded, wiping a tear away before leaning forward to kiss him on the cheek. She glanced up hurriedly at Millers as she passed, forcing a smile as she exited the room, exchanging her place with the two bouncers as they entered. Millers looked at both of them and shrugged. He turned his eyes back to his associate yet remained silent as he took a gulp from the bottle of vodka.

The long-haired man stared to him for a moment before offering him a seat. "What happened to your arm?" he asked, pulling a guffaw from Millers.

* * * * *

Ratliff raced out of the precinct towards the parking garage against the behest of Captain Nolan. He did not care that his superior wished him to stay put until they had more information. Squads were already en route to the location, he had told him. Jacoby did not seem to hear. Or, if he had, decided against the command of no action to run to the aid of his partner. Nolan half-smiled at the notion of loyalty his detective displayed.

Jacoby reached the pavement outside the station just as his cell phone rang. He stumbled down the last step and looked at the display with a sense of panic and relief. "Jo," he hurried into the mouthpiece. "Are you okay?"

"I'm fine," Hartley replied. "I'm fine."

"Where are you? What happened?"

"Relax, Ratliff," she said, diminishing the anxiety of the situation with her tone. "Millers Renholm happened."

"No," he said, though he believed her unequivocally.

"Yeah," she answered. "He must have been casing the place or something."

"Why would he be doing that?"

"I have no idea. But things are starting to come together a little bit, so maybe we'll add that piece of the puzzle to the mystery as well." She paused. "I have Augie with me."

"Who?" Ratliff questioned.

"August Hughes. The red-head from our crime scene."

"What? How?"

"I'll tell you all about it when I get back there."

"Where are you now?"

"Just about to leave James's place. I've got to return the apartment key to James's neighbor and then we'll be heading back." There was a silence on the other end of the line. "Jay?" she said, unsure if she had lost the connection.

"Jo, James and Dane are here. Captain has them in his office."

It was Hartley's turn to bite her tongue. When she spoke, it was in the form of a hurried one word sentence. "Why?"

"They have the box from Verland's. Looks like there might be some interesting things in there."

"Okay. I'll be back shortly. Make sure they don't go anywhere."

Ratliff said his goodbye and placed his phone back into his pocket, tilting his head toward the sky and taking a deep breath. He spun on his heels and halted immediately as he looked to James standing at the top of the steps, leaning and listening intently to one side of the conversation. His eyes expressed worry, yet, at Ratliff's reaction as he hung up, that melted away.

Jacoby started back up the steps and paused briefly behind Graiser. "She's fine," was all he said, stepping through the door and holding it open for James.

* * * * *

The long-haired man sat as still as a statue as Millers relayed the scenario that had played out at James Graiser's apartment building. Every so often he would shift his weight and reach for the smoldering cigarette resting on an antique ashtray at the edge of the desk, only to take a single drag and return to his initial position. His face displayed no emotion, only a focused interest in the plights of Millers Renholm.

When the story was complete, silence encompassed the room, an uncomfortable, eerie quiet that kept Millers glancing over his shoulders at the bouncers and taking small, unsteady sips from the bottle of vodka. The boisterous, over-aggressive state he had when entering Ginger's Trap had long since dissipated into the muggy atmosphere, replaced now by a sense of foreboding and ill-ease. He had been confident in his initial assault on his associate, getting to the point with earnest and a sense of command, feeling in his blood that his new-found authority would lend him some sort of equality in their unwanted friendship.

Yet, now, as the seconds ticked by in utter stillness, two burly, muscular men standing at attention feet behind him, his associate staring from beneath folded hands and dark sunglasses, Millers's confidence faded, escaped into the air surrounding them, seemingly sucked into the man across from him.

The words that broke the silence only shocked and jarred Millers that much more. "You did what you could," his associate said. "You staked the place out and went in like I asked. What the fuck else are you going to do?" Millers remained motionless, feeling a sense of achievement in the other man's eyes. "Listen we have to deal with this. You're right about that. Go get yourself fucking cleaned up, man. I'll be in touch later. You need a ride to wherever you're going?" Millers thought for a moment before shaking his head. "Good. Get out of here. You'll hear from me soon."

Millers nodded slowly, turning his back on his associate and walking out of the room with a small grin on his face, between the two columns that were the bouncers of Ginger's Trap. He gazed at each in turn as they gave him a slight, acknowledging salute. *Finally, a little fucking respect,* he thought.

THIRTY-EIGHT

She tried to be all business, an expression of indifference walking into the pit with a handcuffed August Hughes being directed by her steady hand. She tried to be the cop, the authority figure she had always been, the one who kept those in a tight line with a quick glance and stern directives. She was about the facts. That was what her job called for. Facts and action, split second decisions followed by an operating procedure that had been engrained in her since her days in the academy.

Yet when Jolene's focus connected with James, all that went out the proverbial window, slipped into the bustling streets of Chicago outside the precinct walls. Her business persona was replaced by anger, a raw, unbridled irritation that she knew came from more than just her current case and that of his parents. She wanted to barge into the break room and scream at the top of her lungs about the disappearing act he had pulled so long ago. She felt the urge to grasp onto his shirt and shake him, to question him about his refusal to face the looming past, however painful that may be. Firsthand, she knew she could not completely understand the abyss that lay below the surface of James Graiser. No one had ever been ripped from her life in such a way, leaving in its wake an emptiness that could not be filled. Yet, Hartley *was* a homicide detective. She knew the ins-and-outs of the emotional toll it took, and had seen those torn apart by tragedy force their way through the near impenetrable barrier of grief and come to terms, if just for a brief moment, in order to help along an investigation.

Hartley hardly noticed her brother reclining in the corner of the couch, one foot outstretched to the coffee table, arm draped over the back. He smirked at her, yet held his tongue as she entered the room. James rose slightly, yet was caught off-guard by her response. "Have a seat," she ordered, not looking to him.

She veered Augie to a wooden chair next to the couch and sat him down. "What about the cuffs?" he asked.

"What about them?" she replied, moving opposite the sofa and staring intently at the Londoner to her left. Augie nearly responded, yet remained quiet as Hartley crossed her arms and stood erect next to her partner.

After several moments of silence, James swallowed hard and spoke, his voice weak as he tried to gain some initial ground. "Jo, please," he said. "Augie has done nothing —"

"It's detective," she interrupted, eyes still on Augie.

James nodded and continued. "Detective Hartley, Augie's done nothing wrong. Everything —"

"See, he has, though, James," she answered. "He fled the scene of a crime."

"Was he a suspect?" James asked.

Jolene finally squared him up, her eyes burning as they fell to his, surprised by the lack of intensity countering her glare. "He's a person of interest," she responded. "He obviously has some connection with our victim, since he was in conversation when the whole thing occurred. That makes him very important in our eyes."

"Same with you," Ratliff added quickly, pointing to him.

James glanced to Augie quickly before turning back to the detectives. "We had nothing to do with Korhan's murder," he said, placing a hand on his chest. "Augie was just —"

"I know what Augie was doing for you," Jolene said.

"Then you know he had nothing to do with it."

"I know he didn't pull the trigger. I know he wasn't the one who murdered Korhan directly." She paused, thinking of the words about to form. They were not so much an accusation, however, when she spoke them, they did not fall far from it. "I know Korhan was there when your parents were killed. What I don't know is what your role in this investigation is?"

Ratliff looked sideways at her, pondering the route this line of questioning was taking. "What does that mean?" James asked, a hint of disapproval in his voice.

"It means you had motive to want Korhan dead," Dane said. He could not help but add fuel to the already intense fire.

"Wait," James said, standing. "You really think I could have orchestrated this?"

Hartley halted, thinking back to their first meeting, a brief moment in the precinct long ago when James had confessed to her about an exchange between Benjamin Ochoa and him, a conversation that had been immortalized via the crime scene photographer. She had asked him, in response to his admission of offering Ochoa money for information regarding Daniel Vincent's killer, what the exchange of funds would accomplish. James had replied shamefully, "To have someone kill the man who killed my friend."

Her thoughts returned in a screeching fashion as she became aware James was still standing, hand to his chest as he stared to her. The rest of the room remained motionless, awaiting any form of response, any answer that would turn the conversation in a less accusatory direction. Instead, Jolene matched his glare and responded, "It wouldn't be the first time you wanted someone dead."

The words were like poison, and they tasted bitter on Jolene's tongue moments after they fell. Dane whistled a high-pitched toot, which carried with it a not-so-subtle severity that Hartley knew was meant to point out the harshness in the comment. Ratliff shifted in his position, his elbow making contact with hers on purpose, a sign that he either had her back or he was alerting her to be slightly gentler. However, it was James's reaction that pulled her to the present, slapped her in the face with a realization that perhaps, just perhaps, she was retaliating in a way that was less than professional. Graiser remained staring at her for several seconds before slowly, gingerly sliding back into his seat, eyes down to the table. It was the same look she had seen right before he had entered the taxi after witnessing her and Jacoby kiss. It was the look of defeat.

* * * * *

"Are you okay?" Ratliff asked as he turned into the pit and followed his partner to her desk.

Hartley pulled her chair out, yet remained standing, running her fingers through her long, dark locks, head tilted to the ceiling as she sighed and scrunched up her brow. "Yeah, I'm sorry," she said looking to him with hands clasped behind her head. "I'm just ... I'm just pissed, I guess."

"No shit?" he answered with a grin.

Hartley could not muster a smile, instead shaking her head and bringing her palms together just below her chin. "It's just ... It's just everything that's happened, with this case, with his parents' case."

"With him," Ratliff added, the phrase walking a tight line between a statement and question.

Hartley lowered her head and tried her best *Are you serious?* look, yet faltered. "Everything," she stated.

"Hey, I get it. I do. You know I'm behind you all the way. All this pent-up emotion that's coming out, it's understandable. But, before Nolan gets on your ass, just let me say it: try to remember why we're questioning him. Try to keep some of it bottled up for a time outside of this investigation. Everything in here needs to be focused. Regardless of how absurd it may be, James has a connection to our victim, and a recent one. Not just from his past. He also is tied up with our favorite deceased ex-billionaire." He paused before continuing. "And he has an emotional connection with you. And vice versa." Jolene tilted her head to the side, a feeble attempt at countering his claim. He reached out and grazed her arm with his fingers. "I'm here for you, whatever route you want to go."

Hartley forced a smile. "Put them in Interrogation One."

* * * * *

Detective Jolene Hartley knew the inner workings of the precinct like the back of her hand. She could walk the pit floor blind-folded, brew a pot of coffee and make it back to her desk without spilling a drop. She knew the mood of her superior based on the way he slouched in his chair or which lights he had on or whether or not the blinds to the windows were drawn. She could ascertain the success rate of her requesting additional manpower depending on the fact if Louis Armstrong was pouring from Nolan's office as opposed to The Who's *Teenage Wasteland*.

She also understood the stigma that went along with teeing up a conversation in the cozy warmth of the break room versus cold, bright Interrogation One. The couch, with its soft but worn cushions, whispered safety, tickled at the thought of being your grandmother's home, a living room where one could waste the day away eating cookies and drinking hot chocolate while she waited hand-and-foot on you.

Interrogation, however, was nothing but business. It was a serious, uncompromising room that imposed its will, regardless if an interrogating officer was accompanying you or not.

Ratliff was right: Hartley needed to push her training and experience to the forefront. Everything personally that had happened between her and James had to be left behind. There would be a time and a place for that, but it was not here.

She stared through the interrogation mirror at James and Augie as they sat stock-still at the table, the former leaning forward with hands folded and eyes staring into the past. Graiser did not have the look of a guilty man, and Hartley, in her initial judgment, believed he had nothing to do with Korhan's murder. Yet, she had been wrong before, and regardless of their one-time connection, she needed to see this conversation through.

Augie, hands recently freed from the cuffs that had graced him since before the assault hours earlier, rubbed his chest and glanced around, his gaze randomly falling on that of his neighbor for a brief moment before sliding to the mirror in an attempt to visualize the scene beyond. He appeared nervous, though, again, Hartley believed it to be a reaction from the room itself. She stood for nearly twenty minutes, waiting and watching, hoping an exchange would occur between the two to bring about a starting point for her. It did not happen. Augie seemed to be on the verge of speaking to James on several occasions, however, those uncertain times disappeared immediately. If it had been anyone else, Hartley would have thought the silence odd, as if the story between the duo had been so well rehearsed that it did not need to be studied for another second and the memorized lines would spew forth with little effort and even less conviction.

Finally, she decided to enter. She called out to Ratliff as she moved from one room to the other, stepping through the threshold and into the tension that Interrogation One seemed to hold at all times, like its very own atmosphere of worry and consternation. Ratliff followed close behind, shutting the door and taking a seat next to his partner, across from the pair.

"Jo," James began, but was immediately cut off by her intense glare.

"James," she said sternly, "for the foreseeable future, and especially in here, I'm not Jo. I'm either detective, or Detective Hartley. I'll even go as far as allowing ma'am. But if I hear you call me Jo again, this is going to get a lot more uncomfortable. Do we understand each other?" He nodded his head. Augie chuckled. "And Mr. Hughes, regardless of your assistance today within Mr. Graiser's home, I'd be careful how you handle this interview. London's not that far away, and I'm sure with your recent activities here in the States, the government would have no problem deporting you." Augie clammed up quickly, leaving Ratliff as the only one in the room amused.

THIRTY-NINE

Jolene could feel a pang of guilt course through her body, an uncomfortable, scratchy presence that wrapped its bristly, penetrating tentacles around her insides and squeezed without relent. She was angry at James for everything he did, and did not do, but this feeling, this new, unwanted sensation, arose from the fact that she was formally interrogating her one-time lover in connection with a homicide. It was as simple as that. She had had no qualms when questioning her own brother during the Bartholomew Reed investigation, so why was James any different? As unwelcome as it was, it was necessary, and that is what she told herself as she began. "Why did you contact Korhan?" she asked him.

James leaned forward. "It was the only lead I had. If there had been some other starting point, believe me, I would've taken it."

"Why not come to the police?"

"It's a closed case. Still is, if I'm not mistaken."

"It is, but enough has come to light to possibly open it back up."

"Yeah, but everything that's come to light has been because I came back to deal with it. Not because of what happened to Korhan."

Jolene thought about it for a moment, realizing, for the most part, James was right. Korhan's death, without James and Augie appearing randomly in less than desirable spots, would have been nothing more than the murder of a criminal, an unfortunate ending to a miserable life that should have been played out behind bars. Without James, there really was no headway on the Graiser murders, no obtuse connection to Damian Verland, and no crime scene to place Augie at. Jolene went back to her line of questioning. "What did you hope Korhan would tell you?"

"Anything. I was just hoping he could give me something useful."

"And did he?"

"Pardon the interruption, love," Augie said, "I don't mean to be rude, but didn't we kind of cover this all at his place?"

"Augie, shut it," was all she said.

"What *were* you doing at my apartment today?" James asked with a quiet tone.

"Coming to talk," Jolene responded after a moment. "You've been showing up places within these investigations, and I want to know why."

"Then ask." The phrase was put out there in such a way that Jolene was thrown off-guard. He did not use the words as an attack. They were simply an honest projection, an invitation of sorts into his mind and motives.

Hartley leaned into the table. "Why now? Why get in contact with Korhan now? Why not ... that day?"

"The day you mentioned my father's gun? I didn't want to deal with any of it back then. So I didn't. It wasn't until my friend in Jamaica started hounding me about everything here, in Chicago, that I realized I needed to face it all. Korhan was just the only piece of the puzzle that I had."

"And you didn't think to come to us? Your father's gun could have been the key that opened Pandora's Box on your parents' case. We could have been looking into it all along. Why take matters into your own hands? Why not check and see if anything had come about since you left?"

"Detective, I know what investigations are like, and unless you have an in, or are lucky enough to get stabbed and watched after by the cops themselves, you're pretty much left in the dark." He forced a quick smile, the reference to their initial meeting pulling a fleeting emotion to the surface. "And, in answer to your question, I did try and come to the cops. I just showed up at apparently the wrong time." James glanced between the detectives and looked down to his folded hands. Hartley tried to stay stoic, yet the mention of the uncomfortable occasion forced her to shift in her seat and glance at her partner.

"James," Ratliff said, breaking the silence. "What were you doing at Damian Verland's home? Did you know him? I mean, more than the news coverage?"

James shook his head. "No. Had never met him before in my life."

"So why go to his house? Especially after what happened to Karaca. It seems a little reckless."

"I had gone to Dane for some help —"

"Dane," was all Hartley said, grinding her teeth and shaking her head. "Why?"

James could not help but to giggle. "He's not a saint, but he knows how to research. I went to him because … Well, because he knows how to find things out. He has sources. He ended up finding some information about Verland and his lawyer, and it just seemed like the next logical step."

"Why?" Ratliff inquired. "Why is Verland and Faulk the next logical step?"

James shrugged. "Because Gregory Faulk used to be on my father's research team. I thought it was … I don't know if *strange* is the right word or not. But it intrigued me. Another connection to my parents, you know?"

Hartley scratched her brow and cleared her throat. "I'd like to get back to Korhan," she said. "I know where you were at that time, Augie. Where were you?"

"Drinking coffee, about to go see your brother."

"What about?"

"I needed help."

"And you think Dane would be the type to help out? You remember him, don't you?"

"I do. That's why I brought ten grand with me."

"Wait," Ratliff said, holding up his palm. "You gave that prick ten thousand dollars?"

"Yeah!" Augie chimed in. "You gave him ten thousand dollars?"

James paused as his gaze ricocheted around the room. He pointed at Ratliff and responded, "Yes." He then turned his attention to Augie. "Yes. But you're getting a free place to stay for as long as you want."

"Fucking better be!" he answered, giving James a wink and a tap on the back.

"What was the money for?" Hartley continued.

"At first, I had no clue. I'd done some looking into the case, pretty much internet stuff that I remembered from back then. I looked into every detail I could find, went over every meeting I had had with the detectives in Wisconsin. Nothing really caught my eye. So I went with the only other lead I had. I recruited Augie here to help me out. He was coming over from England and —"

"I understand his role, James," Hartley blurted.

"Then you can understand why I needed to come back and look into things."

"No. No, I can't." James turned his palms to the ceiling, a questioning action meant for her to explain. "I can understand the curiosity that rises in a person. I understand the need to *want* to figure things out. What I don't understand is vigilante work. It's not helpful. To you or to the Chicago Police Department. And it puts us in a difficult situation."

"You mean the police?" Augie chimed in.

Jolene glanced to him before returning her gaze to James. "To the police. Me. Ratliff. Anyone who has a personal interest in what is going on."

"And why is there such a *personal interest* anyway?" James asked. "What does my parents' case have to do with anything that's going on now?"

"Maybe due to the fact that everything seems to be intersecting, James," Hartley retorted, a bit more forceful than intended.

"Meaning what?"

"Meaning Luke Moran."

James turned to Augie with a confused look, his brow furrowed and eyes penetrating, the same countenance spread across Ratliff's face. The Londoner spoke up. "Look, mate, I had to tell her."

"You could have talked with me first," James said.

"Moran?" asked Ratliff.

"No, I couldn't have," Augie responded, sitting up in his chair. "You haven't really been a bloody fountain of truth lately."

"Augie, I told you —"

"You told me what I needed to know. What you wanted me to know. And that's fine with me, mate. I didn't push. But don't get all defensive when I was the one getting backed into the corner."

"Excuse me," Ratliff said loudly, pulling the focus to him. "Luke Moran?" The question was released into the room, yet everyone knew it was directed to Hartley.

"The night James got into the States, he and Augie met with Korhan."

"Where?"

"The same drug house he was killed in front of," Augie said, sinking back into his seat.

"It appears that not only Korhan, but also Luke Moran, were there the night James's parents were murdered."

"What?" Ratliff peered around the room. "Why didn't you come and tell us?"

"I told you already," James said, rubbing his palms against his forehead. "I did try to go to you. Things just … Things just didn't work out." He paused before continuing. "After that, I figured I'd try my luck with your brother."

There was a silence in the room as everyone's thoughts drifted to times of the recent past. Finally, Jolene leaned forward. "Here's the issue, James. This piece of information is a double-edged sword for you."

"How so?"

"The positive side graces us with a new avenue in your parents' case. I'm not sure what, if anything, we can find, but at least we have new information."

"What's the other side?" Augie asked for his friend.

Jolene glanced at Ratliff before returning her focus to James. "That it gives you motive for Korhan's murder."

"Get the fuck out of here!" James said to no one in particular, raising his face toward the ceiling, the phrase something wholly un-James as she knew him. "Do you really think I could do that?"

"Honestly, no. I don't think so. But I can't be certain. People change, James. People can change in short periods of time."

"Apparently," he responded.

Jolene set her jaw, yet took the criticism in stride. "What I need is for you to prove that you had nothing to do with this. Show me that you didn't use Augie to keep tabs on where Korhan was, to tail him until the right moment when you could get payback for what was done to you and your family."

"If I wanted to kill Korhan, I would have done it when he told me he was a part of their deaths. But I didn't."

"Prove it."

"How can I?" he said loudly into the room. "I just didn't do it! You have to take my word on it!"

"If I took everyone's words, there would be a lot of guilty people walking the streets."

"But I'm not guilty of any of this!"

"James, I go on facts! And the fact of the matter is this: Korhan Karaca is dead, killed by three men in broad daylight, with your associate here in attendance. Beyond that, I've got nothing."

"That's right! You've got nothing. You have no proof that I was involved in any of this."

"You *were* involved in it. That I do have proof of. To what extent is the question."

"What can I do? What can I do to make you understand that I had nothing to do with his murder?"

"Whoa," Augie interrupted. "Let's just settle this down a little —"

"Augie, stay out of this," Hartley replied, eyes never leaving James. "Who's Morgan Keller?"

"Who?"

"Morgan Keller. Who is he?"

"I've never heard of her."

"It's a guy, James."

"Fine! I've never heard of *him*."

"Augie?" She watched Augie shrug from the corner of her eye. "Who is he, Augie?"

"I haven't the slightest," the Londoner replied.

"So, neither one of you know who Morgan Keller is?" Silence. "Did you recognize the man in the apartment today, Augie?" Again, a shrug. "He was one of the shooters, Augie. Are you telling me it didn't register in your head that you had seen him before?"

"It's not like I could exactly focus in on the details of the event, mate," he answered, a flustered tone carrying the words.

"Augie, a man was murdered directly in front of you! And you're telling me you can't remember anything? I find that hard to believe."

"Jo," Ratliff said, trying to pull his heated partner's attention to him.

"So I'm guessing the name Millers Renholm means nothing to either of you?"

"Love, I wish I could help, but —"

"Come on, guys!" She yelled.

"Jo," Ratliff said again. "Maybe we should take a break."

She paid no heed to him. Instead, with loaded words ready to spring forward, she turned her gaze to James and halted. The room, ablaze with an exchange that, Hartley knew, would have broken many suspects, had turned cold and silent. Before her, eyes wide and to the table, a stricken look spread across his face, sat her one-time friend. Gone was the annoyance and ill-will he had worn on his sleeve moments before, replaced by a gut-wrenching shock and awe at something she had said. "James?" she said, the fury extinguished. "James?" His gaze slid from the tabletop to her, and she could immediately see the gleam off his tear-filled eyes. "Who is Millers Renholm?"

FORTY

Captain Henry Nolan sat in his chair and gazed between the duo before him, his hands folded underneath his chin, index fingers creating a steeple to his nose. The information relayed to him moments prior was something he had not expected to hear, mainly due to the severity of the cases involved. He bounced between Hartley and Ratliff as they stood prone behind the chairs across from him, looks of steadfast determination etched into both their faces. "And this came from James?"

"Yes, sir," Hartley replied.

"And how reliable is this information?"

Hartley shrugged, glancing to Ratliff. "There's no way to look into it," Jacoby answered.

"But it *is* James we're talking about," Hartley added quickly.

She missed the quick glance her partner sent her way. Nolan did not. "Although, a different version of James." Hartley remained still, letting the comment sink in and knowing her superior was correct. "Could it be part of a story they've concocted?"

"Honestly, I don't think so, sir. The look on his face when I mentioned Millers … It looked real."

Nolan took a moment to think, stewing over each of the answers coming from each of his detectives before responding. He looked to Ratliff. "What do you think?"

Ratliff nodded subtly. "It seemed like the air was stripped from him. And Augie didn't seem like he anticipated Korhan's shooting." Hartley met his eyes momentarily. "I agree with Jo."

Nolan suddenly rose and scratched the crown of his head. "Come on." He led the detectives out of his office and made his way across the pit, snapping at Dane — seated in the break room with the box of files spread before him — to follow. The group made their way to Interrogation One and entered, halting Augie as he paced the rear wall. James, still in the cold, metal chair with his hands folded before him, turned his eyes to the door. "Sit," Nolan ordered Augie.

"Yes, sir," he answered, pulling out the seat next to his friend.

The officers stationed themselves next to the exit and Dane leaned into the doorjamb, arms crossed in the casual way only the reporter could accomplish. "Now," Nolan began, "things have come to light and they require my attention and everyone's compliance. James, you're sure Millers Renholm was the name our victim gave you?"

James nodded. "He only gave me a first name, but I would assume."

"We can't assume anything here. If we don't have a last name, then it's not a certainty that he's our guy. At least not for your parents." Hartley stepped forward, yet was put back in her place with the captain's waving finger. "That being said, it's enough to look into. As of this moment, the Graiser case is reopened. Jolene, Ratliff ... I want you two on this, in addition to the Karaca case. We treat them like separate items, although there appears to be a fine line between the two. If you need more manpower, come talk to me and I'll see what we can do. I want updates. I want to be kept in the loop. Our main objective is getting our suspects into custody. The Graiser caseload is secondary, but don't discount anything."

"What about the files?" Ratliff asked.

Nolan turned to Dane. "Do you have a handle on what's going on in those files?"

Dane smirked. "As well as anyone else in this room, I'd imagine."

Nolan looked between the group quickly. "You two," he said to James and Augie, "are by no means off the hook. I tend to believe my detectives when they say they think you are telling the truth. However, your involvement with Korhan requires me to take precautions. You'll be escorted at all times until I say otherwise. This is for your protection, since, obviously, this Millers character is looking for one of you. Or both. And it's to cover my ass. Agreed?"

"Agreed," they responded in unison.

"Good. Can we set them up someplace?" Nolan asked Hartley.

Before she could respond, James replied, "I still have my hotel. We can stay there for the time being."

"Fine." He looked to Dane. "What about you?"

"I'm going with that box," was all he said.

Nolan eyed Jolene for approval. "He's got the best chance of finding something in there," she said.

The captain nodded his head. "You guys bring them to the hotel. I'll assign some officers to babysit."

* * * * *

"You really fucked yourself up this time, didn't you?" It was the greeting Millers had received from Caprice, a woman he had met years ago that just happened to be associated with the long-haired man he found himself dealing with nowadays.

"Just shut up and fix it," he had responded, roughly pushing past the shorter woman and into her apartment. Caprice was decent looking, definitely not an individual that Millers would kick out of bed, though that was not saying much. He was hardly picky when it came to matters of sexual activity. She was petite, with large, round eyes set in a cherub face. Her dirty blonde hair was cut into a bob, a style she had worn for the past decade and a half, at least. She had a tiny frame, which accentuated the enormous breast implants she had gifted herself in her mid-twenties, a duo that brought in clients and dollars while moonlighting as a dancer at a local all-nude club. In the daytime, however, Caprice was a registered nurse at Rush Medical Center, and a woman that knew how to disinfect a wound and stitch up a bullet hole to the shoulder.

As she finished up cleaning Millers's injury, Caprice waved a hand in front of her face, her fingers slicing through the haze of smoke produced from her patient's exhale. "You're going to fucking kill yourself with those. You know that, right?"

"You mean the bullet's not going to do it?" He laughed.

"Not this time," she responded, rubbing a salve onto the wound and the bruised area surrounding it. "You're lucky."

"I don't call it luck."

"Yeah? What do you call it?"

"I call it knowing how to survive."

Caprice glanced at him with a smirk. "Whatever makes you sleep at night, Mill." She pulled out sterilized medical gauze and lined his shoulder with it, gently rubbing the fabric onto his skin, the salve acting as glue and holding the dressings in place. She turned to a dresser and extracted an elastic bandage, wrapping it firmly around his shoulder and neck, securing the final foot and a half with a metal clamp to his bicep.

Millers reached up suddenly and grasped onto her wrist, flipping her palm to the ceiling and pulling her forearm towards his chin. He slid the sleeve down to her elbow, running his fingers across the smooth, inked skin of her underarm as she patiently waited, watching him all the while. "This a new one?" he asked, referring to a grouping of koi venturing to her fingertips.

"Few years old," she answered calmly.

He studied it longer. "Goldfish? Could have come up with something a little better, couldn't you?"

"They're fucking koi, you idiot."

"What the fucks the difference?" She did not bother to respond, instead shaking her head with a chuckle as he moved his fingers across her skin once again. "You still dancing? Still shaking what the good Lord gave you?"

"Three nights a week," she answered, running her free hand through her hair. "You ought to come by some time. Catch a show. There's a couple dirty broads I work with. Sure they'd love to have some fun with you."

"Why pay for the milk when I can fuck it for free?" He released her arm and slid his hand across her chin and along her neck, halting only briefly before venturing into her shirt to cup one of her voluptuous breasts.

Caprice did not flinch, apparently used to Millers's typical customs. She did, however, grab onto his forearm long enough to extract her augmented asset from his grip. "Unfortunately for you, that ship has sailed." She patted him on the hand just as the apartment phone began to chime. She rose with a smile, reaching up her shirt to place her breast back in its respective cup. "Sailed and is at the bottom of the fucking ocean."

"Come on! Just once for old time's sake?" He chuckled and stood, gathering his shirt and coat and gingerly beginning to dress.

"Old is the keyword there!" Caprice yelled back just as she lifted the receiver. "Hello?"

Millers moved across the room and lifted his injured arm up until the pain became unbearable. He winced and cursed. "You got anything for the pain?" he yelled out.

"Hold on," he heard her say into the receiver. "There's a bottle of Vicodin above the kitchen sink. Grab a couple." Millers made his way to the sink where he rifled through a dozen orange prescription bottles before finding the correct one. He opened the top and pulled out three large pills, popping them into his mouth and swallowing. He returned the top to the bottle and slid it into his pocket.

Out of the corner of his eye, Millers saw Caprice peek her head into the hall and glance to him, a fingernail between her teeth. "Yeah," he heard her whisper into the phone. "I'll try." She disappeared once again around the corner just as Millers turned his attention back to the sink and the window above. His heart stopped. Directly across the street, exiting a black sedan, were the two bouncers from Ginger's Trap, their large frames nearly bursting out of their respective sport coats.

"Hey," Caprice said, coming to a stop near the entrance to the kitchen. "What do you say about sticking around for a drink? You know, for old time's sake?" The smile she displayed was forced.

Millers glanced to her hurriedly before turning his attention back to the window. "Actually, I got to go," he replied. He stepped away from the sink and began towards his host, halting briefly as his eyes fell on the front door at the end of the hall, directly where, Millers realized, the bouncers were heading.

"Come on, baby," Caprice pushed, following his gaze. "Sit with me for a little while. We can … We can talk. Tell me … Tell me what's been going on."

Millers glared at her, perspiration forming on his brow. "Back door," he demanded. Caprice shifted her weight and rubbed her palms together, licking her lips nervously as she stole a glance down the hall. He took a step forward, pulling her attention to him. "Where's the fucking back door?" he repeated.

She froze for only a brief moment before giving in to his imposing demeanor. When she spoke, her voice was weak and shaky. "Through the bedroom on the left."

FORTY-ONE

The early evening breeze was crisp and carried with it a chill that sliced through the thin jacket Jolene had brought with her. She stood outside of the hotel James had been staying at as Augie sucked down a cigarette. Ratliff had taken James inside and was in conversation with the concierge regarding the officers that would be parked outside the building, as well as those that would be making visits to the penthouse where Graiser had taken up residence. The detectives had felt the need to garner as much information as they could about the hotel and its multiple entrances and exits, and Ratliff made a point to urge the concierge that no services, be that room or laundry, were to access the penthouse without police authority until otherwise directed.

Dane had entered the hotel lobby with the two at the desk, and immediately made a B-line for the bar, handing off the file box to James without as much as an appreciative smile. "Ass," James said after the reporter had disappeared into the dimness of the attached establishment.

Ratliff forced out a small chuckle. "That he is."

"Detective," the concierge said as looked up from the computer. "The night manager just got in. Give me a moment to relay the news to him. I'll be back in a minute."

"Take your time," Ratliff replied, sighing as he turned into the awkwardness of his companion.

* * * * *

"This whole bloody thing is messed up," Augie said as he lit another cigarette off of the embers of his last.

"You really need another right now?" Jolene asked, shrugging off, for the moment, his comment.

"You in a hurry to sit in a room with all of us?" Augie answered. "Don't take this the wrong way, love, but you don't seem like the type that likes to babysit."

"Not particularly, no." She shivered off the breeze and caught sight of her partner standing still inside the hotel lobby, James mere feet from him, neither one speaking, eyes to the marbled floor or high plastered ceilings, anywhere but directly at the other.

"I must be nuts," she heard Augie continue. He waited until she looked to him. "To move to Chicago. I must be bat-shit crazy to think it's still a good idea after all this, right? I mean, who watches a man get shot in front of him and says, 'You know what? I think I might get a place near here'?" He took a long drag from his smoke, blowing the gray haze into the air. "I don't understand how you do it."

"Do what?"

"Your job. You're around this for your *career*. I'm around it for ten seconds and I can't get it out of my mind."

Jolene kicked at the pavement. "You learn to separate yourself from it. Or at least try to." She turned her eyes back to the lobby. It was a confusing situation she found herself in, dealing with two cases circulating around something of a common thread, a twisted, obscured focal point that somehow had wrapped herself, her current fling, and ex all in a chaotic package. She could not deny that fact that the lid to the Graiser cold case had been cracked open and she was, no doubt, excited for the opportunity to bring those responsible to justice. It was the company that came along with said case that caused her pause, and as she stared through the glass to James, their eyes met.

* * * * *

"How has she been?" James asked, his voice soft and wavering as he posed the question to Ratliff, his eyes moving from her beauty on the sidewalk to the interior of the lobby.

Ratliff felt his chest tighten, and threw a sideways glance to him.

"I just ... I just haven't been around to —"

"That was your own choice, pal," Ratliff remarked, turning to face him. "Remember walking down the sidewalk and out of her life? Your choice."

James glanced outside once more. "I didn't know what else to do. I … I just thought maybe you could tell me how she has —"

"With all due respect, James, I don't really think it's any of your business anymore. I know you two had a history. I respect that. From what I knew of you, you were a good guy that everyone liked. And that includes Jo. But after what you pulled, I don't think you have the right to ask anything."

"You have to understand —"

"I understand," Ratliff interrupted yet again. "I understand the weight that was put on you, and I wouldn't dare to question that. What I do question, however, is your choice to alienate the one person in your life that was always on your side." The last comment hit home, and Ratliff could tell. He thought for a moment, debating on if he had been too harsh with his words to James. Finally, he gave a little ground. "Look, she's doing fine. She's Jo, you know what I mean? She's a trooper." They both stared out the lobby window at her, watching as she spoke with Augie, a vision next to the wiry Londoner. From behind them, the door to the office opened, pulling both their attentions back to the desk. Ratliff turned to James and made one final comment. "I'm not going to be a middleman for you. Anything else you have to ask about Jo, you can go directly to her."

* * * * *

"You know this has been extremely hard for him, right?" Augie placed the cigarette in his mouth and sucked in deeply.

"What?" Jolene said, turning away from the lobby.

"For James. It's been a bloody awful time for him, you know?"

"I don't, Augie," she replied.

"Well, I'm telling you. He's not a perfect guy, that's for sure. But he is a great one. I know he's had some suspect decision-making over the past year, but he's doing what he can." He paused. "He still cares about you. A lot." Jolene nodded ever so subtly. "Just don't give up on him, is all I'm saying."

She stole a glance once more to James and her partner as the concierge strolled up to the desk once more. "Let's go," she finally said to him. "Put that out."

* * * * *

They settled in their spots throughout the penthouse. Augie nestled into the plush couch and flipped through the channels, coming to rest on European soccer with a smile. James directed his attention to the kitchen table, sliding the brown file box onto the surface as he cleared the few glasses he had left from days past. Ratliff whistled as he walked through the place, checking rooms in an effort to make sure the residence had not been compromised, along with fulfilling personal interests in the sheer size of the place. His detective's salary would never allow him such accommodations.

Jolene stood on the balcony just past where Augie cheered on Chelsea, throwing his hands in the air with a bellow at the shot taken off the free kick. She paced the concrete with her phone to her ear. "This is Officer Hill," came the answer finally.

"Toby, it's Hartley," Jolene said. "Just got off the phone with the captain."

"Yeah," Hill said. "He told me about everything. What time you need us over there?"

"Not sure just yet. We're just getting settled in, so I'd figure it'll be a couple hours. Anything come in on Millers?"

"Nothing," he answered. "We'll be hitting the street for him pretty hard tonight though."

"Great. Just keep us updated, will you?"

"You know it. What room are you guys in?"

"The penthouse."

"The penthouse? Really?"

"Spare no expense," she chided.

"Do I need to check in with the butler before I come up?"

"It's possible. If not the butler, then the front desk, definitely."

"Alright, Hartley. Give me a heads up when you need us over there."

"Will do, Toby. Thanks."

She hung up the phone just as the sliding glass door to the balcony opened. Jolene turned and felt a nervous tingle rise in her stomach as James exited and came to a halt near the railing, his eyes bouncing from her to the world beyond. She forced a quick smile and placed her hands in her pocket, unsure what else to do. "Nice place," she finally said, breaking the ice.

He turned and glanced into the living room as if he were setting his sights on it for the first time. "Thanks," he said. "It's not bad, I guess."

They remained silent and still for several long moments, each wondering if the other was going to say something, enjoying and loathing the quiet that enveloped them. It was an uncomfortable setting, however Jolene did not know what she would have said if a conversation had arisen. The time between the two had definitely, without a doubt, cast a shadow on whatever relationship they still had. Finally, James spoke, the two words falling from his mouth giving her pause. "Thank you." He waited until he realized a response was not coming. "Thank you for helping me."

She weighed her answers, settling on a more professional reply. "I'm following what the investigation gives me." It caused James to deflate slightly. She quickly added, "But you're welcome."

They stood in the breeze, each slightly shivering from the cold, although nerves were definitely part of it. The early evening sky was darkening over Lake Michigan and Chicago, leaving a chilly crispness to the atmosphere. It was not completely unwelcome. There was a calmness that came with this type of weather for Jolene, a heightened awareness she embraced when walking the city's streets.

"How's Jacoby?" James suddenly asked, his fingers toying with the steel railing. His eyes were downcast as the question fell from his lips. She did not answer. "I'm sorry about showing up … You know. I'm sorry. I know I screwed things up when I left, and … I just …" He quieted, though Jolene could tell his mind was racing. "I've thought about —"

"I think we need to get to work," she interjected, curbing wherever the conversation was trying to go, a route she did not wish to venture down at this point.

James nodded. "Yeah."

Inside, he walked straight to the table and situated himself behind the box of files, tilting it onto its side to pull out several dozen sheets of paper. Jolene slowed as she entered the room, sighing and gazing to Ratliff as he approached. "You all right?" he asked, following her line of sight to the kitchen table and the man behind the files.

"I'm fine," she forced. "Let's just get to work."

FORTY-TWO

Dane poured himself another tumbler of scotch and made his way back to the kitchen table to join the group sifting through the contents of the file box, each documenting the dates in which they perused, making certain to keep items in order as pages were passed between one another. He had appeared nearly an hour after they had started their search, smelling of cigarettes and alcohol. Jolene was not too pleased. "I need you to be focused," she had said.

"I am focused," he retorted.

"On getting wasted during my investigation?"

"That's right. It's *your* investigation. Not mine!"

"Dane, the captain is allowing you to —"

"Fuck that!" he blurted back to her. "He's not *allowing* me to anything. I'm the only one out of you shits that knows what to look for in any sort of financial documents. So back off and let me do my thing."

"Just take it easy with the booze," she had stated, regaining her seat and composure.

The only member that had not taken part in the search was Augie, the Londoner by no means an expert in anything other than tracking down junkies in drug neighborhoods and English football. "Come on, you bastard!" he yelled at the television on several occasions, causing those closest to him to jump. "Fucking ref needs to open his eyes." He laughed as he turned apologetically to the table.

"I don't even know what to look for anymore," James finally said, leaning back and rubbing his eyes. Ratliff, too, took a break, standing and stretching his limbs before moving into the adjoining kitchen to pour himself a cup of coffee.

"Did you ever really know what to look for?" Dane said with a smile.

"Can you even read the words on the page with the amount of alcohol you've consumed?"

Dane raised his glass to him. "In fact, I can. Gives me super powers."

James shook his head but slowed, watching as the reporter took a long sip. "Maybe I could use a little extra power too." He pushed his chair out and walked to the kitchen and the bottle of scotch.

"There you go," Dane replied.

Hartley, too, had begun to tire, wondering if they would find anything in the mysterious Verland files. It had crossed her mind that the box before them was merely a ploy, an oasis that would produce nothing more than days of wasted scrutiny. She shifted in her seat and ran her fingers through her hair. "What *are* we looking for?" she heard herself ask.

Those in the room — even Augie — turned to her. "I mean, what could this box of paper show? Anything?"

"It's a financial trail," Dane answered, lifting his tumbler to his lips once more. "Mainly it shows money trading hands."

"No shit?" she replied, her eyes shooting laser beams in his direction. He smirked back.

"Verland told me he wanted me to take them," James said, returning to the table with his own full glass. Dane raised his in a toast, to which James took a sip.

"Why?" Jolene asked.

"He said they were no help to him. He was in too deep over his head to begin with and thought they could benefit me."

"Again, why?"

James shrugged. "I'm not sure."

"I'd say it was a last ditch effort by a guilty fuck," Dane replied.

"What, like to clear his conscience?" Augie asked.

"Why not?" Dane glanced up from the pages before him. "Guy's going down for financial fraud. Going to be someone's girlfriend in some federal prison someplace. He's got no access to money, is on house arrest, and has a cluster-fuck of lawyers and researchers at his place at all times. You figure even a worm like Damian Verland likes to feel good about himself once in a while. Helping out someone like James may have been just that. A last ditch effort at redemption."

"But you've been through these files before, haven't you?" Jolene questioned.

Dane nodded. "A little."

"Tell me what you've come across so far. What stands out to you?"

"You've got papers in front of you. Take a look for —"

"Dane, please! I have a raging headache from staring at this. Just stop being a dick and just give me your take. Please."

He gave in, a moment of compliance to his sister. "Okay, what I see — and correct me if I'm wrong, James — is a grouping of withdrawals, wire transfers, rerouting of funds. You're basic banking activity, all of which seems legal enough. The dates on the files I have now range from … five to six years ago, but I've seen some in there from ten years back."

"I'm in that range," Ratliff stated as he returned to the table.

"The weird thing about this is there are random account numbers and what I would assume to be names blacked out." He held up the sheet before him, displaying a hole cut through the paper. "Or worse. It's like whatever was here wasn't supposed to be. They definitely didn't want these transactions getting into the open."

"Then why not destroy them? Why not get rid of any evidence that could tie Verland to … whatever this is tying him to."

"Leverage," Augie blurted from the couch. Everyone turned to stare at him. He shifted in his seat, digging his knees into the cushion and resting his hips against the oversized back of the sofa. "I mean, why wouldn't you, right? It's always good to have an out. Maybe that was his. Maybe he kept some insurance for himself in case something ever popped up." The thought was intriguing. But why would Verland need insurance? And from what? Or whom?

"I think I have something here," James said suddenly, bringing their collective attention to him. He flipped through the pages before him. "Initials, it looks like."

"Let me see," Dane said, reaching out to retrieve the hand-off from Graiser. He eyed the sheet. James passed one off to Jolene as well, who shared it with Ratliff. "*AG*," Dane spoke, repeating the letters a half dozen times.

"What is that?"

"I'd assume initials, too," Hartley replied. "Look at the dates." They all focused to the respective column and the numbers listed, the earliest starting ten years prior.

"That's a month after my parents were killed," James said. "This can't be a coincidence."

"Or it can," Ratliff answered, pulling James's attention to him. "No jumping to conclusions."

"He's right," Hartley continued. "We'll mark it on our list as something of interest, but a lot of things happen on the same date. It could absolutely be a coincidence." She looked to James. "We don't want to get our hopes up based on a random date on a piece of paper. We want to find something more solid."

They continued through the pages, highlighting on pads of paper the dates and initials as they appeared. Finally, Dane leaned back and took a long sip from his drink, eyes to the ceiling in deep thought. "You know," he said, shifting in his seat, "I think I might have an idea." Jolene watched him carefully, seeing a twinkle in his eye, a fleeting idea that she knew he would milk to the fullest extent.

"Care to share?" Ratliff asked after several moments had passed.

Dane leaned forward quickly and smiled at those in attendance. "Artemis Greer," he stated, surveying the faces before him as they displayed a collective confusion. He sighed, turning to the detectives. "You'd think the name would ring a bell with you two!"

"Dane," Jolene replied, "we've got a ton of shit to do, so if you could —"

"And therein lies the problem," he interjected. "While you cops got *a ton of shit to do*, the media world continues to fight the good fight."

"You mean the fight that benefits you most," Ratliff answered.

Dane shrugged. "That's what I said. Either way, it's something."

"How so? Who is Artemis Greer?" Hartley asked.

"Artemis Greer is a retired financial guru. He was employed with a number of Fortune 500 companies, and probably did consulting work with the rest."

"And you think these initials in here could be his?" she questioned with a raised brow. He smirked and nodded. "Or it could be a wild goose chase."

"It's worth a shot."

"How? It's nothing. It's you ... It's you conjuring up a name from your magic hat. It's me harassing a man for nothing more than a flimsy hunch."

Dane eyed his sister for a moment before conceding and removing himself from the table. He sauntered into the kitchen to fill his tumbler once more before sliding past Augie in the direction of the balcony. The table collectively sighed. Dane turned before pulling the sliding glass door open. "You could be right about my hunch being flimsy," he said, swaying in position. "After all, I am just a drunk investigative reporter. Drunk, being the fun word there." He laughed. "But on the other hand, let's not discount the other two words: *investigative* and *reporter*. Those tend to garner some meaningful feelings. Well, to those who aren't predisposed to my habits, I guess."

"Get to the point, Dane," Hartley replied.

"The point. The point? What was my point again?" He thought for a moment before lighting up a cigarette and blowing the smoke into the room. "Right!" he exclaimed. His smile faded quickly and his drunken gaze turned to his sister. "My fucking point is that Artemis Greer was a financial consultant. He played with the big boys in the fiscal realm, one of them being Congressman Johnston."

"Now Johnston is involved in this?" Hartley said, chuckling to herself and rubbing her temples. "Dane, you're grasping at straws! Involving Johnston seems like a pretty big stretch, if you ask me."

"Thank fucking god I'm not asking you then." His words were laced with heat, a tone that led those in the room to pay close attention to the building momentum that was Dane Hartley. "I'm telling you. So open your fucking ears! We know through my research that Johnston had money in Intervise Securities at one point —"

"That he pulled out well before the scandal."

"— which means Verland was in charge of moving his money around to different investments."

"We don't know that!" Hartley yelled.

"Bullshit! You think a prick like Johnston would let one of the minions handle his funds? Absolutely not. Get your head out of your ass!"

"So how does Greer play a role in this?" Ratliff hurriedly asked, wanting the debate to turn back towards the positive.

"His role was as a financial consultant to Johnston for a time."

"Meaning?"

"Meaning he was the signature to all things monetary for the congressman."

They all faded into their own thoughts briefly, trying to determine what, if anything, had been laid on the table before them. Dane could not help but smile wide as he made a move into the center of the room and let slide the golden nugget Jolene had seen him hide away prior to their exchange. "How about this for a connection: Artemis Greer is filthy rich. He made his money not only being involved in the finances of Fortune 500s, but also in the media world." He paused for effect. "Artemis Greer was at one point, detectives, a board member at *State of Finance.*"

FORTY-THREE

She turned the faucet off and tested the temperature with her fingertips. The water was scalding hot. Steam rose from the surface, rising into the much cooler air and mixing with the fleeting thoughts that evaporated from Jolene's overworked brain into the atmosphere. The walk to the bedroom was forced, pure exhaustion weighing down her body, the adrenaline of the day wearing off just moments ago as Jacoby dropped her off in front of her apartment. He had shown interest in not letting the day end, though Hartley could not, at this exact moment, recall if that concern was ignited from a professional or personal curiosity. Much had happened with the cases before them. And much had happened between her and Ratliff, as well. It was impossible to know which direction her partner wanted to go with the remainder of the evening, and usually Jolene would not have minded either way. It was just not to be.

Jolene fell face-first into her bed, her body sinking into the mass of sheets and pillows and the obscenely fluffy comforter that seemed to cradle her form. She turned herself over to stare at the ceiling. She knew her reasoning for declining Jacoby's offer was warranted; she needed a night to herself, to bathe in the thoughts that churned within her, confront the questions that were rising to the surface and sift through the facts that lay before her. She needed to just be. Fortunately, Ratliff did not seem to mind that much. He knew how she worked, knew she needed time to unwind and recharge her batteries. Every officer needed that. Jacoby was probably refueling his body and soul as well.

At least that was what Jolene wanted to think. He had seemed somewhat deflated as she shook her head and exited the vehicle. However, her apologetic smile had brought forth a genuine grin and an understanding wave of the hand.

She sighed and lifted her hips into the air, sliding her pants down her legs and kicking them to the floor. She stood and pulled at her shirt, tossing it in the direction of the hamper before removing her bra and underwear. She ran her fingers across her hip, fingering the bruise left by the doorknob from the attack in James's apartment. It stung, but was nothing that would keep her down, especially after the wounds she had received within the last year.

She moved from the bedroom and into the hallway, hurriedly making her way back to the bathroom and the cauldron that waited. She stepped into the heated water and shivered, goose bumps traveling across her skin as she lowered herself into the warmth. Jolene took in a large gulp of air and submerged, feeling the heat caress her muscles and flow between every strand of hair on her head. She clutched her hands together on her chest as if praying, flexing and relaxing her biceps and shoulders numerous times before exhaling, the light bubbles floating to the surface, tickling her face and getting caught in her eyelashes.

She came to the surface and wiped the water from her eyes, running her fingers across her scalp and down her neck. It felt good, the soothing embrace of super-heated liquid wrapping every inch of one's body. It was calming and comforting, a way to feel safe and secure in the chaotic world she sometimes felt she lived in.

Especially since the return of James. The alone time they had shared on the balcony of his penthouse had been absolutely awkward, a convoluted ball of pent-up anger and confusion. She knew without a doubt there was a definite, possibly irreparable, rift between them. It tended to happen with exes. And she did not care. At least, she did not seem to care as much as she would have thought. A large part of her believed it to be the fact that she and Jacoby had something in the making, though there was a nagging feeling that the Graiser murders played a role, pushing her into this fading relationship based on the fact that an outcome to a cold murder case was beginning to rise from the ashes.

They had made progress in the Graiser case, much more than in the previous decade. Suspects had been named. Leads had been generated. Impossible links had been tied to current or ongoing investigations. There was a lot to think about. The Karaca case, however, remained stagnant. Sure, Morgan Keller and Millers Renholm had been tagged as shooters in the murder of Korhan, but other than that, nothing. Keller had turned into a dead-end after Ratliff's interview with Sarah Bernice. Patrol had, as of yet, been unsuccessful to pinpoint Renholm's whereabouts. The driver of the van still remained a mystery. Tips on the murderer had not garnered anything worth looking into. They were at the mercy of Renholm's stupidity, and, at the moment, it looked as if he was lacking that much needed ignorance.

Jolene ducked under the surface of the water again, clearing her mind and remaining completely still, feeling an air bubble escape her nose and slowly roll its way up the contours of her face before detaching and rising to the surface. The stillness was breathtaking, the absolute peace underneath the water all-consuming. The steady *thump-thump* of her heartbeat was the only noise within her ears, the shockwave of the concussion sending minute pulses through the liquid picked up by the tiny hairs covering her skin.

She re-emerged again and sat up, the water droplets forming rivulets coursing from her hair, across her shoulders and down her back and chest. The coolness of the air brought with it a renewed mental awakening. Her thoughts rushed back once more, morphing into a singular point and landing on her brother, the man she once again found herself dealing with. Jolene hated to admit it, but he was absolutely someone that brought benefits to her investigation. The initials *A.G.* would have been lost upon her and Ratliff — possibly even the forensics unit that would be getting the files as soon as James signed them over. But here was Dane, her ass of a brother, producing a name out of the tension-laden air of the penthouse.

Artemis Greer.

Jolene had not had time to research the name since Dane mentioned him. It would be yet another addition to her list for the following day. She wanted to make sure what she was getting into, not chase ghosts brought on by an individual with his own, extremely selfish, agenda.

* * * * *

He walked quietly from the kitchen, the soles of his Wolverine boots clicking along the tiles leading into the sitting area where Augie slept, head thrown over the armrest, hand gripping the remote control. The Londoner's mouth was open and a small amount of saliva was suspended from his bottom lip, waiting the eventual drop to the upholstery inches away. Late night replays of the day's football highlights continued in succession, rotating amongst overseas teams and Major League Soccer and back again quickly. James had retired to the bedroom twenty minutes ago, desperate for some shut-eye before starting anew the following morning. He left his guest to his own devices, which consisted of finishing his tumbler of scotch. The door had closed to the adjoining room, and Dane Hartley had found himself alone in the kitchen with an abundance of financial records at his mercy. It had taken him only a minute to conjure up his next course of action, setting into motion a series of events that he knew Jolene would consider questionable. However, he could truly not care less. The only thing that plagued his mind at the moment was finishing a story he had started months prior.

* * * * *

She moseyed down the hall in her skin, letting the crisp air of the apartment cool her heated limbs. Droplets of water fell from the tips of her soaked locks, descending down her back in tiny streams or cascading through the expanse to collide with the backs of her legs. Jolene turned into the bedroom and opened the armoire. She retrieved a pair of worn, gray sweatpants and an oversized shirt — an ancient relic from Debarsi — and slid into them, the fabric hanging about her frame as she climbed into bed.

It took a while to fall into a fitful sleep, her eyelids not wanting to remain shut, her brown orbs peering past the darkness to the ceiling, the city's lights dancing across the room. She had had an epiphany while nearing the end of her soak, an idea that, as she thought about it, was proving to build momentum to the point that the itinerary for the following day would have to be postponed. Jolene had thought of sending Ratliff a text to share her notion. In the end, she did not, feeling that she needed a full night to herself before jumping headlong into the case once more.

Documents, she had thought to herself. *Financial money trails.*

It was brought on by Dane. He had found the initials. He had summoned the name from his research into the Intervise-*State* fraud. He had connected some dots that indirectly pushed her to an individual that could possibly shine some light on things.

If only Jolene could bring her back into the picture.

* * * * *

Dane slipped the night manager a hundred dollar bill. "Come on, pal," he said. "Just unlock it for five minutes. That's all I'll need." The man, a mid-twentysomething with slicked back hair, chubby cheeks and a missing jawline, grinned nervously, glancing between the journalist and the copy room, which had been closed for the last three hours. "Look, here's another fifty." Dane flipped through the bills and tossed the amount on the desk. "Five minutes, that's all I'm asking. Five minutes of your time just made you a hundred and fifty bucks."

In the end, he won out. The manager escorted Dane to the entrance of the copy room and unlocked the door. "Can you work with the lights off?" the employee asked. "I'd rather not have anyone see you in there. We're supposed to have this closed until the morning."

"As long as the copy machine is running, I think I'll manage." Dane patted the young man on the shoulder and entered the room. He made his way to the large Xerox WorkCentre printer and opened the manila envelope, his eyes falling on a section of the financial records Jacoby had perused earlier in the evening. There were three dozen or so pages, each displaying the initials *A.G.* a handful of times. Dane fingered the papers carefully before tapping the whole lot of them against the printer's top, leveling the items and setting them into the slot for the automatic feed of the copier.

He reached into his pocket and woke his phone, pulling up the text messaging application and searching through his contacts until he came to the letter *M*. He grinned as the image of an attractive Chinese woman displayed next to the entry field.

Need a favor, he typed.

He pressed the send button and placed the device on the table next to him. Dane turned his attention to the printer and started the copying process, the whir of the machine before him growing as the seconds ticked by, the internal guts of the contraption warming up to the late night activity.

A chime from his phone drew his focus once more as his request was answered. *No favors. $$ is how things work today. Only $$.*

Dane shook his head as the Xerox printer began to work, pulling and pushing pages into and out of the mechanism furiously. He punched in a series of letters. *Only money? Where'd the fun go to?*

He grabbed the stack of papers from the output tray and sifted through them, flipping the pages and letting them roll off his thumb in a whir. He exited the room and waved to the manager at the front desk, the relieved look spreading across his face as he hurriedly turned the corner to lock the copy room door.

Dane stopped on the sidewalk outside of the lobby and lit a cigarette, taking in a long drag as his phone sounded once again. *I'm always fun. Monk's Pub. 30 minutes.* He smiled and placed the device back in his pocket, turning down the pavement to the taxis lining the adjacent road.

FORTY-FOUR

Ratliff entered the precinct the following morning and headed directly into Captain Nolan's office to join the meeting already underway. Jolene sat in one of the chairs, their superior on the phone pacing a three-foot path between his own luxurious seat and the nearby end table. Hartley glanced up to her partner and grinned her hello. She was clothed in a white form-fitting blouse, dark blue jeans and a pair of black, faux leather boots from Nine West that stopped just below her kneecaps, an ensemble that Jacoby knew was well beyond the dress-code set by Nolan himself. Regardless, she looked ravishing. "Hey," he said in response, taking the seat next to her.

"You call the guys and tell them to stick around longer?" Hartley asked, referring to the officers babysitting James and Augie.

Ratliff nodded. "Didn't seem all that happy about it, but yeah. What's going on?"

"Shhh!" Nolan said suddenly, waving erratically at the pair. Hartley placed her finger over her lips and turned to listen to her boss. Ratliff, confused, allowed the scene to play out before him. "Yes, I'm here," Nolan said into the mouthpiece. "Yes … That's correct … The utmost. We don't want to put anyone in danger either … Absolutely. Officers will be with the entire time … Yes. Yes, I understand the severity of the witness. But it is detrimental to my investigation to interview those who may have inside knowledge … Understood … Great! Thank you. What …?" He looked to his watch. "Sounds great. I'll relay the message to my detectives. Thank you." He hung up the phone and ran his fingers through his thinning hair. Nolan's gaze connected with Jolene's. "You better know what you're doing."

"So, it went through?" she asked.

Henry nodded. "It's approved." He paused before adding, "Ann Carroll will be here a little after noon."

* * * * *

Dane sipped lazily on his venti non-fat mocha with two extra shots of espresso. His head had been pounding upon waking up early this morning, however, a quick shower followed by three ibuprofen had seemed to do the trick. He had received a text message nearly an hour ago stating that his contact from the previous evening had completed her research into the file and would meet him shortly, after a quick shower and bite to eat.

Dane found himself wiping away the residual sleep and picking at the protein box filled with a hard-boiled egg, some grapes and several pieces of cheese when he received the follow up message. *Hotel Sax. Room 906.* He pushed himself out of the seat and tossed his breakfast in the trash near the door.

Hotel Sax was not far, just a mere fifteen minutes at a leisurely pace. However, Dane did not feel much like walking the distance, his body still feeling the effects of the scotch from the night before. He hailed a cab as he exited the coffee shop and gave the driver his destination. The man behind the wheel glanced at him for a moment before accepting that he would not be getting the best fare or tip. "No smoking in here, sir," he yelled to the back seat as Dane placed a cigarette in his mouth and flicked the lighter to life.

Dane eyed the driver momentarily before extinguishing the flame. "Come on," he pleaded. "I'll even pass one up to you."

"No, sir. No smoking in this vehicle."

Dane succumbed to his demands, placing the cigarette back in its pack. "It would make this fucking cab smell a little better, you know?" He shook his head and glanced out the window as the driver stared to him with contempt.

* * * * *

"Ann Carroll?" Ratliff asked. "What's she have to do with this?" He stopped at her desk and waited for Jolene to answer.

She leaned back into her seat and crossed her legs. "I was thinking last night about the documents. About whatever importance they carry, and how, unfortunately, Dane really *is* the expert. It got me thinking about where we are with the Karaca case."

"Nowhere?" Ratliff said with a chuckle, wheeling his chair over and taking a seat directly in front of his partner.

"Not *nowhere*, just at a standstill. It really boils down to what we know and who we can question. Morgan Keller led us to Sarah Bernice —"

"Who knew nothing."

"Right," she agreed. "Because it's been such a long time since she was connected with Keller. I bet you if we met with her again, all we'd find would be random notes or pictures of them when they were together."

Jacoby shrugged. "Most people tend to get rid of that stuff after a certain amount of time. Unless there's still something there."

Jolene smiled. "Unless there's still something there. Augie said yesterday that Verland probably kept those documents for leverage. Something to have, just in case."

"Yeah. Protection, maybe."

"Could be. I didn't think of it until last night, but Verland was in this mess to begin with because of documents that Ann Carroll kept."

Ratliff leaned forward and nodded. "Right. She had copied all those files and shipped them off to Bart Reed." He paused.

"You think she could know something about all this? Maybe she came across some of those files at one point?"

"It's a possibility. But I'm more wondering about what role she played initially. Ann was at *State of Finance* for a long time. She had to have seen something. Late night meetings. Mail. Email. Hell, she was the office manager! She had to route calls. I want to see who was in contact with O'Dowd and Walker."

"And Artemis Greer," Ratliff added.

* * * * *

Mei "Maggie" Tien had not heard from Dane Hartley in nearly a year and a half, not since his run-in with some young, rough-and-tumble thugs in Chinatown. And even that meeting had been merely an exchange of information followed by the inevitable thank you screw in her apartment. She did not mind. Maggie — as those outside her family called her — understood his disconnected ways. She, too, was a venomous snake, a member of the greedy up-and-coming world of journalism, and knew that her success was fickle in the grand scheme of things. The next Dane Hartley could, in fact, be her. Or it could be some guy writing in his spare time from the basement of his tri-level in the far suburbs. Which is why she kept an ace up her sleeve, a true gem in her otherwise lackluster career. That golden nugget just happened to be her younger sister, a hacker, a virtuoso of a computer programmer that could garner information when needed.

Maggie had become accustomed to burning bridges, throwing those less deserving under the proverbial bus in order to advance her own career. Yet Tien also understood how to reel in the ones she had disgraced, mainly by tempting them with her physical beauty and shameless sexual behavior. She was, in a way, Dane's exact mirror image, his doppelganger in the feminine form.

Maggie stared out the window overlooking the street, the roof of The House of Blues rising prominently below. She watched as throngs of men and women zigzagged through the mobs of tourists setting out early to bombard Chicago with cameras, city maps and awestruck expressions. She cracked the window and lit a cigarette, holding the Marlboro to her thin lips and sucking deeply, laughing to herself as a group of individuals nearly knocked over a hurried businesswoman, the assemblage sporting bright turquoise shirts and what appeared to be fanny packs as they goofily sidestepped the natives.

She could not believe the way tourists lacked any sense of fashion. Pastel shirts atop knee-length, black jean shorts. Rhinestone baseball caps splashed with Disney characters of all sorts. Haircuts that seemed straight out of the '80s. It was beyond her. Mei Tien was the exact opposite. She was a woman who had been dipped into the fashion pool by the gods themselves. It did not hurt that she had been blessed with a frame that could make anything look appealing and hip. Her tanned complexion and straight, jet-black hair had proved enough to draw the opposite sex in since her teenage years. Her slim, athletic build and toned ass atop long legs had driven the boys wild from high school till the present. Yet it was the breast implants she had gifted herself at the ripe age of twenty-two that pleased her more than anything. They had proved to be the determining factor in whether or not she would break into world of journalism with a bang.

* * * * *

Dane entered room 906 without a knock, testing the handle and pushing the door inward to the smell of cigarette smoke. He laughed at the no smoking sign posted underneath the peephole and knew he was in the correct spot. He edged his way farther into the room and halted at the end of the small corridor, staring to the beautiful Chinese woman leaning against the desk, one leg thrown to the surface and swinging as she blew the smoke out the cracked window. "Took you long enough," Maggie said.

Dane looked around the room, the extravagant furnishings unlike anything he had seen before in a hotel. His eyes fell on the two manila envelopes laying on the end table next to the bed, one the folder he had given to her the previous evening, the other Maggie's research in the physical form. "What can I say?" Dane finally replied as he moved to the envelopes. "I have better shit to do."

Maggie shook her head. She was happy to see him, although the *I have no time for you* look forever splashed across his handsome face had always left her wanting more. He was a prick. That was well known. Dane Hartley did nothing for anyone unless it benefited him as well. To get in his way meant a slight that could throw a serious wrench into one's career advancement. At least that is what she had been told. Yet Maggie knew how to read people, and what she had read on Dane's face when meeting the other night was he needed her help. His celebrity status as of late seemed to come with a price: sources were not easily at his disposal anymore. The thought of names being leaked to the public was something that those in the shadows most definitely did not want. Anonymity was what they cherished, and a connection with a reporter on the front pages of newspapers and the pixels of a television screen absolutely went against the grain.

"You're an asshole, you know that?" she finally said, extinguishing her cigarette in a cup half filled with water.

"I do," he responded, opening the new envelope and sifting through the pages. His eyes widened and a smile formed on his face. He glanced up to her before sliding the papers back into the pouch. He reached down and retrieved the originals. "But I pay well when I need something." Dane pulled out a stack of bills contained by a red rubber band and tossed it on the bed.

Maggie barely had to focus on the money. She knew it was short. "That's not what we agreed to," she said defiantly.

Dane stalled momentarily, a grin forming on his face. "Well, that's all I got on me, so you're going to have to deal with it." She advanced toward him, shaking her head all the while. She reached down and flipped through the bills before tossing it at him. Dane did not make an attempt to catch the money, instead letting it fall to his feet as Maggie moved past him and into the corridor leading to the door. She turned the locking mechanism and swung the hinged metal hook into place. "Don't take this the wrong way, babe," Dane replied, "but if you're going to get physical, you may want to rethink."

"Don't underestimate me," Maggie answered. Dane squared up to her and watched eagerly as Tien grasped onto the bottom of her shirt and lifted it easily over her head, her large breasts close to popping out from the black satin bra, a silver choker necklace with a pendulum hanging almost to her navel.

Dane sighed. "I don't have time for this, Mei."

"You don't have the money for that," she responded, pointing at the envelope tucked under his arm. "So I figure it's money or your next best asset."

"My charming personality?"

"Your dick. Believe me: your personality isn't worth shit." She stepped up to him and grasped onto his belt, unhooking it quickly and unzipping his pants.

He focused on her before looking to his watch. "How long will this take?" he asked.

She smiled. "As long as I want it to."

FORTY-FIVE

Ann Carroll looked different. At least, different in the mind of Jolene Hartley, who had only met the ex-office manager at *State of Finance* a handful of times, the last at the prosecutor's office when Carroll was placed in protective custody after agreeing to appear as a witness against Seamus O'Dowd, Kyle Walker and Damian Verland. The direct line of danger in regards to the Bartholomew Reed case had been stopped within the warehouse of the magazine with a well-placed bullet in Luke Moran's skull, however, as things had been, there was no way to tell if there were any other less than savory characters about on orders from Walker or Verland.

So Ann Carroll had been taken away, hidden in a remote suburb, put up in an extravagant penthouse until her time on the stand. For all Hartley knew, Ann had been placed in a bunker on some government airfield with restricted access. But here she was, waiting in Interrogation One while Jolene and her partner stared at her from behind the mirror.

Ms. Carroll's hair was cut short, much shorter than eight months prior, and dyed a dark brown. She had definitely aged since their last meeting, most likely a result of her own remorse in the fraud that had played out between Intervise and *State of Finance*. Ann's guilt or innocence was still being debated, however, the prosecution knew full well the defense was going to attack her character, pinning Ms. Carroll as one of the early embezzlers.

And she possibly was. Hartley and the rest of the team knew, without a doubt, that Ann Carroll had played some role in the fraud. Whether that was being a full-blown accomplice, or just knowingly allowing the illegal activity to proceed, the detective did not know.

Nor did she care. As Jolene stared to the woman seated behind the table, all she wondered about was what information could Ann Carroll provide them. What inside knowledge did she possibly possess that could further along their current investigation, as well as the Graiser case.

"Ms. Carroll," Hartley said as she and Ratliff entered the room and took their seats across from her. "Thank you for coming in on such short notice."

"You're welcome," she replied. "Is everything all right? Did something happen?"

"No, Ms. Carroll," Ratliff said. "Everything's fine. We just have some questions is all."

"Oh," she said, somewhat surprised. "Well, I hope I can help. I'm not sure what else I can answer, especially without my lawyer."

"Ms. Carroll," Hartley stated, "you're agreement with the District Attorney —"

"Is why I'm here," came the interruption, the door to the interrogation room opening and allowing and elderly man with a salt-and-pepper beard and thinning hair to enter and take a seat next to his client. "I'm George Naple, Ann's attorney." He shifted in his seat and removed his glasses, wiping the grime from the lens on his tie before extending his hand to the detectives in turn.

"Mr. Naple," Hartley said. "I'm Detective Jolene Hartley, and this is my partner, Detective Jacoby Ratliff."

"Pleasure," he replied with a grin. "You guys haven't begun any questioning, have you?" He turned to his client without pause. "They haven't started the questioning yet, have they?"

"No, Mr. Naple," Hartley replied. "Though this line of questioning really won't have anything to do with Ms. Carroll's agreement with the DA."

"Everything has to do with Ms. Carroll's agreement with the DA. You do realize she has immunity, correct?"

Hartley nodded. "Yes, we do."

"Good. Then we understand each other when I say to not goad my client into confessing to anything. If I so happen to feel a question —"

"Mr. Naple," Hartley interjected sternly. "Let me remind you who you are talking to. I am a detective in the Chicago Police Department with a lot of sway. And let's not forget that the people Ms. Carroll was testifying against are all dead, which means that Ms. Carroll's immunity may be less beneficial to the city at this time. Do we understand each other?"

Ann and her lawyer glanced at one another. "We understand," she finally said.

"Great. Ms. Carroll, the case we're investigating has some ties to Damian Verland and *State of Finance*. That's the only reason you're here. We're not questioning your involvement in the embezzlement. Honestly, I don't care." The phrase brought a brief grin to Ann's face. "What I *do* care about is my murder investigations. Do you understand?"

"I'll help as much as I can."

"Good." Hartley paused for a moment, reigning in her thoughts before she opened her mouth. "I'm sure you've heard by now that Damian Verland is dead."

"Luckily, they did give me a television to watch, so yes, I did see that."

"Do you remember seeing Verland in the *State* building ever? Or at a function through the magazine?"

Ann thought. "He was there at times."

"How many?"

She shrugged. "I can't remember, detective. He was there though. Early on."

"What about phone calls?"

"I can't recall. I'm sure he had Seamus's and Kyle's direct lines."

"So you don't remember him ever calling?"

She shook her head. "I'm sure he did, but I can't remember."

"What about others?" Ann stared to her with questioning eyes. "Congressman Harold Johnston, perhaps?" Ann shrugged yet again. "You don't know? Or you won't say?"

"Detective," her attorney said. "Is that necessary?"

"Is it necessary for your client to dodge direct questions?"

"I'm not dodging," Ann stated. "I just don't remember. Did Verland have contact with Seamus and Kyle? Yes. Did Harold Johnston? I don't know. I would assume Verland and Johnston did, since some of the congressman's money was tied into Intervise. But other than that, I'm sorry, detectives. I just don't remember."

Hartley sat back and eyed the woman before her, wondering if there was any reason for her to keep close-lipped. She could not think of one, other than Ann Carroll simply not knowing. "You kept a copy of files from the embezzlement, is that correct?"

Ann laughed. "That's correct, Ms. Hartley. It's pretty much what the case against them was based on."

Jolene eyed her. Before she could protest to the tone of her comment, Ratliff chimed in. "Ms. Carroll, we have in our custody some documents that were part of Damian Verland's collection. They range from about ten to five years ago. Do you know what these documents would encompass?"

Ann waited for a moment, looking between the two. "How would I? I'd have to see them."

"What my partner means to ask," Hartley added, "is do you have any knowledge of the files of Damian Verland from ten years ago? Were you tracking what Verland was doing at that time?"

"The documents I kept records of weren't so much to keep track of the VP of Intervise, or anyone for that matter. He just happened to become a major component of the whole thing. I just felt I needed some security, and in the end," she glanced to her lawyer, "it looks like I was right."

"Does the name Artemis Greer mean anything to you?" Hartley asked.

Ann nodded her head. "I didn't know Mr. Greer, but I knew of him."

"Did you ever meet him?" She shook her head. "Can you tell me what you knew about him?"

"Well, Mr. Greer was on the board at *State*. Early on."

"How long ago?"

"If memory serves correct, I'd say fourteen or fifteen years ago. He only served as a member for three or four years though."

"How much say did he have in the direction of the company?" Ratliff questioned.

"Hard to say. I don't think much. It was pretty much Seamus's show. And then Kyle's, when he came on board. I maybe saw Mr. Greer at the building once or twice. No more than that though. I know *State* was more of a side project for him."

"How do you mean?"

"Well, Mr. Greer was a finance guy. I know he had other ventures throughout the city, one of them being a cog in the wheel of Congressman Johnston's empire."

"Do you know anything about Greer's relationship with Johnston?"

"Not much. Just that his initials were on some of the items that I saw."

"What sort of items?"

Ann shrugged. "It was a long time ago, detective," she said. "If it helps any, I'd say whatever those transactions were, they were probably legit. I don't remember any of them throwing any flags for me. Not like the things O'Dowd and Walker were into." She paused, her eyes open but elsewhere, her memories floating into the past. "I'll tell you one thing, though," she finally said. "I bet you a million bucks that if Mr. Greer hadn't been on the board, none of this would have happened." She snapped to and looked to the detectives. "The murders. Bart. I bet you it wouldn't have happened at all."

"Why do you say that?" Hartley asked.

"Well, mainly because Kyle wouldn't have been there." She continued after seeing the confusion on Hartley's face. "Mr. Greer was the one that got Kyle the job at *State*. He recommended it to the others to hire him into the position of Assistant Editor."

FORTY-SIX

Millers stood in the alleyway a half block from his home, nervously shifting back and forth as he sucked down his third straight cigarette. He kept playing the scenario at Caprice's pad over and over in his mind. The phone ringing. Caprice becoming distracted, trying to get him to stay. The bouncers walking to her front door. He felt betrayed, yet knew in the life he led — the life he chose — it was just part of the system. The situation, however, had definitely brought him into the light. He realized he was absolutely not getting the respect he deserved. Instead, he was being targeted for execution.

His associate, although showing concern for his wellbeing after the altercation with the detective in Graiser's apartment, was only masking what was truly going on, throwing smoke as a distraction to have him killed for becoming such an enormous liability. And it was exactly what he had become, and Millers knew it. The police obviously knew who he was. The female detective had called his name out in the apartment before he had employed the door as his own personal battering ram, which meant only one thing: the police were after him. And his remaining partner in the scheme that killed Korhan Karaca seemed to be after him as well.

Which was why his trip back to his home was such a risky move, and why he had found himself standing guard and surveying the area for the past hour. He had seen no movement through the windows, at least from the vantage point he now held, nor had he witnessed police cars or out-of-place characters moving through the vicinity.

He had not thought out his immediate plan as well as he would have liked. There were two options that faced him, and neither one shined bright with a positive outcome. On the one hand, Millers could run, flee the Chicagoland area, even the state, for greener pastures. That meant starting over though, something that he did not wish to do. Finding himself in Los Angeles or New York or Seattle in search of a new crew was harder than it sounded, and the likelihood of someone taking him in on a whim was nearly implausible. Plus, he did not want to start over. Chicago was his home, just as much as it was his associate's. He had a right to the streets, to the life he had led for decades.

The other option, a notion that did not sit well with him either, was to face the onslaught with open arms, to embrace the maliciousness that was directed to him and sway the opinion of his murderous cohort into something less violent, something that left Millers alive and well. The odds of this direction working to plan were slim. Never before had Millers seen his partner deal in mercy. Humans were dispensable, items to be tossed to the side when they benefited him least. Millers would know. It was how he worked as well.

He stared to the garage and took a deep breath in, exhaling slowly before sucking on the nearly extinguished cigarette. Millers flicked the butt into the alleyway and started toward the building. His boots clicked on the pavement, limbs shaking and arms darting from side to side, his nervousness nearly overtaking him. He needed to get in and out. His lone goal was to get the shoebox full of cash he had hidden away nearly six months ago after a string of successful robberies. After that, he would decide his course of action.

Millers made it to the brick building and slid between the exterior wall and an overgrowth of weeds, inching west toward the back yard and the detached home he hoped was empty at the moment. The access door was closed, so Millers reached out and slowly turned the knob, pushing it open with a slight squeak, a noise that was like a bomb going off in Millers's ears, yet would not have been heard a mere two feet away.

He entered the garage and left the door cracked, relieved he had made it this far. The interior was dark and smelled of cigarettes and booze. Broken bottles littered the area, and a haziness floated just about his head like smog over a city. Light eked through the windows that faced the home, yet the stacked boxes and grimy curtains created enough of a hindrance that Millers felt safe enough climbing into the rafters to collect his stash.

He stepped onto the rickety stool to his right and pulled himself toward the ceiling, his wounded shoulder straining and creating a pain that shot into his back. "Fuck!" he whispered to himself. Millers took several deep breaths and bent his knees, mentally counting to three and jumping from the stool and onto the platform above. The space provided was just large enough for him to army-crawl into, a deep and dark alcove primarily used for additional storage. His had been cleared out long ago, not that he kept much in the way of extra stuff. Millers lived simple.

He pulled himself a good three feet into the space before reaching to his left and grasping the dilapidated shoebox. The weight told him his money was still there, though he could not see in the darkness that surrounded him. He would not have checked even if he could. Millers was in a hurry. He had accomplished his goal. Now onto phase two: get out.

Millers exited the hole and hung at the waist, his legs dangling in the air in search of the stool, his torso resting upon the dusty plywood of the storage space. Suddenly, a hand grasped his ankle and pulled, dislodging him from the second level and sending him tumbling onto his back with a sickening thud, the air escaping him, the box of money flying to the side and ejecting bills onto the floor of the garage. Millers tried to regain his breath as he rolled to his side and looked up. Before him, near the doorway he had just entered, stood the two bouncers from Ginger's Trap, each one resting on either side of the threshold.

"You're fucking stupider than I thought," came the unmistakable voice of his partner. Millers turned just in time to receive a boot to the ribcage, a strike that sent him to his side. He tried to crawl but could not. "Why the fuck would you come back here? Huh? I mean, I knew you were a fucking dunce, but I didn't realize you were this stupid." The long-haired man lowered his head and stared to Millers through dark-tinted sunglasses, an eerie grin crossing his face. He shook his head before running his fingers through his locks.

"Wait," Millers heard himself say, his mind going a million miles per hour, trying, unsuccessfully, to picture a way out of this predicament. "Wait."

"Wait? No. I don't think so," he responded, pulling his hair into a ponytail. "I'm done fucking waiting. Fortunately for me, I haven't caught word of the cops knowing who *I* am. I'd like to keep it that way." He paced before Millers for a moment before stopping. "Sit up, you fuck." He reached out and pulled Millers up by the shirt collar, cocking his arm back and sending a jab to Renholm's chin that sent him back to the concrete floor with stars forming. "Goddamn!" the man yelled, shaking his hand. "That one will leave a fucking mark, I tell you!"

Millers woozily ran his hand over his jaw and spit, a stained yellow tooth rattling across the floor. His associate laughed, an evil, skin-crawling chuckle that resonated throughout the interior of the garage. Millers rose to his knees and immediately was sent back to a lying position from a boot to the back. He felt the whiplash throughout his neck and into his shoulders, but was with it enough to catch himself from face-planting onto the hard pavement.

He was going to die. He knew it without a doubt. His associate was a strong man, and where he lacked strength, he made up for in pure, unadulterated craziness. There was no way Millers was going to make it out of here alive, even if he could make it over to where his tools lay. The tire iron would make a good weapon, however, three grown men — two of them the size of small oak trees — were no match for it. What he needed was deadly force. He needed a live wire or a nail gun.

Or a gun.

Millers's eyes went wide. He did not keep a gun in the garage. Anything he owned would have been in the crawl space of the home behind the loose cinder block just below the kitchen floor. Guns in the garage were just too accessible for thieves. Unless one had been left by a thief. Or better yet, an associate from the robberies months prior who was feeling some heat and needed to stash his weapon.

Millers shot a quick glance toward the workbench behind his attacker, just under the windows looking out over the back yard. He needed to trade places with his associate, needed to somehow get behind him to grab the gun that he knew was still there, just behind the box containing the power drill.

Millers lifted from the floor and turned to open his mouth, but was met with a debilitating punch to the right shoulder, a direct contact with his gunshot wound. He let out a piercing groan and fell to his side. "You sound like a fucking pig," his associate said. "Is that what you are? Huh? A pig? A squealing fucking little piglet that's caused me enough trouble up till now?" He delivered the last line with a toe to the back of

Millers's right shoulder, pulling from Renholm yet another scream.

"Please!" Millers begged, lifting an arm. "Please stop!"

"Oh, fuck you!" The man lashed out again, this time striking anywhere that Millers left exposed. "You don't tell me what's happening right now! You hear me?" He sent another boot towards Millers's ribs and connected, tipping the bloodied man onto his side into the fetal position, his watery eyes looking up to the three men that stood above.

The long-haired man knelt down. "Unfortunately for you, the cops know who you are." He smiled as Millers glanced up to him. "You don't think I know? You think I'm a fucking idiot? Like you didn't drop your gun at the scene? You think I don't do my research? You had a fucking record before we ever met, you stupid shit. You don't think I knew you would be tagged for Korhan?"

"I won't say —"

"Shut up. You shut the fuck up! Don't open your mouth until I tell you to."

"Please! I —" The statement was cut short by a blow to the chin.

"I said shut the fuck up!" Millers raised a hand above his head in submission. The man nodded his head and stood. "You know why we went to end Karaca, right? You remember?" He turned and walked towards the bouncers before stopping and looking over his shoulder. "You can talk now," he said, his tone borderline encouraging. Millers nodded, his eyes searching his surroundings, determining his chances of making it to the worktable. "We searched him out because he knew too much. Because he became a fucking burden to both of us. And when someone becomes a burden, you know what we do, right?" Millers stared to his associate and watched as the evil grin formed on his face. "Get him up," he said to the enormous men near the doorway.

It was the only moment he had, that point when his associate's back was turned toward him and the attention of both bouncers was on the directive of their boss. It was only a split second, but it was all he had. Millers pulled his knee to his chest and set his foot underneath the weight of his body. He suddenly pushed with all his might and shot from the middle of the garage to the workbench. The long-haired man turned quickly, obviously surprised by the movement, his shift in position edging one of the bouncers out of the way.

The other made it to Millers in a single bound, reaching out and grasping onto Renholm's left shoulder and spinning him toward the doorway. Millers reacted by swinging the hammer from the top of the workbench and connecting with the side of the bouncer's head. The large man stumbled backward, woozy from the strike, and shook his head furiously before taking a focused step back toward the bloodied individual before him.

Millers ducked under the grasping arms of the bouncer and handled the gun underneath the table, pulling it into the light with one quick movement and squeezing the trigger, the bullet ejecting from the chamber and embedding itself into the thigh of the man before him. Another shot rang out in the garage, this one grazing Millers's abdomen as he turned to see his accomplice aiming at him.

Millers bounced to the side and pulled the trigger in succession, missing each and every time as the long-haired man and his cohorts dove behind tables or out of doorways, allowing Renholm to make the quick decision to leap over his workbench and through the glass facing his home. He landed with a thud in his yard, rolling onto his side and propelling himself into a sprint past the lone tree standing near the right of his property. A single shot sounded in the air, the projectile ricocheting off the hard wood of the oak. Millers raised the gun behind him and pulled the trigger, hearing the soft click of an empty weapon as he ran with reckless abandon through yards and over fences, losing himself in the adjacent houses in hopes he could extended his miserable life a few more minutes.

FORTY-SEVEN

Jolene and Jacoby sat in a waiting area at the Robert H. Lurie Comprehensive Cancer Center of Northwestern University. They had made the call to Artemis Greer's home to schedule a meeting with the retired financial consultant, but were made aware by his wife, Lynette, that he was indisposed for the rest of the day, in and out of treatment for pancreatic cancer. They had given their quick condolences at the news, however, Mrs. Greer assured them her husband was a fighter, and guaranteed the detectives he would welcome them at the offices and answer whatever questions they may have between sessions.

"That's really not called for," Jolene had said.

"Oh, please, dear," Lynette had said. "He would love the company. I assure you!"

So while Lynette Greer called her husband to let him know two detectives from the Chicago Police Department were en route to question him, Hartley and Ratliff found themselves making their way to the Northwestern Memorial Hospital,

436

their thoughts on the case before them and the unusual circumstances that surrounded a dying cancer patient.

They had entered the building and made it to the twenty-first floor of the Galter Pavilion, checking in with the receptionist and learning that Mr. Greer had entered his second round of tests and would not be available for roughly the next thirty minutes. "Lynette called and told us you were coming, so please, help yourself to coffee or a pastry." The receptionist was jovial and sincere, an attribute, Jolene thought, one needed when dealing with the murderous rampage cancer brought. The detective smiled and moved to the cushioned chairs in the waiting area, her partner tailing close behind.

"How do you want to go about this?" Ratliff questioned. The inquiry treaded lightly on eggshells, the need for the truth within their investigation softened by the absolute acknowledgment to their current location and plight of their newest person of interest.

Hartley looked to Jacoby. "As any other murder investigation," she replied. "Mr. Greer's condition doesn't exclude him from any responsibility if he's involved." She paused and watched as a young woman, no older than herself, pushed through the doorway and to the receptionist. She was pretty, however, her cancer had sunken her eyes and made her cheeks stand out underneath a hairless, scarfed head. She walked slowly, shifting her weight and swinging the large walking boot she wore over comfy black sweatpants. Hartley swallowed. "Leniency can't be given by us," she finished, her eyes cast to the floor.

"Agreed," Ratliff stated, backing the plan.

"Do you recognize the name Leary?" Hartley asked after some time.

He thought for a moment before nodding. "Yeah. Didn't your guy in Philly mention the name Leary in connection with Kyle Walker?"

"Ronny. And yes, he did. And it's the family Walker's great-aunt married into, remember?" She did not wait for a response. "Debarsi told us when Walker was in Ireland, he ran into some family that paid his way into University College Dublin —"

"Right, right. Graduated with a business degree, if I'm not mistaken."

"— and then came back to the States to a cozy spot at *State of Finance.* How much you want to bet that Greer is linked to the Learys?"

"But didn't everything point to Verland paying for Walker's education?"

Hartley shook her head. "That's what I thought. But nothing has been found within any seized financial documents that show Verland paying for any student enrollment."

"Maybe he hid it?"

"Why? College tuition doesn't really scream for investigation."

Ratliff shrugged. "But it may be a whisper for someone without kids."

She turned her attention to the wall directly across from her. "Either way, if Ann Carroll is right, and you tie that into what Debarsi said about the Learys, Artemis Greer has to be connected."

* * * * *

Millers stumbled and fell face-first into a crumbling gravel walkway cutting through a neighborhood park. His reached his hands out before him and slid across the pavement, feeling the loose stones dig into his flesh. It would have caused him some pain, if not for the excruciating ache that centered on his wounded right shoulder.

The owner of Ginger's Trap had done a number on him: missing and cracked teeth; possible fractured ribs from the steel toe of his boot; broken thumb from the eight foot drop from the storage space to the concrete floor. He was in pain, yet alive, which, at this moment, was all he cared about.

He scrambled to his feet and came to a crouch at the edge of a maintenance shed. He cursed and spit a mouthful of blood into the weeds to his left, eyes immediately turning to his surroundings as a car door slammed from across the field. An elderly man made his way up his driveway and disappeared into the home.

Millers's thoughts raced, dispersing as quickly as they appeared. He attempted to catch onto one, to reign in a wisp of a coherent idea that his mind circulated at a furious pace. He finally took a deep breath and stood, knowing he had to keep moving, to find a more reclusive spot where he could tend to his wounds. The problem, however, was that Millers had nowhere to go. He had no real friends, just acquaintances and cronies that would give him up for a case of beer. His money, or lack thereof, was spread out across his garage or traveling with the long-haired man in the disintegrating shoebox. Either way, it was out of his reach.

He turned the corner of the building and watched as a young couple made their way out of a house and paused between the brick exterior and an old Buick. They embraced and kissed in a passionate exchange of young love. Millers scowled at the pair, yet found himself wondering what the young woman tasted like, how smooth her skin was and if she was any good in the sack. Her straight, red hair fell about her shoulders and, even from this distance, Millers could see she had perky breasts. He almost smiled, but was instead pulled from his fantasies by the squealing of tires in the distance, the direction of the noise coming from where his home stood. He needed to get out of here, and quick.

The couple did not see his approach, their eyes closed and mouths and tongues working in overdrive, his hands up her shirt as her leg pulled his pelvis into hers. They stopped only as Millers yanked the back of his shirt away from the girl, their shocked expressions mirroring one another as they realized they were not alone.

"What the fuck!" They were the only defense the young man displayed before Renholm brought the gun down with a smash, instantly splitting open the skin on his cheek and sending him to a heap on the blacktop of the driveway. Before the red-head could scream, the gun was aimed at her head and a finger brought to his own lips. "If you make any noise, I'll fucking kill him and do worse to you. Do you understand?" She remained still, back pressed against the cold brick, tears streaming down her flushed cheeks. Millers stepped forward and pressed the gun to her jaw, his lips coming extremely close to her own. "Do you fucking understand?"

"Yes," she whimpered.

"Good," he answered. "Now get in the fucking car. You're driving."

* * * * *

The detectives followed a frumpy nurse in pink scrubs down a hallway. They passed rooms with open doors, doctors and patients seated and speaking in quiet voices, or laughing with tears streaming down their respective cheeks. They turned down an adjoining corridor and stopped. "Here you go," the nurse said, opening a door to their right and raising an arm for them to enter. "Take your time. We'll be by in a little bit to steal Arty from you."

"Thank you," Ratliff said.

Artemis Greer was a frail, bald-headed man in a wheelchair, with large glasses over a wide nose. His mustache, obviously at one point full and bushy, was short and scraggly, and there were random hairs sprinkled across his aged, wrinkled face. Hartley could not tell his age and immediately felt a lump in her throat. There were points in her career where she felt that the right course of action came with negative repercussions, mainly on her own soul. This was one of those times.

Artemis Greer, however debilitated physically, was mentally with the rest of the world. He knew at first glance that the female detective before him was wavering the moment she stepped in the door. "Don't worry, my dear," he said, pulling her eyes to his. "I've done a lot of despicable things in my past. Feel free to ask anything you need to."

"Thank you, Mr. Greer," she said, stopping in the middle of the room with Jacoby by her side.

"No, no, no," he said, shaking his head. "You can call me either Artemis or Arty or just plain Art. I'm not going to have this Mr. Greer bullshit." He smiled. "But I'm not going to call you ma'am or sir either. Now, Lynette phoned and told me your names, but, I apologize, I've forgotten them."

Hartley nodded. "I'm Detective Jolene Hartley."

"And I'm Detective Jacoby Ratliff. You can call me Jay."

"Jolene and Jay. Great." He smacked his legs and folded his hands. "Before we start, would either of you like some coffee?" He did not wait for a response. "Susana? Susana!" A petite nurse with long blonde hair entered the room. "Ah, Susana. These are my friends, Jolene and Jay."

"Nice to meet you," she said in a high-pitched voice. She turned her attention back to Artemis. "You know, buddy, there's a call button. You don't have to scream down the hallway every time."

"But if I used the call button —"

She rolled her eyes. "I know, I know. That'd make me a call girl. He's hilarious, this one." She thumbed at Greer. "What can I get you?"

"Three coffees, please."

"Surely. Cream and sugar?"

"You know how I take mine. Jolene? Jay?"

"Black will be fine," Hartley responded.

"Same," Ratliff answered.

The nurse rounded the corner and disappeared into the hall. "Got to keep them on their toes," Greer finally said, "seeing I won't ever get back on mine."

"Due to the cancer?" Ratliff asked.

"Car accident," Artemis answered quickly. "Six years ago. Driving on some back road in Manteno. Deer came out of nowhere. They said the car flipped a half dozen times. Broke my back and both legs. Fractured my pelvis."

"Wow," Ratliff replied. "Sounds like it was pretty serious."

Artemis waved a hand in the air. "It was six years ago and I'm still kicking. For the moment, anyway. Now, you didn't come here to talk about my accident. Lynette said something about an investigation?"

Before Hartley could speak, Susana reappeared in the doorway carrying their coffees. She handed one to each of the officers in turn, and then to her patient. "Thanks, dear," Artemis said as she left. "Now, please, what can I do for you?"

"Mr. Greer," Hartley began, stopping as he raised a finger to her. "Sorry. Artemis, we're investigating a murder and through some roundabout ways, your name has come up."

He raised his eyebrows. "Really? A homicide, and my name's coming up? I can't imagine why."

"Like I said, sir, it's pretty indirect, but we need to follow-up on every lead."

"Sure." He paused and looked between the duo. "What would you like my help with?"

FORTY-EIGHT

"I'd like to ask you some questions about *State of Finance*. About your time there as a board member." Hartley pulled up a chair and sat between the door and her interview subject. By no means did she think Artemis was going to make a break for it. It was merely a habit, an ingrained action to be an obstacle in case matters should escalate, an extra wall or shut doorway should an escape be in the works.

"Sure," Artemis responded. "What would you like to know?"

"How long were you a board member there?"

He lifted his eyes to the ceiling and stretched his neck, thoughts meandering back to a time long ago. "I was on the board at *State* for a little over four years, if memory serves. I started about fifteen years ago at the behest of my good friend Christopher Cunningham, who was also a board member."

"Is he still there?" Ratliff chimed in.

Artemis shook his head. "No. Chris died years ago of a brain aneurysm." He trailed off with the final word and the expression on his face faded to sadness.

Hartley waited only a moment to pull him back from the tragedy. "Why did you leave *State* after only four years?"

"Well, I was never *really* fully at *State*, you see. It was purely a side interest."

"One that made you a lot of money, no doubt."

"It was a lucrative position. But I assure you, not as lucrative as you think."

"So, why did you leave after such a short time?"

He waved a hand in the air before them. "Jolene, I was always more of a finance guy. I was good at it and made a fortune helping those that weren't. Many people got rich because of me. Many Fortune 500 companies skirted around and through loopholes to maintain a wealth that the average man can't even dream of. I left the position at the magazine because it was not my calling. It was fun, don't get me wrong. However, I had other items that needed more time from me."

"Such as Eric Sheehan?" The question escaped her lips more hurriedly than intended, pulling Ratliff's gaze to her momentarily.

Artemis stared to her for a second before responding. "By the look on your face, I'm assuming you are the detectives behind what happened at *State*?" Hartley remained quiet. Greer nodded his head. "I was sorry to hear about Kyle getting killed. He was ... He *tried to be* a decent man. Guess it just wasn't in the cards for him."

"How well did you know him?"

"Well enough, I guess. He seemed like a good kid."

"Did you know about his past?" Ratliff asked.

Greer nodded. "I knew he had had some troubles. But he said he was over that. He was trying to get his life in order, and that meant going to college and getting a job. I had no reason to believe otherwise. He seemed very sincere."

"Were you close with him?"

"Not overly so. Detectives, I am a man that has many different interests. Helping people was one of them. Still is. But I don't see the need in sticking around to watch how one's work turns out. Seems a little selfish to me." He leaned forward. "Pardon me, but what does Kyle have to do with anything?"

"Artemis, Kyle Walker was a major part in the case we worked last year. His death is a tragedy, but if he was still alive, he would be in a federal penitentiary for the rest of his life."

"So it is true then? The reports about him and the murders?"

Hartley nodded her head. "We had a hunch about Walker from early on, and had help from the FBI regarding his whereabouts before he ended up at the magazine. We tracked him to Ireland and learned that he entered the University College Dublin by way of a gift from the Leary family. After graduation, he came back to the States, changed his name, and ended up at *State of Finance* as Assistant Editor." Artemis nodded, waiting for more. Hartley glanced to her partner. "You know all of this?"

"I do," Artemis said. "I was the one who got him the job at the magazine, after all."

"How do you know about Walker's schooling in Ireland?" Ratliff questioned.

"My wife and I paid for it." Hartley and Ratliff looked to each other. "I'm confused," Artemis replied. "This all seems like common knowledge between us. I don't mean to be blunt, but what exactly are you asking me?"

"I guess I'm wondering how you are associated with the Leary family," Hartley said.

"Ah," he answered, sitting back and tapping his thighs. "That's an easy one. Leary is my wife's maiden name."

"So your wife is related to Kyle Walker? Or, I guess, Eric Sheehan?"

He shrugged. "In some long distance sort of way, yes. But we never had him over for Christmas dinner or anything."

"So you're wife knew Kyle?"

"To my knowledge, not before his appearance in Ireland."

"Then how did he get onto your radar?"

"My wife makes quarterly trips back to *the motherland*," he said, the last words in an accomplished Irish accent. "On one of them, she had a chance to meet Eric Sheehan and learn about him. Lynette's a giving soul, like me. She likes to help out those less fortunate. So, after a couple meetings, she was convinced to give Eric a chance."

"Convinced? By whom?"

"If memory serves, I believe it was her nephew. Dante Leary."

"Was Mr. Leary in contact with Eric Sheehan from before the trip to Ireland?" Ratliff questioned.

Artemis shrugged. "I have no idea. We're not really in touch with Dante nowadays."

"Why's that?"

He lifted a palm in the air and stalled. "He just kind of … faded out of our lives."

"Do you know his whereabouts?" Again, Artemis shook his head. "When's the last time you talked to Dante?" Hartley asked.

"Six years ago." He answered confidently, watching as the assertiveness drew a minute reaction from the female detective. "I remember that because it was a couple weeks after the accident. I was in a medically-induced coma to keep some swelling down on the brain, and when they brought me out, Dante showed up."

"That's surprising," Hartley said.

"How so?"

"Well, you said you weren't particularly close with your wife's nephew. Seems odd that he would be someone that shows up at the hospital in your hour of need."

"Circumstances, Jolene. It's all about the circumstances." He smiled.

Jolene grinned back. "Maybe you could enlighten me then."

"Surely, my dear!" He leaned forward and shifted in his wheelchair. "Dante is actually the reason I'm still alive today." He paused for effect and waited.

Finally, Hartley acknowledged the silence and humored the sickly man. "What do you mean by that?"

"Dante was in the car wreck with me. He pulled me from the car moments before it exploded."

* * * * *

"Turn here," Millers said coldly, glancing at the girl behind the wheel, the empty gun aimed at her ribs. They had gotten in the car after his assault and kidnapping and made their way through the neighborhood. He did not have a plan as of yet, only that he needed to get out of the area as quickly as possible. It did not go unnoticed by Renholm that the man he had pistol-whipped into unconsciousness would, at some point — most likely — wake to a splitting headache and missing girlfriend and alert the authorities. Millers knew the car they now drove in would be searched for with intense diligence in the coming hours or minutes. He could only hope the boyfriend was still in the driveway and had not woken up.

The whimpers from the driver's seat pulled him from his thoughts with jarring force. "Shut the fuck up!" he yelled, jabbing the barrel of the gun into her ribs. She gulped and held in the air, eyes trying to clench as she forced them back to the road.

"Okay! Okay! Please!" Her whispers were nearly lost amongst the sobs.

"I need to fucking think!" He shouted at her, rising from his seat and leaning into her shoulder. "Shut the fuck up or I'll make you!"

At that moment the rear end of the car crashed in toward the back seat with a deafening boom and the vehicle spun in a half circle. Amidst the flying glass and mangled upholstery, the girl screamed at the top of her lungs, clutching onto the steering wheel in an unsuccessful attempt at curbing their spiraling twist. The Buick slid into a parked taxi with a force that nearly wrenched the girl from her current location and into Millers's lap.

He looked up just as a bullet was released into the air, the projectile piercing the front window and burying itself into the console directly between Renholm and his chauffeur. Millers looked up for a split second at the SUV facing them and knew he was in great peril. From behind the bent and broken hood of the larger vehicle, Millers could make out the owner of Ginger's Trap, gun in hand as he tried to aim it over his ruined auto.

"Go!" Millers yelled, throwing the gearstick into reverse and pushing down with all his might on the girl's leg. The car's tires squealed on the pavement, a gray smoke rising as the rubber burned from the friction. Finally, they lurched backward, scraping metal on metal along the parked cab to their right. The SUV began to pull forward, yet suddenly came to a halt, the engine dying in the middle of the intersection.

"Get the fuck out of here!" Millers yelled again, yanking the wheel to the right as the girl tried to control the speed.

They crashed into another vehicle, the alarm sounding in the atmosphere. The girl popped the gearstick into drive and slammed her foot down on the gas, accelerating hurriedly down an empty one-way street until they came to a fork. "There!" Millers yelled, pointing to an alleyway perpendicular to their location. "Down there!" The girl turned the wheel and propelled the Buick into the dim lit road, following her captor's demands to turn left and right, his panicked, deranged tone leaving no wiggle room for questions. She cried, tears streaming down her cheeks, adrenaline pumping to the point where she felt like she may vomit.

Finally, after what felt like hours, Millers directed her onto a main street, watching as the red and blue flashing lights zipped by. "Good," he said in a calm voice, hand grasping onto her thigh. "You did well."

FORTY-NINE

"I hate to keep asking questions," Artemis said, holding up a withered finger as Hartley opened her mouth to speak, "but you said you were investigating a murder. Why are you asking about my past at *State of Finance* and Dante?"

"I assure you," Hartley replied, "there's a method to the madness."

"There always is." He smiled at her and lowered his hand.

Jolene took it as a sign to continue. "The murder we're investigating involves Korhan Karaca. Did you know about Mr. Karaca?"

Artemis shook his head and then halted. "Just what I've seen on the news. I know that he's Ahmet's son. But that's about it."

"So you know Ahmet then?" Ratliff asked.

Artemis nodded "We had built up a mutual respect for one another throughout the years. Don't really keep in touch anymore, but there was a point where I would have considered him a friend."

"When's the last time you spoke with Ahmet?" Hartley inquired.

"Here and there. Holiday cards. Well wishes at New Year's. That sort of thing." He paused and took a long sip of his coffee. Hartley was about to follow up when his eyes widened and he removed the cup from his lips. "Now that I think about it, the last time I talked to Dante, Ahmet was there."

"At the hospital?" Ratliff asked.

Artemis nodded. "I remember talking briefly with Dante and then Ahmet coming in. Dante left shortly after that, if I recall. That's the last time I spoke with him in person."

"But you've had contact with Dante other than that?"

"Used to talk to him on the phone when he'd call to check in on Lynette. Christmas cards." He shrugged. "Like I said, Jay, we kind of drifted apart."

Jolene thought for a moment, taking the seconds to sip her coffee and write a couple notes in the pad she cradled in her lap. Finally, she chose a different route. "Mr. Greer, does the name James Graiser ring a bell with you?"

"I recognize the last name. Hard not to if you had any sort of business in Chicago." He paused and cast his eyes to the floor, lost in the past. "I remember the murders well, too. Horrible thing. They were decent folk. Had a good vision for the city and a lot of pull politically throughout the neighborhoods. It's too bad what happened to them, especially their boy. James, you said it was?"

"That's correct."

"Terrible. I had the honor of meeting the Graisers on several occasions and I could tell they were involved for all the right reasons, not just to make money. In fact, that's where I initially met Ahmet. Some city function that we all attended." He chuckled. "I spent most of the night rubbing elbows with Ahmet near the bar. It was a great evening."

"Did you know Daniel Vincent?" Hartley asked.

Artemis nodded. "Oh, yes. Daniel was a good man, as well. That whole group consisted of good people, respectable people. It's too bad Robert Thames's son went off the deep end and did what he did. Daniel could have done much more for this city then anyone could have imagined."

"How did you come to know all of these individuals?" Ratliff asked. "Was it through your association with Congressman Johnston?"

Artemis slowly nodded his head, a smile forming across his aged face. "I got it!" he said, holding a finger up to Hartley. "I can place you now! See, my mind's still sharp, but old age does slow you down a bit." He leaned forward. "You're the officer that brought Johnston down. You really get around, huh?" He laughed. "In answer to your question, Jay, yes, I met the foresaid individuals through my association with Harold Johnston. I knew of the Graisers before that, of course, but working with Harry is how I came to know them."

"That must have been a strange relationship," Hartley interjected. "I mean, with all the feuds that were said to have happened between Johnston and Mr. Vincent."

He bounced his head from shoulder to shoulder. "It wasn't the ideal situation, no. But I'm not one to care much what others think. If I want to associate with this individual and do business with that scoundrel, then so be it. Both parties will just have to deal with it."

"Are you calling Congressman Johnston a scoundrel?"

Artemis paused and leaned. He folded his hands on an armrest of his wheelchair and stared right to Jolene. "No, Harold Johnston is not a scoundrel," he said. "He's a downright crook, to the highest degree."

* * * * *

Caprice ran her fingers through her hair as she hurriedly made her way from the sidewalk to the door of her apartment. Her workday, although ten hours in, was not over, only at a brief hiatus to exchange the pink scrubs and tennis shoes for a sparkly gold thong and fuck-me boots. She had only fifteen minutes to eat and change out of her hospital garb and into a warm-up suit, her attire for traveling to and from the strip club. Once at the gentlemen's club, Caprice would quickly don her favorite pieces, dance seductively whilst losing articles of clothing at certain musical cues, and eventually spread eagle for ogling eyes to survey.

It was not the dream job she had once conjured up, however, it did pay extremely well, enough so where she had trouble pulling the trigger to quit and focus solely on her nursing career. Instead, the extra couple grand in her pocket a week kept her shaking what she had, allowed her mind to turn off when groping hands in the back booths found areas they were not supposed to venture to.

She had allowed things to happen in her past, her youth and one-time devil-may-care attitude allowing inhibitions to drop to the floor along with her clothes. She had, at points, allowed the groping of her breasts, thick calloused fingers caressing her skin from shoulders to knees. On several occasions even, for special regular gentlemen she had grown accustomed to, she had even allowed sexual contact, penetrating fingers and curious tongues, and, once, intercourse.

However, that was in the past. Her views on the job had changed. She had grown up. Unwanted relationships had been set aside. All-night binges on alcohol and drugs were extinct in her life. Dancing for money was exactly that. Sure, there were times when she still felt the euphoria of being on stage, lights flashing, music pumping, all eyes turning to the platform where Andrea — the chosen name for her stint at the latest establishment — was about to step onto. She still felt sexy, at times, while strutting across the surface, staring to the mirrors lining the walls to take in the moves she had perfected throughout the years. She had become the veteran of the place, the younger, fresh out of high-school girls — and that was what they were — looking up to her for guidance in the business of erotic dancing.

She had long ago learned she was not the prettiest, and was quite content with it. That title belonged to the tall, lean twentysomethings that took the stage with reckless abandon, bouncing their asses off the platform and wiggling their hips in a frenzy to work their clients into a yearning they no longer felt at home. They were beautiful. Caprice knew it. However, she also understood the art of the dance. She knew the brush her body could become on a canvas such as that. But it was also something she knew would come to an end, be it by a well thought out decision or the inevitability of age. Either way, her days on the stage were numbered.

Caprice yawned and reached into her purse, sifting through the jingling contents until she found her keys. She unlocked her front door and entered into darkness, tossing her purse to the floor before stepping in and kicking off her shoes. She turned to the door and shut it, reaching to the left to flip the light switch and illuminate her aging abode, yet another item she wanted to be rid of.

Her breath caught and her heart skipped a beat as she felt the cold metal of a gun barrel press against the base of her neck. Thoughts flooded her mind rapidly and her mouth dropped open to scream. An arm wrapped across her body and she was immediately quieted by a forceful grip muffling her cry. The strength of the intruder's hold spun her around and she came face to face with Millers Renholm. She began to speak but was silenced as he lifted the gun high in the air and brought it down with brutal force against her temple, sending her to the floor in a whimper.

Colors erupted in her vision as she tried to move, her limbs heavy, like weights had been strapped to them in the previous split second. She glanced up and tried to focus as the blackness faded in. The only thing she could make out was the confused, scared look spread across Millers's face.

FIFTY

They had taken a break for a short period as Artemis's nurse came in to check on him. Hartley and Ratliff had taken to the halls and paced back and forth, stretching their limbs and debating internally on the route their investigation was going. Artemis, indeed, seemed like a viable source, however, Jolene could not determine the importance of his role. The link Greer had created between himself, Kyle Walker and Dante Leary was something special. It had closed part of the mystery surrounding their previous case regarding Damian Verland and the Editor and Assistant Editor at *State of Finance.* Now, Hartley needed to figure out where Greer came into their current case. The best spot she could start was where he had left off, with his connection to the congressman. "Tell me about your work with Harold Johnston."

"I was never that fond of Harry," Greer answered finally, his nurse wheeling him in front of the chairs where the detectives sat. He thanked her and smirked to Hartley and Ratliff. "Actually, that's understating it. I despised him."

"Then why do business with him?"

"There are always people you won't like in the business world. Especially when dealing with politicians. The upside is that they usual pay well."

"We know you were a consultant to Johnston. What did that entail?"

"You've done your research, haven't you?" He seemed impressed. "I came on board to oversee some of his investments. Like I said, I was good at what I did. Part of that dealt with the management of allocated funds into stocks and bonds, that sort of thing. All legit transactions, I assure you. Eventually, he asked me to become more of an accountant for him, which I accepted. Not as interesting of a position, but the pay grade increased substantially."

"What were your responsibilities there?" Ratliff asked.

"Along with the stocks and bonds? The usual suspects: balancing checkbooks; opening and closing accounts; signing off on transactions."

"Were any of those transactions through Intervise Securities?" Hartley questioned, his response throwing a cautionary flag.

He nodded. "Absolutely. That was considered my main responsibility. I was directed to pull dividends out from time to time and wire the funds to account numbers that were given to me."

"Do you still have these account numbers? Or remember who the funds were wired to?"

"Sorry, detective. I don't. There was never a name associated with the account numbers. And to be honest, I never asked, although I'm thinking maybe I should have now."

Hartley smiled. "That would have been too easy if you had. Do you recall any of the sums that were sent?"

He thought for a moment before responding. "Not exact amounts, but most were substantial."

"Give me a range."

"I'd say between fifty-thousand and half a million."

"That's quite a range," Ratliff added.

"There were many organizations and individuals Harry dealt with."

"Like who?"

"Take your pick. He's a politician in one of the biggest cities in the United States, not to mention a businessman at heart. There's no saying who he *hasn't* done business with."

"Tell me about the end of your consultation. What were the terms of you leaving the employment of Johnston?"

"The short of it? My employment was terminated. I was brought into his offices to sign non-disclosure forms for the umpteenth time and given a large severance package. Then I was shown the door." He sat up and stretched before continuing. "Didn't really matter that much to me. I was only consulting, and had many other ongoing obligations."

"Isn't it strange to receive a severance package for consulting work?" Hartley asked.

He agreed with a quick nod of the head. "Extremely," he said.

"Why do you think it was given to you then?"

"I think there was really only one solid reason why: Robert Thames."

* * * * *

She came to with a headache like she had never felt before, the constant, unrelenting pounding in her temples reverberating throughout her body until the nausea became almost unbearable. She felt herself gag, a wrenching coursing through her torso for several moments before subsiding and allowing her a brief moment of calm and relief.

Caprice gingerly opened her eyes, her surroundings sluggishly coming into view before her mind could process them. The tape over her mouth suppressed the sounds she tried to emit as she realized she was tied to the frame of her bed, hands over her head, feet restrained together with that of another individual.

She lifted her eyes to her right and looked upon a young woman no more than twenty years of age, duct tape covering her mouth, hands tied in the same fashion as her own. The girl looked back with sorrowful eyes. She seemed in a much better state physically, no gash to the side of her head with encrusted, dried blood forming clumps in her hair. Mentally, however, Caprice could see the turmoil behind her eyes, the confusion and chaos that clouded her thoughts.

There was no relief Caprice could instill on her guest. She could not tell her everything would be all right, even if the duct tape had not been placed over their mouths. For all she knew, Millers had gone off the deep end and was planning on killing them both, or worse. She had heard stories from those that knew Millers. She knew from the gossip between their mutual acquaintances of what Millers was capable of and that his mental status, at times, hung by a thread. Caprice had seen firsthand his aggressiveness toward the opposite sex, yet had never felt the brutality of it until this very evening.

There was no solace she could give the girl next to her. Caprice was scared as well.

* * * * *

"Why Robert Thames?" Hartley pushed.

"I was never really that convinced that Robert had done anything wrong. Granted, I had nothing to do with Johnston's political endeavors, and Robert did, but he just never seemed to me to be that type of guy. He was hardnosed and to the point, but, up until the investigation into him, he was always on the straight and narrow."

"People can change."

"That they can, Jolene. That they can. But everything that came about was just too ... cozy for me. Things were wrapped up in too nice of a little package." He paused and thought briefly, eying both of the detectives for a moment before continuing. "As I said when you walked in, detectives, I have done things in my past that are undesirable. Not illegal, mind you, just not up to my standards today." Again, he stalled.

"However, the items behind Robert Thames's downfall and imprisonment may be partially my doing."

Hartley furrowed her brow. "How do you mean?"

"Well, as I said, I signed off on a lot of transfers. In those days, pretty much everything was coming through me. I was inundated by the amount. After I was released from Harry's services, I didn't think much of it. I was happy to get on with my other ventures and be rid of Johnston. But as the details came out on Robert, things didn't add up to me. I remember vividly some of the accounts and transfers being on my lists. I recalled signing off on those and being shocked when they were mentioned in relation to the Thames scandal. It was baffling."

"Why not come to the police with the information?"

"Because they already had their guy. And there was no proof. I wasn't allowed to keep the documents."

"But you were behind the scenes. You could have brought reasonable doubt to the jury's sway."

"And a prying eye into my life."

"But you said what you did was legal," Ratliff added.

"It was, at least from my understanding. But I was the one signing off on the transfers that put Thames away."

Hartley thought for a moment, placing her head in her palm as her brain raced. "Wait, wait," she finally said. "Wait. Something doesn't make sense to me here." She sat up and pulled their focus to her. "If you signed off on whatever put Thames behind bars, why aren't *you* the one in jail?"

"My only guess is that whatever happened around that time involved those documents being switched to show Robert as the source." He stopped and looked to the duo. "You have to understand, I had no intentions of ever helping Johnston with any of his less than respectable business transactions. And I definitely did not know I was playing a role in putting Robert Thames in jail."

* * * * *

A shift in lighting brought each woman's attention to the doorway of the bedroom, to the shirtless man stepping into the threshold, gun held near his waist as he loaded a magazine into the handle. "Hope you don't mind me taking this," Millers said to Caprice. She stared to him yet did not respond. Her eyes scanned his naked torso, looking upon the right shoulder and the fresh bandages wrapped around his frame, a patchy, unprofessional attempt at doctoring a wound.

Millers stepped forward and knelt next to her, running his eyes across her frame. He reached up and turned her head savagely, bringing forth a muted grunt as he surveyed her bloodied head. "Now, I want to talk to you, Caprice. You understand? I'm going to remove the tape in a second, but I have some rules." He smiled and lifted the gun to the red-haired girl's head, pressing the barrel firmly against her as she tried to wriggle away. "If you scream, I'm going to fucking shoot her in the head. If you don't answer my questions in a timely manner, I'm going to fucking shoot her in the leg." He moved the gun to the girl's thigh. "And if I find that you're lying to me in any way …" he said finally, moving the weapon from the girl to Caprice's jaw, pushing her face skyward as he edged in closer to her. "If you give me any shit, I'm going to have some fun with you before I put a bullet between your eyes. Understood?"

* * * * *

A light lit in Jolene's mind as she thought about the information Artemis Greer had given her thus far, a notion about something he had said in regards to the Robert Thames's fiasco. "You said you think the files must have been changed? The ones you had signed off on?"

"That's right," Artemis answered. "It's the only reason why I can think that I was never questioned."

"Who took those files over?"

Greer thought for a minute before responding. "They were taken by Damian Verland and his legal team, at the behest of Johnston."

Hartley leaned back into her chair and glanced to Ratliff, who in turn stared with wide eyes back to her. "The files," was all he said.

FIFTY-ONE

The nurse had come in shortly after that, and Hartley and Ratliff found themselves exiting the building as night fell upon the city. Artemis Greer had proved to be a useful individual in the chaotic mess that they called their cases. As he had wheeled away, he had stopped and turned to the officers. "Anything I can help with, you let me know. Anything at all." He smiled.

"We may call on you," Hartley had responded, handing him her card. "And I hope when we do, you'll come forward." They had left then, watching for a moment as the nurse wheeled Greer to his next test.

Hartley turned onto the sidewalk and ran her hands through her hair. "What do you think?" Ratliff asked, stopping next to her and flipping through the notepad he had scribbled in while speaking with Greer.

Before she could respond, her phone began to ring. She reached into her pocket and pulled the device out, staring to the screen. "It's James," she said, pressing the answer button and putting the mechanism to her ear. Before she could even speak a greeting, her brow furrowed. "Whoa! Hold on!" she yelled back, holding a hand in the air. "What do you mean he took the files? ... Did he bring them back? ... All right. All right. Tell everyone to sit tight. We'll be there shortly. I don't want anyone to move!" She hung up and swore.

"What's going on?"

"Dane is going on," she replied as if that answered the question entirely. She looked upon Ratliff's confused face. "He stole some of the files and shared them with someone. Apparently no one knew until he came back to the room. With some woman."

"Perfect," he replied. "Captain would love this."

"Yeah," she agreed with a chuckle. "Captain's not finding out about this one. Let's go."

* * * * *

The yelling could be heard from outside of the room, and the officer stationed there only shook his head as Hartley and Ratliff entered. The scene was heated, yet neither side appeared ready for physical altercation. James and Augie had set themselves in the den area, the section of the large room that the Londoner had called home for the duration of his stay. Meanwhile, Dane exited from the kitchen, drink in hand, and eyed his sister as she stopped before him. "Hey sis," he said, raising the tumbler to his lips.

"Is it true?" she asked.

"Yeah, it's true!" Augie yelled from the couch.

"Fuck off!" Dane yelled back. "I don't see you motherfuckers doing anything to help move this stalling investigation on."

"It's not your investigation to move on, Dane," Hartley responded.

He turned and chortled. "Don't fucking start with me. Without me, you're —"

She stepped to him and swung with an open palm, connecting with her brother's chest as he stepped back, surprised. Ratliff reached out and grasped onto Jolene's waist, lifting her easily off the floor and spinning her away from the reporter. He set her down, yet kept his hand on her, waiting for another assault that did not come.

Suddenly, a woman appeared from behind the table, a folder in her hand. Hartley had never seen her before, but immediately did not like her, the smirk across her face making the detective wish Ratliff was not holding her back. "Maybe you want to take a look at what we've found, instead of assaulting the citizens of the city."

"Who is this?" Ratliff asked, staring intently to Dane.

"Allow me to introduce Maggie Tien," he answered. "Good reporter, decent human being, and a fantastic lay." He smirked.

Maggie eyed him for a moment. "Prick."

Dane turned to Ratliff. "When you're done with her, Maggie'd be perfect for you." He barely got the words out before James turned the corner and struck him across the jaw with a quick jab, a stunning blow that caused Dane to stumble and drop the crystal tumbler to the floor, the container shattering and splashing scotch throughout the kitchen. Dane pushed himself off the wall and began to step towards James. Graiser, however, was not done, and flung himself into the reporter with enough force to cause the pair to slide across the floor and crash into the cabinetry. Ratliff and Hartley bounded after, grabbing past flying fists and kicking legs to pull the two apart and set them at opposite sides of the kitchen.

"Knock it off!" Hartley finally yelled, her hand pressed against James's chest, eyes bouncing between him and her brother who had been subdued by Jacoby. James glanced to her and caught her focus, noticing the slight curl to the corner of her mouth, an amused thank you of sorts for doing what she legally could not. His face lost its ferocity, eyes softening as he nodded.

"Are we done?" Ratliff asked Dane, who pushed his arms away and smiled across the distance to James.

"You hit like a woman," the reporter said to him.

"Enough!" Hartley exclaimed. She turned her attention to the middle of the room where Maggie had backed to. "Who the hell are you and what are you doing here?"

Maggie stepped towards her with her hand out. Jolene held hers up to halt the woman and shook her head, a tired look spread across her face. Maggie stopped and cleared her throat. "I'm Mei Tien. People call me Maggie. I'm a reporter, like Dane, except not as big of an asshole."

"That's debatable," Dane chimed in, ever the jokester.

"And I have a source that helps me find things better than anything your brother has. That's why I'm here."

"Without her," Dane added, "you wouldn't have the information we found."

"And what information is that?" James asked. "Something you had to steal these files for?"

"I assure you, James," Maggie said, "The files are back. The copies Dane made for me have been destroyed, and there's no trace of our search."

"What do you mean?" Jolene said, stepping into the center of the group. "No trace? Why would you need to worry about someone tracing what you did?"

"Because it's not exactly legal."

Hartley turned to stare at her brother. "What the fuck did you do?"

He held up his hands in defense. "Just listen —"

"Dane, I swear to god, if you compromised my investigation, I will throw your ass in jail without a second thought. And you're friend, too."

"Jolene!" he said loudly. "You need to listen. Maggie found names."

"What names?" James asked. Jolene shot him a glare.

"Names to accounts listed on these papers," Maggie answered.

The room quieted. Everyone, including Augie, who had positioned himself on the couch, away from the mayhem, turned and perked his ears up to take in the phrase. Jolene stared at Dane for several moments before asking, "How'd you get the names?"

"Does it matter?" Maggie answered. "It's not something you can use in court."

"It matters to me."

"Well, I'm not giving up my source."

"Maggie, I really don't have time —"

"Give me your word," she interrupted. "My source doesn't come into this unless I say so, and I'll give you the information we found." She let the option hang in the air, waiting for some sort of response from either of the detectives in the room. "Listen, it may not be admissible, but it's the truth. What I have is fact. I can give you items to move on, names to look into."

"Illegally generated items and names."

Maggie shrugged. "Take it or leave it."

* * * * *

Jolene sat back in the chair at the end of the kitchen table and sighed. All eyes were on her, including Augie, who had muted the program he was watching and sat on his knees to take in the gathering. They had all agreed on hearing the information from Maggie in a much less hostile state, Dane and James placed at separate ends while Tien and Hartley faced each other through the slim portion of the table, as they would in Interrogation One. Ratliff paced the floor near Dane, a position he refused to give up in case the reporter once again opened his mouth to expel venom.

What Maggie Tien had found was breathtaking, the kind of information one could only come upon by illegal means, skirting around access points and securities to pilfer data that was not rightfully yours. "So you're a hacker," Hartley said bluntly.

Maggie shook her head. "My *source* is a hacker. And a damn good one." The conversation had started by revealing the actions taken to garner the information she now had printed on pages for the detectives' viewing pleasure. Her source had taken the information from the Verland files and hacked into the mainframe computers at many of the world's leading banks and financial institutions. Through a script that had been written prior to Maggie's behest — "I did not ask the reasoning behind it, so don't ask me" — her source was able to gain entry into various networks and eventually break through firewalls undetected. "Pretty much, they were able to get to points that you and I can't."

"We have people on our payroll that can do this. Legally," Jolene said.

Maggie smiled. "Not like this. And not in the short time it took. How long would it take to get warrants for all this?"

Hartley remained quiet, knowing Maggie's statement was true. The information in the documents from Tien would have taken weeks to gather, which included requesting those warrants. But that was only if they could gather enough cause. "So these are all the names your source found?"

Maggie pointed to the pages before her. "I'm sure with enough time, they could find more. But that's a good start, from what Dane has told me."

Hartley remained fixed on her for a moment before turning her attention to the pages in her hand once more. She sifted through them again before halting and focusing on her partner who had not, as of yet, perused the material. "What's it say?" Jacoby asked, coming around the table.

"Are you sure about this?" Hartley questioned Maggie. She only nodded, a grin across her face. Hartley rose and paced a few quick steps.

Ratliff read through the names one by one, his eyes alive as he looked up to Hartley. "I told you you'd like it," Dane said from across the room as he rose and tapped a cigarette out of his pack.

"What are the names?" Augie said from the couch.

Jolene eyed her partner once more before turning her attention to James. "They appear to be the names associated with your parents' murders."

James sat up in his seat and folded his hands on the table, rubbing them together as he tried to work up the nerve to ask his question. Finally, swallowing hard, it came out. "Who's on the list? Karaca?" Jolene nodded. "Renholm? Moran?"

"Yes," she replied, though her focus hovered on him for a moment longer.

"Who else?" he asked, confused.

"Chris Pennington, Lindsey Pratt and Emmett Eckland." She watched as his face fell to the table, and witnessed the questioning look from Augie, Maggie and Ratliff. "Pennington and Pratt were the first responders at the scene. Eckland was Oneida County's medical examiner."

The silence that followed was deafening, a black hole that sucked the air from the room, leaving a cold, uncomfortable abyss in its wake. James remained in place, staring with glistening eyes to the table's surface, ringing his hands together as he tried to piece everything together, a muddled mess of a past that Hartley realized he could have left behind. Even Dane, never the one to let a moment pass, stayed put, quietly taking in his surroundings and allowing the seconds to tick by undisturbed. After several minutes, James opened his mouth and asked, "Whose account is it from?" No one answered, just solemn faces staring to him. "Whose account?" he finally yelled.

"We don't know," Maggie answered. "Whoever transferred the money did so with extreme caution. My source wasn't able to find where it originated."

"But they were able to find who it went to?" Augie asked, pulling some of the attention away from his friend. Maggie nodded.

"How's that possible?" Hartley followed.

"What do you mean?"

"I mean, your source is able to find a path to those people, but not where it came from? Don't you think whoever moved that money would want to cover all possible trails? Why leave the possibility to track down the recipients?"

Maggie nodded her understanding. "Maybe a way to point the finger at who was involved from behind the curtain, so to speak."

"Leverage," Augie chimed in. "It's all about leverage."

FIFTY-TWO

The trip back to the precinct was more than Hartley or Ratliff had anticipated. After agreeing that they needed to return to their home base to look into the findings, James insisted that he was coming with. "You need to stay here," Hartley had said, stepping to the balcony where Graiser and Augie were having a cigarette. Dane leaned into the balcony railing away from the group, puffing away at his own smoke. "We have things we need to —"

"No," he had replied, adamantly.

"James," she had tried, "I know this is a lot, but Jay and I can do a lot more without —"

"I don't care," he said, turning to her, his tone fierce, yet his expression soft. "This is my family. My life! Don't you understand that? I'm coming with."

Jolene stood still, taking in the brief verbal assault with class. She opened her mouth but was cut off by Augie. "Where he goes, I go," the Londoner said.

Hartley nodded her head and turned to glance through the window, watching as Ratliff returned to the room with two officers in tow, Maggie seated at the table with legs crossed as she waited for the next step. She turned to Dane. "Dane, I have to —"

"I know," he had said. "Although I doubt Maggie's going to be happy about it."

"I don't really care what Maggie thinks."

He turned and smiled to her, flicking his cigarette into the air, the glowing ember swinging in the breeze as it fell to earth. "Neither do I," he said.

"Fine." She glanced among the men on the balcony. "Put those out. Let's go."

* * * * *

Maggie was none too pleased to be placed in handcuffs and escorted out of the hotel by Ratliff and his fellow officers. She had definitely not seen it coming. Dane, on the other hand, followed leisurely, a smile spread across his face. Hartley had told Ratliff that their only option was to arrest the pair, their crime going well beyond the hazy line that sometimes officers found themselves straddling. Should Maggie's illegal seizure of the sensitive files of secure bank documentation see the light of day, this would not place a cloud over the Chicago Police Department. Whether or not charges would be pressed was another matter. The main purpose was, as Captain Nolan said, to cover their asses.

At the precinct, Dane and Maggie were seen to their respective holding cells, and James and Augie were placed in the break room with pastries and coffee, the leftovers from an impromptu meeting by some of the other detectives. Hartley moved to her desk and fired up the computer monitor with the shake of the mouse, simultaneously watching as Ratliff followed suit. She leaned back and sighed, the length of the day catching up to her. "Are you hanging in there?" she heard Jacoby ask.

She turned to him and grinned lazily. "Trying," she answered. She forced herself to sit up. "How are you doing?"

"Ha!" he said, picking up the receiver to the phone. "I could sleep for days."

"Maybe we should call it a night then?" He glanced to her with a sly grin. "You know what I mean!" she said quickly.

"I know." He punched in a series of digits. Hartley smiled at her Freudian slip and leaned into her desk. She yawned and removed the pages of Maggie's trace from the envelope, slowly scanning the documents with weary eyes. She had looked upon them and noticed the highlighted last names of those involved, each one receiving a considerable amount deposited into their respective accounts.

Or, at least, the accounts set up for them. Hartley had trouble believing these were the individuals' everyday sources of fast cash. Any sensible criminal wiring money between recipients would no doubt know to set up an account to route money through, mainly an offshore bank that had an extremely intense privacy policy.

Augie had been right when mentioning the curious nature of the somewhat easily traceable recipients of the funds. Why were they not able to produce a source? Why was the originator of the payments shrouded in the ever-looping mess of routing and rerouting? Could it be just as Augie said? Could it be the reasoning behind the find was leverage?

"Jo," she suddenly heard her partner exclaim. She turned to see him sitting straight in his chair, tapping the eraser of his pencil on the desktop furiously.

"What?" she said.

He paused, phone still to his ear. Finally, he hung up and faced her. "I think we had a Renholm spotting."

Hartley perked up. "Where?"

"Happened earlier. A young couple was assaulted. Kid got knocked unconscious by a pistol across the head, and his girlfriend is nowhere to be found."

"What? He kidnapped her?"

"Seems like it. Stole the car too."

"Do we know —"

"The car? Yeah. They found it smashed up on the west side near a bus stop. Bit of blood on the front passenger seat. No one in the area saw anything."

"How do we know it's Renholm then?"

"The kid at the scene — the one that got pistol-whipped — remembered turning around and seeing a man with a large scar across the side of his head. Matches Millers's description."

Hartley sat back again and stared to the ceiling. "So he now has a hostage. That's great."

"Hey, look on the bright side. He didn't kill the boyfriend. Maybe he won't do anything to her."

She shrugged. "We put out an amber alert?" Ratliff nodded. "Good. That should get some heat on him." She rubbed her eyes and exhaled deeply into the room.

Ratliff wheeled over. "You okay?" he asked.

She turned to face him and smiled, reaching her hand out to place on his forearm. "Yeah. I'll be fine."

"How about a cup of coffee?"

"From the place on the corner?"

He smiled and shook his head. "I was thinking the kitchen."

Hartley gave him a disgusted look but nodded. "That'd be great."

He stood and made his way across the pit, sidestepping several other officers as they darted through the opened area. Hartley turned her attention back to the pages. She did not know what she was looking for, or if she was looking for anything at all. It had become habit to survey something a multitude of times, to let her eyes fall on items over and over just in case there was something she missed. With this, however, she could not tell if there was anything out of place. It was like reading Sanskrit. She would not know if she found something unless it jumped off the page and —

She reached out and grabbed the remaining papers, skimming across the highlighted last names and amounts, running her finger down the columns until they intersected with an adjoining row. She followed her pointer across the surface, her nail creating a noise akin to that of a chalkboard. There was something. She had just seen it. It was right in front of her —

"Ratliff!" Hartley yelled, causing officers and city personnel meandering by to cast a sideways glance to her. She looked up and saw him take a step from the kitchen. "Jay, get over here." He hurriedly stepped back into the kitchen and grabbed the coffees.

Jolene stood and handed him the sheets as he approached. "What?" he asked.

"Look at the names," she replied. He perused the documents, flipping between them. "See anything?"

"Am I supposed to? Renholm. Karaca. Pratt."

Jolene's index finger pointed to a column just to the left, smashed between the date and a random ten-digit bank code. "Initials."

"Okay," he said. "What about it?"

She rolled her eyes and stepped closer, her body pressing into his. "*M* Renholm," she said, pointing to the column associated with the highlighted last name. "*L* Pratt."

He focused on the next one, the initial causing his eyes to widen and Jolene to smirk. "*A* Karaca," she said aloud. "Korhan wasn't getting money funneled to him."

He finished the statement. "Ahmet was."

* * * * *

"Sir, I need to be there," Hartley said to Nolan. She and Ratliff had entered his office with the documents and immediately filled him in on the proceedings as of late. He was not overjoyed at the thought of hacking into financial institutions, however, things as they were — mainly Dane and Maggie in a state of arrest — he had decided questioning Ahmet was a good next step. He had also decided, however, that Ratliff was to go, and not Jolene.

"Jay can do this one," Nolan said. "I want you to follow up on this Dante Leary guy."

"Sir, it's a dead end, I'm —"

"Really? Have you checked him out already?" Hartley remained silent. "Well, then, it looks like that's our course of action then."

"But, sir —"

"No buts," he said, smiling to himself. "Sometimes I feel like a kindergarten teacher here." He refocused on her. "Look, Leary is the connection to Walker. A lot was left open with our last case —"

"Except for our murderer and his handlers being figured out and killed."

"— so I think you need to look into it. Don't give me the whole run-around here, Jo. These cases seem too close to let something like this slip through the cracks. Jay is very capable without you by his side."

In the end, the boss won. Hartley followed Ratliff from the room and fell into her seat. Jacoby halted near her desk and grinned. "I'll keep you updated on what I find out."

"Fine," she said, running her hands over her face and through her hair.

"Maybe later …" He paused as she looked up to him with tired eyes. "I'll give you a call after I talk with him." He started off towards the step and yelled back. "Call me if you find anything on Leary."

Jolene sat for a moment longer, staring to the ceiling, wondering — dreaming — of her plush comforter and fluffy pillows, craving the dim light of her living room or the piping hot cauldron of her bathtub. It was not going to be this evening, she determined after a few moments. Tonight — or what was left of it — would be spent hunkering down in front of her computer, searching the internet and police databases for Dante Leary, a man unknown to her other than through a deceased Kyle Walker and a dying Artemis Greer.

FIFTY-THREE

"This is fucking useless!" Hartley said to herself as she tossed her computer mouse to the desk in a clatter, her frustration shining through. She stood and pushed back her chair, the wheeled seat careening with the station directly behind her. Jolene turned to apologize, but realized no one was there. The precinct was sparse, random detectives working late on cases, drifting, zombielike, through the paperwork and online searches, not unlike her.

She found herself turning into the break room, eyes searching the two men seated in chairs directed away from her, their gaze half-heartedly on the television before them. Jolene smiled. This room did not have a television on normal days. It was used as a sort of waiting area for those coming in to meet with officers, a less intrusive atmosphere than the interrogation rooms. She had no doubt that James, with his likeable demeanor and whimsical charm, had procured it from one of the detectives on duty, throwing his genuine smile their way to gain access to the cable box and remote control.

But then again, that was not the James she now looked upon. He looked like the old James, but darker, settled into a chaos that centered on himself, swirling in an abyss that funneled into a black hole. He had no place to run, no place to turn to, no escape from the cloud hovering overhead. His eyes lacked the life she had once known, his body seemingly folding in on itself in desperation and despair. And, at this moment, Jolene could understand why.

She stepped back into the pit without being seen and refilled her cup of coffee, slowly inching her way back to her station and the searches that inevitably continued. She connected to the police database and waited as information on Dante Leary loaded. Not much was known about the man. His traffic record was clean. No warrants had been issued. There was also no known whereabouts, which was not unheard of. People moved cities, countries. They left homes and relatives behind. It was just the way of the world.

An entry from long ago caught her eye, however, a record from nearly twenty years prior. For battery. She read the brief description of the incident and settled back into her chair, sighing at her misfortunes. Dante, in his late twenties, had been involved in a scuffle at a Chicago nightclub, an event that left one man hospitalized with a concussion and multiple abrasions. Leary, it seemed, had been on the winning end of the battle, and had thus been arrested and placed into police custody before posting bail. The occurrence did not make it to court, with the defendant dropping the charges, stating the fight had been "a drunken thing that needn't be made any bigger."

Jolene scrolled down the page until she came to a link for Dante's mugshot. She clicked it and stared at the image before her. Dante looked like any other individual out for a few drinks with friends. His dark hair was cut short, disheveled from the encounter, and his eyes appeared slightly intoxicated. Other than what appeared to be a split lip, he was your average party boy, someone Jolene may have had a few drinks with back in her college years.

She navigated through the record, trying in vain to find something worthwhile. Finally, she came upon it, a note made by an Officer Hanson fifteen years prior, an update on Leary's last known whereabouts and occupation, which was listed as Humboldt Park and entrepreneur, possibly a restaurant or a bar. Hartley wrote the address on a Post-it note and picked up her phone, dialing Ratliff's number.

He answered on the second ring. "Hey."

"You there yet?" Hartley asked.

"Stuck in traffic. It's a parking lot. Want to trade? I'll check on Leary and you go talk to Ahmet?"

Hartley chuckled. "I'll pass. I think I'll keep my assignment, as much fun as yours sounds. I'm going to step out now to see if I can track him down."

"Yeah? You got something?"

"Not at all. A note on a past address is about it. I'll go check it out and see if he's still there."

"What's the address?" Jolene gave it to him. "Okay. You sure you don't want to wait for me?"

"You're not the only officer more than capable of doing their job." She hung up the phone and walked to Nolan's office, catching from the corner of her eye as James stood and stretched his limbs, head turning to connect with Jolene's gaze through the break room window. Hartley forced a quick smile before stepping just inside the captain's door and pulling his attention to her.

"Find anything?" he asked.

She shrugged. "An address from fifteen years ago."

"That's it?"

"That's it," she replied. "Picture doesn't match anyone we've seen. No warrants. No recent arrests. Nothing."

"So, what do you think?"

"I think I'm going to head out there and see if I can chat with him."

"Yeah?" Nolan lifted his wrist watch in the air and gazed upon the face. "Getting kind of late, don't you think?"

Hartley glanced to the wall clock above his head. "He's probably not even around anymore. If he is, we'll chat a little and then I'll head home."

"All right. What do you want me to do with the pair in the break room?"

She thought for a moment, determining the likelihood of their return to the hotel was slim. "If they won't head back to their room, maybe offer them a pillow and blanket?"

Nolan smiled. "Sure. It'll be like old times."

"Yeah. Old times." The thought was refreshing to her.

"Where's Leary's last known address?"

"He was listed as an entrepreneur in Humboldt Park. Maybe a bar or restaurant or something. There were question marks next to the entry." She lifted the Post-it and read off the address, shrugging to him and saying, "Like I said, it's from fifteen years ago."

"Okay. Ratliff know where you're heading?" She nodded. "Give me a shout when you're leaving there."

"Will do," she said, waving her goodnight. Hartley reached her desk and grabbed her cell phone, typing the address in to her navigation and tossing the Post-it into the receptacle before turning and making her way to the steps and out of the precinct.

* * * * *

Anxiety rose in James. He had placed himself just inside the break room door, a position that allowed him to eavesdrop on the conversation between Jolene and Captain Nolan without being seen. Twice he had had to hush Augie, the latter trying to determine what his friend was doing, pressed against the wall with his ear inches from the hallway.

James peeked out just as Jolene threw the Post-it into the trash and exited the area. His eyes followed the pink square of paper as it fluttered into the bin, the sheet making contact with the other trash at the exact same moment he formed a plan. He looked to Augie. "You want a smoke?"

The Londoner glanced to him. "Yeah, but we're not really in the position to get outside. We're pretty much prisoners here." He thought for a moment. "Not prisoners like Dane and that woman, but prisoners, nonetheless."

"I'll get Nolan to let us go," James said. "Come on." Augie relinquished his seat in front of the television and followed James out of the room and to the captain's office. They knocked on the door and entered as Nolan looked up. "Hey, Henry," James said.

"Hey, gents," he replied, though he did not move from the papers on his desk. "What can I do for you?"

"We were wondering if we could step out for a cigarette."

Nolan glanced up. "You're smoking now?"

James smirked nervously. "Bad habit I picked up just recently."

"That shit's going to kill you."

"I plan on quitting before that happens. Believe me."

"Yeah, spoken like every other smoker." He paused. "Look, I meant what I said before. You two are under our supervision. You're not out of the woods completely. There's still a lot going on with this case. I can't have you two walking around in the open by yourselves."

"We'll take him along," Augie said suddenly, pulling in an officer as he strolled by. The young man, a rookie on the patrol beat, stopped and joined in the conversation, reveling in the fact that he was in the captain's presence. "He can babysit us."

"Murphy, is it?" Nolan asked.

"Yes, sir," Officer Murphy answered with a smile.

"You busy at the moment, Murphy?"

"I, uh … I can make some time," he responded nervously, not wanting to seem bored, but also not wanting to turn down his superior.

"Good. Take these gentlemen out front for a cigarette. They are not to leave your sight, do you hear me?"

"Yes, sir," Murphy answered.

"Thanks, Henry," James said. Nolan waved his hand and returned to his papers. James and Augie followed Murphy out of the captain's office and towards the stairs, the Londoner making small talk with the officer as they moved out of the pit. At the last moment, James turned and reached into Jolene's trash bin, pulling the crumpled Post-it from the receptacle and sliding it into his pocket. He hurried after the officer and Augie, catching them on the first landing, grateful neither one saw him near Hartley's desk, unaware of the plan forming in his mind and the anxiousness gathering in his chest.

FIFTY-FOUR

Ratliff finally pulled up to the Karaca household and threw the cruiser into park, tilting his head back and sighing as he rubbed his hands over his face. He glanced at the lit up home quickly, the living space shining bright through the sheer curtains with the television displaying a commercial for the newest line of automobiles from Ford. It was an obvious sign someone was home, although he could see no movement from within.

He stepped to the curb and was about to reach for his phone to text Hartley when his eyes rose and he realized the front storm door was open, swaying in the breeze and giving him a look into the front room of the home. Ratliff halted, taking in the scene before him, as well as the yards to the left and right of the Karaca's. Something was off. He spun in place and looked to the street. Cars were parked at various intervals with no individuals behind the wheel. An elderly man a half dozen houses down was exiting onto the sidewalk and making his way up his steps.

Ratliff hurriedly strolled to the side of the Karaca's home and glanced through the kitchen window, surprised at what his gaze fell upon. Inside, amidst dirty shoe prints and broken glass sprinkled across the floor and counter, were droplets of blood. He glanced to the yard between the houses and found divots in the grass, fresh imprints from small feet that had collected dirt and grime and tracked it onto the concrete sidewalk.

He retraced his steps and made his way to the front of the house, pulling his firearm as he neared the opened entrance. With a cautious glance into the home, Ratliff pushed the door open and yelled out. "Police! Mr. Karaca? Esra? It's Detective Ratliff! I'm coming in!" There was no answer. He stepped into the room, eyeing a blanket on the ground and the television on mute in an otherwise overly cleaned home. Table lamps and candles lit the interior brilliantly, showering the area in a warm glow.

"Ahmet? Esra?" he yelled again, receiving no response. Jacoby halted as he reached the hallway, the corridor empty, the home quiet. He glanced into a bathroom to his right, checking the linen closet and shower before moving deeper into the Karaca's abode. To the left, he could see the kitchen counter through the threshold, the glass on the floor reflecting the overhead lights. He stepped into the room and inched his way across the linoleum floor, trying to stay clear of the mayhem. It was nearly impossible. The pilsner, as Jacoby came to realize, was everywhere. There was no missing it all. The best he could do was try to retain the footprints covering the floor and stay away from the blood splatter.

He hopped over the items and came to a halt at the kitchen table, bending slightly to inspect a small puddle of blood pooling on the plastic tablecloth. Suddenly, from behind him, someone entered the room, shifting noisily as they made their way across the linoleum, shuffling hurriedly as Ratliff turned and raised his weapon. "Police!" he yelled, causing a curdling scream to escape Esra's throat. She threw her hands up in defense and shut her eyes tightly, obviously unaware who was standing in her kitchen. A bottle of hydrogen peroxide fell to the floor and burst open, spilling the contents.

"Please, don't shoot!" she answered.

Ratliff held his breath for a moment longer before exhaling and lowering his gun, his heart thumping rapidly. "Mrs. Karaca!" he said. "What's going on here?"

She opened her eyes and let loose a small hiccup, tears forming and beginning to run down her full cheeks. "You scared the life right out of me!" she yelled, placing her hand on her chest. "What are you doing in my house?"

"The front door was wide open," he explained, holstering his weapon. He looked to the counter and floor. "What happened here?"

She waited for several seconds, composing herself as she bent and picked up the spilled bottle of peroxide. When she rose, she stared to him. "Ahmet dropped a glass and cut his hand. What are you doing in my home?"

"I'm sorry," Ratliff said. "I came to talk with Ahmet. When I got here, the front door was wide open and I saw broken glass and blood."

"The door was open because I ran to the garage to get this!" She held up the bottle and reached into her pocket, pulling out a cylinder of medical gauze and tape.

"I'm sorry," Ratliff said, raising his hands in apology. "I really didn't mean to startle you." She sighed again. "Is he all right?"

"He'll be fine. He's in the basement." She walked over to him and pushed the medical supplies into his chest. "Since you're here to see Ahmet, take this down to him. I'll clean up this mess."

* * * * *

James did not know quite how he was going to execute his plan, nor could he decide upon how he would alert Augie. There had been something Jolene had said when speaking to Nolan that caught James's ear, tugged at every fiber of his being and pulled him back to his first meeting with Korhan. It had been a heated exchange, emotional, to say the least. Korhan, through his drug-induced haze over the past number of years, had been struggling to come up with any information other than the names Luke Moran and Millers. He had, however, shared with James a nugget that, up until this point, Graiser had deemed useless, a piece of data that led him nowhere and proved nothing. It was not until the conversation between Jolene and her boss that James became increasingly aware of its possible importance.

* * * * *

"Who is this, Ahmet?" Ratliff asked as Karaca exited the laundry room.

The elderly man made his way to the seat across from Jacoby and looked at the photo the detective shared with him. He stared at it for several moments before sliding it across the table. "I don't recognize him. Should I?"

"Depends," Ratliff answered, wondering how to proceed, thinking of the line of questions Hartley would open with. "You've never seen him before?"

"I don't think so. Not that I can recall."

"Does the name Millers Renholm mean anything to you?" Again, Ahmet paused. Finally, he shook his head. "Nothing?" Ratliff pressed.

"No, detective. I'm sorry. What is this about? Is it about Korhan's case?"

"More or less. Mr. Karaca, your son's murder seems to be more than we originally thought."

"How do you mean?"

"Well, for one, it's brought another case into the spotlight. It's also led us to you."

Ahmet stared at Ratliff for a moment, trying to comprehend the words coming from his mouth. "I'm confused," he finally said, scratching his brow. "What case?"

"The Graiser murders," Ratliff answered quickly, keeping the old man's gaze.

Ahmet's confused look did not falter, no recognition registering with him. "How does that lead you to me?"

"We're not sure yet, but I was hoping you could help me with that."

"How?"

"By telling me why money was being deposited in your account just after the Graisers were killed." Ahmet's confused expression slid to the floor in an acknowledging heap.

* * * * *

"Do you have any more?" James asked Augie. They stood on the precinct steps, chatting with Officer Murphy as they smoked their cigarettes. Murphy, they came to learn, was a fan of soccer, having played intramural ball at Purdue University after blowing out his knee in high school after an All-American season. James stood on the same step as the officer as he asked the question to his friend.

Augie patted his pockets until he found his pack and tossed them to James who dislodged one and returned them with a soft lob. Augie placed one in his mouth as well, flicking the lighter to life and igniting the tobacco in his smoke. "Throw that here," James said. He caught the lighter and lit his cigarette, sucking deep and feeling the burn as the smoke poured into his lungs.

As Augie started up the conversation once more with Officer Murphy, James fingered the lighter, running the smooth plastic between his fingers, working up the nerve to put his required plan into action. His thoughts turned to Jolene, en route to wherever she was going, alone. He was not usually a man of action. He remembered a life where he lived by the seat of his pants, playing everything by ear and making spontaneous decisions at a whim. This was not one of those times. This required action. And immediately.

"Here you go," James said, tossing the lighter back to his friend. His aim was purposefully off, careening to the right and bouncing off the left shoulder of the officer, rattling to the concrete steps at Murphy's feet. "Sorry about that," James said.

"No worries," Murphy answered, bending at the waist to retrieve the lighter for Augie. As the officer rose, James jumped into action, watching his friend's eyes widen in utter surprise as Graiser reached under Murphy's left arm and, in one quick motion, unlatched and removed the Taser strapped to his chest.

* * * * *

"I'm going to need you to answer my question," Ratliff said sternly. He had been watching as Ahmet took the time to retrieve a drink from the nearby bar and nervously lift the glass to his lips, hand trembling all the while. "Why were you receiving money?"

Ahmet remained silent, even as Esra made her way down the steps and froze, noticing, feeling, the tension within the basement. "What's going on?" she asked, concerned.

"Everything's all right, dear," Ahmet said to her.

"It doesn't look all right." She glanced to Ratliff. "What happened?"

"That's what I'm trying to figure out," Ratliff answered, his eyes never leaving the man by the bar. "Ahmet?"

Esra gave her husband a questioning look, eyebrows furrowed. "Ahmet? Tell me what's going on."

"Why were you receiving the money?" Ratliff asked.

"What money?" Esra questioned.

"Let's talk in the garage," Ahmet said.

"Ahmet," Esra pushed, "what's he talking about?"

"I know there were multiple deposits," Ratliff continued. "We found documents and traced it to you."

"Ahmet?"

The silence that followed was palpable. Ratliff had him by the neck, submitting him with what could only equate to a bluff in the long run, the documents from Maggie only a lead due to the nature of their reemergence. "I think you need to come with me to the station," Ratliff finally said, taking a step toward the elderly man.

"Wait," he said, holding up a hand. "Just wait." He looked to his wife apologetically, tears lining his eyes. "I'm sorry," he said. "This was never supposed to happen."

FIFTY-FIVE

They found themselves running, sprinting like they had never sprinted before, down the sidewalk, away from the steps and Officer Murphy. James cut into an alley, followed by Augie who yelled after him to stop, wondering what had just happened and why. They turned into an alcove surrounded on either side by overflowing dumpsters, pausing briefly to catch their breath.

Augie pulled up next to James, hands on his knees, trying to gather in his breath. "What the fuck was that, Jimmy?" he said, reaching out to shove James into the nearby wall.

"Augie, wait," he tried, only to be pushed once more, with enough force that it caused him to tumble backwards.

"Are you fucking kidding me?" Augie continued, his voice raising an octave.

James put a finger to his lips. "Shut up!" he said.

"Fuck you!" Augie yelled back. He threw his arms in the air and began pacing back and forth, unable to come up with any rational reason why the recent events had occurred. "I'm absolutely getting fucking deported now, thanks to you!"

"Augie, quiet down." James pushed himself off the ground and moved towards his friend, receiving a quick jab to the chest that stopped him in his tracks.

Augie's face morphed into a scowl, a look James had never seen on him. Then again, James had never put his friend in such a position before. "Do you know what you did? Do you *really* know what the fuck you did?"

"Augie!" James said sternly, stepping forward and grasping onto the Londoner's chest. "Listen to me. You need to be quiet. You —" He froze, as, from down the alley, the sound of police sirens erupted in the night, coming to life and echoing loudly, bouncing off the numerous buildings surrounding their current location.

James pulled Augie deeper into the darkened alcove and waited, peeking out and staring between the building and dumpster as several police cars raced by. Finally, when the mayhem nearest them calmed, he looked to his friend with serious eyes. "Listen!" he said fiercely, tapping his index finger into Augie's chest viciously. "I'm sorry. I couldn't tell you —"

"Why the fuck not?" Augie whispered back.

"Because you wouldn't have gone with it."

"Because it's not something you'd normally do! You fucking tased a cop, James. A cop! Do you understand that, mate?"

"Augie, listen! Jolene's in trouble."

"How do you know that? Huh? How do you know she's in trouble?"

"Because I listen, Augie," he replied. "I listen, and I keep track of things."

"The fuck you do," Augie answered, shoving his arms from him. He stepped into the alley and rubbed his hand over his face. He stared at James for a moment before shrugging. "What do you know? How is she in trouble?"

James stepped to him and kept his gaze. "Because of this," he answered, pulling the pink Post-it from his pocket and holding it between him and his friend. Augie did not try to read the address written on the crumpled piece of paper. Instead, he looked up to James for an explanation, one that James was happy to give him. "Think of what Korhan told us, that first night."

* * * * *

"I never kept the money," Ahmet said, standing in front of his wife.

"What money?" Esra pushed.

Ahmet stalled, his mouth moving, but the words unable to form. Ratliff answered for him. "The money for the murders of Michael and Amelia Graiser."

Esra's expression was that of confusion and disgust. She turned to her husband. "What?" she asked, her voice faltering.

"I'm sorry, Esra," Ratliff replied. "Our investigation has shown that your husband was accepting money dealing with the Graiser murders."

"Is this true?" she inquired, her submissive character looming large.

"Wait a —"

"Is it true?" she interrupted.

His shoulders slumped, tears flowing freely down his cheeks. "Yes," he admitted. Esra raised a hand to her mouth and seemed nearly to tip over. She waddled to the closest wall and leaned into it, the weight of the current situation pulling her down. "But I had nothing to do with the murders," he added after several moments. "And neither did my boy."

Ratliff watched the elderly man for several seconds, glancing to his wife and weighing his next comment. "Ahmet, your son was there the night the Graisers were killed. He was at the lakehouse."

Esra looked up in utter disbelief. Ahmet answered before she could respond. "But he wasn't involved! He had no clue where he was or what was going on! I promise you!"

"How can you promise that?"

"Because he told me."

* * * * *

"Are you serious, mate?" Augie replied as they walked from the alley and sprinted across the street. "Korhan was a fucking goon. He was cracked out of his mind. You're basing this off of what he said?"

"I'm serious, Augie," James replied. "Think. What did Korhan tell us about my parents' murders?"

"I don't know," he responded with a shrug. "Not much."

"He knew the names Luke Moran and Millers, right?" Augie nodded. "If you think he was such a fuckup, how'd Millers Renholm turn up at my apartment? Huh?" Augie remained silent, remembering the occurrence with Jolene and the crazed individual. "Do you remember how Korhan and Moran met?"

The question sent Augie flying back to the meeting with Korhan and James, the first time Graiser had stepped foot in the States since his untimely departure eight months prior. He was right back in that drug den, James facing Korhan with a resolved steadfastness, Paw-Paw inching his way towards the exit.

* * * * *

Ahmet and Esra sat down at the table willingly, the ultimatum put forth by Ratliff to take Ahmet into custody more than she could bear. "I swear to you," Ahmet began, speaking more to his wife than to Jacoby. "I didn't know about Korhan's involvement until after the fact."

"When?" Ratliff questioned. Esra remained silent, stoic.

Ahmet lifted a hand into the air and let it drop back to the table. "I don't know. A week. Maybe two."

"Did he tell you?"

Ahmet nodded. "When he learned what happened, he came to me. He told me he was high and didn't remember most of it, but he knew for a fact that he was there."

"What was his role?"

"To stay in the car. He was the driver, apparently."

"And he didn't know what was actually going on?"

"No. He was told they were there for a robbery. From what I understand, Korhan didn't know about the killings until a couple days later."

Ratliff thought for a moment. "From what I understand, Amelia Graiser was brutally raped. How did that not register with your son?"

Ahmet's look was pleading. "Korhan was an addict, detective. There were certainly a lot of things that probably didn't register with him." He paused, lost in thought. "That was the breaking point in our relationship. After that, he didn't come by as much, and I didn't look."

"That doesn't explain the money, Ahmet. The documents we have don't shine a positive light on you right now."

"I know," he said, nodding his head. "The money was deposited in an account I had."

"What account?"

He thought. "It was an investment account. I don't exactly remember which one."

"What happened to it?" Esra finally asked.

He turned to her. "Everything was donated to charity. I didn't want that money."

"Why?" Ratliff questioned.

"Because it was blood money. It was money for the murder of my friends that I had nothing to do with."

"The financial trail begs to differ," Ratliff said.

"I promise you. I wanted nothing to do with it. If I could have gone to the police, I would have."

"Why didn't you then?" Esra questioned.

"Because of you. Because of Korhan and you."

"What do you mean?"

He took a deep breath. "A couple weeks after Michael and Amelia were killed, two men came here. They knew everything about us. Where we lived. Where our cabin was. Who you were. Your sisters. Nieces and nephews. They knew everything. They told me if I was to say anything to anyone, especially the police, that they would kill me and my family." Tears began to flow freely. "They told me that they would kill everyone and make you suffer. I couldn't let that happen, Esra! I couldn't let that happen." He wiped his tears and took a sip of his drink. "For my silence, they said there would be random deposits in one of my accounts." He looked between his wife and the detective. "You have to believe me," he pleaded. "I had nothing to do with it. All the money went to charity. I didn't want it. Any of it."

Ratliff held up a hand. "Do you know who the men were? The men that came to visit you."

"At the time? No. I just thought they were Korhan's fellow druggies. Now ..." He stalled, sniffing several times before locking gazes with Ratliff. "I remember. It was that guy on the news last year, and the other one with the scar."

"The guy on the news? Who?"

"Luke Moran. The guy from the *State of Finance* shootout. One hundred percent."

"And the guy with the scar? Is it the same guy you said came by looking for your son? The cop?"

"Yes. But he wasn't a cop."

"Then why not tell us then? Why lie?"

"Because I was afraid."

Ratliff thought a moment. "Do you remember his name, Ahmet?" Ahmet nodded. "Who is it?"

The words that formed and spewed forth fell from Ahmet's lips in slow motion for Ratliff. He could not believe his ears. He stared at the couple before them, not hearing as Ahmet asked if everything was all right and Esra reached out to touch his forearm. He went into a state of shock for a brief moment, his mind traveling back to the precinct, back to his partner and her beautiful face.

He suddenly leapt from the chair and bolted up the steps, clearing three at a time as he sprinted from the house, praying as he went that he was not too late.

* * * * *

The air was fogged, a cloud hovering above the inhabitants of the room. Paw-Paw had lost his fiery rambunctiousness and now sulked in the corner, waiting for the perfect moment to escape into the hallway and make his exit. He had seen horrible things happen from less intense situations than this. Augie stood in the middle of the room, arms crossed, a joint hanging from his lips as he looked between the pair before him.

James looked nervous, yet wholly confident in the route he had taken since exiting the airplane a mere hour before. His eyes portrayed a hesitation, not due to the current events, but the route in which his life now found itself taking. It was the look of a man not ready for an outcome, not seeking an answer for the questions he so gingerly pursued.

Korhan turned to Augie, tears in his eyes. "What the fuck is this?" He tried to rise, but Augie reached out a hand and easily pushed him back into the seat. Korhan continued his rant towards James. "I know you! I know you!" he said "Why are you here?" He turned to Augie. "Why is he here?"

"Mate," Augie said. "He just wants to talk."

"I don't want to fucking talk to him! Let me the fuck —"

"Do you know who I am?" James asked, waiting for a moment before repeating the question. "Korhan, do you know me?"

"I know you," Korhan replied. "You're the Graiser kid."

"That's right. My name's James." He paused and thought of his best approach. Finally, he decided a direct route was best. "I'm looking for information on my parents, and you're the only one that may know something." James spoke the words based on the information Jolene had given him months ago, about his father's gun being found at the scene after Korhan and Luke Moran assaulted her in her apartment. What fell from Karaca's mouth nearly buckled Graiser's knees, and caused Augie's jaw to drop.

* * * * *

Augie looked to James, his expression completely understanding, as if the tasing of Officer Murphy had never happened. The words that came from his mouth were practically verbatim. "He didn't remember everything," Augie said, following James towards the street as Graiser flagged down a taxi. "He thought he was the getaway driver for a robbery."

"Right," James said as the cab pulled to the curb. "But do you remember what he said about Luke Moran? About where he met him?"

Augie's face began to mirror James's, a countenance of concern and anxiety. "He said that he met him at a bar in Humboldt Park." Augie practically smiled.

James held up his phone, the display showing a Google map of the address Jolene had written down while in the precinct. Augie looked at it briefly before nodding to James and stepping onto the street, arms wide as he stopped the approaching cab. James glanced to his device and the location given: Ginger's Trap.

FIFTY-SIX

Jolene parked across the street from the address she had found in the report, turning the key to kill the engine as she stepped onto the sidewalk. The vicinity was empty at this hour, odd, considering the location she was headed to was a bar in Humboldt Park. She stood on the curb and looked around, taking in her surroundings as she always did when on the job. Or off the job. Everything seemed to meld together nowadays. Her life had become one solid entity, no gray areas of questioning, besides Ratliff.

And James.

She knew what she had going with her partner was good. That was a definite fact. Her time with him had been beneficial, personally and professionally. Yet that lingering effect James had left her with bothered her, drove her to think about past occurrences that had no bearing whatsoever on her current state. She did not know if it was because of the current investigations or not. She had not had time to think about it. All she knew was she was here, waiting for an interview with an unknown individual, the last item of the day before she fell into her plush comforter, and dreamt of better days, calmer days, where she could conjure up a future with Jacoby Ratliff.

She waited for a bus to pass before crossing the street, jogging the two lanes to the opposite sidewalk and making a left. To her right was a parking lot for the establishment, a six-foot high chain-link fence creating a not-so-secure space for cars to park while visiting, the gaping twenty-foot wide entrance lacking the security cameras needed to deter criminals from entering the private property and causing mischief.

The parking lot contained a variety of vehicles: a Mercedes, an antique from the late '80s, beaten and bruised, yet, by the looks of it, still running; a Toyota Corolla, paint-chipped and rusted; two Studebakers, both sitting atop cinderblocks and waiting for remodeling. Another vehicle caught her eye as she walked by. A large SUV, a newer model, was backed into a spot, the front end smashed in, the damage appearing new to her detective's eye.

Jolene continued down the sidewalk, passing the neon sign of the establishment. Ginger's Trap, from the outside, seemed like a small, rinky-dink bar, a place that lacked any normal crowd and most likely served only the regulars of the near vicinity until closing, which was probably early evening, on most nights. From the looks of things, tonight seemed like a slow night.

She pulled on the door of the bar and it opened with a screech, the bottom rubber guard catching on the pavement momentarily before allowing her access. Jolene stepped inside and paused, allowing the door to close behind her as she moved from a darkened alcove and into the light to look around. The establishment was nothing special. A bar lined the left wall, arching into the middle of the room and jutting at a ninety degree angle, dissecting the interior in half until it reached about five feet from the back wall and abruptly stopped. The shelves behind the bar were stocked with various liquors, tequila and whiskey topping the list.

Jolene walked to the corner of the bar and waited, watching as the homely barkeep made her way to her with a not-so-pleasant acknowledgement, leaving a large, sweaty man at the other end of the room to whatever demons were shrouding his soul. "Can I help you?" she asked, her tone not welcoming in the least.

Hartley moved her eyes about the room, noticing the Quentin Tarantino movie posters and antique film paraphernalia gracing the walls. She finally looked to the woman. Before she could speak, she noticed a stain on her shirt, a red splash on her lower abdomen that Jolene had seen many times before: blood.

The woman shifted positions before forcefully asking, "What can I get you?"

Hartley connected with her gaze. "I was looking …" She stopped, watching out of the corner of her eye as the man at the end of the bar doubled over in pain. "I'm sorry," she said. "Is he okay?"

The bartender did not avert her eyes, instead quickly answering, "Yeah. He's fine. Just cut himself on a broken bottle. What can I get you?"

Hartley moved her focus to the woman. "I'm looking for Dante Leary. Is he here?"

"Who?" the woman asked.

"Dante Leary," Hartley repeated, the volume of her voice rising above the music spewing from the jukebox.

The bartender stared at her for a moment, perplexed, it seemed, until she picked up a towel and wiped off her hands, glancing to the man at the end of the bar quickly. "You going to be okay?" He nodded his head. She turned her attention back to the woman before her. "Let me see if he's here. Who's asking?"

Hartley raised her silver star. "Detective Hartley with the Chicago Police Department."

The woman backed away slowly. "Let me see if he's here," she repeated. Hartley watched as she exited the bar and entered a short corridor that knifed between the restrooms on either side. She pushed through a swinging door and into an adjoining room. Jolene surveyed the area once more, noticing the emptiness, save for the man in the last stool. She pulled out her phone and checked the time. It was definitely not the normal bar hour. She had been part of that many times, Kim Banneau usually pulling her to a random location no earlier than ten o'clock.

It took several minutes for the barkeep to reappear. When she did, she slowly made her way to the detective, who had taken a spot at the bar. "Dante's in back. Go through there." She pointed to the corridor.

"Straight through there?" Hartley asked.

"Straight down the hall. Swinging door, then to your left. That's the office." Jolene rose and made the short walk into the corridor, shooting a sideways glance at the man at the end of the counter, watching as he shifted a rag on his leg, the red bloodstain noticeable on the brilliant white fabric.

Her phone buzzed in her pocket just then, a vibration that caused her pause as she reached the swinging door. She pulled the device from her coat and pushed through the divider into the back area, halting in the threshold as she looked down at a missed call notification from Ratliff, her service bars blinking between one and two, neither one enough to garner any meaningful connectivity. Movement out of the corner of her eye caught Hartley's attention, and she turned to watch the bartender move to the front door, flipping the neon sign to *closed* and switching the door to a locked position.

At that exact moment, the happenings within the bar did not immediately register with Jolene. Whether due to the fact that she had been working non-stop on multiple, confusing investigations, or that the hour was getting late, Hartley's mind did not click into gear as it should have. The neon sign being turned off was not an issue. Hartley understood by the lack of customers that the bar could be in the process of closing down, shutting its doors for the evening. The locking of that door, however, eventually created some unwanted anxiety in the detective. She glanced hurriedly between the barkeep and the area before her, thinking, trying to wake her mind from the lackadaisical state it was now in. She lifted her eyes to a corkboard nailed into the wall directly in front of her, the surface covered with a collage of photos of the bar at busy hours, employees and patrons alike smiling wide for the camera.

Hartley quickly scanned the board, skipping between smiling faces and drunken expressions, bartenders from years past to the woman who currently wiped down the counter. Young women, all pretty and perky and no more than nineteen years of age, huddled in close to older, grizzled biker men, their eyes drifting to the soft, clear skin of the underage girls.

And then it was there, in front of her face, causing her breath to catch and her focus to throw the red flag in her mind. In the upper right of the corkboard, held by a red plastic pin, was an image of a man she had seen before, his long, dark hair and goateed face bringing her back to Korhan's shooting, to the driver of the van as he turned the automatic weapon in her direction. She leaned in, noticing the large, grotesque scar coursing through his left eye.

Just as she reached into her pocket and pulled her phone out, a door to her right opened and she heard the click of a cocking hammer, the barrel of a gun pressed to the flesh behind her right ear. From her left, another man appeared, just as large as the one seated at the bar. He roughly pushed her arm out of the way and pulled her firearm from its holster, sliding it into his waistband and taking a step back.

Dante Leary lowered his weapon and turned the detective to him, removing his sunglasses and putting on display for her the scar that graced his face, slicing through his eyebrow and ending just below his cheek. His eye was opaque in color, the injury removing any pigment in his iris that once matched his right orb. "This just got a little more complicated, wouldn't you agree, Scott?" Dante asked the bouncer, lowering his weapon and forcing a grin to Hartley.

* * * * *

James and Augie exited the cab just behind Hartley's cruiser, Graiser running his hand along the exterior of the vehicle as Augie stared to the building. "The open sign just went out," he said to this friend, pulling James's gaze to the unlit neon in the window. "What do you think?"

James did not respond, instead passing by the Londoner with a tap on the back to get moving. They crossed the street with ease and came to the front door, each of the men jogging to the entrance. James reached the handle and pulled, feeling the resistance of the rubber bottom catch on the ground momentarily before halting completely. He tried again, this time pushing. Again, the door did not budge. He glanced to Augie with worry in his eyes.

Augie leaned toward the window and glanced inside, instinctively staying out of sight by peeking between several flyers that were taped to the glass. "Do you see her?" James asked.

Augie shifted positions, lowering his body to get a better vantage point between the table directly in front of him. "She's there," he answered. He stepped out of the way. "In the back. Talking to someone it looks like." James looked through the same spot, squinting through the glare from the overhead streetlamp. He saw her, Jolene's beauty shining brightly in an otherwise dismal atmosphere. "What do you want to do?"

"I don't —" The words stalled in his throat, catching in a lump and refusing to exit. The man between the window and Jolene stepped slightly to the side, giving James full view at the detective. Her expression was calm, though serious, her body language like that of someone trying to gauge the options before them. However, it was something else that caused James to stumble verbally, allowed his mind to race and body to tense: an empty holster.

FIFTY-SEVEN

He checked the gun once more, ejecting the clip to make sure the bullets were loaded before once again sliding the firearm under the driver's seat. Millers had left Caprice's with the weapon and a box of bullets, protection for the otherwise undersized woman, if the situation ever arose. He also had decided to take her car, needing some way to get to his destination. Caprice and the red-haired girl he had left tied to the bedframe, having another go with the duct tape to ensure neither one would have an easy escape.

Caprice had shared with him, through angry sobs and desperate pleading, that Dante was indeed gunning for him, wanted him removed from the situation sooner rather than later. "He won't stop!" she had cried as he grabbed a handful of her hair and yanked her head back, tears and blood streaming down her cheeks and neck, soaking into her scrubs.

"He told you that?" he asked with a growl. "Answer me, bitch!"

"No!" she yelled back. "I just know! I know him. He won't stop. Please, just let us go!"

He had released her head with a quick jerk, her bedframe clanging loudly as the back of her skull crashed into it. Caprice had only let out a small, audible sob before Millers taped her mouth shut, looping the adhesive band around the back of her head several times. Then he had left.

He had no plans to return. He could care less if both women starved to death and rotted. All he needed at the moment was a bit of time, an hour or so to carry out what he needed to do for his own survival. It was his way of preserving his future, to live another day before taking on the obstacles that were sure to come.

* * * * *

Ratliff flew down the Kennedy Expressway, lights flashing, sirens blaring, heart pounding. He felt the vibrations of his phone on his lap, saw the display light up. He picked up the device and opened his mouth to answer, yet was beat to the punch by James. "Jolene's in trouble!" he said.

"Where are you?" Jacoby asked.

"Ginger's Trap. In Humboldt Park."

"Ginger's …? Why are you there? You're supposed to be at —"

"Listen!" he said. "Jo's inside the bar and the door's locked."

"What? Why's it locked? What's going on?"

"Jay," Graiser said, his tone serious. Ratliff perked his ears up, the use of his shortened first name falling from James's mouth a definite first. "They took her gun."

Ratliff's heart sank. He realized the seriousness of the situation was far graver than he had originally thought, immeasurably more critical than when Ahmet let loose the name Dante Leary as being one of the men who had come to threaten him. He tried to focus, tried to reel in the next course of action. Finally, he turned his attention back to James. "Can you see her?"

He heard James move the phone and relay the question to Augie. "They just took her into a back room. Augie can't see her." He paused. "What do we do?"

Ratliff weighed his options. "Nothing. I'm going to be there as fast as I can."

"Nothing? But Jo's in there —"

"James, just sit still. I'm calling for backup now."

"But Ratliff, I —"

"I have to go. Stay put!"

* * * * *

James stared to his phone for a second, feeling anger towards the detective and his commands. How was he supposed to just sit still and wait while he knew Jolene was in there, alone and without her gun? He did not know the circumstances, though figured they could not be beneficial for Hartley.

He squeezed the phone in frustration and nearly threw it to the ground. Instead, he placed it back in his pocket and looked to Augie. "We need to get in there," he said.

Augie nodded. "You still got it?" James reached into his jacket and, from the inside pocket, pulled the Taser he had taken from — and employed on — Officer Murphy. "How do you want to do this?"

* * * * *

"So how's it that you're in my bar?" Dante Leary said as lifted a leg onto his desk and sat directly in front of Jolene, who stood in between him and the folding chairs he had set up for guests. She did not respond, instead staring to him. "Was it Korhan?" Again, silence. "Renholm?" She turned her head and looked around the room, trying to determine if engaging this man in conversation was the route she wanted to take.

Jolene was a ball of nerves, though she was not, as of yet, out of control. She had gauged the individuals in the establishment and was pretty sure she knew what faced her. Dante was not a large man, though that could have been due to the fact that his bouncers were enormous in comparison. She knew he could probably handle his own in a fight, however, so could she, and she had been professionally trained. The bouncers, on the other hand, could pose a bit of a problem. Jolene, in her mind, checked off the injured man at the end of the bar. Bottle wound or not, the amount of blood loss and the way he writhed in pain led Hartley to the vision of taking him out with a well-placed shot to the leg, a kick or punch that dug into the injury with a buckling force. The woman behind the bar was definitely not high on Jolene's priority list either. She knew she could handle her.

What she did not know for certain, however, was how many weapons were in the place. Guns, knives, baseball bats: they were all items she had to worry about and, with the people she was currently dealing with, the number could be endless. She already knew of two firearms in their possession, her own and Leary's, which he had slipped into the front of his waistband as they pushed into the office area. Luckily, for her, they had not taken her side piece, a small gun which she holstered to the outside of her calf beneath her clothing, an item that had proven useful in the past. At least she had —

"Scott," Dante said, waving his bouncer into the office, his eyes never drifting from the detective before her. The large man made his way to stand just beside Jolene and awaited instructions. "See if she's got anything else on her." With that, the man turned to her, his large hands flipping her arms wide and beginning to pat her down, a rough frisk from an individual that obviously knew the ins-and-outs of criminal behavior. His fingers traveled into her pockets, over her chest and down her torso, sliding over her backside before traveling down her leg. Finally, he came to her extra piece, pulling up her pant leg and looking up to Dante as he unlatched it and set it on the desk. Leary smiled at her. "You came prepared."

A sudden loud knocking pulled their attention to the office door, an audible banging that gave the tension in the room a brief pause, but only for a moment. "Should I go?" Scott asked, thumbing toward the hallway.

Dante thought for a minute before returning his eyes to Hartley. "Nah," he said with a wave. "Antonio's out there with Mary. They can handle whatever drunk's looking for a watering hole. Why don't you stay here? Who knows what this cop's capable of?"

* * * * *

"Open up!" Augie yelled, striking out with his fist on the front door of Ginger's Trap. He pounded several times in succession, each accompanied by a shout for the door to be unlocked.

Mary, the homely barkeep, yelled back from near the bar. "Go sleep it off! We're closed!"

"Closed?" Augie asked. "I don't see any hours listed on the window!" He moved into view and cupped his hands over the glass, leaning in to gaze through at the woman staring to him with arms wide. "What bars closes this early?"

"Piss off!" she yelled again.

"Come on, love!" Augie said loudly. He waited several seconds before stepping back and shrugging. "Fine. If you don't want the message from Millers, then fuck off!" He stalled briefly and noticed the woman stop in her tracks. She glanced over her shoulder at the man outside before turning her attention to the injured bouncer.

Augie moved away from the window and started slowly from the building, leisurely strolling down the sidewalk until he heard the click of a lock and the door swing open. "Hey!" the woman yelled to him.

"No!" Augie said with a wave. "I don't have time for this. I told Millers that!"

"Stop!" she said sternly, stepping from the building to follow.

The plan was anything but foolproof, and James and Augie knew it. However, it was the best they could come up with in the limited amount of time they felt they had, especially with Jolene's potentially unhealthy situation.

With a swiftness, James leaped from behind the door and pressed the Taser's metal prongs to the base of the woman's neck, pulling the trigger and holding it in place for several seconds. She let loose a gurgling growl before slumping to the pavement, falling sideways into a lamp post suddenly and knocking her head into the concrete curb. Augie sprinted over and knelt beside her, looking at the lump forming on her head. "Shit, mate!" he said. "What now?"

James looked up to him. "I don't know I didn't think that far ahead," he admitted, rising to his knees and taking in his surroundings. "Where's Ratliff?" he asked rhetorically.

"Not sure," Augie said, tapping his friend on the shoulder and extending his finger. James followed, his eyes falling on the opened door. "But we can proceed with your plan now, if there's any more to it." They stood, each glancing between the entrance and the woman at their feet, unconscious on the city sidewalk.

"What about her?" James asked.

Augie looked about him before reaching down to grab under her arms. "Get her feet," he said, the pair lifting the smaller woman off the ground easily and moving to the side of the building. They set her in a space between the bar and the adjacent establishment, propping her up against the bricks. She moaned softly, yet remained still. "Give me that," Augie said, grabbing the Taser from James's grasp and placing it against the woman's leg.

James reached out and halted him before he could engage the trigger. Augie looked to him. "We're going to need that." Augie nodded and followed Graiser toward the front of the bar. They stalled out front, each staring to one another, their minds working to the interior and what awaited them.

FIFTY-EIGHT

"Look," Hartley began, "I don't know what this is about, but I suggest you rethink what you're doing."

"Yeah?" Dante said with a small chuckle. "Take a seat, detective." He waited for her to comply, and, when it was apparent she would not, his smile dropped from his face like a ton of bricks. "I said take a fucking seat!" Hartley felt her muscles tighten, yet remained stoic for a moment, finally acquiescing to his demand and sliding into one of the folding chairs. Dante's eyes never left her. "Now, how about we try this again? I want to know what brought you to my doorstep? Which one of those fools was it? Karaca? Renholm?" He shook his head. "Those fucks. Should have gotten rid of them immediately. Won't be a mistake I make again." His index finger wiggled before her.

"Why did you kill Korhan?" Hartley finally asked.

"Huh? Me? I didn't kill Korhan," he replied.

"I saw you. You were there, driving the van."

Dante shrugged. "I'm not sure what you're talking about."

Hartley stared up at him. "This won't work, you know. This whole act. We have you at the scene of Korhan's murder."

"Prove it," was all he replied. "From what I read in the papers, there was a crazy amount of shooting going on. With all those bullets flying, I'm sure it was pretty difficult to determine up from down. Or so I heard."

Hartley assumed, by the looks of it, that Dante was merely jerking her around, not intending in the least to use the *I don't know what you're talking about* card as a means to separate himself from the situation. He looked like he was having fun, enjoying the cat-and-mouse game, the back-and-forth banter between the good guys and bad. It was something that put her on edge. People like this, like Dante Leary, did not turn themselves in based on the fact that they were guilty and could be linked to the scene of a crime. People like Dante fought. They scratched and kicked and bit until they freed themselves. They killed for their potential escape from a lengthy stint at a penitentiary.

Hartley decided her only chance at finding her own freedom was to engage verbally. "Why kill Korhan?" she asked. He frowned and cocked his head to the side. Hartley sighed. "Hypothetically, why would someone have reason to kill Korhan?"

"Ah, well, *hypothetically*, Korhan was a fucking weasel. He was a crook compromised by the pungent bliss of drugs. I'm sure in your line of business, you know how easy someone like that turns. One minute they're doing what you hired them to, and the next, they're hunkered down in some fucking motel, ratting you out to the highest bidder." He paused and shrugged. "Sometimes people just like to cut their losses early in the game."

"And sometimes they forget to until it's too late," Hartley added.

"Too late? I'm not sure what you're talking about. I don't think it's too late." Dante stood and bent at the waist, his face inches from hers as a grin formed. "Not for me, anyway."

* * * * *

From the back of the bar, Antonio worked his cell phone diligently, pressing a series of numbers over and over, the ringing constant in his ear until the inevitable sound of her voicemail message. "This is Caprice. Sorry I'm not able to take to your call. Leave your name and number, and I'll get back to you soon." He hung up and tossed the device onto the bar in frustration.

"Fuck!" he growled, reaching to pull the makeshift tourniquet tighter about his leg. He needed the petite dancer. Her association with Dante should have made her answer the phone on the first ring. There was no reason he should be required to call back multiple times. The amount of blood he was losing was significant, and a professional nurse without ties to a hospital was required.

From the front of the bar, Antonio heard the door close, the draft created by the heavy entry taking several seconds to reach his sweaty face. It was dark in the alcove near the entrance, the light having long ago burnt out and never replaced, much like the bulbs elsewhere in the building. He cocked his head to the side in an attempt to see, but was unsuccessful, instead maneuvering a little too much and causing a jolt of heated pain to streak up his thigh. He sneered and bit down hard, giving the tourniquet another much needed twist.

"Mary," he said, glancing once again to the front of the bar. There was no answer. "Mary! What the fuck's going on?" The silence caught his attention. Mary was not a big talker, that much was for certain. She barely had the time of day for anyone in the place, including Dante. What she lacked for in social skills, though, she made up for in loyalty, having been an alibi for numerous individuals in tight spots. No, the fact that she did not respond did not surprise him. However, her appearance, or lack thereof, after nearly half a minute since entering the bar, did.

Antonio pushed himself off his stool and tested his leg. The pain was excruciating, but he was still on the job. Something was definitely off in Ginger's Trap, and he was going to be the one to make sure it was straightened out.

* * * * *

Hartley's jaw clenched. "So you mean to kill me then?" She waited for him to respond, yet continued when he did not, instead leaning back into his desk with arms folded. "Are you really that dumb? Killing a police officer? You wouldn't survive five minutes. This entire city would be all over your ass."

"There are other ways to deal with you, if need be," he replied.

Hartley glared at him. "If you so much as look at me the wrong way —"

"Come on now!" he answered. "You're pretty, but that's not my way. I'm more of a … fixer. I take care of things that happen to pose problems for me. That's it."

"And that includes murder."

Dante shrugged. "I don't know about that. If someone happens to piss me off and then a week later they are found, I don't know, floating down the Cal-Sag, it's no sweat off my brow. Accidents happen."

"Like Korhan? Was he an accident?"

"Korhan was a blemish on the planet," he answered quickly, raising his arms and running his fingers across the crown of his head. "He was an idiot to the highest degree. Fuck Korhan. The world's better without him." Scott laughed, pulling Dante's smiling face to him as the two shared the moment.

It was a moment Jolene could not pass up. Without hesitation, she darted up from the chair, one hand extending towards the gun in Dante's belt, the other reaching for his throat. Leary's eyes widened instantly as she approached, clearing the few feet between them in a matter of milliseconds. He tried to sidestep her, but she had already read his next move. As he brought his limbs down, Hartley grabbed onto his thumb and spun him, his arm being drawn behind his body and towards the ceiling in one quick motion, the pain from the maneuver causing his blood to boil and his face to morph into a sneer.

Scott reacted slowly, not sure what was happening in the brief couple seconds. He hurriedly lunged at Hartley, forgetting about the detective's gun within his waistband. She twisted her body enough to parry the much larger man, ducking behind Leary and kicking out with her leg, her foot making contact with the bouncer's ribs with enough force to send him tumbling backward, his balance lost as he collided with the folding chair and fell head-over-heels to the floor.

Her movements to deter a strike from the bouncer lessened the pressure on Dante's arm, and he rose up on his toes while pushing backward, his body coming into contact with Hartley's and slamming her into the solid desk. He landed on top of her and was immediately free, rolling to the side and reaching for the firearm at his side. Jolene reached out with both hands and grabbed onto his, forcing the weapon and his extremity downward, back into his waist, the hold not allowing Leary to pull the gun on her and utilize it.

What it did permit, however, was a free shot at the defenseless officer, one that Dante took instantly. With his free hand, Leary reached over and grasped onto the detective's neck, squeezing with all his might as he pushed her away. He righted himself and straddled her, one foot firmly on the ground with his other leg bent and resting on the surface of the desk, Jolene's body sprawled beneath him.

Hartley fought to free herself, struggled against his grasp to gain some maneuverability in an attempt to breathe. She felt her head begin to pound and stars formed. Finally, she released his wrist, allowing him the chance to pull the firearm and bring the barrel to within inches of her face. He removed his hand from her throat and Jolene gasped audibly, sucking in a large breath and swallowing hard. Dante leaned in close. "You fucking try that again, and you're a dead woman! You understand?"

* * * * *

By the time Antonio reached the front of the bar and glanced into the alcove, he was woozy and out of breath. Sweat dripped from his brow, a small waterfall cascading down the immense cliff that was his nose. His tourniquet was soaked through with the blood he was losing at a rapid pace and his hands were beginning to shake.

So when two men jumped from the darkened recess at him, his heart jumped and he nearly toppled to the side. Augie flew through the air and rammed into the bouncer, fists flying as he tried to strike out at Antonio's face and neck. The assault was lackluster, in the bouncer's eyes, a battle waged by a weaselly man with a jab like a four year old. However, in his weakened state, Antonio stumbled backward, catching himself on a nearby table as another man dove low, an object extended in his hands.

The metal prongs of the Taser connected with the bouncer's ankle. Just as James was about to press the trigger, the man moved, twisting his weight and shrugging Augie off of him, the Londoner tumbling into Graiser and knocking the electroshock weapon from his hand. James watched the device skitter towards the bar, bouncing off of the wood paneling perpendicular to the tiled floor. He looked up just in time to see a fist barreling down on him, felt the contact to his chin, a glancing blow that dropped him to the floor with stars in his eyes.

Meanwhile, Augie renewed his attack, pulling a chair from underneath the nearest table and swinging with all his might, an assault that caused the bouncer to back away, his forearm out to ward off the battering. James shook his head and regained his feet, lashing out with his fists and connecting with the bouncer's jaw, spinning him around to meet the newest onslaught. Graiser glanced down at the towel tied to his leg and immediately struck out, his hand jabbing at the wound and pulling from the much larger man an ear-piercing scream.

Antonio tilted his head to the ceiling in agonizing pain, a rage rising to the surface as he looked upon the pair assaulting him. In one swift movement, he grasped onto the chair swinging towards him, stopping the motion of the makeshift weapon and heaving it backwards, the man attached to it flipping over the nearest table.

In the time it took for the bouncer to deal with Augie, James moved to the bar and retrieved the Taser, standing tall and reaching out with his right hand to aim the weapon at the larger man, the laser sight pinpointed on his chest as he turned to Graiser, eyes wide at the sight of the weapon in his hand.

Before James could pull the trigger, a concussion exploded within the bar, a loud popping sound that made everyone freeze in place, including the bouncer mere feet from him. Augie jumped at the sound, hands to his ears. "James?" he said, the tone of his voice disbelieving and laced with worry as he looked to Graiser.

James turned his attention to the back of the bar, his eyes meeting those of Jolene, her own glassy with tears, hands raised to her mouth in utter shock as she tried to break free of another bouncer's firm grip. He did not understand what had happened, only that *something* had happened, something serious enough that both Augie and Jolene were reacting in unprecedented ways towards him. Things seemed to stall in the bar, everyone freezing in place, eyes to him.

Then it was clear. He glanced to the left of Hartley and gazed upon a long-haired man, a scar running through his eye and down his cheek, standing just outside of the corridor leading to the rear of the building, an angry scowl spread across his face as he lowered the firearm. Graiser lifted his left hand to the right side of his chest, running his fingers across his shirt, feeling the blood ooze from the bullet wound and soak into his clothing. He looked down and took a labored breath before glancing at Jolene once more. He felt himself stumble, take an unsteady step or two backward. His arm lowered and he crashed into the bar, sliding between the stools and to the floor as darkness clouded his vision and eventually took over.

FIFTY-NINE

Jacoby exited the cruiser just outside Ginger's Trap and watched Officer Toby Hill turn onto the street with lights flashing. Ratliff waved his hands in the air and Hill extinguished the light bar, pulling to the side of the road and exiting his vehicle to meet the detective on the sidewalk. "What do we know?" Hill asked.

"Jolene's in there," Ratliff answered. "Not sure where James and his friend are though."

"They're here?" He sounded surprised.

Ratliff nodded. He took in his surroundings, noticing his partner's car. He opened his mouth to speak and immediately shut it as the sound of a single gunshot from inside the bar erupted into the air. The officers looked at one another and jumped into action, Ratliff pulling his firearm and running toward the building's entrance. Hill jumped on the radio and called it in, giving their location and the request for backup.

Ratliff tried the door, but it did not budge. He sidestepped to the window and glanced inside, his eyes taking in the scene before him. He saw Hartley, tear-streaked and awestruck, trying to break through the barrier that was a large man's arms. Augie was nearer to him, pushing past another giant of an individual to run to a form lying prone on the floor, squeezed uncomfortably between two barstools. It was James. As Augie shifted his position, Ratliff could see clearly the blood forming on his chest and underneath his body.

At that moment, a man stepped forward from the rear of the room. Jacoby had not initially seen him, his focus drawn immediately to those he knew. Now, however, he could see the long hair and grotesque scar. His thoughts traveled back to the murder of Korhan, the vision of the driver of the van morphing into the forefront of his mind from a crystal clear reverie.

"He's got a gun," Hill said from his side, pulling the detective's vision from the recent past and to the here and now. Ratliff saw it as well, the weapon held firmly in the man's hand as he neared the front of the bar.

Jacoby stepped back and looked around, trying to find anything that would serve the purpose at hand. It took a moment, but he finally spotted it: a wrought iron bench with splintering wood for the seat and backrest. "Help me," Ratliff said to Hill. They each grabbed an end, pulling an old rusted chain from the armrest that had once secured the seat to the parking lot fence. They moved quickly to the front of the building, setting themselves before the large plate glass window, the pair of them in view to the individuals inside as if splashed across a movie screen. Ratliff's eyes connected with

Jolene's for just a moment, enough to grace her with the notion that help had arrived and allow her the chance to once again jump into action as the officers outside cocked back the bench and let it fly, the heavy, decrepit seat crashing into the window and sending thousands of glass shards spewing in every direction.

* * * * *

The moment was a rollercoaster, a long dive into the abyss followed by a soaring ascent into the light. They had heard the initial crash within the bar area, a somewhat welcoming sound that forced Dante to remove his leg from over her waist and pull the firearm from her face. "What the fuck was that?" he had said, looking to Scott as he picked himself from the floor and walked off a twisted ankle. Jolene did not move. She breathed deep, her fingertips running across her neck, the pounding in her head lessening with every ticking second.

Before she knew it, she was being pulled from the desk surface by the large bouncer, his strong hands yanking her to her feet and grasping firmly onto her arm as they followed Dante from the office and down the short corridor. They stopped in their tracks and watched the melee unfold, James and Augie waging war with the injured bouncer, the man swinging his arm in anticipation of the assault from the chair-wielding Londoner.

Hartley could not come up with a solid reason of why the two were there. She stood still, trying to think, her mind empty as to how the pair were standing a dozen yards away and not sitting peacefully within the precinct break room. She shook her head and jumped as the engaged bouncer screamed, her eyes watching as he grabbed onto the swinging chair and shoved backward with all his might, sending Augie tumbling head-over-heels.

Amidst the commotion, Jolene had not seen James jump to the side and retrieve the Taser. She had watched as Augie tried to regain his feet, oblivious as Graiser stood and aimed the electroshock weapon at the bouncer's chest. She had not, however, missed Dante, in one swift motion, lift his armed hand into the air and compress the trigger, sending the projectile through the space between them to pierce James's chest, tearing flesh and striking bone. She had watched through tear-filled eyes as he slipped to the bar and fell to the earth.

It was horrendous to watch, and it felt as if her mind was replaying it over and over again, warp-speed through her memories, a skipping visual record that was stuck on the absolute worst scene. She felt herself trying to disengage the bouncer holding her. She shrugged away his hand and took several steps forward before being corralled and lifted easily back into place, this time his arms wrapping around her frame as a makeshift prison, the bars rock-solid muscle.

Then, just like that, she was staring to a new hope, a vision she hoped and prayed was not a figment of her shocked and compromised imagination. Officer Toby Hill appeared with Ratliff, both men carrying the bench she had seen outside prior to entering this nightmare, swinging it back once before allowing the heavy bomb to blow apart the picture window running the entire front of the building.

She had caught Ratliff's eye, and in that moment, a connection was felt, a warning, a signal, something that told her to get moving. Act. James was wounded, possibly dead. There was no time to think upon it, no time to stall on the fate of her friend and the possibility that he was no longer part of the world. Dante Leary had just shot him *in front of her*. The odds he was going to leave any witnesses, especially cops, alive was slim. So she did what she needed to. She acted. She followed suit, watching the bench crash through the window and scatter fragments of glass throughout the building.

Dante turned at the last moment, catching the movement from the corner of his eyes just as the men outside the bar released the bench. He instinctively threw his arms up for protection, the gun still held firmly in hand. Scott, holding fast to her, turned his head to witness the mayhem, allowing Hartley the leeway to make her move. With a quick jerk, she brought her heel down on the top of the bouncer's foot, crunching bone and stripping an angry growl from his soul. "Fuck!" he yelled, relaxing his grip on the detective slightly. Jolene shot her arm up, her fist connecting with the man's jaw and jolting his head back. She ducked immediately and slid from his grasp, spinning on her toes as she tried to gain some much needed space.

Unfortunately, there was not much ground to be had. Hartley bounced off the nearest wall, her shoulder colliding with a shelf housing napkins and stemware, the lasting remnants of a restaurant long since extinct. As she regained her footing, she felt a firm hand grasp the back of her shirt and reel her in, her body slamming into the bouncer's as he tried to bring her under control once more, his arm wrapping around her shoulders. Jolene tried to free herself, yet his grip was strong. She twisted and turned, unable to inch her way out of the unwanted hug, her mind trying to corral her next step.

"Jo!" she heard her partner yell, just before bullets began to fly.

* * * * *

"Jo!" Ratliff yelled, his vision searching the rear of the bar until he focused on his partner in the clutches of a large man near a small back hallway. He nearly stepped through the front window after her, but was tackled suddenly by Officer Hill and knocked to the ground, the pair rolling to the side and coming to a halt next to the door as several shots rang out, the bullets following the pair along the sidewalk. Ratliff popped up onto a knee and pulled his firearm once more. "You okay?" he asked Hill, who rose and armed himself in turn.

"Yeah," he said, reaching to the radio strapped to his shoulder. "Shots fired! Repeat: shots fired! Need backup at Ginger's Trap in Humboldt Park! Address —" Two consecutive concussions ricocheted off the windowsill near their current position, causing each of the men to duck into the door and out of harm's way.

"Ratliff!" came the accented shout of Augie. "No!" Ratliff turned into the opening and watched as the long-haired man aimed the gun towards the Londoner and fired.

* * * * *

Jolene heard Augie's shout and the gunshot that followed straightaway. A crash, moments later, led her to believe that Augie had met a similar fate as James, that he had taken a bullet and was now lying lifeless next to his American friend. The thought did not sit well with her, boiling her blood and pushing her into action that was borderline reckless. She suddenly lashed out, pushing the bouncer's arm toward the ceiling and flashing her pearly whites, sinking them into his flesh as he screamed in pain. Scott yanked his limb free, trying to shake the sting from his forearm.

Jolene spun and reached for her gun in his waistband, nearly grasping the weapon before he slapped her hand away and threw an open palm toward her face. He connected, but the blow was lessened as Hartley arched her head backward, taking the strike on the chin and splitting her lip open with a searing pain. She nearly fell to the floor but caught herself and watched as the man before her reached to his belt and pulled the firearm free. Jolene did not wait to see how he planned to use it, instead turning and bolting through the swinging door as the large, armed bouncer yelled after her, his footfalls rapidly following as she turned into the office and collided with

Millers Renholm, the collision stripping the air from her lungs as she fell to her hands and knees on the tiled floor.

SIXTY

The sands were cool on the beaches of Ocho Rios. White light shone brightly from the lampposts, like little stars hovering above the rolling tides. The dark blue of the sky was shifting to black, miniature twinkling pinpoints covering the canvas overhead.

He kicked his feet into the billions of granules of sand, wiggling his toes and feeling the particles slide against his skin. For a time, he stood there, not willing himself to move on, to trudge along the beach in no particular direction. He remained stationary, feeling the briny breeze cross over his face, the saltiness of the air catching on his lips as he closed his eyes and breathed deep.

He felt lips press to his, sweet and delectable, and he parted his own to let a tongue come forth and caress. Fingers worked their way into his hair, stroking the back of his head. A hand slid across his waist, coming to rest on his lower back and pulling him in. He reached his arms out and wrapped them around a slim body, coursing his digits along a linen shirt and to the shoulders of the being embracing him.

They parted, his eyes remaining closed, lost in the exchange that had just happened. "You don't have to go," came the familiar Caribbean twang of Mattie, her brown skin and short dreadlocks filling his mind. He could taste her on him, could feel the smoothness of her legs. Her scent wafted into his nostrils and he opened his eyes to look upon her.

Only it was not Mattie he gazed upon, but Jolene, her inexplicable beauty radiantly glowing as she smirked to him, flipping her head back in order to remove the strands of hair from her eyes. He found himself leaning into her, his lips gracing small, meaningful kisses along the muscles of her neck, his tongue tracing lines across the hill of her esophagus and back to the spot where her shoulders came into play. He pulled at her linen shirt, bringing the fabric down below her shoulder, her tanned skin and toned arms displayed before him as she raised her head back up.

"You don't have to go," she said. He closed his eyes and pulled her in for an embrace, breathing deep and smelling the sweet aroma of marijuana float from her being. When he opened his eyes again, Mattie stood there, her fingers toying and twirling his wavy hair, her lips glistening in the light of the lampposts. "I have something for you," she said, grabbing onto his waist and pulling him slowly to her. She leaned back, leading him to the sand, his grip gracefully laying her down to stare up at him. He kneeled before her, straddling her legs, watching as she slowly began to unbutton her thin shirt, pulling the fabric apart cautiously, playfully, until he stared upon her flawless skin, a flat stomach and perfect breasts.

He returned his gaze to hers, his eyes taking in the display before him — Jolene. "I have something for you," she said, reaching up to pull him to her. He reached out and ran his palm up her side, feeling the tiny hairs on her skin stand at his touch, goose bumps rising under his fingertips. He etched the hills and valleys between her ribs. He cupped and squeezed slowly and deliberately her breast, leaning forward as her mouth parted and her tongue invited him in.

At the last instance, however, she titled her head back, her gaze streaming down the sands, an arm reaching above her head to point down the beach. "There," she said, her voice not seductive in the least, businesslike and matter-of-fact. James halted and stared to her, glancing to her body underneath him, her slacks and white blouse buttoned and tucked in, his hand cupping the breast of a detective of the Chicago Police Department.

His eyes followed the direction of her finger, traveling down the sands of Ocho Rios, over the wind-blown cracks and crevices and past the wrinkled palm leaves skittering along the beach. His eyes journeyed the expanse and fell upon a couple standing at attention, their fingers intertwined, bodies close. Their expressionless faces stared back. James caught his breath and pushed himself from the ground. Jolene was no longer there. Neither was Mattie. It was only James. James and his parents, all standing at attention, staring to each other with questioning, unsure eyes.

* * * * *

"Ratliff!" The scream reverberated within his ears, a sound deafeningly close and desperate. He opened his eyes and tried to focus, blinking a multitude of times in rapid succession before he could make out the form just to his right. August Hughes.

He could also see the man standing in front of them, the long hair disheveled, the crooked eye taking aim at his friend. It was not until the gun in his hand raised, however, that James fully awoke from unconsciousness, the sight of the barrel pointing towards Augie sending the adrenaline coursing through his body. "No!" Augie yelled.

James shifted slightly, trying to rise. He felt something in his hand, a hard plastic and metal object he immediately recognized as the Taser he had taken earlier, the weapon still held in his grasp. He reached up and set the laser sighting on the man before him, pulling the trigger and ejecting the probes into his chest, the electric current taking effect at the moment of contact and sending fifty thousand volts into his system, a growl escaping his opened mouth, his muscles flexing as he squeezed off a round. The bullet sailed wide, missing both Augie and James and embedding itself in the wall just to their right.

Augie leapt forward, slapping the firearm from Dante, the weapon dancing across the floor and coming to rest toward the rear hallway. He caught Leary as he stumbled away, grabbing onto the man and pushing him roughly to the floor as the electricity coursing through his body subsided. The Londoner's momentum carried him into Antonio, the bouncer's fragile existence collapsing into the tables as Augie collided with him, his limbs finally giving way from the loss of blood.

Ratliff appeared at his side, pushing him back and yelling, "Go help James!" Augie nodded and turned, sliding across the floor to where another officer knelt over the wounded Graiser.

James looked up to him and coughed, blood dripping from his chin. "Where's —" He tried to push himself from the floor, but Hill placed a hand on his shoulder. "Jo. Where's ... Jo?" He coughed again, this time leaning to his right and spitting out a glob of red-tinged saliva.

Augie glanced up, his head on a swivel as he met the gaze of Ratliff, the detective pulling his handcuffs from his belt and lining them up with Leary's wrists. Eruptions from the back made everyone in the area halt, the concussions of gunfire cracking wood and mortar through the back wall. Hill and Augie turned just in time to watch Ratliff fall to the side, a splatter of red forming on the left side of his abdomen, just above his waistline. "Jay!" Hill yelled, stepping toward him before a shower of bullets rained down between the officers, causing Toby to dive to the side.

Ratliff rolled to the far wall, cursing through the pain and realization that Dante Leary was regaining his motor skills, the long-haired man shifting his weight and charging towards the back room and the unknown battle being waged.

* * * * *

Millers climbed the parking lot fence from the rear of the lot, falling into a crouch and taking a moment to gather his thoughts. Ahead, smashed and damaged, sat the SUV that had rammed him earlier. Alongside it were a number of cars, all vehicles he had seen on his last visit. He did not know if Dante was inside, but walking through the front door and announcing his own presence was not the cards he planned to play. He was here for survival, and by any means necessary. Sneaking in the never-used side entrance and placing a bullet in Leary without him noticing was fine by Renholm. Shooting a man such as Dante in the back was, by all means, legal play.

He hurried to the side of the building, sliding a panel of plywood across the gritty surface of the brick façade and stripping away the vines and weeds that had overrun the rusted door over the years. He looked at the padlock. It was nothing but a hiccup in his advancement, the wall onto which it was attached having been chipped away long ago by the elements. Millers grabbed firmly onto the lock and, with a quick yank, pulled the mechanism free. He tossed it to the side and entered.

Inside, the room was a cluttered mess. Water-stained boxes and dilapidated pallets of ages past lined every wall, overflowing with yellow papers and stale napkins and file boxes that Millers was sure had long-since been forgotten. Rat droppings littered the floor, and an ancient raccoon skeleton lay at peace in the far corner, its carcass picked clean by the scavengers that called Ginger's Trap home.

Millers pushed through the debris and entered the room, pulling the gun he had taken from Caprice as he walked toward what appeared to be a lighted hallway. He turned the corner and came to another door, this one shut and secured in place with two-by-fours and bent and crooked nails. He swore to himself, edging closer to the stream of light that poured in from the office just beyond. He realized he needed to be quick. There was no telling what was on the other side of the door.

He took several deep breaths and, with a fury, lashed out with his boot, the gate snapping inward, two-by-fours falling to the ground, splintered and broken, nails bent in every direction. Millers jumped through and raised the gun.

He was alone in the office, yet commotion from the front of the establishment told him something was definitely going on. Millers thought for a second, his mind telling him flight might be the best scenario. Yet he moved forward, approaching the door that led to the hallway and the bar beyond. Fleeing would only buy him some time. It would not allow him the freedom from Dante Leary that he so yearned for.

Just as he reached the door, it suddenly opened, his eyes going wide as Detective Jolene Hartley burst through, ramming at full-speed into him and falling to the ground in a gasp. She glanced up at Millers with a questioning glare, no doubt wondering where he had come from.

The look, for some reason, incensed him. Perhaps it was his tussle with her in James Graiser's apartment. Maybe the mounting stress of his unwanted association with Leary, coupled by the fact that he was a target, caused him to react the way he did. But in that moment, as she gazed up at him — eyes wide, blood dripping from her lip, her beauty undeniable — Millers became enraged.

He snarled at her, pointing the gun in her direction and reaching down in the same instance, grabbing a fistful of hair and pulling her to her feet. Hartley, regaining her breath, saw the hatred in Renholm's eyes. All at once, she reached out, taking a handful of his shirtsleeve and locking her arm at the elbow. She moved into his body and took several quick, succinct jabs to his midsection, an attack that caught Millers completely off guard. The strikes were not debilitating, however, and he quickly regained focus, grasping onto her hair once more and twisting her to the side, the motion jerking her head back and spinning her on her heels. The movement caused Hartley to release his sleeve, allowing Millers freedom with the firearm.

Fortunately for Jolene, however, the bouncer walked through the door, shocked to see Millers standing feet from him. Their eyes connected momentarily, each of the men simultaneously raising theirs guns and firing. Millers stumbled backward, two bullets entering his hip. His own initial shots sailed wide, though they flew close enough where Scott was forced to take cover, jumping to the side in a chaotic maneuver. Millers released several more, each one careening through the wall and into the hallway beyond.

Jolene rolled to the side, cowering behind an end table near the side wall, waiting for an opportunity — any opportunity — to exit the battlefield. Suddenly, from the front of the establishment, she heard a yell, a name released into the atmosphere that caused her heart to drop. "Jay!"

SIXTY-ONE

Dante charged forward, slipping and sliding on the tiled floor until he reached the office door. The shots that had rang out and struck the officer about to handcuff him had been surprising, to say the least. He could only assume that Jolene had outsmarted Scott, somehow wrangling the gun away from the much larger bouncer and employing it in a life or death battle against the man.

It was the farthest thing from reality, however. As Dante burst through the office door, another gunshot rang out, piercing the air and nearly toppling Leary to the side. From his left, Scott suddenly heaved backward into the wall, groaning loudly before face-planting into the hard floor, blood oozing from the fatal wound inflicted and pooling underneath his oversized body. Leary turned his focus to the desk before him, to the source of the blast, surprised to see Millers Renholm doubled over, one arm slung about his waist, gun in hand as he tried to bring his eyes back to the room before him.

Dante raced forward and grasped firmly onto Millers wrist as he attempted to level the gun at the owner of Ginger's Trap. Leary yanked the piece free with ease and tilted the wounded man to up with his free hand, pushing him up by the neck until he was at eye level. The unwanted movement pulled a shriek from Millers. Their eyes met, and hatred crossed between them, a river of indignation amongst crooks flowing freely between the pair. "What the fuck are *you* doing here?" Dante yelled, not waiting for an answer as he brought the pistol high overhead by the barrel. He followed through with enough force to split skin and chip bone, Millers's cheek exploding from the blow, blood erupting like a fountain.

There was nothing Millers could do to curb the assault, however. The bullet wounds he took in the hip were debilitating, a fiery cauldron that radiated into every slight movement he made, causing him an unprecedented amount of pain that halted all voluntary motor activity. He collapsed onto the desk surface, stars forming in his vision, his legs dangling over the edge, arms wide as, for the moment, the pain in his body subsided, stepping aside for the numbness that associated itself with the trek into unconsciousness.

Dante stepped back and wiped the splatters of blood and rivulets of sweat from his face, breathing deeply as he stood over his useless partner. He cursed his bouncers for not having taken care of this mess when they had the chance, thinking back on their ineptitude and the lack of effort made by Caprice to stall Millers.

"Millers," he said. "Millers, look at me." Renholm semi-shrugged off the stupor that had set in to gaze upon the man above him, recognizing through the blur the gun aimed in his direction, the tingling feeling overwhelming his senses blocking the survival instinct he had lived by in his recent plan of attack. "Consider our association over." Leary smirked and set his finger on the trigger.

Before he could do the deed, however, Jolene bolted from her place of cover, diving shoulder first into Dante's exposed back and tackling him to the floor. He gasped for breath and pushed himself to his knees, yet was stung with quick series of jabs to the ribs, strikes Jolene put all her weight behind, throwing her body forward in the assault as well as her fist. Dante folded without hesitation, pulling his gun-wielding arm toward his knee in an attempt to block any sort of additional melee from the desperate officer.

The movement brought the weapon into Hartley's line of sight and she immediately reached for it, tugging and twisting in an attempt to free the firearm from Leary's grip, a struggle that proved difficult for both parties as they tossed elbows and leaned into one another. Dante held fast, however, the much needed air coming back to him, a tackle that would have put most individuals down for the count. Yet Leary battled, regaining his composure slowly but steadily. It was a battle of survival, one in which Jolene had no other option than to win. Dante had already shot James in front of her — blatantly disregarding the fact that a cop was present — and had just proceeded in pistol-whipping another man. The only outcome for her in his mind, she surmised, was death. It was the only way to allow himself any sort of leeway when it came to deniability.

Leary breathed deep and suddenly set his left foot underneath his weight, grounding himself as he mounted an attack. Jolene recognized the movement and wrapped her arm across his back, clinging to the front of his shirt at the exact moment he forced himself up, springing from a crouch and hurtling the detective back with him. Hartley, fortunately, had countered his move, spinning suddenly at the last possible moment and locking her right leg, her heel set into the floor as Leary flew to her left. The momentum carried her with him, though her left leg acted as a tripwire, knocking him off balance once more as he spun on a dime, losing the weapon into the air, the piece clattering to the floor and coming to a stop three feet from the wall.

Dante, feeling the maneuver benefiting Hartley, tried jumping to the right, his feet tangling with one another in a last ditch effort to gain some space from the detective. He fell into the corner of the desk and tumbled backward, his feet kicking upward into the sky, hands pushing the chair back as he collided with the floor in a grunt. Jolene, too, lost her balance, making a three-sixty with legs wide and catching herself just before she slid into a door at the rear of the office, a curious opening that had not been there before. Hartley instantly determined it to be the entrance Millers had taken to gain access into the establishment.

As she came to her feet, she froze, staring to the room before her, Millers swaying back and forth, the gun she had just freed from Dante's grasp in his hand, the barrel aimed in the direction of the desk where Leary now stood. The owner of Ginger's Trap — to Hartley's surprise — was also armed, her backup piece held aloft in the direction of Renholm, two lifelong criminals staring down the barrels at one another.

"What now?" Dante asked, out of breath, eyes jumping between Millers and the officer to his right. "This what you want to do?" he asked, his voice surprisingly low and calm. "This how it's going to be? Me and you gunning for each other from here on out?"

"Fuck you, man!" Millers yelled, his tone the exact opposite of his counterpart. He tried to shift into the center of the room and winced in pain. "This was your call. What choice did I have?"

Dante stared at him. "Leave fucking town," he answered, as if the question bordered on the absurd.

"Like you wouldn't come after me."

"Be better than you sticking around here!" he yelled. "You're kidding me, right?" Renholm did not respond. "You're fucking dumber than I thought. You think I could let you stick around with all the heat on you? You're just like that fucking Turk! You would've caved the second you got into the interrogation room."

"Don't call me a fucking rat!" Millers shouted back. "Things could have been different between us, Dante. I've never done anything but what you hired me for. I've never —"

"Is that right?"

"Yeah!"

"What about the Graiser lady?"

Millers paused. "What about her?"

"Did I pay you to beat and rape her? Did I pay you to force yourself on her? Fuck! She wasn't even supposed to be touched! But you and your ... your fucking sickness had to take matters into your own hands."

"I'm not the one that fucking put the knife in her," Millers retorted.

"I ended what you started! And I should have ended you right then, too. You know as well as I do that Graiser was the target. Not the woman!"

"That's where *you're* the idiot. You don't think this would have all happened if we left her alive? You think this bitch wouldn't be here asking questions?" He pointed to Hartley, who watched the proceedings with a wary eye.

"They would have kept quiet," Dante answered. "I would have seen to that."

At that moment, the office door burst open and Ratliff stumbled in, his hand clutching his side where he had taken the bullet, blood coating his shirt and dripping down his pants. "Jay!" Hartley exclaimed, her eyes glassy as she took in his current state.

"Put ... Put it down," Ratliff directed between breaths, leveling his gun on Millers, who shifted to the side in surprise, his own firearm still aimed at his accomplice.

From behind Jacoby, Officer Hill appeared, his attention on Dante as he slowly inched from behind the desk in the direction of Hartley. "Don't move!" Hill screamed, stopping the man in his tracks.

"Jay?" Hartley looked to Jacoby with fright, watching as he struggled to remain standing, sweat beading on his forehead, shoulders slumping. He glanced back and blinked, a slow, lasting action that revealed to her that Ratliff was in desperate need of medical assistance.

Dante noticed it, too. "Bullet wound to the abdomen? Who knows what organs were hit."

"Shut up!" Hill yelled, though he peered at Ratliff from the corner of his eye, realizing the situation was indeed grim. Jacoby took two short steps backward and leaned into the wall, his weight pulling him to the floor, the gun — still in the palm of his hand — resting on the tiles.

"Ratliff!" Hartley yelled, trying to rouse her partner.

"Pal," Dante said to Officer Hill, "you have two options right now. One: we stand here pointing these fucking things at each other, in which case he dies. Sure, we'll have our go at one another, but you seem to be outnumbered." He looked at Jolene and grinned. "I don't think that sits well with you. Two: you put down that gun and get the first-aid kit in the hallway just outside and he gets a fighting chance."

Hill looked upon his fading comrade and tried to weather the storm. "Toby," he heard Hartley say.

"Make the right choice here, Toby," Dante pushed, smiling as he let loose the officer's first name.

"Shut up," Hill said, though this time his tone lacked the intensity it had moments ago. He looked throughout the room, recognized the anxiety in Millers standing before him, the steadfast resolve in Leary's countenance as he took the reins of the situation. He felt the helplessness along with Jolene, the utter lack of control coursing through his body.

"Your choice," Dante said, taking a quick step to his right to put Renholm between him and the officer. In the same movement he swung his arm up and aimed the barrel at Hartley's head.

"No!" Officer Hill yelled. "No, okay!" He raised his hands in the air, the weapon dangling on an extended finger. "Okay. I'm putting my gun down, okay? Don't shoot."

Dante smiled and turned his focus to Hartley. "Get over here." She did not move, her focus still on her partner, bloodied and unconscious, his head slumping towards the floor. "Get the fuck over here!" he yelled, taking a step forward and grabbing her arm firmly, jerking her to him and setting the gun against her head.

"My gun's down!" Hill yelled.

"Then I suggest you go get the first-aid kit." He pulled at Hartley's arm and led her backward towards the rear exit, halting just inside the threshold. He yanked Jolene furiously, running her into the doorjamb, the large pieces of splintered wood poking into her skin and drawing blood. She instinctively winced, a small cry escaping her lips as she drew her hand back.

Millers, standing in the middle of the office, felt some relief. His life was still in danger and the wounded hip was causing him enough pain to where he found himself fighting to not faint. Yet the company of police officers had definitely taken the focus off of him, and with it the anxiety that had been weighing him down since stepping foot in the bar. It had been replaced by hope, an idea of escape, stepping free of the establishment and the police that hunted him, avoiding the looming threat that was Dante Leary.

He took an agonizing step toward the rear exit and turned just in time to watch Leary raise the gun over Hartley's shoulder with a grin. "Bye-bye, you fuck," Leary said, pulling the trigger and sending a bullet rocketing into the cheek of Renholm. Millers dropped the gun to the floor in a loud clang as his head whipped back, his hands coming to his face in a desperate attempt to stop the bleeding as he felt the life rushing from him.

SIXTY-TWO

Hartley saw it happening, but could not force herself to react in time. Her thoughts had been racing between James near the bar and Ratliff feet away. The moment directly after Dante pulled the trigger — after the blast so close to her head caused her to jump and lose the hearing in her ear; after Millers lurched forward and fell to the floor, writhing in chaotic convulsions as the bullet seared the insides of his head and he became still — was when Jolene reacted. She moved quickly, grasping onto the outstretched forearm of Dante and pulling it into the space where her neck and shoulder met, restricting his movement as she looped her own extremity around his, locking it against her body. She felt him try to pull free, felt his palm between her shoulder blades and the force with which he tried to gain his limb back.

She lashed out with her elbow, sending it into his ribs and buckling him. Without hesitation, she threw it again, this time connecting with his nose, hearing the crack of cartilage and the growl that escaped his lips. Dante righted himself quickly and cocked his arm back, sending his fist across her cheekbone and past her lips, splitting the wound she had suffered earlier even further, the blood coursing down her chin and falling through the expanse to the floor below.

Hartley remained locked on his arm, however, unwilling to let it go. The blow Dante had just graced her with caused her to stumble, and she fell roughly into the doorjamb. She yelped in pain and caught her breath as a large, pointed piece of the broken jamb connected with her side and sank in. She grabbed at it frantically, putting her palm against the threshold when she felt herself veering into the dagger with more force. She glanced over her shoulder and saw that Leary had caught sight of her new issue, using his full weight to push her forcefully into the makeshift blade, the jagged piece of wood sinking farther into her body and yanking from her a tearful sob.

Hartley desperately rammed her free hand into the doorjamb again, locking her leg against where the threshold and floor met. The piece of wood was nearly two inches into her side and the pain was excruciating. She felt Dante raise his arm into the air and bring it down, though the blow was diminished by his awkward positioning. Hartley had sunk her head into her shoulders, using her frame as would a boxer.

From the office doorway, Hill appeared, a concerned look on his face as his eyes glanced down at the lifeless form of Millers Renholm. He carried with him a white first-aid box, though dropped it to the floor as the gun Dante held aimed in his direction and fired. He jumped to the side, diving across the floor and coming to rest against the far wall.

Hartley felt Dante raise his hand again, but as he did, she made her move, kicking off the door frame and freeing the protrusion from her body, gasping as the wood slid from her flesh, the dozens of minute splinters it left behind causing an extra amount of sting to the wound. Hartley held onto the ten-inch weapon and was surprised when it broke from the rest of the doorjamb, coming loose in her hand. Without thinking, she twisted Dante's arm and pulled down, his elbow resting on the top of her shoulder and bending the absolute wrong way, the scream, which quickly gained momentum, pulled from Leary until the hyperextension emitted a loud pop and the gun clattered to the floor.

Hartley released his arm and spun, swinging the makeshift dagger with all her might and sinking it into the upper left side of Dante's chest. He caught his breath and grabbed hold of the protrusion, wincing as it moved ever so slightly. His agony turned to rage as he tried to breathe, lashing out with a crazed blow that struck Hartley in the chest, sending her flying backward to slide across the floor and come to a halt just at Ratliff's feet. She immediately pushed herself up, her hand reaching for the gun in her partner's hand. She turned and held it aloft, aiming toward the doorway in which she had just battled Leary.

Yet he was not there. The space was empty, an opening into a darkened room welcomed by a splintered doorjamb. She remained aimed at the space, waiting for Leary's return, for the moment when he erupted through the entrance with another weapon in hand, guns blaring as he finished the battle that had been waged within the bar. His return did not happen, however, and Jolene found herself pushing up from the floor as Hill retrieved his service piece.

They made their way to the opening, Hill flipping on his flashlight as they quickly breezed in, clearing hidden alcoves and mysterious chambers as they went, finally reaching the side door and the exterior of the building. Hartley swung her weapon to the alleyway and hurriedly stepped into the night, edging her way around the back of the building and into the silence of the emptied parking lot.

Dante Leary was nowhere to be found.

* * * * *

"Jo!" she heard from the insides of the building, her partner's lazy voice echoing through the back room of the bar to reach her ears.

Jolene holstered her weapon and hurriedly ran past Officer Hill, hearing him on the radio reporting the incident once more, requesting an immediate lockdown of the surrounding area. She vaguely recognized the flashing lights bouncing from the nearby buildings, somewhat captured the scene down the alleyway near the front of the building as a paramedic talked to the woozy bartender of Ginger's Trap leaning against a nearby fence.

However, her mind did not register the events until well after they happened. Her thoughts carried her feet, her heart directing her through the darkened back room and into the office area where Ratliff, eyes opened, tried to push himself from the floor. "No!" Jolene said, sliding next to him and pushing him down by the shoulders. "No! Stay where you are. The paramedics are here."

"Jo," he said, looking at the blood surrounding his wound, the blood pooling on the floor. Jolene glanced to the area as well and placed her hands over his, applying pressure in an attempt to curb the bleeding.

"Don't talk," she said, lifting into a crouch. "I need help!" she shouted desperately.

Hill appeared behind her. "What can —"

"Get me the first-aid kit!" she yelled. He jumped to the side and pulled the case to her, opening the lid as she began to rummage through its contents. It was sparse, to say the least, a collection of items that had not been replenished in years. She grabbed a package of gauze and ripped it open, pulling the sheets out in a rush and placing them underneath Ratliff's shirt, pressing down, leaning into him, as he cursed in pain. "I'm sorry," she replied, though she was definitely not, the action an absolute requirement in the situation. "Help!" she yelled again.

Hill gained his footing and bolted through the door, only to turn around and pop back in, holding the entrance open for a pair of medics to come through and take positions on either side of Jacoby. "Detective, I need you to back up," one of them said, tapping Hartley on her shoulder. She did not move, instead holding fast to her partner and applying the necessary pressure needed for such a wound, trying to lessen the amount of —

"Detective, please!" the paramedic repeated, his voice louder and sterner. Hartley glanced to him through glassy eyes, the look spread across her face pleading. "We have this," he said, his tone carrying with it an acknowledgment of the importance of this injured individual. Hill moved to her shoulder and pulled her back, the pair watching as a gurney was carted in and Ratliff was placed upon it. They quickly moved through the office door and into the adjoining hallway, Hartley rising to follow.

"What hospital are they taking him to?" she asked no one in particular. "Where are you taking him?" No one answered, the medics hurrying through the establishment and to the waiting ambulance. "Where …?"

"We'll find out," Hill said, stepping aside and rushing after them.

Hartley stood alone, shifting her weight to the left and right, her feet shuffling along the bar floor. Yet she saw nothing, her mind shutting off the outside world, a euphoric feeling of floating encapsulating her body. She was not there. She was no longer standing in the bar. She vaporized into the atmosphere, her molecules escaping through the large broken window and into the Chicago air.

The darkness of the bar gave way to an eruption of light, and she was led onto the sidewalk, helped into the back of the ambulance and seated on the right hand side of the cabin. She heard her name spoken aloud, yet could not focus on it. She felt fingers touch her arm, and turned, slowly, to gaze upon the face of Officer Toby Hill. "Do you understand me, Jo?" She stared. "You go with him. I'll take care of the initial statement. I'll meet you at the hospital." She felt her head bob up and down, though she could not recall doing it herself. "Graiser is en route. Okay? Do you understand? James is on his way to the hospital, too. I'll bring Augie."

"Detective," another voice echoed. "You're bleeding pretty badly —"

"I'm fine." It was her voice, but she did not realize she had spoken.

"Let's go!" someone yelled, closing the rear doors, the vehicle shooting into the city streets and whatever outcome was in wait.

* * * * *

Jolene sat on a non-descript table in a random room within Mount Sinai Hospital, staring blankly at the wall before her as a nurse placed another layer of gauze over her stitched up side. The incision caused by the lengthy, jagged piece of doorframe had been deep, yet luckily had not struck any major organs. After some thorough cleaning and a detailed inspection to remove any residual splinters, she had been cleared, free to her own devices, or whatever was currently on her mind. The nurse had insisted on checking out the detective's lip as well, however, after looking into Jolene's empty eyes and seeing the war waging within brought on by the day's events — events the entire hospital was soon privy to — she let it go. "I can take care of it later," she told Hartley, to which she received only a disinterested nod.

Hartley remained seated on the table even after the nurse left, staring at the wall, her right arm free of her shirtsleeve, the medical tape the nurse had placed on her clinging to her skin and the red-tinged pad of gauze. She envisioned the happenings at Ginger's Trap over and over, wondering how things had played out as they had. She wondered if she could have done things differently, if she should have waited for Ratliff before entering the building by herself. She knew everything that had happened was beyond her control, yet, with the state of James and Ratliff at this exact moment, she could not help but question herself.

From the doorway, Captain Nolan appeared, pulling her eyes from the wall to his face, a solemn expression etched across his façade. He stalled by the door momentarily before stepping forward. He said nothing at first, his presence, like that of a father figure, enough to bring her some solace in the turmoil she had been living in. Henry pulled her shirt and gently laced her hand through the sleeve, careful not to touch her wound and cause her more pain. Not that she would have noticed.

Finally, he placed his hands on her arms and gazed down upon her. She looked to him for only a moment before the tears began to stream, flowing freely as convulsions wracked her body, her sobs echoing through the halls of Mount Sinai Hospital as she fell into the arms of Captain Henry Nolan.

EPILOGUE

Kim Banneau found Jolene pacing the hallway, wearing a track along either side of the corridor in a lap that had lasted nearly forty-five minutes, a continuous oval that paused briefly only for the doctors and nurses coming to give updates in intervals. Hartley wrapped her arm across her stomach, the other bent at the elbow and leading to her mouth, where her fingernails were being chipped away by anxious teeth.

The bullet Jacoby had taken had caused severe blood loss and internal injuries that required immediate emergency surgery. They had rushed him through the double doors and into one of the rooms beyond, leaving Jolene standing outside with watery eyes and a gaunt expression. There was nothing she could do. His life was in the hands of professionals, and no matter how much she hoped and prayed for his survival, nothing was for certain.

James, she had been told, had flatlined twice, once in the ambulance and another while on his own operating table. The prognosis, as told to her by the numerous nurses and surgeons that made their way through the hall, was bleak, yet did have a silver lining. "He's already pulled through twice," several of the hospital employees had told her upon passing the distraught detective. "He's in the best hands at the moment."

Kim said nothing as she approached her friend, standing at attention and waiting for Hartley to make the first move. She did not know whether or not Jolene was in need of someone to talk to or just an embrace to allow the release of pent-up emotions. She could not fathom the depths at which the day had reached, the chaotic tendrils that squeezed the detective's every sense with unrelenting purpose. The only thing she was sure of was that Hartley was thankful for her just being there.

From behind her, she sensed someone approach, and Kim turned to see Captain Nolan take station at her shoulder. He handed her one of the two coffees he had brought with him from the cafeteria down the hall. "How's she doing?" he asked.

Kim shrugged. "I haven't talked to her yet."

"Well, I'm glad you're here. I'm sure she is too."

"What happened today, Henry?" Kim questioned, turning to him.

Her superior took a sip of his coffee. "Everything you don't want to see happen as a police officer."

"I mean, how did James get in the middle of this?"

"James was always the middle of this," he responded. "This whole case has revolved around him. He just happened into our lives at the right time to bring everything to the light."

"And what is *everything*?"

He paused. "I think we're still trying to figure that out. But we will. I assure you that much."

"So what about the case? Karaca's case, I mean."

"From what we figure, Morgan Keller, Millers Renholm and Dante Leary were the perps. Obviously, two of them are deceased."

"What about Leary?"

Nolan shook his head. "Units didn't come up with anything besides some blood on the parking lot fence. Other than that, nothing. We brought the bartender and one of the bouncers in for questioning. Not sure what we'll get from them. They seemed pretty tight-lipped."

Kim's line of sight connected with Jolene down the hall as a doctor exited the double doors and came to her side. "What about Jo?"

"What about her?" Nolan asked.

"With Leary still out there, is she in danger?"

Nolan glanced to her. "No more than every other man or woman who puts on that star. We'll keep an eye on her."

They halted their conversation as they tried to will their hearing the length of the hall, tried to pick up any of the words falling from the doctor's mouth. They could not, and, at the moment, neither Nolan nor Banneau felt the urge to interrupt Hartley's current trance. The doctors knew Nolan was on the premises. It was only a matter of time before they made it to him to relay whatever news was coming from the emergency room.

* * * * *

The concrete and steel cage Maggie had found herself in suddenly buzzed to life. She glanced to the door swinging open and her gaze fell upon the face of Dane Hartley, followed closely by a uniformed officer. "What the fuck is going on?" she stated abruptly.

Dane shrugged. "Not sure, but I'd recommend curbing the language, unless you want to spend the night here."

"No thanks," Maggie answered. "I think I've had enough of jail cells."

Dane laughed. "You were never that good of a reporter to get yourself holed up in one anyway."

"You're an ass," she stated, sliding by him and into the hall. "Seriously though, what's going on?"

"I've been told to release you and bring you two upstairs," the officer said.

"What for?" Dane questioned.

"We'll find out when we get there." They turned in unison and began down the hall, turning right and exiting into another corridor where they took an immediate left.

Dane rode the elevator in silence, his mind on the documents Maggie had illegally procured. He wondered how the rest of this would play out, who they would find behind the curtain pulling the strings for the past ten years filled with murder. He had his ideas, but, in the grand scheme of things, could care less. It was a tragic story, young Graiser's, and one that he felt he had become a large part of. But the majority of his interest fell into the realm of exclusivity to the story. He was a prick, and he knew it, however, that was how he was able to live with himself.

The elevator doors opened and the duo walked out upon a somber, serious Jolene Hartley, her bloodshot eyes and bruised, scarred lip facing them. "What the fuck happened to you?" Dane asked.

"Follow me," Jolene said, turning immediately and leading them past the interrogation room, away from the break room, and into a side office stacked full of file boxes. She turned and faced them with a stern look. "Close the door," she ordered. Maggie paused for a second before complying.

"Am I being charged with anything?" Maggie asked, her voice forceful, yet her demeanor showing a lack of confidence.

Hartley glared at her and opened her mouth to talk, yet could not, the emotions from the day rising and causing her eyes to tear. She cleared her throat and fought through. "Who was behind the payments?"

Maggie glanced at Dane before answering. "I don't know."

"Bullshit!" Jolene muttered. "Your source couldn't have found all of that information but not who generated it. Now I want —"

"Detective!" Maggie said loudly, holding her hands up in defense. "I promise you! My source wasn't able to find anything in such short notice."

"You expect me to believe that?"

Tien swallowed hard. "You can believe what you wish. But fact's fact. There was nothing attached to what we found that led us to any source."

Hartley placed her hands on her hips and put her eyes to the ground, shifting her weight. Dane caught a glimpse of the bloodstain covering her side. He stepped forward. "What happened to you?" he asked, his tone, for once, carrying some worry. "And where is everyone? Augie? James? Your partner?"

Jolene held her emotions at bay, instead glancing back to Maggie with teary eyes. "How long?"

Maggie was confused. "How long, what?"

"How much time do you need to track down where the money came from?"

Maggie shrugged. "I don't know," she answered. "I'd have to talk to my source."

"Do it," Hartley said without hesitation.

"You do understand none of it will hold up in court, right?"

"I'll deal with that when it comes up." Jolene stepped between the pair and opened the door.

"Are we being charged with anything?" Maggie said, to which Hartley turned and glared at her.

"Mei," Dane answered, placing his hand on the small of her back. "Just shut up and walk." They exited the room and began towards the stairs leading out of the building, following Jolene until she turned and collapsed in her chair. Dane paused as he reached the top step and turned, his eyes falling on his sister. He moved away from Maggie and his exodus of the precinct and knelt in front of Jolene. "Jo," he said, pulling her eyes to him. "What happened? Where is everyone?"

* * * * *

"What are you doing here?" Captain Nolan said as he entered the precinct an hour later. She did not answer him, nor did she avert her eyes from the monitor before her. Henry moved away from his office and stood next to her desk. "Jo," he said.

"Any news on Leary?" she asked.

Nolan stalled, wondering what route he should take on the matter. Finally, understanding the way Jolene Hartley processed, he gave in. "No. Leary hasn't been seen. We received a call about a stolen car about an hour after everything."

"Where at?"

"It was found thirty minutes ago in a parking lot of an abandoned building near the Kennedy."

"And we're sure it was him?"

Nolan sighed. "No. But there was blood in the driver's seat."

"We send it to the lab?"

"Already on its way."

"Good." Jolene seemed to think. "What about —"

"Jo," he interrupted. "You need to go home."

"I need to get some work —"

"No, Jolene. I need you —"

"I need to be here!" she said, her voice carrying through the pit.

Nolan edged closer and took a seat on the edge of her desk, putting himself in line with her vision. "This is not a request. I'm ordering you to leave the station, Jo." She glanced to him. "I'm putting you on a leave of absence —"

"Why?" she exclaimed.

"Because. What happened today isn't something to be taken lightly. It *won't* be taken lightly. I need you to go rest. You need to go home and —"

"Going home to sit on my fucking couch isn't going to make me feel better!"

Henry nodded. "You're right. It won't. But circumstances as they are, an investigation into what happened —"

"An investigation? Into what?" She paused, looking to her superior with eyes ablaze. "Into doing our job?"

"Into everything. Leary. Renholm. James and Augie leaving the station." He stared to her. "You and Jacoby."

She threw her head back with a laugh. "We did our fucking jobs, Henry!"

"I know!" he agreed, leaning forward. "But we have two dead bodies, an officer in critical condition, and a civilian, under the watch of the Chicago Police Department, in a coma with a gunshot wound to the chest. Things don't look good right now, Jo."

Jolene lowered her face into her hands and slowly shook her head. "So what happens now?" she finally asked.

Nolan sighed. "I'm putting you on a leave of absence."

"For how long?"

He glanced to the floor, his teary eyes showing his true feelings. "Indefinitely," he answered. He continued to speak hurriedly as she opened her mouth. "The review board will look into what happened and question those involved. After that, we'll see." He paused briefly before reaching out to place a hand on her slumped shoulder. "You did everything right, Jo."

She glanced to him and nodded ever so slightly, rising from her seat. "Doesn't seem like it, Henry." She lowered her gaze to the floor briefly before reaching to her waist and unlatching her silver star, holding the badge in her hand and running her fingers across the smooth metal. She connected with the captain before tossing it to her desk and moving to the steps, leaving the pit for what felt like the very last time.

ACKNOWLEDGMENTS

Thank you to everyone for your continued support. These manuscripts continue to be challenging and fun, so any feedback (good or bad!) is much appreciated as this story plays out.

My first thank you needs to be to my dad, who has consistently gone through OTLOH, OTEOG and, now, OTRTC with a fine-toothed comb. Your advice, criticism, ideas, directions, encouragements... It's led me to where I am today. Thanks, Old Guy!

And then there's these people...

Mom. Billie. M & H. Aunt Lynn (congrats on your book!). Angie Berglund. Sean. Samantha. Aunt Theresa.

I am forever grateful.

Thank you.

RJP